SHAE CONNOR

KIERNAN KELLY

KAGE ALAN

JEVOCAS GREEN

J.P. BARNABY

TC BLUE

BUTT BABES IN BOYLAND

SHAE CONNOR

KIERNAN KELLY

KAGE ALAN

JEVOCAS GREEN

J.P. BARNABY

TC BLUE

WILDE CITY PRESS
www.wildecity.com

Butt Babes In Boyland © 2015
Shae Connor, Kiernan Kelly, Kage Alan,
Jevocas Green, J.P. Barnaby and T.C. Blue
Published in the US and Australia by Wilde City Press 2015

All rights reserved. No part of this book may be reproduced or transmitted in any form or by any means, electronic or mechanical, including photocopying, recording, or by any information storage and retrieval system, without permission in writing from the publisher. This book is a work of fiction. Names, characters, places, situations and incidents are the product of the author's imaginations or are used fictitiously. Any resemblance to actual events, locales, or persons, living or dead, is purely coincidental.

This book is licensed to the original purchaser only. Duplication or distribution via any means is illegal and a violation of International Copyright Law, subject to criminal prosecution and upon conviction, fines and/or imprisonment. This eBook cannot be legally loaned or given to others. No part of this eBook can be shared or reproduced without the express permission of the publisher.

Published by Wilde City Press

ISBN: 978-1-925180-67-1

Cover Art © 2015 Wilde City Press

CONTENTS

The Half Life Of Pumpkin Pie 1
Shae Connor

Elf Confidence 19
Kiernan Kelly

It's A Wonderful Lube 67
Kage Alan

Overnight Delivery 137
Jevocas Green

The Isle Of Misfit Sex Toys 161
J.P. Barnaby

For Fox Sake 205
T.C. Blue

THE HALF LIFE OF PUMPKIN PIE

SHAE CONNOR

Wilbur Johnson hated pumpkin pie.

He hated his name, too, and the whole holiday season, which only served to remind him that he was alone. No family, no boyfriend, only a handful of friends—who, he was convinced, spent all their time when he wasn't around pointing and laughing behind his back.

Okay, so Wilbur—or Wil, as he preferred to be called for obvious reasons—was having a bad day.

He'd gone to Thanksgiving Day dinner at his closest friend's house the day before, trying his best to be buoyed by the long weekend and the prospect of a big feast with some people he genuinely liked, an improvement on the sad little office party they'd had on Tuesday. Turkey roll-ups, a veggie plate, and store-bought apple turnovers did not a holiday make. Wil had asked Rob what to bring for the friendly feast, and Rob had suggested pumpkin pie "with lots of whipped cream!" Wil agreed readily, already thinking of the bakery down the street with the cute guy behind the counter and the apple turnovers that tasted homemade, not like the supermarket stuff procured by Peggy in accounting.

Wil showed up to Rob's perfectly on time, two gorgeous-looking pumpkin pies in hand, along with a bag that held both a can of real whipped topping and a container of the fake stuff—which, truth be told, Wil preferred on pumpkin pie. He'd cover a slice so completely that it just looked like a pile of fluff, and that was perfect.

Dinner was amazing. The beautifully browned roasted turkey was moist and flavorful. Perfect mashed potatoes almost dripped with fresh butter and, to gild the lily, an equally rich gravy came on the side. Add in a huge platter of roasted vegetables, sweet-potato casserole covered in marshmallows, and two different kinds of rolls, all of it served with a selection of wine, tea, and cider, and Wil was soon pleasantly overstuffed.

The dessert course was where the trouble started.

Rob's oldest friend, Marcus, had brought apple pie, but not just any apple pie, oh no. From the oven, where it had warmed while they ate, he produced an oversized latticework-topped miracle, oozing with juice and smelling like cinnamon heaven. He'd picked up a half-gallon of high-end French vanilla ice cream too, and when he set his offerings on the table and everyone *ooed* and *ahhed* in admiration, Wil almost didn't want to break out his dessert. How could cold pumpkin and spray-on cream measure up?

He'd brought the pie and toppings out anyway, but as expected, everyone filled up on apple-y goodness. Rob, as host, and Marc, probably feeling bad for stealing the sweet spotlight, had each taken a small slice of Wil's dessert and made the appropriate yummy noises, but everyone else begged off as too full.

When Wil headed home, along with a plastic-wrapped plate of turkey, potatoes, and veggies, he carried one complete, untouched pumpkin pie and an unopened container of whipped topping. He'd left the more-than-half-uneaten second pie and canned cream behind and didn't even care what happened to it. Let Rob feed it to his dog.

Friday morning, Wil got up still grumpy. He drank a cup of coffee and stared balefully at the refrigerator door, imagining the pie inside smirking under its bakery cover. As hard as he fought the battle of the straight-skinny-gay-fat body type, if Wil had to eat an entire pie by himself, he'd blow up like a pumpkin.

But he couldn't quite bring himself to throw it out, either.

His phone rang. Happy for something to do other than contemplating squash-induced obesity, he grabbed for it and answered without even checking the screen. "Hello?"

"Hi, is this Wilbur Johnson?"

All else aside, he really did *hate* that name.

"Wil," he corrected automatically. "Who's calling?"

"Hi, Wil," the man replied. He sounded like he was smiling, and it made Wil want to smack him. "This is Vin down at Hammel's Bakery. You bought a couple of pies from us on Wednesday?"

Oh my God, don't remind me. "Yeah, I did. Is there a problem?"

Vin chuckled. "Well, I'm sure it's just a glitch, 'cause I know you've been in before and we've never had an issue. But it looks like your credit card didn't go through right. I wanted to double-check to be sure we had the number right and all that. Or you can come down and use another card or pay cash if you prefer?"

What he wanted to do was go down and smash the leftover pie all over the bakery floor, but that would be a bit excessive. "I'm off today," he replied. "Give me an hour or so and I can come down. Will that work?"

"Perfect." Vin was smiling again. Or still. Whatever. If he was smiling in person, Wil would have to resist the urge to punch him in the face.

"See you then." Wil hung up and, resisting the urge to growl at the world in general, headed to the shower. Maybe shampoo and shower gel would wash away his mood.

He wasn't counting on it.

Vin looked up when the bell rang over the door and couldn't help smiling when he saw Wil walk in. Vin had been trying to convince himself for months that his gaydar was right and he should ask the other man out. Wil's messy hair, big eyes, and long body flipped every switch Vin had. All legs and arms, he looked like a cross between a newborn racehorse and a Muppet, in all the most adorable ways. The slightly geeky glasses only added to Wil's charm in Vin's eyes.

Today, though, the Muppet he resembled most was Oscar the Grouch. Well, that, or one of those inflatable yard decorations that had sprung a leak. Wil looked like he'd lost half his air, and Vin's smile slipped a notch, but he wasn't giving up that easily.

"Good to see you, Wil," he forged ahead, hoping to brighten the guy's mood by sheer force. "Sorry about the problem. Did you decide how you want to handle it?"

Wil stopped at the far side of the case and gave a sort of grunting sound. "Cash, I guess." He shrugged and reached into a back pocket. "The pie was good. I mean, the one that got eaten. The other one's still in my fridge."

"Oh." Vin himself deflated a bit at that. He'd made all the pumpkin pies for the holiday, so he hoped he hadn't messed anything up. "Not a family favorite?"

Wil flipped through his wallet. "Wouldn't know. Haven't seen them in years. Took it to my friend's place. Got overshadowed by the best apple pie in the history of apple pie."

"Oh." Vin held back a wince. "Sorry about that."

A sharp shoulder shrugged. "Not your fault." Wil pulled out some cash and went to hand it to Vin, but his hand brushed the edge of the cake stand atop the display case, and before Vin could react, the whole setup toppled over.

Letting out a yip like a lapdog, Wil jumped back out of the way, but thankfully, the stands Vin used were solid acrylic, not glass. The stand bounced one way, the cover the other, and the three doughnuts that had been on display rolled across the floor in three different directions.

"Shit!" Wil scrambled to pick everything up, moving so quickly that Vin barely had time to come out from behind the counter to help. He grabbed the doughnuts and tossed them toward the trash can, then turned to Wil, who held out the cake stand in shaking hands, his cheeks apple red.

"S-sorry," he stuttered. "I'm such a klutz."

As Vin reached for the stand, a brilliant idea popped into his head. "I know how you can make it up to me."

Wil couldn't figure out how going to a party with Vin would make up for anything. He'd paid for the pies, of course, once he'd gotten over the immediate embarrassment of knocking over the doughnut display. He'd tried to pay for the doughnuts, too, but Vin had said they were on the verge of being tossed for fresh anyway and wouldn't take the extra money. Instead, he'd made it sound like going to the party was the very last thing he wanted to do, but he had some kind of obligation Wil couldn't quite figure out.

"I mean, it's not going to be horrible," Vin assured him. "It's just there are so many holiday parties, you know? And this one is all toy themed. Bring a gift for Toys for Tots for admission, and they're going to have toys for us to play with. Which could be fun, I suppose, but what are we going to do, dress Barbie dolls and push around Tonka trucks?"

Wil had agreed eventually, mostly because Vin had told him he could bring the pie in place of a toy. Vin already had one—"and it's really two, because it's a set of twin dolls, right?"—so he assured Wil that plus the pie would be plenty. They agreed to meet in front of the bakery at seven, closing time, and go to the café across the street for a quick dinner before walking the five blocks to the house where the party was being held.

Wil got home feeling a bit like he'd been railroaded but also a bit relieved to have something to do other than contemplate his lot in life and angst over the leftover pie. He ate a turkey sandwich for lunch, spent his afternoon doing laundry, and stressed himself out over what to wear.

Finally ready, dressed in khakis and a button-down shirt, he slid his feet into his loafers, pulled on a light jacket, and opened the front door…then mentally smacked himself and headed back to the kitchen to collect the pie he'd almost forgotten.

Finally ready for *real*, he headed out, hoping he wouldn't do something else dumb like trip over his own feet and give Vin a pumpkin pie facial.

❖ ❖ ❖ ❖

Vin hadn't known what they'd be walking into. He really, really hadn't. But he wasn't at all sure Wil would believe him.

They arrived at the party a fashionable ten minutes late, after eating soup and salad specials at the café, Wil guarding the pie on the table next to him like it was the second coming of Jesus. Their conversation had started off slow, but Vin had turned his charm up to eleven and gotten Wil to smile a handful of times before they'd finished. Vin had insisted on paying for dinner, too.

"I invited you," he pointed out. "And you paid for dessert. You can get the next one."

The smile Wil gave him at that bubbled inside Vin like champagne all the way down the street and right up to the door of Linda's house. Then Linda opened the door, wearing an outfit that Vin could only dub "sex-starved housewife"—breasts rounded over the top of a bright pink corset, a micromini pleated skirt, impossibly high stilettos, and a string of incongruent pearls. After that display, it was all Vin could do to introduce Wil and hand over their food and toy offerings without turning and running for the hills.

All his questions were answered a few moments later when Linda ushered them into the living room, where the coffee table was covered with the toys for the party.

Adult toys.

And a lot of them.

Vin swallowed hard as his gaze ran over the collection of dildos, plugs, rings, paddles, and other implements spread across the shining wooden surface. A dozen or so other people stood or sat around the room, most of them laughing, a few flushed the color of the largest of the items on display: a fat pink fake cock with an even fatter set of fake balls attached, which appeared to be suction-cupped to the center of the table.

Vin couldn't bring himself to guess if the fifty shades of flushed faces on the other partygoers were from embarrassment, excitement, or a little of both.

He stood frozen, staring at the tableau spread out in front of him, and tried desperately to get his mind to work. How the hell was he going to extract himself and Wil from this situation without ruining any chance he might have had with Wil?

And then Wil started to laugh.

Vin turned to look at him, and Wil looked back through a helpless wave of giggles that soon morphed into full-blown guffaws. He flopped onto the nearest seat—the ottoman to an overstuffed chair—and dropped his head into his hands as he laughed and laughed and laughed.

Vin felt the corner of his mouth twitching, and then he had to laugh, too. Seriously? He finally gets a chance to go out with the cute guy he'd been eyeing, and *this* is what they walk into?

Wil glanced up at him, eyes twinkling with mirth. "Well," he managed through residual chuckles. "It sure brings new meaning to 'thank you for coming'!"

The party turned out to be plenty of fun. Sure, Vin was still a bit miffed that he'd been tricked into a sales event, but the hostesses—Linda's best friend, Connie, actually ran the show—kept things light and silly and didn't pressure anyone to buy. The guests made all the expected jokes and generally acted immature in all the most enjoyable ways. But most important to Vin, Wil seemed to be on board and having a great time.

Maybe years from now this would be a story to tell their grandchildren.

Or, on second thought, be careful *not* tell their grandchildren.

Best of all, Wil's pumpkin pie disappeared in a flash, and everyone who had a slice gushed over it, which made Vin even happier, especially since Wil made a point of telling everyone where he'd gotten it.

Vin tried not to pay too much attention to the toys, though it was hard…*difficult*, when people were pointing and touching and, in the case of one particularly talented guest, juggling. Despite a few tempting moments, Vin didn't make a purchase and neither did Wil, but there were door prizes, and he and Wil each ended up holding a small pink-and-black striped bag stuffed with tissue paper and offering no clues about the contents.

"Don't worry," Connie assured them with a wink. "The party gifts are all unisex."

In the ensuing flurry of order-taking from a brave few, mixed with chatter and laughter at increasing volumes, Vin and Wil said their good-byes and headed out, minus the pumpkin pie that started it all but plus a couple of sexy surprises. Well, Vin hoped for sexy, anyway, because he also hoped he'd be invited in at Wil's and they could open their prizes together.

Sure enough, when they reached the sidewalk leading to Wil's door, Wil graced Vin with a lopsided smile. "Come in for coffee?"

"I'd love to," Vin replied.

Wil couldn't remember the last time he'd brought a guy home after a date. Hell, Wil could barely remember the last time he'd been *on* a date. Not that Vin was just some guy, and not that they'd been on a date, exactly. Or maybe they had, but….

Shut up, Wil told his brain.

He led the way into the kitchen and nodded toward the small table by the window. "Have a seat, and I'll get the coffee started."

Wil turned toward the counter, but before he could take a step, Vin's body pressed along the back of his.

"I've got a better idea." Vin's voice, low and gravelly, had parts of Wil's body that *also* hadn't had a date in a while popping up to say hello. "Why don't we open our prizes together and see what we've got?"

Vin brushed his lips against the tender skin behind Wil's ear, and Wil couldn't have stopped the full-body shiver if he'd tried. Then Vin nudged his nose along Wil's neck, and Wil had to grab for the counter to keep from sliding to the floor in an undignified puddle. He'd already shown off his lack of dignity enough.

Get it together, he ordered himself, and he spun around to face Vin.

"I think," Wil said, ignoring the way his voice squeaked, "that these prizes are best opened in bed. Naked."

Vin let out a slow, shuddering breath and then grinned. "Lead the way."

Vin didn't look around Wil's bedroom. It didn't matter one bit to him if it was painted white or blue or zebra striped, or if the furniture matched, or if there was a mirror on the ceiling. There was a bed, and Wil was tossing his gift bag on the mattress and then fumbling for his belt, and Vin could not possibly care less about anything other than that.

Vin had his own clothes discarded in record time and crawled onto the bed to watch Wil, who hesitated at the waistband of his plain white briefs.

"C'mon," Vin murmured. "Show me whatcha got."

Wil flushed bright red, but he shoved his underwear down and kicked them away before lifting his gaze to meet Vin's.

Vin let his gaze wander over all that smooth flesh, winter pale and sprinkled with freckles. He smiled and held out a hand. "Let's open our packages."

Wil barked out a laugh. "I thought we just did."

Vin smiled wider. "Well, then, let's open the *other* ones, and then we can see about putting all four to good use."

Wil climbed onto the bed and sat with his legs crossed. He reached for his prize with one hand. "I have a confession to make."

Uh-oh. Vin paused before he tore into the tissue paper. "What's that?"

Wil flushed again, his gaze trained on the gift bag. "I've never used a...um..."

Vin leaned closer. "A sex toy?" Wil's face darkened another shade until it nearly matched the hot-pink shade on their prize packages. Vin reached for Wil's free hand. "Well," he said as he moved in closer, "unless a repurposed bathrobe sash and some ice cubes count, neither have I."

The last three words were murmured against Wil's lips just before Vin took his mouth in a firm kiss. Wil moaned deep in his throat and opened to Vin's tongue, and Vin got his first taste. Wil had skipped the pie at the party, but he'd had a couple of glasses of punch, and Vin could taste the lingering tart sweetness of cranberry juice and ginger ale. He slid closer, deepening the kiss, slipping one hand behind Wil's neck and the other across his thigh, the rough hair there tickling his palm. He let his fingers wander, playing along Wil's skin, moving inexorably closer to where Wil's body strained to meet them.

Vin made himself stop, though. He drew slowly out of the kiss, lingering for a few final touches before pulling away. "Sorry," he murmured, though he was anything but. "Got a little carried away." He slid his hand away from Wil's leg and hooked a finger around the ribbon of his toy bag. "Presents first?"

Wil's heart and cock throbbed in a syncopated beat that left him even more breathless than Vin's kisses had. His hands trembled from equal parts anticipation and nerves. He was no virgin, but his list of "never-have-I-evers" was piling up fast: bringing home a near stranger, ending up naked in bed with him before they'd so much as kissed, and now…whatever they were about to find in their gift bags.

Anticipation won out, and Wil reached for his bag. He caught Vin's gaze and watched as his mouth turned up in a smile somewhere between dirty and silly.

"On three?" Vin lifted his eyebrows, and Wil nodded. "One…two…go!"

In unison, the men grabbed at the tissue stuffing their bags and tossed it in all directions until they were surrounded by puffs of pink. Wil tilted his bag to look inside and felt his skin flush.

Is that...a butt plug? He couldn't tell for sure from that angle, but he couldn't quite bring himself to reach in and grab the thing, either. It was red, though, that much he could tell. Bright fire-engine red. At least it wasn't pink.

He tilted the bag for a better look, and something else flopped down across the plug, covering it up. A black satiny-looking mask of some kind.

No, his mind helpfully corrected. *It's a blindfold.*

Wil swallowed.

Hard.

Vin couldn't tear his eyes away from Wil's face. He didn't yet know what either of their bags held, but from the way Wil's eyes darkened and his skin flushed, it sure seemed he liked whatever he had.

Vin scooted closer. "What do you have there?" he rasped out.

Wil's gaze darted up from the bag to Vin's face. "Um...." He stopped, and without another word, he upended the bag, letting the items inside fall onto the bedspread. Vin looked down at the two packages and felt his own face heat.

"Um." He reached out and ran his finger over the silk of the blindfold. "I..."

Wil shot out his hand out and grasped Vin's wrist. "Uh-uh," he scolded, though his voice shook. "Not until you show me yours."

Vin lifted an eyebrow and nodded to where Wil's fingers gripped Vin's arm. "You gotta let go of me first."

Wil's return smile was slow but wolfish. "Promise not to run?"

Vin would have felt whiplash at Wil's mood swings from nervous to confident, except he was experiencing the same things. "Not going anywhere," he assured, and Wil slid his fingers away, leaving Vin free to tackle his own prize.

He didn't mess around, just grabbed for his bag and dumped its contents onto the bed. A shower of tiny packets scattered out around a larger item, and it took a long moment for his brain to make the connection. At least two dozen condoms in bright rainbow colors surrounded a box that displayed an image of a woman with her head thrown back—in pain, ecstasy, or both—with an evil-looking set of clamps on her bare nipples, a chain hanging in between.

"Holy fuck."

Vin's head snapped up at Wil's words, and he nearly keeled over when he saw Wil's face. If he'd thought Wil the picture of arousal before, this would have to be him on the verge of total wanton abandon. His eyes were black, his face red, his breath coming in short, raspy pants.

That was all Vin could stand. He pounced.

The toys on the bedspread scattered, all but forgotten in Vin's rush to get his hands all over Wil, who tumbled back against the pillows as Vin landed on top of him. Vin caught Wil's mouth under his, the kiss a little lopsided at first until they got things lined up right. *Every*thing, as it happened, since the sensation of their cocks slotting into place side by side between their bodies had Vin moaning into Wil's hot, wet mouth. Wil gripped Vin's hips and ground against him, and Vin moaned again as he slid his fingers into Wil's hair.

Fuck it all, his brain demanded. *It's time to get off.*

Vin rotated his pelvis, adding friction to the alchemy between them, and the rumble that vibrated up from Wil's chest told him to keep right on going. He yanked a hand free and spit into his palm before lifting up just far enough to take their cocks together in a firm grip.

Wil pulled out of the kiss with a gasp. "Yeah," he breathed out. "Oh *fuck* yeah."

Vin grinned and nipped at Wil's lower lip as he worked their dicks faster. "Gonna make you come so fucking hard," he panted. "Wanna feel you come all over me."

"Oh *fuck*!" Wil shouted it that time, and Vin was only a little surprised when Wil's body jerked so hard he nearly bucked Vin right off. Suddenly the movement of Vin's hand was slicked by a gush of hot come, and just the feel of it, paired with Wil shuddering under him, was enough to set Vin off, too. He let his hand fall away and thrust slowly against Wil's abdomen, riding out their climaxes until lethargy washed over him and he rolled to one side.

Something bit into his back, and he turned his head far enough to get a glimpse of a cardboard box. He laughed and turned back to Wil, whose eyes were still unfocused.

"Best laid plans," he said. "We totally forgot about the toys."

Slowly, Wil smiled. "Well, we'll just have to put them to use the next time."

Wil jerked awake to bright sunlight from the window and the sound of a turkey gobbling in his ear. He fumbled around until he got his hand on the phone sitting next to his head, though it wasn't until after he swiped to unlock the screen and click on the text message alert that he realized he hadn't set that ringtone.

Morning, sleepyhead, the message read. *Didn't want you to think I just ran off. I'm getting breakfast. Handy dating a guy whose family owns a bakery, right??*

Wil blinked at the screen. *Dating?* Well, he supposed last night was a date. *And a damn good one*, his body reminded him.

He flopped back on the mattress and stretched, enjoying all the little tells of a night well spent. As it turned out, they'd dispensed with the toys last night entirely—for the moment, anyway—and concentrated on just each other's bodies. Wil wasn't sure if he could really break up their night into separate sessions of sex, but he knew he'd had three strong orgasms and nearly managed a fourth before his well-sated body waved the white flag.

Nature called Wil out of bed and into the bathroom. The steamy air and damp towel on the bar told him Vin had helped himself to a shower before heading to the bakery, not that Wil begrudged him in the least—though a shared shower would've been nice. Wil jumped in for a quick wash himself and was drying off when he heard noises. He flicked the exhaust fan off and listened until the sound came again: loud knocking on the door.

Oh, he realized. Vin didn't have a key, and he must've locked the handle behind himself when he left.

Wrapping the towel around his bare hips as he went, Wil hurried to the door and flipped the lock, staying behind the door as he opened it to let Vin and a blast of chilly air inside.

"Brrrr!" Vin said as he grabbed for the edge of the door and pushed it shut. "Damn, it got cold overnight!"

He stopped then as he caught sight of Wil standing there in nothing but a towel that threatened to slide right off his body. Vin stepped in closer. "Now there's a sight for sore eyes," he murmured. "I'd be all over you right now, but I'd better warm up a little first or I might freeze off something important."

Wil blushed and clutched the towel to keep it in place. "Let me put on some—"

Vin stopped him with a quick kiss, careful not to let anything else touch Wil's bare skin. "Put on some clothes," he agreed with Wil's unfinished statement, "but only because it's too cold to run around naked."

Wil nodded toward the box. "What's for breakfast?"

Vin stepped away far enough to flip open the box he held to display an assortment of fruit-filled croissants. "I was so tempted to bring a pumpkin pie, you wouldn't *believe*." He grinned. "But I figured you'd appreciate something different."

No longer caring about the damn towel, Wil reached for the box and folded the lid back over the pastries. "I think," he said, as he reached to set the box on the table just inside the front door, "that what I'd appreciate most right now is you, naked, and in my bed."

Vin stood stock-still for a moment before he grabbed for the zipper of his jacket. "Last one there has to make the coffee later!" he yelled and took off toward the bedroom.

Wil turned to follow, then paused and picked up the bakery box. "On second thought," he murmured, "I bet these would taste awesome eaten off bare skin…"

ELF CONFIDENCE

KIERNAN KELLY

CHAPTER ONE

The workday was proceeding smoothly, to Zook's surprise. He checked his pocket watch, which he always wore pinned to one of the twin leather straps crisscrossing his hairy, naked chest, and nodded to himself. Perfect. If everything kept going the way it was, they might actually make their quota for the day. He was almost afraid to be optimistic, since if they did hit it, it would be the first time they'd done so in months.

Zook's tight black leather pants creaked and his boot heels tapped the floorboards with a steady beat as he strode up and down the aisles watching his crew of Elves work. His riding crop kept time in soft beats against his thigh, lashing out only occasionally to hurry a dawdling hand or startle a daydreamer back to the present. He paused now and then to glance with a critical eye over the shoulder of a worker, spot-checking for errors. If he spotted a mistake, his crop would encourage the worker to correct it posthaste. Otherwise, he would nod and continue on, ignoring the inevitable sigh of relief expelled in his wake.

The only sore spot in the day so far was that a few of the reindeer had gotten inside the workshop again, despite Zook's explicit orders for the Elves to keep them out of the area. The deer might be magical, they might fly, and some might even have body parts that glowed in the dark—although Zook privately suspected that was less magical and more because the Boss had flown them too close to Chernobyl one time too many—but the one thing they *weren't* was housebroken. He sidestepped a pile of droppings and shot Blitzen a dirty look.

He was about to address the issue for the millionth time when suddenly there arose such a clatter from the workshop's subbasement that everyone, himself included, froze.

The Artists stopped painting, a rainbow of fat droplets dripping from their brushes onto the floor at their feet. The Woodworkers stopped carving, the ever-present snowfall of wood chips ending, settling in soft mounds over their curly-toed boots. The Battery Inserters stopped popping AAs into place, the Slickers stopped prelubricating, and the Quality Assurance Inspectors froze, the toys they'd been testing popping out of their asses and hitting the floor, bouncing once or twice like penis-shaped rubber balls.

The boom was loud enough to shake the building. Toys fell off the shelves, along with a variety of tools. The windows rattled in their frames, and bits of dust and plaster drifted down from the ceiling like snowflakes.

Smoke followed the noise, billowing up from the narrow staircase leading down into the bowels of the workshop. A tall, lean figure emerged, coughing and rubbing his eyes. Soot blackened his face as well his uniform, dulling the usually vibrant reds and greens.

"Timothy!" Zook's deep voice thundered, rattling every nerve in the room and literally scaring the crap out of the reindeer. The stench of fresh reindeer dung joined the odor of bitter smoke permeating the workshop.

Distracted from the commotion by the pooping ungulates, Master Zook pinched his nostrils closed with two fingers and continued to bellow, although the nasal result sounded far less intimidating than he would've liked.

"Who let the fucking reindeer in here again? Was it you, Ernest? I know it was you. You must have some kind of weird fucking antler fetish. Well, *you* let them in, and *you* can bloody well clean up their shit."

He stepped over a fresh steaming pile and approached the choking, sooty figure who'd emerged from the subbasement.

Still holding his nose, Zook fanned the smoke-filled air with his other hand and continued to yell. "Timothy! What in the blue fuck did you do this time?"

Cough. "'Sploded." *Cough. Hack.*

"*What* exploded? I sent you down there for a box of paper for the copier!"

"Yes. It exploded." *Cough.*

"Copier paper does not explode."

Hack. "It does when it's soaked in nitroglycerin."

Pain began to throb at the base of Master Zook's skull, and for the briefest of moments, he wondered if he was having a stroke. Then he decided he wasn't that lucky. He drew in a deep breath, trying to calm himself. Unfortunately, that resulted in a lungful of noxious smoke and his nearly coughing up a lung.

"How, might I ask, did the copier paper become soaked in nitro-fucking-glycerin?"

"Well, I had to put the dynamite *somewhere*."

Zook's lips attempted to form an intelligent reply, but could only manage a string of expletives so foul his beard began to smoke from the toxicity. The smell of burning hair joined the odors of smoke and reindeer droppings, serving to make Zook's temper flare hotter. Rather than risk complete spontaneous combustion, he jerked his thumb toward the door and led Timothy outside, his boots stamping the floor hard enough to leave indents in the wood.

As soon as they were alone, Zook pushed Timothy up against the workshop wall and held him there with one beefy hand planted flat against Timothy's chest. A miniature avalanche of snow loosened from the roof and fell with a soft plop on Timothy's head and shoulders. He looked like he had the world's worst case of dandruff.

"Why? Just…*why*, Timothy? Why can I not trust you with the most simple of tasks? Why do you make every day an exercise in frustration? Isn't it bad enough that our workshop is already the redheaded stepchild of the North Pole? Do you really think all the crap you get up to isn't noticed by the Big Boys over at the Head Office?"

"I…I'm sorry, Chief. I don't mean to screw up. It just sort of happens." Timothy's eyes were wide, and his apology was clearly heartfelt. He looked so innocent, so contrite, that Zook couldn't stay irritated with him. Timothy might mess up a lot, but he really did *try* to do well.

Zook sighed and felt his anger rush out of him like air from a popped balloon. "I know you don't, kid. It's just that we're already the laughingstock of the compound. Everyone else makes toys, electronics, books, jewelry… What do we make? Dildos and butt plugs. Ho-fucking-ho." He locked his hands behind his back and began pacing back and forth, his boots carving deep imprints in the snow. "How many kids want to wake up and find battery-operated boyfriends in their stockings? Not one, that's how many. These are not child-friendly creations we're making. They're for adults only. That's why none of our designs ever make it into the Santa's bag on Christmas Eve."

Timothy shook his head and shoulders like a puppy, spraying little clots of snow everywhere. He looked startled, his big blue eyes wide as he blinked snowflakes from his eyelashes. "Then why do we keep making them?"

"Where do you think Santa gets the bankroll to make the other toys and presents year-round? How do you think he gets the cash to maintain the Compound, make payroll, buy raw material and reindeer feed? From selling our stuff to the big adult box stores and on Amazon, that's where. Yet we still get the stink eye from all the other Elves. Bastards look down their button noses at us just because our stuff doesn't make the sleigh ride."

"That's not fair. Sounds like if it wasn't for us, there wouldn't *be* a Christmas."

"You're right, there wouldn't be. I've been saying it for years, but nobody listens. There's a double standard in place. Our goods pay for everything, and everyone is happy to reap the benefits, but Headquarters believes we're useless, pervy idiots belonging at the bottom of the Elf totem pole. That's why they assign all of Elfdom's fuckups to us. Who got stuck with Snap, Crackle, and Pop after the scandal about their orgy with the M&M guys broke in the media? We did. Until we trained them, all they were good for was making cereal noises with their armpits.

"Where did Legolas go after the Elves in the Undying Lands revoked his membership card for sneaking that roly-poly dwarf, Gimli, in there with him? Here, that's where. He might've been a great archer in Middle Earth, but up here he couldn't inject a mold worth a shit until we trained him."

Zook shrugged a broad shoulder. "Even me. My brothers and I were Keebler Elves. That name commanded respect once upon a time. We were worth our weight in fudge crème. Then Ernie started gambling, and the Tree went into foreclosure…well, it's a sad story. You don't want to hear it." He turned away and cleared his throat, waiting until he had his emotions under control again. "Anyway, we had nowhere to go but here. Because scandal tainted our reputation, they assigned us to Workshop 69 even though we knew nothing about making sex toys. We learned, though, and now we're the best at it."

Timothy kicked a mound of snow with the curly toe of his boot. Jingle bells rimming the boot's ankle tinkled softly. "I'm a fuckup, too, like the other guys. Everything I touch turns to shit."

Zook tried to smile reassuringly and thought he even managed to get halfway there. He patted Timothy's shoulder. "That's not…well, it's not *completely* true. You try hard. You really do. Now tell me, where did you get the dynamite?"

"Oh yeah, that. I got it from Mab, who said she got it from Roger."

"Roger?" Zook frowned and tried to place the name. "Roger, Roger… Red suit, white collar? Sort of a devious-looking smile? Likes to hang out on shelves?"

Timothy brightened and nodded. "Yeah, that's him! Mab said he told her to give it to me and tell me Santa said to hide it in the basement where the house Elves couldn't find it. It made sense to me—you know how mischievous Kreacher and the rest of those little guys are. Mab suggested I put it in the box of copier paper."

Zook swore and punched the workshop wall, succeeding in loosing another fall of snow from the roof and causing an agonizing pain to shoot through his knuckles. "Those rat bastards! You were set up, Timothy. They knew the dynamite would leak nitroglycerin into the paper. They've been after Santa to close Workshop 69 for years. Roger and his far-right conservative cronies, like Mab, Honeythorn Gump, and Robin Goodfellow, formed S.E.M.E.N., the Society for Elf Morality, Education, and Normality. I believe one of their main directives is to get us to close up shop."

Timothy cocked his head. "Doesn't that spell…"

"Yeah, it does. I never said they were overly bright." Zook motioned for Timothy to follow him back into the workshop. "They must've known the box of copier paper would explode. It's one more thing they can throw up in our faces at the next Weekly Workshop Conference at the Head Office. If they can make Santa believe we're a threat to ourselves or others, Santa would be forced to close us down."

He opened the door for Timothy to enter the workshop, but Timothy paused. "What are you going to do, Zook?"

Zook smiled, although there was no humor in it. It was the Elf equivalent of a pit bull baring its teeth. "I'm going to go have a talk with Roger."

"Ooh. Can I watch?"

Zook blinked. Timothy looked positively eager, as if "talk" was code for something far more entertaining. "No, you can't. You'd better start cleaning up the mess the explosion made. And find some unexploded copier paper, please. Nathan needs it in the design room."

He thought he heard Timothy grumble something about Zook having all the fun, but shrugged it off and left the workshop.

CHAPTER TWO

He found Roger sitting on a shelf.

Well, not exactly a *shelf*, per se. Not unless one could consider a window ledge on the top floor of the Administration Building a shelf.

A small crowd had gathered at the foot of the building, craning their necks, the better to see the soles of Roger's dangling, curly-toed shoes. Zook elbowed his way through them until he stood nearly directly below Roger's feet. He looked up, shading his eyes with his hand.

"Roger? What are you doing up there?"

"What's it look like I'm doing?"

"Truthfully, it looks like you're getting ready to jump. Are you? Going to jump? You'll count to three or something first, right?" Zook wasn't being facetious. If Roger really was going to take a dive, Zook wanted a little warning so he could get the hell out of the way. He was in the splash zone, so to speak.

"Sorry to disappoint, but I'm merely getting some fresh air."

"On the window ledge?"

"I like the view."

"Uh-huh. Well, look, Roger, I need to talk to you."

"Take a number."

"Funny. It's about the, er—" He glanced at the crowd around him and decided discretion might be the better part of valor. Speaking openly might cause a panic or, at the least, a distasteful heightening of curiosity among the Elf masses. "—*package* Mab gave Timothy to hide in Workshop 69's basement."

"Please, take a number."

He refused to rise to Roger's bait. "It was dangerous, Roger, and in really bad form. You should be ashamed of yourself!"

"Are you deaf? I said take a fucking number!"

Zook scowled, but a finger tapped his shoulder, distracting him from what no doubt would be the deliciously brilliant and scathing reply his mind was scrambling to compose. He turned on the tapper, only to see a line of Elves snaking into the Administration Building, each holding a tiny yellow slip of paper. The tapper, an Elf named Leonard, waved his paper under Zook's nose. It read, "Number 167."

"Are all of you here to see Roger?" Zook jerked his thumb up toward the ledge. Head after head nodded.

Huh. No wonder Roger was out on a ledge. Zook would consider jumping too, if one hundred sixty-seven Elves were waiting to unload their problems on him. Zook's smile was smug. *Well, that's what you get when you're head of the Elf Satisfaction Department. Nobody forced him to apply for the job. Roger probably just figured it would look good on his résumé when he runs for President of the Elf League next year.*

Still, Zook admitted it was a difficult job on the best of days. Every Elf at the Pole brought their troubles, arguments, complaints, and general frustrations, large, small, and every size in between, to the Elf Satisfaction Department for mediation.

Does your mother want to move in with you and the Missus? Come to the Elf Satisfaction Department for an intervention.

Does your teenager want to get a tattoo of his favorite band, The Throbbing Elfhoods, on his ass? The Elf Satisfaction Department will run interference for you.

Did the surgeon confuse your tonsils with your testicles? The Elf Satisfaction Department will bring suit against him *and* get you a job singing First Soprano with the Holiday Choir.

Zook held no sympathy for Roger, though. No, sir, not a bit. Roger's S.E.M.E.N. had been burning Zook's ass for the last six months, and their efforts to shut down Workshop 69 had added complications to Zook's life he absolutely did not need. This latest fiasco with the dynamite sealed the deal. All Zook cared about was getting the bastard to quit making his life so fucking difficult, and he wasn't about to wait for one hundred and sixty-seven Elves to yak Roger's ear off about their piddling problems before he could get to it.

He began to push his way through the line. "Let me through. Elf emergency. Grave circumstances. Life or death. Mutant weather patterns. Puppy smuggling. Disaster. Tragedy. Shaved kittens. Armageddon. Make way."

The Elves in line muttered and growled into their beards, but let him pass. He took the elevator to the fourth floor. Stepping out, he saw the densely packed rows of cubicles comprising the Elf Satisfaction Department. There was a red line painted on the floor in front of him and a small, white sign reading, "Wait here for your number to be called." Hanging from the ceiling was a digital counter.

As he watched, the glowing red numbers clicked over to twenty-three.

An Elf stepped around Zook, waving a slip of paper. "I'm twenty-three! Twenty-three here!" he yelled and dashed over the line, disappearing into the labyrinth of cubicles. Zook wondered if anyone would ever see the Elf again, or if he was doomed to wander the warren of cubbies for all eternity, trying to get whatever problem irked him solved.

He shook his head and remembered why he was there. The ledge on which Roger dangled was on the west side of the building. It was the fourth window, the last one near the far corner. Zook headed in that direction, weaving between cubicles and scaling the cubby walls, boosting himself over by standing on desks and the occasional Elf head. Every Elf he passed wore an expression that seemed frozen halfway between surprise and horror, obviously shocked that someone had the gall to jump the red line out of turn.

The fourth window was wide open, and the icy Arctic air blew in, shuffling papers and creating a terrible draft. *Someone over in Accounts Payable is going to have a shit fit when the heating bill for this month comes in*, Zook thought.

Roger was still sitting on the ledge, his back to Zook. Zook reached out and grabbed the back of Roger's white fur-trimmed red tunic and, giving a mighty yank, jerked him back through the window. Roger tumbled backward and landed on his ass, legs sprawled wide and pointy Elf hat askew.

"What the fuck?" He blinked, looking slightly dazed, confused, and a bit nauseated, until his eyes focused on Zook. Then he was furious. "You!"

Zook was not about to be intimidated. He puffed out his hairy chest and growled, "Yes, me. I said I needed to talk to you. What the hell did you mean by telling Mab to give Timothy a stick of dynamite? The kid can barely walk without tripping over his own jingle balls. You're lucky he didn't blow himself up along with everyone else in the workshop!"

"What in the fuck-all are you talking about?" Roger climbed to his feet and dusted off the seat of his pants. He tugged down the hem of his red tunic and straightened his hat. "What dynamite? What would I be doing with dynamite? And who's Timothy?"

"Timothy. You know who I'm talking about. The blond, blue-eyed Elf?"

"Oh yeah, that's a help. Your description covers three-quarters of Elfdom, myself included."

Zook grunted. He couldn't argue. There *was* a predominance of Nordic features among the Elves. Not himself, of course. Zook prided himself on his swarthy complexion and his dark hair and eyes. Got it from his mother's side. Her people came from Ireland and were what was commonly referred to as *Black Irish*. Some folk claimed there was more than a trace of Fae blood in his lineage as well, but that was only a rumor, unless you counted Zook's Uncle Jerome who believed himself to be a great horned owl. Aside from that, Zook didn't remember any relatives with actual wings.

"He's the lanky one with the long nose and a birthmark on his forehead shaped like a holly berry."

"He has a birthmark shaped like Halle Berry? Holy shit, Catwoman, he must've been popular with all the kids' dads at birthday parties."

"Not *Halle* Berry. *Holly* berry." Zook threw his hands up, frustrated. "He's the skinny one who always seems afraid of his own shadow."

"Oh, *him*! Sure. Shy kid. Nice, but too quiet. What about him?"

"You had Mab give him dynamite!"

Roger looked genuinely confounded. "I reiterate my prior statement. What would I be doing with a stick of fucking dynamite, and even if I had one, why would I have Mab give it to Timothy?"

"You…you and your S.E.M.E.N. want Workshop 69 to close! I guess you figured if Santa wouldn't do it, you would do it yourselves—by blowing it up!"

If Zook didn't know better, he would've sworn Roger's expression of dismay was authentic. "You're nuts! S.E.M.E.N. couldn't care *less* about Workshop 69."

Zook chewed his inner cheek and tried to contain his temper, but it was difficult. It was bucking and heaving and trying its best to break free all over Roger's face via Zook's fists. "S.E.M.E.N.—the Society for Elf Morality, Education, and Normalcy? Workshop 69 makes all the sex toys."

"And…?"

"What do you mean, 'and'? You want us shut down!"

"We do not. Our purpose is to promote safe and responsible sex among the Elf population. Why, just last week, we gave out candy-cane flavored condoms during Junior Elf League Reindeer Castration Weekend. And Rudy Flowerbum gave a wonderful speech about how important it is to play safe during the Ladies Auxiliary Gingerbread Cookie and Tea Party."

Zook blinked and shook his head. "I'm confused. You *don't* want to shut us down?"

"Of course not. Who told you we did?"

"I… I just assumed the Morality thing meant—"

Roger made a rude noise. "This is what happens when you assume. You make an ass out of you and me. Especially the 'you' part."

"You're just so conservative. I naturally thought you'd be against anything—"

"That promotes sex? Don't be stupid. I *love* sex. Have it as often as I can, which isn't much since I rarely get out of this office until late and work most weekends." He glanced out the window at the line of Elves that now curled out of sight around the corner of the building, and sighed heavily. "I should've never taken this job. Did you know I could've had a position up at the Big House? Yup. You're looking at the guy who could've been Third Assistant to the Fifth Associate to Santa's Chief Helper. But no, I had to throw it all away to become the guy everybody bitches at." Roger's big blue eyes looked sad, and his shoulders slumped.

Zook didn't want to be distracted by Roger's good looks or the fact that Roger not only liked sex but also had it as often as possible, and he *definitely* didn't want to think about what Roger looked like *while* having sex, which was the normal progression Zook's mind favored for that sort of train of thought. He didn't want to start feeling sorry for Roger either or, Santa forbid, *liking* Roger, which he feared he might actually start doing any minute now, and so brought the conversation around full circle.

"But the dynamite…"

Roger cleared his throat and turned back to Zook. "Did this Timothy kid tell you *I* gave him dynamite?"

"Well, no. Like I said, he told me Mab gave it to him. Said she told him you gave it to her."

"Mab is an Elf-shaped pile of bitch in size seven shoes. We kicked her out of S.E.M.E.N. six months ago because of her extremist leanings. Look, you're a smart guy, Zook. You run the entire operation over at Workshop 69. That's no easy feat. It takes intelligence to do that. Tell me the truth—does this story about the dynamite sound even *remotely* feasible to you? Think about it, Zook. Who even *uses* dynamite anymore? Doesn't everyone use C-4 nowadays?"

"I don't know. I'm not familiar with the most fashionable methods for blowing shit up."

"Well, I am. I wouldn't even know where to get a stick of dynamite! Whatever Mab is up to, the explosive didn't come from me or from anyone at S.E.M.E.N. I swear it, Zook."

Despite wanting desperately to do the contrary, Zook actually believed him. "Then you think it was all Mab's idea?"

"I think you should be asking Timothy that question."

Zook slowly shook his head. "Timothy? Nah. He's a good kid, but not very bright. I just can't believe he'd be in on some scheme to destroy Workshop 69. He's happy there."

Roger scowled, his lips pressing together into a thin white line. "It might not be Workshop 69 they were trying to destroy."

"What do you mean?"

Roger's searing blue gaze met Zook's. He held a hand up before Zook could interrupt. "Listen first and then tell me if you don't think this makes sense. Mab was kicked out of S.E.M.E.N. because her ideas were too extreme and frankly more than a little batshit crazy. She blames me for it, I know she does. Suppose she wants revenge? What does she do? She gets Timothy, who's either too naïve or thinking with his dick, to go along with her plot to damage Workshop 69 and blame me for it. She's probably hoping you'll take it to Santa and get me kicked out of S.E.M.E.N. Hell, she probably hopes I'll get exiled from the Pole altogether."

Zook shivered at the thought of exile. For an Elf, it was a fate worse than death. There weren't many options for an exiled Elf other than touring county fairs in Elf-tossing events or working in a fur suit on children's programming for the Public Broadcasting Service.

"What you're saying makes sense, but I still can't believe Timothy would be in cahoots with Mab." He chewed on the inside of his cheek for a minute, thinking. "Let's go have a talk with Timothy. Between the two of us, we should be able to get at the truth."

Roger nodded and motioned for Zook to follow him into the labyrinth of cubicles. They made their way through so many plastic-and-Plexiglas twists and turns that Zook fervently hoped Roger knew the way back out because *he* couldn't possibly hope to find his way to the elevator again.

Finally, Roger halted in front of a cube identical to all the others. Within it, a moon-faced Elf looked up from a book he was reading. His cheeks blushed crimson, and he tried to slide the tome under a pile of papers, but not before Zook read the title: *Fifty Shades of Elf*.

Zook had tried to read it once, but when he found himself wanting to punch the heroine's Inner Goddess in the head just three pages in, that was the end of that.

Roger didn't seem to notice or just flat-out didn't give a shit about what literary sludge his underlings read on duty. "Melvin, I'm taking off for the day. You'll have to take my cases."

Melvin turned fifty shades of nauseated before finally settling on a nice, puke green pallor. "I…you…them…"

"Verbs, Melvin. They're useful. Learn some. Also, you may want to reevaluate your literary choices. Just sayin'. Toodles." Roger turned and led Zook away. Behind them, Zook imagined Melvin was still trying to formulate a response, because he could hear slightly strangled noises coming from behind the cubicle wall.

After a moment, he heard Melvin call out, "McJingles gave the book to me! It's his fault!"

"What kind of name is McJingles?" Zook asked. "It sounds like something you order during the holidays at McDonald's."

"From what I understand, McJingles's parents lost a bet."

Roger led Zook back through the maze to a bank of elevators separate from the one he'd come up on. "These are the freight elevators. I don't want to go anywhere near the line of Elves waiting to get in out front. If they saw me, it'd be a stampede."

Zook heartily agreed. The sooner they got to Timothy, the sooner he'd have answers.

CHAPTER THREE

The elevator ride was quick. Sidestepping an Elf pushing a handcart loaded with boxes of envelopes and another pulling a pallet piled high with reams of copy paper, they left the building through the rear cargo bay doors. Roger set off at a brisk pace toward the small, snowy square that separated the office buildings from the workshops. At its center was a giant statue of Santa holding the Good List in one hand and the Naughty List in his other. The names inscribed on the lists magically changed every year, depending on which child made which list.

The sidewalk continued past the statue and through the park toward the area where the workshops were located. As Zook followed Roger, he tried to keep his mind focused on the questions he needed to ask Timothy and not on how nicely rounded Roger's ass was or how perfectly it filled out the seat of Roger's pants or how hypnotically it hitched to and fro with every stride.

Tried.

And failed.

All he could think about was grabbing a double handful of Roger's butt, and that was a surefire way to get on the Naughty List.

Of course, if copping a feel got him on the Naughty List, then he might as well go for broke and say, de-pant Roger, right? Pull those red leggings down and get an eyeful of that firm, round ass up close and personal. Touch it. Knead it. Maybe nibble it a bit? Spread those twin mounds of fine, firm flesh and take a peek at the pretty little hole between them.

Then, oh then Zook would spin him around and get a mouthful of the throbbing Elfhood that made Roger jolly. Oh, Roger would like it too. The noises he would make while Zook sucked him, the grunting and the groaning, and at the end when Roger would come in salty hot spurts, he'd strike a note sweet enough to rival the Hallelujah Chorus.

"Oomph."

Zook walked directly into Roger and bounced back, nearly knocking himself off his feet. So caught up in his naughty little fantasy, Zook hadn't realized Roger had stopped walking. He felt his face heat up, cheeks burning, and became conscious of the hard-on straining at the fabric of his pants caused by his naughty mental porn movie.

Worse yet, Roger noticed it too. He glanced down at Zook's crotch, then back at Zook's face, arching one sleek blond eyebrow.

Zook cleared his throat and tried to avoid eye contact. Unfortunately, averting his eyes directed his gaze back to Roger's personal Elf puppet. It was hard, too, and perfectly outlined under the thin material of Roger's red leggings.

Roger suddenly grabbed Zook's hand and pulled him behind the statue of Santa. Zook found himself roughly pushed back against the statue, his head giving Santa's rotund stone butt cheeks a wedgie.

"Ow." Stone butt cheeks, Zook realized, did not make for comfy headrests.

For a moment, he thought Roger was going to punch him. Roger was scowling, eyebrows knitted and upper lip curled in a snarl.

"What is going on here? Huh? I'm trying to figure out who wants to sabotage my reputation and possibly have me thrown into the brig for destruction of Elf property, reckless endangerment, and possibly attempted murder, and all I can think of is stripping you naked and sucking you so hard your eyeballs invert."

Roger either thought his question was rhetorical or simply didn't want to wait for Zook to answer because he smashed his lips against Zook's and began rubbing their bodies together hard enough to create sparks of static electricity.

Zook's mouth popped open in surprise, and Roger took it as an invitation to move his tongue in and take over. He swirled it over and under Zook's tongue, bullying him relentlessly, until finally, Zook overcame his shock and began to push back.

Roger performed a frontal assault, sliding his hands up over Zook's naked chest, fingers threading through the patch of hair curling under the twin straps of leather until he found Zook's nipples and took them prisoner. Sweet torture followed, as Roger tweaked and twisted Zook's nipples into stiff nubs, sending a delightful ache through the rest of Zook's body.

Zook decided it was all-out war and went directly for Roger's battle command. He molded his hand over Roger's hard, hot cock, squeezing it until Roger moaned his surrender. Sadly, the skirmish was over before any eyeball–inverting–suction maneuvers could be accomplished, but Zook counted it as a win anyway.

In a flurry of rubbing, squeezing, and noisy tongue wrestling, sizzling with static electricity, looking like a pair of Fourth of July sparklers, they climaxed one after the after.

In fact, the war was short, messy, and left them both with wet spots on their leggings, but both sides claimed the victory.

"What was that about?" Zook unzipped his pants and poked at the wet spot spreading across his crotch. It wouldn't show so much on his black leather, but there was no hiding the messy blotch on Roger's thin leggings.

Roger knew it too. "People are going to think I either blew my wad in my shorts or lost control of my bladder."

Zook figured he'd prefer people to think the former, although the strong smell of sex wafting up from the region might be a deciding factor.

"It's my fault." Roger was fanning his own groin, as if he could air-dry the wet spot there. No such luck, though. "It's been a long while since I got any. I've been practically chained to my fucking desk at work. When I realized you were checking out my ass and getting hard, I just lost it. Sorry."

"Don't be sorry." Zook took out a handkerchief from his pocket and began dabbing ineffectually at the wet spot on the inside of his pants. It was going to ruin the leather. He just knew it. "Been a while for me too. Running the workshop doesn't leave me much time for, er, fraternizing."

Roger chuckled. "No, I don't suppose it does."

Zook crumpled the handkerchief into a ball, stuffed it back inside his pocket where it artificially added to the bulge nature gave him, and zipped up. "This is no use. We can't walk into Workshop 69 like this. The Research and Development guys will smell us coming a mile away and be all over us, wanting to know what we did, how we did it, what we used, and trying to take samples…"

Roger blinked and shook his head. "I don't think I could give a sample so soon. I'm not that young anymore."

Zook nodded and looked around, frantic to find a solution that didn't involve them wasting time by running back to their respective homes and changing clothes. Down from his orgasmic high, he finally realized his feet were freezing. They'd been standing ankle deep in the snow while they'd…

Of course! The snow! He threw himself down on the ground and began rolling back and forth. "Get down here," he ordered Roger. "Get yourself all snowy. If we're wet all over, it'll hide the stains and hopefully dull the smell."

Roger seemed doubtful, but he did as Zook asked. The two of them rolled around on the square, pausing only long enough to make Elf angels in the snow as required by Elf Law. In no time, they were covered with globs of frosty white. It seeped into their clothing and chilled them to the bone, but it did the job. When they stood up, shivering, the stains had blended in with the rest of their wet pants.

"C-come on, b-before it d-dries!" Zook stammered. His teeth were chattering so hard he was afraid he'd bite off his tongue if it got caught between his chompers. He took off at an awkward splay-legged gait in a half-hop, half-run toward Workshop 69.

Once inside the workshop, the heat hit them and they began to drip. It didn't matter—the snow had done its job and camouflaged their indiscretion.

What it *hadn't* done was hide them from the eyes of the workshop. There wasn't an Elf in the place who hadn't been called to the windows to watch Zook and Roger having a vertical rub-off under Santa's butt and their subsequent roll in the snow.

The Research and Development Elves were waiting for them, Petri dishes and test tubes in hand. Before Zook and Roger could blink, the R&D Elves were trying to pull Zook's and Roger's pants down, clamoring for shavings and scrapings. Zook had to grab a broom from a nearby workstation and use it to herd them into another room, locking them in.

"What in the fuck, Zook?" Roger had pulled his leggings up practically to his neck, trying to keep the waistbands out of the R&D Elves' grabby little hands. His eyes were wide, and he stared at the door behind which the R&D Elves had disappeared. "Just…what in the fuck?"

"Sorry. R&D gets a little overzealous sometimes." He realized the other Elves in the workshop were still staring at them. He put his game face back on, stalked to his desk, and picked up his bullwhip. When he swung it, it cracked loudly and sliced the pom-pom cleanly off the hat of a nearby Elf. "Get back to work!"

Instantly, everyone in the room with the exception of Roger found something that needed doing. The air filled with the sounds of tapping hammers, swishing brushes, and buzzing vibrators.

"Better." Zook didn't even try to hide his satisfied grin. Even knowing his workers had watched him furiously frotting under Santa's stone ass, he could still literally whip them into shape when necessary. "Come on. Timothy should be in the back, shelving copy paper or huffing toner or whatever the fuck it is he does when nobody's looking."

He led Roger past worktables at which Elves all appeared studiously working, none even glancing up as they passed, although if one listened carefully, one could hear bony Elven knees knocking together.

"You mean you don't know what Timothy *does*? I thought you were in charge of this workshop?" Roger paused briefly in the Quality Assurance Section, watching an Elf test one of this season's new glow-in-the-dark candy-cane-shaped butt plugs. He nodded his approval. "Nice texture, good form, tight fit…I give it a nine out of ten."

The Elf testing the butt plug clenched his cheeks a little tighter, smiled, and gave Roger a thumbs-up.

Zook grunted and pulled on Roger's elbow, hurrying him along. "I *am* in charge!"

"Then why don't you know what's in Timothy's job description?"

"I do! I mean, I should. I just…well, truthfully? I don't really remember hiring him. He just sort of showed up one day."

Roger dug in his heels, effectively pulling Zook to a halt. "And you didn't question that? You didn't find it funny that somebody just insinuated themselves into your workforce?"

Zook shrugged. "It happens sometimes. We get so many cast-off Elves in this place it's hard to keep track of them all. Anytime an Elf is caught doing something embarrassing or scandalous or is found otherwise unsuitable for the hoity-toity Elf community up at the Head Office, they send him or her here. It doesn't matter if they have no experience in making sex toys or if they can't paint worth a shit or sculpt or hammer a fucking nail into a piece of wood or whether or not I have an abundance of labor already. I *have* to take them and find them something to do."

Zook gestured toward the Elves, all diligently working. The sound of knocking knees had quieted now that Zook had moved on. "And I do it. When I noticed Timothy, I figured he was just another throwaway Elf. He was one of the worst of the lot too. Couldn't seem to do anything right. I had to invent a position for him. I made him the official gofer, which means whenever something needs to get fetched, he goes for it. Need paint? Send Timothy to the Color Shop. Need a new jigsaw? Send Timothy to Tool Requisitions. Need copy paper? Send Timothy into the basement office supply storage."

"Zook, we need to talk to Timothy. I have a feeling you've been snowed."

"What do you mean?"

"Well, let's think about this. An Elf shows up with no paperwork and just sort of infiltrates the workforce. He's nonthreatening and so stupid you need to make up a position for him—one that allows him the freedom to move around the Complex freely without suspicion. He has downtime in between jobs, too, am I right? Where does he go and what does he do during that time? Most importantly, who sent him here and why?"

"I figured he was sent because he was too incompetent for the Head Office or any of the other workshops." Zook's vision narrowed as he felt himself scowl. "Why do I suddenly get the feeling I was set up?"

"There's only one person who knows the answer to that."

Zook nodded. "And his name is Timothy. Let's go."

CHAPTER FOUR

The sign over the back room read, "Elf Storage." It was a long, narrow room lined with ceiling-to-floor shelving units. At the far end, a lone Elf was bent over a lower shelf, studiously fiddling with something.

Zook led Roger into the room. "Timothy! I want to talk to you."

The figure looked up. It wasn't Timothy.

"Ernest? What are you doing back here, bro?"

"Looking for the original schematic for the F1000 Ultra Thin Super Sensitive Glow in the Dark French Tickler. There's something wrong with the Synthe-lamb formula. They keep springing leaks. The problem is so bad we might as well be making the condoms out of Swiss cheese. Of course, you'd know that if you weren't outside bumping uglies with Mr. Uptown Elf, there."

Zook frowned, but ignored the jibe. "Where's Timothy?"

Ernest laughed, although there wasn't any humor in it. "Who knows? He took off shortly after the basement blew up. Which reminds me, where did you run off to? This place was a disaster. Do you know how hard it is to get the smell of smoke out of edible underwear? We finally had to label them Barbeque Flavor."

"Damn it! We missed him. He could be anywhere by now!" Zook pounded his fist on a shelf, rattling a pile of blank requisition forms. He scowled at them as the uniform stack collapsed, papers sliding every which way. "I'll be so fucking glad when the North Pole finally catches up with the rest of the world and computerizes. Honestly, Santa needs to get a clue. Things would be so much easier and flow so much better, not to mention save tons of time, if they'd only go paperless."

"Ha!" This time there was humor in Ernest's laugh. "That'll be the day! Santa likes to do things the old-fashioned way. Translation? The hardest fucking way possible. I'm more surprised that he let the Techie Elves install those surveillance cameras around the Compound. Of course, the only reason he did *that* was to stop whoever was letting the reindeer fly over and crap on the his statue in the square."

Roger cocked his head, and his eyes grew wide. "Surveillance cameras? Zook, do you know what this means?"

"Yeah. Our little bump and grind is probably being uploaded to Facebook as we speak."

Roger rolled his eyes. "True, but I wasn't thinking of that. The cameras might show us where Timothy went."

Zook could practically feel it when understanding clicked into place. "Of course! Come on. Security should have the footage."

He led the way out of the back room and through the workshop. Tossing his bullwhip back on his desk as he passed, he ignored the collective sigh of relief that swelled in his wake.

"You're some tough taskmaster, huh?" Roger was grinning and seemed to be pushing to keep up.

They crossed back over the square. Zook noticed absently that a reindeer had shit on Santa's statue again. "I've gotta be. We get way more orders to fill than Santa's precious children's toy workshops do, and we don't get all year to fill them, either."

"Yeah, I suppose so. I never thought of that before."

"Nobody does. Like I said before, everybody likes to pretend we don't exist, but they'd all be fucked sideways if we didn't bring the money in." He stopped in front of a one-story building with a cedar-shingle roof and knotty pine walls. Gingerbread trim graced the roofline and porch.

A sign hung above the front door. It read, "Department of Elf Defense." Zook opened the door and stepped inside, followed by Roger. There was a large desk, behind which several rows of video monitors showed various images. Zook noticed one showing the Elf Emporium, the square and Santa statue, of course, and several other locations around the Compound.

An aged Elf, his beard so long necessity forced him to plait it and wrap it around his head like a turban, sat behind the desk, watching the monitors. There was a small brass bell next to him. Zook hit it.

Ding.

The elderly Elf continued to watch the monitors.

Zook hit it again. *Ding, ding.*

There was no reaction from the Elf behind the desk.

Ding! Ding! Ding! Ding!

Roger caught Zook's hand in midair and forced it down. "For fuck's sake. The guy is obviously stone-cold deaf. Stop banging on the damn bell."

"I'm not deaf. I just wanted to see how long you'd keep hitting the bell. Had a fella in the other day, went for fifteen minutes straight. Dang fool gave me a headache. Thought he'd never give up." The old Elf turned around and smiled at them, showing all three of his teeth. He nonchalantly slid the bell out of Zook's reach. "I guess if it wasn't for your friend here, you might've gone even longer."

Zook frowned and opened his mouth, but Roger beat him to it. "We really need to speak to the person in charge of Security, please."

The elderly Elf opened a drawer of the desk, took out a ball cap, and placed it on his head. The cap had Chief of Security written across the front. "How do. Name's Oberon. How can I help you?"

Zook blinked. "*You're* head of Security?"

"Sure am. Assigned by The Claus, himself."

"When? In the Dark Ages?"

Roger elbowed Zook in the side. "Excuse my friend, please. He's a little overwhelmed. You see, there was a terrorist attack on Workshop 69 earlier today, and we think Zook, here, might've been a target."

Oberon raised a bushy white eyebrow. "You don't say? Now who'd want to go and hurt such a polite, upstanding Elf like this fella here?"

His sarcasm was not lost on Zook.

Zook glared at Oberon. "I've been in charge of Workshop 69 for a long time. How come I've never seen you before? What happened to Eddie? Wasn't he Chief?"

Oberon suddenly found a scratch on the desktop that demanded his complete attention. He picked at it with a fingernail. "Oh, Eddie. Yeah, sure. Eddie was my stand-in. I was on assignment for The Claus. Deep undercover, you understand. Very Super Sekrit. Eyes Only clearance. Real 007 stuff."

Roger exchanged a puzzled—and extremely doubtful—look with Zook. "Is he kidding?"

"There's sure something screwy somewhere." Zook scowled at Oberon. "You want to tell us what really happened, or do I need to call the Front Office right now to find out the truth?"

Oberon growled and then looked side to side, behind him, up, and down. "Look, this could ruin my street cred if it got out, so keep it between the three of us, okay? I'd checked into the Betty Crocker Clinic. I had a little problem with fudge brownies." He sighed and sat back. "It was the Clinic or the heave-ho. I made the right decision. It's a relief to have that chocolate monkey off my back."

"Well…good for you," Roger said.

"Yeah. Glad you got help." Zook glanced pointedly at the wall clock. "Oh, look at the time. We need to see the security footage for the area around Workshop 69 starting at about midnight and going until noon or so today."

Oberon cocked his head. "What for?"

"It's for a new reality show. *Elves Gone Wild*." Zook kept his face expressionless, but his voice bled sarcasm.

Roger elbowed him…hard. "Again, please excuse him. We think he needs his meds changed. We'd like to see the footage to see if we can identify the person or persons who tried to blow up the workshop."

"Oh yeah. That. Sure. Give me a minute." After shooting Zook an ugly black look, Oberon shuffled off into a room situated behind the desk.

Roger shook his head, but waited until Oberon was out of earshot to speak. "As Security Chief, I would think he'd be more interested in a bombing at one of the workshops."

Zook made a rude noise. "Probably, if it wasn't Workshop 69. I told you how our workshop is thought of by the rest of the community."

"Well, I think it's time for that to change."

"Change is good, dollars are better, and plastic is best of all."

"What does that have to do with anything?"

"Nothing at all. Don't waste your time, because nothing's going to change anytime soon."

"You know what I like about you? You're such an optimist."

"Oh, no. You're the optimist. I'm a realist. There's a big difference." Zook turned away before Roger could start lecturing him on why he should be more optimistic. Optimism was in most Elves' blood, but not Zook's. He was a firm believer in the "prepare for the worst" mode of thinking, minus the whole "hope for the best" crap.

Oberon reappeared a couple of minutes later. He gestured toward the bank of video screens behind him. "Keep your eyes on monitor eleven. It's going to play this morning's footage from the areas around Workshop 69 and the Square."

The footage was definitely not high-def. Santa might have sprung for the cameras, but he didn't go as far as getting good-quality video. It was darkish and grainy, and pixilated every so often.

"There he is!" Zook shouted, pointing at a lone figure running from the direction of Warehouse 69. As he reached the edge of the monitor, he disappeared from the screen and reappeared on the clip at the Square.

"Is it Timothy?" Roger pushed against Zook, peering at the screens.

"Of course it is. Who else can it be?"

"He's not the only Elf who likes to wear leggings and the traditional stocking cap."

Zook had seen enough. He turned away from the screens. "It's him. I'm sure of it. He went into Workshop 17."

"That's the Weapons workshop. Toy swords, guns, knives…" Oberon observed.

"Oberon, I need Security backup on this. We don't know who put Timothy up to this. I don't want to walk into Workshop 17 unprepared." Zook looked toward the screens again. "Who knows what they're planning next? For all we know, they could be plotting a complete overthrow of the current regime."

Oberon's eyes grew wide, and the color drained from his face. "You don't mean…"

Zook straightened up, lifting his chin. "Yes. A full-on Santapocalypse. It's possible."

Roger shook his head. "We have no proof of that, Zook. Earlier you thought it was me and S.E.M.E.N. behind this. You were wrong about that, right?"

"Maybe. But this is different. You saw him run."

"I saw *someone* run. Neither of us could tell if it was Timothy." Roger put his hand on Zook's shoulder. It felt warm and steady.

Zook shook it off. He couldn't afford to let anything deter him. "Even if it wasn't Timothy, somebody sure as hell tried to blow up Workshop 69!"

Roger nodded. "You're right about that much. Okay, let's do this. Just remember that if you see Timothy, everyone deserves the benefit of the doubt until proven otherwise."

"Yeah, yeah. Let's go. Oberon? Who can you spare to go with us?"

CHAPTER FIVE

Oberon's sarcasm seemed to dissipate in the face of the much larger threat of a North Pole coup. "Come with me," he said and motioned for Roger and Zook to follow him through the door behind the desk.

The door led to a vast office complex very similar in design to the Elf Satisfaction Department. It was obvious in the layout that the same designer conceived of both offices. Rows of tightly packed cubicles filled the room. The only thing missing was the long line of Elves waiting to voice their complaints.

Each cubicle had a small, tasteful brass nameplate next to the entrance. Roger read them silently as they passed. Agent Smart, Agent Smith, Agent Orange… Oberon led them past all without stopping.

"Oberon, what about all these agents? Can't you assign any of them to us?"

"No. They're all busy working. Who do you think assembles the Good and Naughty Lists each year? Santa?" Oberon snorted, and Roger heard chuckles arising from nearby cubicles. "He hasn't written his own Lists in centuries. The world is too big, my friend. We do the investigating and gather evidence, then compile the Lists."

"Where do you get all the information?" Zook stopped and peered into a cubicle where an agent was watching a monitor with single-minded focus.

"Mostly Facebook, Twitter, and Instagram. School records. Everything is electronic these days." Oberon waved a dismissive hand. "Still, it takes a lot of time and Elfhours to complete the investigation in only a year's time. Now, enough questions. Shake a leg and follow me." He led them through the room to another door at the rear.

The second door opened into a vast warehouse-like space mostly filled with shelving. "This is where we stored the old Lists, before we went digital." Oberon led them down the center aisle to the back of the room, where the shelves ended in an open area that stretched from one side of the building to the other. "Here's what I wanted you to see. I can loan you these to help you out with your search for the bomber." He shot Zook a sly look. "Anything here look familiar to you?"

Zook gasped and stared openmouthed at what filled the space.

Zook glanced at Roger, and saw him gape at what lay before them. It was obvious Roger didn't know what they were when he asked, "What the fuck *are* they?"

Before them stretched line after line of posture-perfect six-foot blue-eyed dark-haired wooden soldiers, all dressed identically in carved and painted red coats, black pants, and shiny black boots. Tall, furry black hats sat on their heads, their hands covered with pristine white gloves. Each carried a wooden rifle tipped with a bayonet.

In addition, each soldier sported a long, thick, wooden erection proudly poking out from the painted fly on their pants.

"I…I thought they were all destroyed after the Toyland debacle!" Zook gasped.

"So you and everyone else were led to believe. We had reason to think they might be useful in the future, so we stockpiled them here."

Zook turned in Oberon in a fury. "You bastard! Why would you keep them? Why?"

"Zook?" Roger stepped between Oberon and Zook and placed a hand on his chest to keep Zook from smashing a fist into Oberon's face…which was exactly what Zook wanted to do. "What's going on? Why are you so angry?"

"Don't you see? These soldiers are the reason Workshop 69 is the laughingstock of the North Pole!"

"What do you mean?"

"Back in the early part of the last century, some nitwit in Workshop 69 misread an order from Santa. Instead of six hundred one-foot-tall erect soldiers, they built one hundred six-foot-tall soldiers with erections. It was a disaster at first, but after Santa caught a few Elves selling the soldiers as synthetic sex partners, he realized there was money to be made by catering to the sexual appetite. Sales have only gone up as the years have gone by, and we, of course, have greatly expanded and improved on our inventory. The origin of the incident may have been forgotten, but the stigma remains."

Roger gave out a low whistle. "That sounds crazy."

"It is, but that's what happened. Now I come to find out that the damn things are still here!" He turned to Oberon. "And you want me to turn them on and take them out of here? Do I look stupid to you?"

Oberon huffed at Zook. "Stand down, boy. I'm old enough to be your Grandpappy Elf's Grandpappy's Grandpappy. Show some respect." He gestured toward the rows of wooden soldiers. "Now, as I see it, this is your chance to put an end to all the crap you and your workshop have been taking on account of these fellas. Take 'em, let 'em help you. They may look ridiculous, but they're good soldiers, every one of 'em. I remember when they were made—a lot of ingenuity and magic was put into them."

Zook looked more than doubtful. "But—"

Roger whispered in Zook's ear. "We need the help, Zook. We don't know what we'll be facing going into the Weapons workshop. If nothing else, they'll make a good shield."

Zook didn't look happy, but he finally nodded. "Fine. But I still say this is a bad idea." He stepped up to the first soldier in line and began examining it. "Where's the button that turns it on?"

Oberon chuckled. "Didn't have the technology for that back when they were built, sonny boy. These are run by clockwork, which means you need to wind them up. Want to guess where the handle is?"

Zook frowned, puzzled, until his gaze happened upon the thick, stiff erection poking out from the soldier's wooden groin. "Oh, come on. You've got to be kidding me."

Oberon's chuckle grew into a full-bellied laugh, and Roger couldn't help sniggering as well. "Nope! We had a sense of humor back then. Not like today. All business, you Elves are. No imagination. Now, go on. You got a lot of jerking off to do."

Zook's eyes narrowed as he glared at Oberon. "I really hate you right now." He pointed at Roger before Roger could even open his mouth. "Not a word. I swear. You do not want to speak right now."

Roger was trying to hide his grin until Zook turned his back, but Zook saw it when it slipped his control. It seemed to take him a long moment to wrestle his features back into a somber expression.

Oberon didn't bother to hide his enjoyment of Zook's discomfort. He roared, his beard bouncing, holding his sides as if the hearty laughter might shake something inside him loose. Not even the murderous looks Zook shot him could silence his guffaws as Zook gripped the soldier's wooden dick and pumped it a few times.

There was a scratchy whirring noise, the sound of gears long motionless beginning to move again. Then the soldier shouldered his weapon and snapped his hand to his forehead in a salute. The movements were a bit jerky, and his glass eyes seemed a little unfocused, but for a toy left to rust for almost a hundred years, Zook figured it was a miracle he moved at all.

"Well, don't just stand there. Help me!" Zook jerked his thumb at the next row of soldiers.

Roger blinked. "Me?"

"No, the Easter Bunny. Yes, you! It'll take me all day to turn all of these soldiers on by myself."

"That's not what was written on the bathroom wall at the Head Office," Oberon said and began to laugh all over again.

"Enough! Think what you want, but I will not allow someone to destroy my workshop or see good Elves die because of anyone's fucked-up opinion of me. Now, shut up, old man, and start jerking."

Oberon looked startled, although not for long. He was mumbling under his breath something about uppity Elves who should know their places. Still, even as he said it, he hobbled to the third row of soldiers and began pumping their penises.

"I've got to say, Zook, this really takes some guts. I wouldn't think you had it in you." Roger smiled as he hurried to the next row of soldiers and began enthusiastically jerking each penis in turn. "You spent years breaking your ass to make Workshop 69 a success, even when you had problems of your own, and even when the whole North Pole laughed. That takes brass balls, and at these temperatures, it ain't easy to sport a pair. I'm impressed."

Zook smirked but said nothing. He got the feeling Roger was being sincere, and the praise coming from Roger felt damn good.

One after another, the dusty soldiers came to life of a sort, snapping to attention amid the raspy grinding and popping sounds of old, tarnished gears. In less time than Zook would've thought, all one hundred soldiers were wound up, awake, alert, and waiting for orders.

Zook corrected himself. *One hundred and* one *soldiers. I think Roger has officially joined my Army.*

His thoughts were confirmed when Roger smiled and snapped to attention at the end of the row. "Orders, General Zook?"

Zook snorted, but when he looked out the window toward Workshop 17, there wasn't the slightest trace of scorn in his expression. "Yeah. Don't get dead."

✧ ✧ ✧ ✧

His plan was simple. The majority of soldiers would surround Workshop 17. No one was to get in and no one was to get out without Zook's express permission. The rest would act as a shield for Zook and Roger as they infiltrated the workshop. Their first and only order of business was to find Mab and Timothy. No matter what happened today, Zook was determined to find answers to his questions and put an end to the attacks on Workshop 69.

The soldiers took up positions at every entrance and window, wooden guns at the ready. The guns didn't really fire, but the bayonets would make up for the lack of firepower. They were also wooden, but were filed to a very sharp point. Back in the early part of the last century, the Consumer Product Safety Improvement Act didn't exist to protect children from dangerous toys. The bayonets on the guns the wooden soldiers carried could be deadly.

Eight soldiers surrounded Zook, Roger, and Oberon, bayonets facing outward, and after Zook gave the order to open the workshop door, the eleven of them shuffled slowly inside.

"Halt! Turn around and leave immediately. Only Elves with Level Five or higher clearance are allowed inside this workshop." An Elf dressed in a black flak jacket stood blocking their way. He had an electric assault paintball rifle trained on them. Beside him stood several other Elves, all dressed and armed similarly.

"We want to speak to the Elf in charge of this workshop. Where are Mab and Timothy? I demand you bring us to them immediately!" Zook's voice rang out from behind the wooden soldiers.

"Turn and leave. This is your final warning!"

Zook refused to back down. "Where is your Chief Elf?"

The flak-jacketed Elf didn't answer. Instead, there was a loud popping sound. Paintballs hit the wooden soldiers, exploding upon impact, staining their wooden skin with several different colors.

The wooden soldiers never flinched. Instead, at Zook's prodding, the entourage began to move forward again, taking small steps. The sharp tips of the bayonets encouraged the flak-wearing Elves to scurry out of the way, although they continued to shoot at the invaders.

Not a single paintball made it through to Zook, Roger, and Oberon. Within their wooden cocoon, they remained whole and unpainted. On the outside, though, the wooden soldiers were taking a beating. Bright splotches of orange, red, and green decorated their formerly uniformly painted bodies.

Still, inch by inch, they kept on, moving inexorably toward a door at the rear of the room. Zook's head snapped up at the sound of gunfire coming from above their heads. He had time to see another Elf in a flak jacket standing on a high shelf, firing over the heads of the wooden soldiers.

"I'm hit!" It was Oberon. He clutched his right shoulder, where a dripping blotch of blue was spreading from under his hand. "Damn that stings like a mother!"

"Keep your heads down!" Zook ordered. "Move faster! We need to get through the door into the next area."

More gunfire erupted from all around them, but no other shots penetrated the wooden soldier shield that protected them. They made it at last to the door. One of the soldiers opened it, and they moved through, closing it behind them. The multiple paintballs hitting the door from the other side rattled the door on its frame and sounded like firecrackers.

They were in a large office. Zook peeked between two of the soldiers and spotted a familiar face standing behind a desk on the far side of the room. "Timothy! Come here, boy. You and I have a talk coming."

"Oh, hey, Zook. What's with all the soldiers? Why do they all have hard-ons?" Timothy's voice was cheerful, as if a gaggle of six-foot, paint-splattered, bayonet-wielding wooden soldiers was an everyday sight. "Hey, is that Roger in there with you? Hi, Roger. Long time no see."

Roger elbowed Zook and whispered, "He really isn't all there, is he?"

"I told you so. You're the one who said he was some sort of criminal mastermind."

"Guess I was wrong."

Zook huffed. "Yeah, I guess you were." He pushed past the soldiers. Timothy stood behind the desk. Mab was seated in a chair, her fingers frozen over a computer keyboard. "Ah, Mab. I suppose *you're* the brains behind the bombing at Workshop 69."

Mab shook her head vehemently and stood up, moving away from the desk with her hands up. "Me? Hell, no. I was just following orders. I swear it, Zook! She told me to give Timothy the dynamite and tell him to put it in the storeroom."

"Who's 'she'?" Roger joined Zook outside the protective flank of soldiers. Oberon remained where he was, safely ensconced in the circle of wood. "And why should we believe you?"

"I've got no beef with Workshop 69. I swear it! But I couldn't say no to her. I couldn't!" Mab's voice was shrill with fear. "Not even you could say no to her. Of course not!"

"To who, Mab? To who?" Zook demanded. "I want to know whose idea the bombing was and why!"

A new voice startled Zook and Roger. Neither had realized anyone else was in the room. When they turned toward it, their eyes bugged out like boiled eggs. "Oh, come on. It can't be! Not you!"

CHAPTER SIX

Mrs. Claus, white-haired and round, wearing her traditional red velvet dress and white frilled apron, stood in a corner of the room. She held a paintball revolver in her pudgy hand. "Why *not* me?"

Zook shrugged. "Because…because you're Santa's wife!"

She barked a short laugh. "And? Listen, I've been relegated to the kitchen for eons." She imitated her husband's deep voice. "Bake me some gingerbread, woman. Where are my stockings, wife? Get this taffy out of my beard." She pointed the gun first at Zook, then Roger, then back at Zook. "I'm sick of working my fingers to the bone making sure everything runs smoothly up here at the Pole, and who gets the credit? Santa, that's who."

"What's that got to do with trying to blow up Workshop 69?" Zook demanded.

Mrs. Claus waved a dismissive hand at him. "I didn't really try to blow it up. I just wanted to disable it for a while. Without the income generated by Workshop 69, there'd be no way to pay for parts and labor for the toy making. Christmas would've come to a complete halt this year. The scandal would've forced my husband to step down as Commander-in-Chief Elf, and I would've gladly filled the position. No more baking cookies. No more knitting Elf caps until my fingers bleed. No more singing carols until my throat burns. No more tinsel in my bra or glitter in my teacup. All I'd have is one night of work a year. One night! Then I'd be the one to kick back and have somebody fawn all over me for the other 364 days."

The door behind them suddenly banged open, and a deep voice boomed, "JESSICA!"

Everyone froze at the familiar voice of the Commander-in-Chief Elf. Framed in the doorway, Santa's bulk filled it from side to side. "Jessica, how dare you plot against me? I thought you loved me!"

Mrs. Claus gasped and clasped her hands to her shelf-like bosom. "Why…um, darling! Of course I love you. Whatever makes you think otherwise?"

"Oh, I don't know." Santa walked around the gaggle of wooden soldiers and stood between Zook and Roger, and Mrs. Claus. He reached over to the desk and pressed a button on the phone console. "Maybe because the intercom was on and I heard every word you said? Along with every employee of Workshop 17."

"I… I…" Mrs. Claus seemed at a loss for words.

Not so her husband.

"Get your ass back to the house. We'll discuss this when I get home." Santa's expression brooked no disagreement. Mrs. Claus ran off as quickly as she could, which was quite a bit faster than Zook would've thought, considering her bulk.

Santa gestured toward the wooden soldiers. "Who jerked my Wooden Army awake?"

Zook lifted his chin. "I did, sir. I felt we needed the protection coming in here."

Roger stood tall next to Zook. "He's not the only one to blame, sir. I helped."

"And me." Oberon's voice rose from within the flank of wooden soldiers.

"Oberon? Is that you in there?" Santa chuckled. "You old goat. You're still getting into trouble, I see." He turned toward Zook and Roger again. "Never fear. I'm not angry. I'm glad to see someone in this Compound was using his head. Coming into Workshop 17 unarmed would've been foolish." He clapped a beefy white-gloved hand on each of their shoulders. "I'm sorry about my wife's plot. I hear she did some damage to the basement of Workshop 69."

Zook and Roger exchanged a glance. "Nothing we couldn't handle, sir."

"You know, I could use a couple of smart Elves like you up at the house. How'd you both like to come work with my crew and me?"

"Us? At the Big House?" Zook and Roger blinked in unison, both of them equally stunned.

"Yes. What do you think?"

Zook bit his lip. "Well, sir. I appreciate the offer, I really do. It's an honor. But I feel I have a responsibility to Workshop 69. I wouldn't feel right leaving it to the care of someone who's not trained. The entire Compound relies on the income generated from our sex toys."

Santa nodded. "That's true, and you've been doing a splendid job, Zook. Don't worry. I understand, and I appreciate your dedication." He turned toward Roger. "How about you? I don't think you're too anxious to go back to the Elf Satisfaction Department, are you?"

"No, sir, I'm not." Roger glanced toward Zook. "But to tell the truth, while I'm also honored at your offer, I really think I'd like to learn how to make sex toys."

Zook couldn't hide his smile. He hadn't thought much beyond finding out who was behind the bombing and stopping them from setting off any others. Now that it was over, he realized he didn't want to say good-bye to Roger. They worked well as a team. Moreover, he really wanted a repeat of their frotting session—this time in private and sans clothing.

Santa's lips curved in knowing smile. "Oh, you do, huh? Ho, ho, ho. Well, I suppose that could be arranged. Very well. Off with the two you now." He waved his hand toward the door. "Remember to put the wooden soldiers back where you found them, and clean them off before all that paint dries."

Zook snapped off a salute. "Yes, sir!"

"Hey, what about me?" Oberon piped up. "I helped too. Don't I get an offer to go the Big House?"

Santa sighed. "Oh, fine. You can be in charge of House Security. I just had one of those newfangled security systems installed, and it's so fucking sensitive, every time I fart I set off the alarm."

❖ ❖ ❖ ❖

They'd just finished scrubbing the last bit of paint from the final wooden soldier. The soldiers once again stood in long, straight lines, their erections waiting to be jerked to bring them to life when next they were needed.

Zook cleaned his hands on a rag, then tossed it into a trash barrel. "It's been a long fucking day. I need a shower."

"Yeah, me too." Roger arched his back. The sound of his spine realigning was like popcorn popping in a microwave.

"Okay. My place or yours?"

Roger blinked in surprise. "Huh?"

"What? Do you think I'm deaf or suffer from dementia? I distinctly remember you offering earlier to suck me until my eyeballs inverted."

"Yeah, I remember, but…"

Zook held up his hand. "Oh no, you don't. No takey-backsies."

"Well, since you put it like that…" Roger grinned at him. "Let's go. It takes a good deal of time and a lot of sucking power to invert someone's eyeballs. I may need to have my own pump primed first." He cupped his crotch, and his smile grew lecherous.

"I believe that can be arranged." Zook's grin matched Roger's.

Roger laughed, grabbed one of the straps crisscrossing Zook's hairy chest, and snapped it. "I never doubted otherwise. I have complete confidence in you."

IT'S A
WONDERFUL LUBE

KAGE ALAN

For Martha Davis
Merry Christmas!

Are you ready to add some magic into your life and earn money while doing it? Are you ready to develop sustainable strategies in the workforce and be a responsible corporate citizen? Do you possess the sincere desire to make merry and the gift of wonder in imagining the look on every man, woman, and child's face when they unwrap the perfect holiday gift? If so, then you'll want to apply for one of our many positions at Santa's Workshop here at the North Pole!

Santa Holdings Incorporated Technologies (SHIT) is a management company offering competitive wages and packages close—but not identical—to similar companies located in third-world countries not part of the United Nations, discounted flights for when you get homesick*, room and board, and opportunities for advancement as well as lateral moves for valuable flexible work experience. There's also reindeer games, but no elf tossing, please!

We're looking for installers, electricians, technicians, statisticians, tacticians, wrappers, ropers, dispatchers, debriefers, stuffers, shufflers, fluffers, quality control specialists, consultants, coordinators, genealogists, gynecologists, meteorologists, and overall team players full of sunshine & joy and not afraid of working occasional overtime**.

Our company is your company, and your SHIT is committed to compliance with all applicable equal employment *laws we consider worth recognizing and deem as benefiting our associates most. We are an equal opportunity employer***!*

SHIT provides basic job application instructions in English and Broken English, so if you're ready to join our team of dedicated men, women, reindeer, and elves in a fast-paced, rewarding, and exciting career working for the man who lives to come down your chimney and shoot back out once a year, then submit your resume today!

*All discounted flights are Coach Class or Freight, and any miles accumulated using this privilege must be credited to Santa's corporate account.

**Occasional may refer to daily overtime and include working with disgruntled employees on third shift.

***We may not explicitly or implicitly discriminate on the basis of any prohibited factor unless we have a very good reason to be bothered by your race, sex, religion, national origin, disability, age, or sexual orientation. In the rare case we do, SHIT will be all over you.

✦ ✦ ✦ ✦

'Twas a late night in July

At the North Pole up high;

Frigid air surrounded Santa's toy shop with impenetrable squalls,

Uninviting to anyone working there, especially if they had balls.

All was merry each evening until someone got plastered,

Causing security to remove the little elf bastard.

To third shift he went,

Until his attitude was spent;

For if his work ethic didn't level,

He was bound to run into the elf terror known as Tall Devil.

Here was the man, the myth, someone with no history,

And what he was doing at the North Pole remained a bit of a mystery.

So it's here our story starts with a little elf fury,

And his run-in with a young security intern from Missouri.

❖ ❖ ❖ ❖

"No!" Glans Maximus, the second-shift sleigh maker, screamed at Jameson Wallace, security officer, and Barbara Barletta, the middle-aged and questionably competent head of Human Resources.

The ruckus caught the attention of all the third-shift elves in Warehouse Eleven, which was where the sleighs were built. The elves knew the drill, though, in that there was always a bit of noise when someone was brought in this time of night for disciplinary action, especially since *he* arrived. And as assuredly as there was noise, there would also assuredly be quiet and order soon enough…after *he* showed up. The mood was currently a stark contrast to the Christmas trees, fake snow, smell of pine, and twinkling LED lights that helped create their merry work environment.

And then there was the music. Most of it was tolerable, but if they had to listen to Mariah Carey sing "All I Want for Christmas Is You" one more fucking time, there'd likely be a homicide.

"You're not sticking my ass on third shift with these other asshats and that emotionless, unholy whack job you soulless corporate management minion wardens hired. I didn't do anything wrong. And if that teasing bottom bitch of a quality control intern wants to say different, I'll go before the fat ass in the red suit and get him to vouch for me. And if he won't, I'll tell everybody where he stores all the granny-porn videos he downloads illegally on the dedicated T1 line in his office!"

"It's only for a week or two," Barbara attempted to soothe him in her matter-of-fact business tone, "just until we work out your little behavior issue…and move the intern to a safer location, preferably somewhere you'll never see him again. You don't want a mark in your file to turn into something bigger. Corporate won't like that. And it leaves us open to too many lawsuits."

"Behavior issue?" Glans's nostrils flared. "Fuck you and your files! I'll show you a behavior issue." He grabbed a hammer off the nearest worktable and raised it. "Now you put me back on second shift and stay the hell away from me. I told you, I didn't do anything wrong."

"You told him you'd only insert the tip." Jameson raised his open hands in front of him in an attempt to keep the little shit's attention directed toward himself and Barbara. Provoking a pissed-off elf never ended well. Well, it didn't used to anyway. Things had gone a bit differently lately.

"I did!" the elf insisted.

"He didn't know you were deformed," Barbara countered.

"I'm not deformed. I just happen to be a weapon of ass destruction and proud of it." He waved the hammer toward them. "And nobody, *nobody*, is going to stick me on a shift after all those stories I've heard about that heartless, soulless, dickless, elf-hating, malcontented motherfucker you have making their lives a living hell and…"

Jameson and Barbara looked at each other nervously.

"He's standing right behind me, isn't he?"

"Take off, Jameson," security intern Wesley Lee instructed his partner in a low, icy tone. "I've got this."

Jameson slowly backed away and closed the warehouse door behind him. He'd be waiting outside, ready to rush in if things went badly. The situation wouldn't take a turn for the worse—they never did with this intern—but he'd be ready anyway.

Meanwhile, all third-shift eyes were on the remaining three.

"Now put the hammer down." Wesley spoke politely but firmly, leaving no room for negotiation.

"Tall Devil…" Glans bolted toward Barbara, grabbed a hold of her leg, then whirled around and stared at his worst nightmare come true. "I'll bust the bitch's kneecaps!"

"That's not very smart"—the security guard remained calm—"especially since we're not just going to let you walk out of here if you do."

"We?" Glans looked around. He had one of them by the leg who could be hit or easily pushed to the ground, and he was sure he could outrun the other, at least long enough to escape the warehouse. The other elves wouldn't get in the way or stop him. "Who's 'we', sucker?"

"Black and Decker—and me." Wesley brought out the nail gun hidden behind his back he'd picked up from one of the other tables. Jameson had been nice enough to make sure the little minion kept his attention forward in order to make it possible. "And since this is their latest model, a Twelve-Volt Cordless Eighteen-Gauge Brad Nailer, the most powerful nail gun in the world and can blow four hundred nails clean through you before losing its charge, you've got to be asking yourself one question."

"Do I feel lucky?"

"Don't be a cliché," Wesley warned. "You have to be wondering how many holes I can make in your body before you even get close to busting the bitch's kneecaps."

"Excuse me?" Barbara objected to being referred to as the "b" word.

"Shut up!" Glans snapped at her, then hefted the hammer and glared at the guard. "I swear I'll do it."

"Go ahead—" Wesley aimed the gun at the elf's head and used his thumb to power it on. "—make my sleigh."

Several tense seconds passed and nobody wavered. Finally…

"All right. You win this time, copper." The elf slowly set the hammer down on the floor, then stood up and stared at the head of Human Resources. "Two weeks, lady. You got two weeks to put me back on second shift, so go do what you gotta do. And you—" He turned to Wesley. "—how do you sleep at night?"

"With my eyes open and my asshole puckered."

Wesley thumbed the switch on the gun to OFF and set it back down on a worktable.

"Don't fuckin' tease me now, bitch. You coulda had this"—Glans grabbed his crotch—"if you'd played your cards right and hadn't acted so hard to get."

"Yeah, not like you," an elf nearby called over. "Jesus, Glans. You gave in easy. A gay twenty-eight-year-old stared you down? That's embarrassing."

"Yeah, Glans," another called out. "You just got busted by Dirty Mary."

"Dirty Mary?" another voice piped up. "The guy's name is Wesley Lee. What kind of parent does that to a child? Sounds like I'm fucking stuttering whenever I say it."

"Swell." Wesley stared at the elves.

◆ ◆ ◆ ◆

"Well, that could have gone a whole lot worse." Jameson sighed and leaned back against the wall of the corridor outside Warehouse Eleven.

It was but one of many hallways extending out like a spider web from the main building—which contained all the housing and kitchens necessary for the workforce and connected to all the other warehouses. The main level of each workshop was the assembly level, while all completed stock or kits were sent one level below for packaging, then whisked away for storage below the launching area of Santa's sleigh. That in itself was an impressive system and went a hundred levels or more below the surface, each intricately cataloged and automated to load the sleigh based on whatever course weather conditions dictated each Christmas Eve.

"I agree." Wesley eyed his partner and saw both fatigue and something else he'd feared had been developing since they'd first met two months earlier. The fatigue was the main problem for the moment, though, since they still had another four hours to go and had to write up incident reports. Speaking of which… "The stack of paperwork for killing an elf is a hell of a lot thicker."

"I think we both know that wasn't going to happen." Jameson shook his head. "You have a knack for anticipating what they'll do, what they won't do, and how far they can be pushed. I don't know how the hell you do it, but I'm glad you do."

"I understand them, whereas most people don't. Just read the folklore. We're all raised on the belief that Santa's elves live in harmony at the North Pole, singing, laughing, playing with the reindeer, shitting rainbows, and making toys year round for that one magical night. If the world knew the truth about their libidos and how much trouble they enjoy causing from thinking with what's between their legs, someone somewhere would have a trophy room with all of their heads nailed to the wall." Wesley paused for a moment. "Some of them aren't so bad. They just need to know exactly where you stand."

"I guess it's a good thing they keep the female elves separated from the males during work hours, otherwise it'd just be one giant fuck fest in the warehouses." Not that it hadn't come close to becoming one anyway when the elves got their hands on the interns. "Have you ever been tempted to, you know, try elf sex at least once?"

"I'd rather take a steel brush to Vladimir Putin's ass in a phone booth full of lighter fluid than fuck or be fucked by one of those gremlins."

"Well all right, then." Jameson chuckled, then studied the twenty-eight-year-old intern he'd been partnered with.

Wesley was about six foot two, had dark brown hair, absolutely piercing brown eyes, prominent cheekbones, a finely chiseled jaw that was rumored by the elves to be able to cut glass, and the body of a fitness model. The only thing he lacked was a fire to melt the ice around his heart and the clothes off his body, which everyone who saw him—man and elf alike—would have fucked each other over in order to get into his good graces and gaze at. Quite frankly, Wesley had driven the elves into a frantic sexual frenzy his first day on the job, each one vowing to get into his pants for bragging rights.

Jameson was a bit opposite in looks, though by no means ugly. He had the blond-haired, blue-eyed thing going for him, but since he was only five foot seven, the other security officers and interns tended to be taller than him. This made his stock plummet in the eyes of the elves, and they therefore considered him a lesser prize. This was especially true since he'd reached the age of thirty, the same age that most men disappeared in the eyes of the gay community and officially became senior citizens. Not that he'd slept with any of the elves. And not that any of them had asked him to, especially with a fresh batch of interns coming in every three months. It used to be every six months, but the turnover rate tended to be quite high when the elves were feeling frisky. And, really, when weren't the little anus raiders feeling frisky?

They didn't leave Jameson with many options for extracurricular proclivities.

"You know—" He looked down at the ground, then back up at Wesley, and summoned as much courage as he could. "—they're not the only ones who get lonely. I mean… I really want…and I'm sure you'd want to be discreet about it, too…but I'd like to…um… I wouldn't mind stocking your stuffing."

"What?" Wesley's brow furrowed.

"I mean…" Jameson stammered, "I want to stuff your stocking."

"You've been hanging around the elves too long." He dismissed the come-on, then opened the door to the warehouse and walked back in. "And if you can't say it right the first time, maybe there's a reason you shouldn't be saying it at all."

The door closed behind him, leaving Jameson feeling like he wouldn't be needing a cold shower for a least a month after their exchange.

"Damn…you *are* cold."

✧ ✧ ✧ ✧

"Where's Tinkles?" Wesley called out while making his way around several of the busier aisles.

"He's over here, Tall Devil," one of the elves yelled out.

He steered himself in the direction of the voice and finally found the little troublemaker. The elves' nickname for him hadn't bothered Wesley in the least. In fact, it made it that much easier for his reputation to spread, not to mention they tended not to cross him and instead left him alone, which figured into his agenda perfectly.

"Tinkles," Wesley addressed the elf, who actually managed to look like he was legitimately working.

"My fucking name is Twinkles"—the elf continued stacking several boxes onto a conveyor belt—"you tall, stupid, sniper's first target!"

And thus their dance began.

"And here I thought your name was Tinkles since you spend so much time in the bathroom tinkling."

"He ain't tinkling," Chipper, the elf working next to him, clarified. "The inspiration for *Honey, I Shrunk the Kids* is in there laughing manically and beating off to pictures of Justin Bieber and Austin Mahone."

"Inspiration for *Honey, I Shrunk the Kids*..." Another elf laughed. "That's a good one." And raised his hand. "Low five!"

They smacked hands.

"Bieber, Mahone, and laughter?" Wesley stared at Twinkles, the corner of his mouth turned up in the faintest of smiles. "Then I guess that would make you the Twinkler."

"What do you want, cock jockey?"

"Cool it, Rumple Foreskin. You usually work in Warehouse Sixteen. I need to know which locker in the holding area the prototype dildos are held in."

"That's not your jurisdiction, flatfoot deadfuck. The SHIT engineers are the only ones who are allowed access to those lockers, which is why none of us have seen that area in years. Not that I don't know, though. Some fresh, warm, milky white elf love, or as we call it in the hood, Elfer's Glue, has a way of making tight-ass corporate types spill their secrets when it's added to their coffee." Twinkles leaned in closer in order to whisper the next bit, forcing Wesley to kneel down. "What's in it for me if I tell ya, fuckrudder?"

"For starters, spunk bubble, I won't tell Barbara Barletta in HR that you're putting elf fizz in the coffee since I happen to know you bring her a cup sometimes, too. Second—" He thought for a moment at what he could possibly offer to sway the little shit demon's mind. "—I had an embarrassing moment the other night, and someone saw me naked as I was stepping out of the shower. They're sworn to secrecy and will unequivocally deny it when asked due to the confidentiality agreements we all have to sign, but I know you have your ways. You tell me what I *need* to know, and I'll tell you what you *want* to know."

Twinkles glanced around to the left, then to the right.

Satisfied nobody was close enough to hear what he said, the elf leaned in farther and whispered something into the security intern's ear.

Wesley stood back up, made a mental note of the number and letter combination of the locker, then stared into the elf's eyes and searched for any sign of deception. The little bastards would lie, cheat, and steal to get the upper hand when it came to gossip, only this one apparently wanted it bad enough to tell the truth. Now to keep his end of the bargain.

"The person you want to get close to is my partner, Jameson," Wesley admitted with fake trepidation. "He took a good, long, explicit, wet, detail-oriented look." He stopped, opened his mouth to say more, stopped, sighed, then continued. "He's been trained to resist, so it may take several of you to wear him down, along with some unspeakable acts of pleasure. That's all I'm saying."

"And that's all you have to say, Tall Devil." Twinkles grinned.

"No, it's not." He reached over and picked a box cutter off the nearest table. "If you ever stick your tongue in my ear or nibble on my earlobe again after you've whispered something into it, your name is going to change from Twinkles to Twinkleless."

"Tease…tease…tease…" The elf chuckled and started stacking boxes again. "Your kind always teases before they fall victim to my throbbing elfhood."

"Throbbing elfhood?" one of the other elves, who'd been trying to eavesdrop, shouted out. "Bitch is so small, bacteria laughs at it." Then he wiggled his eyebrows at Wesley. "Give it up to me instead, RoboCock. What do you say? Ready to worship my pole in your hole?"

"The only thing that gets a boner at the thought of you fucking me is my middle finger." The intern turned and strolled toward one of exits that had a connecting hallway to another warehouse. "Go dry hump a pasta strainer, Spicket."

"Sparkle! My name is Sparkle!" the elf snapped. "I'll put the sparkle up your ass, you cock teasing meat wallet."

"You couldn't reach my ass with that snot slinger without a highchair," Wesley called back over his shoulder and shut the door behind him.

"I fucking heard that!"

There was seldom rest for the wicked, which explained why the elves always seemed to have plenty of time to be up to no good. On the other side of things, the corporate engineers only put in exactly the amount of time they had to. They were there for the paycheck, nothing more. The elves were there to blow their Mr. Sniffles in every mangina possible. And none of it went unnoticed by Wesley, which meant behavioral patterns could be predicted and manipulated as needed. All he had to do was coordinate what he'd learned from Twinkles with what he'd observed in executive security protocols over the last two months to know exactly where all the weaknesses were. It also helped he had the man of his dreams from *in* his dream helping him, but that was still a secret.

It took him less than twelve hours to put his plan into action. Absolutely nothing could be allowed to get between him and his mission.

Wesley arrived at Jameson's room and knocked on the door at exactly six thirty that evening. It typically gave them fifteen minutes to catch up on whatever needed to be followed up on or discussed from the previous night/morning before the staff meeting at six forty-five; then they were on duty for their eight hours, covering half of second shift and half of third.

"You ready?" he asked after Jameson met him at the door.

"Yeah."

"Here." Wesley handed him a thumb drive.

"What's this?" Jameson eyed him cautiously, expecting it to be a PDF of SHIT's sexual harassment policies because of what he'd said the previous night. "An assignment?"

"No." Wesley ignored the sarcasm. "You told me last night when we were coming off shift that you didn't have anything entertaining to watch. I just downloaded a made-for-SyFy movie, some new franchise called *Monkeybots vs. Killer Penguins*. Figured I'd give you a copy."

"When I said entertaining, I was kinda talking about porn." Jameson sighed and gripped the thumb drive in his hand. "*Monkeybots vs. Killer Penguins*? Seriously?"

"It sounded…entertaining as a one-off. I mean, really, what's the likelihood it'll ever make it to a part eight?"

"Listen…" Jameson paused. "About last night…"

"Apology accepted."

"I wasn't apologizing."

"Oh." Wesley's brow furrowed. "Awkward."

"I just want to tell you up front, no-holds-barred and in complete honesty"—he locked eyes with his partner—"that I really want to get in your pants."

"I know."

"That's it?" Jameson was already frustrated and this wasn't helping. "That's all you have to say?"

"You haven't exactly been subtle about it. What more do you want me to say?"

"For starters"—he folded his arms across his chest—"you could tell me how you feel about it."

"That usually tends to work against me, but all right. Since you've asked, the least I can do is honor your request out of professional courtesy." Wesley thought about it for a moment. "I already have someone in my life, but I feel we need to get this out of your system. You should go back in your room, get naked, and play Hide-and-Go-Fuck-Yourself for the next fifteen minutes. That way you won't be thinking about it all night because it's really getting in the way of your work. Our performance reviews are coming up, and I don't want them to suffer because you're distracted. It's not fair to me. How's that?" Several long seconds of silence passed between them. "What?"

"I'd call you a cunt, but honestly, you lack the warmth and depth of one." Jameson glared. "How's that for 'what'?"

"It raises a question."

"Only one?"

"How the hell do you know what the depth and temperature of a—"

Jameson slammed the door shut.

"I'll wait outside here until you're finished." Wesley looked around for something to pass the time.

***

The two security guards raced from one warehouse area to the next, only checking things out peripherally instead of their usual in-depth inspections. Their presence was typically enough to help the shift foreman or foreelf keep everybody in line, and things appeared to be running smoothly on second shift. That wasn't uncommon. Third shift was the headache, but that was still several hours away.

"You didn't look the least bit surprised they're calling a town hall meeting tonight with the big guy in red and the missus." Jameson stopped and studied one of the production sheets to make sure everything was filled out properly. "Everybody else was. It's like you knew it was going to happen even before they did. Do you mind explaining how?"

"There's a certain symmetry to it," Wesley replied nonchalantly. "Besides, we're security. How would it look if we walked around acting surprised every time something unexpected came up? The last thing we need going around are rumors about our efficiency."

They entered one of the hallways that took them to an adjoining warehouse.

"Speaking of rumors…" Jameson chuckled. "I've heard one for a couple of years now that a horny Afghan Hound once got out of the kennel and had its wicked way with an unlucky elf."

"Bestiality? That's funny to you?"

"Not that specific part, no." Jameson realized it sounded kinda bad if it had. "The part where he allegedly kept screaming he was getting fucked by Cousin It was."

"I'm not even sure who I feel more sorry for." No, Wesley was pretty sure. "Leaning toward the dog."

"Yeah, well, I never found out if it really even happened. And speaking of things that may not be real, I'm not buying that shit about you having a significant other in your life. Nobody would put up with your shit."

They opened the door to Warehouse Thirteen, where most of the science fiction toys were made, and headed for the foreelf's desk. It didn't take long for the elves to notice them.

"Well, lookee lookee," Topper Winky called out. "It's the Bone Ranger!"

"And his sidekick, the Artful Throbber!" Bling-Bling, the elf working next to him, teased. "What do ya say, Security Guard Jameson? Wanna go back to your place and reenact *Jurassic Pork*? I'll be all up in your moo shu, cutie."

"It's too early for this shi—" Jameson stopped in his tracks. "Did he just call me 'cutie'?"

"Yes, he did." Wesley feigned confusion. It looked like word had gotten around that his partner had seen something he shouldn't, and now they were willing to pay him a little attention to find out some details after all. One thing was for sure, the elves didn't disappoint when it came to their libidos. "Something you want to tell me?"

"Hey, no minions in my moo shu, okay? They've gotta be messing with me for some reason." Did they really need a reason? "Or they're just bored."

"Just you and me." Bling-Bling winked and sauntered toward Jameson, thrusting his hips up and down as he went. "My dick is so big that my mother was in labor two extra days."

"Oh, please." Topper Winky gagged. "Your dick is so small, you make it disappear just by breathing in and out." The elf grabbed another elf passing by and pointed to Bling-Bling. "You ever see his dick?"

"Yeah," the worker admitted. "I haven't laughed that hard since he showed me his balls."

"That is some cold shit!" Bling-Bling's seductive voice turned right to anger, and he whirled around to face Topper Winky. "Why are you talking about my Vlad the Impaler like that? As I recall, the last time you got frisked by security and they got to your crotch, they asked if you had a sex change. And you—" He turned to other elf. "—I'll have you know my dick is so big that it came in first, second, *and* third in a big dick contest!"

"As fun as this isn't"—Wesley tapped his partner on the arm—"come on, we've got work to do."

And with that, they continued toward the foreelf's desk.

"You're in a hurry tonight," Jameson remarked. "You'd usually just stand there until you made one of them cry."

"The shit sometimes even wears on me." He sighed. "Have any of these gremlins ever boned anything other than an intern?"

"Well"—Jameson stopped and pointed to an elf two tables over—"I know that Nipper over there once bragged about fucking Jack Frost."

"Jack Frost?" Wesley's eyes narrowed. "*The* Jack Frost? How do we know when the sneaky little bastards are telling the truth?"

"Hey, Nipper?" his partner called out and got the elf's attention. "How's production today?"

"Right where it should be!" Nipper shouted back, his voice several octaves higher than it had any business being.

"Oh man." Wesley shook his head. "That's seriously fucked up. His dick froze, didn't it?"

"Balls and all. Snapped off like an icicle from what I heard, but it was painless."

"That reminds me." He pulled Jameson into a small room used for meetings and to make plant-wide announcements. "Do you remember that issue we were briefed on regarding some of the more adult-oriented prototype toys going missing and then magically reappearing?"

"Yeah. What about it?"

"I figured out a way to catch our thief, and based on what I was able to arrange earlier today, we've got a good chance of nailing him at tonight's Town Hall meeting right in front of the big guy and missus." Wesley stopped to make sure he had his partner's full attention before continuing.

"How?"

"I have a source…"

"Of course you do."

"...who told me the latest dildo model, the Deluxe Ally Blue Blunt Instrument of Orificial Pleasure Palace Pleasing G-Spot Stimulator Simulator, was just added to a holding area locker. I borrowed and installed one of those mini megavibrating motors used in the new Magic Fingers mattresses that responds to clapping. Now, whoever's been stealing these toys hasn't been caught with them in their room during searches, and that means it's on their person. I'm betting they're not only walking around with them, they're also using them while they're walking around because it's the only chance they'll get to try them out. We just have to find an excuse to clap a couple of times tonight and watch for a reaction. Once we have that, we can nail whoever it is."

"That'll look pretty good on our reviews, too." Jameson mulled it over. "Do I want to know how you managed to get into a security area even we don't have access to?"

"If something goes wrong," Wesley warned, "it might be best if you had plausible deniability. You won't have to lie about something you don't have any information about."

"I know I've said some unkind-yet-true things about your negative personality and general disdain toward your coworkers and probably humankind as well, but I do appreciate and trust your dedication to the job, and that's what counts." He grinned. "Let's catch the son of a bitch."

"We'd better get back out on the floor. They're going to announce the meeting any second now."

The two guards hadn't gotten more than ten feet before they heard the *squee* over the loudspeakers. The North Pole intercom turned on and the sound of Barbara clearing her throat reverberated throughout the entire facility.

"Anyone want to lay odds on whether or not she'll call us minions again?" Squeezy asked while gluing the plastic barrel onto an official Spacehunters toy Shimmer Pistol frame.

"I'll take that bet." Bubbles grabbed the piece Squeezy put together and inserted the battery-operated mechanism that provided real-life laser sounds into the chamber compartment.

"Attention all minio…mini-associates…and full-size associates…"

"Yeah, that didn't sound remotely like a fuckup!" Squeezy yelled at the closest speaker.

"Seriously," Bubbles agreed, "who did that bitch piss off to get sent here anyway?"

"I have a special treat for you all tonight!"

"She's back on Percocet?" Puddin' Pants asked while grabbing the Shimmer Pistol from Bubbles and adding the light-up panel to either side of the barrel.

"The Kringle family, that's Mr. and Mrs. Kringle, or Santa and Mrs. Claus as they're known throughout the world…"

"Who? The who?" Squeezy asked everyone around him. "The which family? I'm just so confused as to who she might be talking about."

"If this was a real gun"—Bubbles hefted the piece of plastic in his hand—"I'd shoot myself in the fuckin' head so I don't have to listen to her finish this announcement."

"…cordially invite you to a surprise, festive Town Hall meeting in half an hour! All employees are expected to be there to greet Mr. and Mrs. Claus as they personally provide us with the State of the Company address and discuss…um…the state of the company…and where it's at this particular time during the fiscal year."

"Has anybody ever seen this bitch walk, talk, and chew gum at the same time?" Puddin' Pants rolled his eyes. "How the hell she doesn't get fired and wind up on elffare is beyond me."

"All foremen and foreelves are to release your shift in exactly fifteen minutes, with shifts resuming within fifteen minutes of the meeting's conclusion. Everyone off-duty should report there now. And since tonight is a special occasion, there will be spicy eggnog and green cornflake wreaths served during the report!"

"Oh good." Bubbles shook his head in disgust. "Because putting that much food dye into an elf is always a good thing. Last time that moron did this, I shit green for two days, and when I went to the elfirmary, the corporate doctor thought I'd gone vegan."

"Didn't you fuck the corporate doctor?" Squeezy asked.

"Don't be an idiot. I just proved to him I ate meat." He giggled. "It got me two days off with pay."

"So are you ready to have some fun tonight?"

"Absolutely," Puddin' Pants answered. "On your mark, get set, go fuck yourself!"

"See you soon!"

✧ ✧ ✧ ✧

The Commons was the only place, besides utilizing one of the warehouses, where all the employees could be gathered with any amount of comfort. There were a hundred round tables that sat six to eight people, with room to spare in case of guests or a convention. Believe it or not, there were companies found throughout the world willing to pay through the nose just to be able to brag that they held a function at Santa's workshop at the North Pole.

SHIT only ever had one issue with the original setup, and that was with the tables and chairs. The company had ordered two different sizes of each so that the elves could sit with each other and everyone else didn't have to. The arrangement didn't last long, because once the male elves took one look at the first batch of interns all those years ago, they threatened to strike if they couldn't be eye-to-eye with the objects of their desire. New tables were ordered that were all uniform, along with new adjustable chairs, thereby allowing anyone to sit at any table, elves or non-elves. The interns were less than pleased.

There were large entrances on the east and west sides of the room, while the south side allowed access to the kitchen serving line, and the north side featured a large stage with video monitors. As for décor, there were the usual Christmas trees from one end of the room to the other, decorated to represent every region of the world, LED Christmas lights strung along the walls and ceiling, wreaths above doors with lights that blinked in patterns or to music, and snow globes in the center of each table that could be switched on for further illumination.

All of the off-duty interns were already in attendance and sitting next to each other for protection. They knew the drill. The corporate engineers, other various support personnel, and the female elves kept to themselves, too, but also in close proximity of each other.

Shift foremen and foreelves released their workers, and it was mere moments before the elves surged through the doors in an effort to spy the intern they wanted to sit next to and hit on.

Barbara stood on the stage in front of a microphone stand and looked out at the chaos in front of her.

"Let's be orderly, people," she instructed. "And—hey!" She pointed to several of the elves. "Go find a place to sit where there are empty chairs and leave those interns alone. We're not a bunch of wild banshees."

"Fuck you!" One of the elves flipped her off, then leapt onto one of the tables and slid across it toward an extremely good-looking—though now terrified—twenty-two-year-old male Latino college intern. "*Elfnado!*"

"Get your ass over here, McDiddles."

A hand reached out and pulled the screaming elf off the table before he could make contact.

"Watch the shirt and vest, Tall Devil!" The worker righted himself. "And unless you want multiple swift kicks to the shins, my name is McJingles."

"You kick me in the shins and your name will be McSingles," Wesley growled. "As in testicles."

"Oh, chill the fuck out and go read *Fifty Shades of Elf*, will ya, you dickless bean pole?" McJingles straightened his shirt and vest out, then went in search of an empty chair a few tables away. "Who the hell did I loan that book out to anyway?"

Meanwhile, back on stage, Mr. and Mrs. Claus entered through a private hallway and were assisted to their seats with a couple of other corporate types nobody knew the names of.

Jameson wandered over to Wesley.

"Is this everybody?"

"I think so. Keep your eyes peeled. I'm going to make my move in a moment."

"Okay, settle down." Barbara attempted to bring the meeting to order. "Settle down, please. Before we begin, I do want to thank all of you for…"

"We want a sing-along!" one of the elves shouted, interrupting her.

"Yeah, we always had a sing-a-long before the management company of Sucks Hairy Icy Tampons put you in charge of HR!" another called out.

"Change the title and add one little verse in 'O Come All Ye Faithful All Over My Face', and suddenly it's an issue because somebody might be offended!" yet another one shouted.

"Hey!" Wesley strode in the direction of the three troublemakers, which conveniently put him in the middle of the room, exactly where he wanted to be. "Let's give Barbara your attention." He waited for them to mumble their response, which they did. They couldn't help themselves. That's when he clapped three times. "Knock it off!" And then he stood perfectly still, waiting for someone, anyone, to make the slightest noise.

"*Ohhhhhhhhhhh!*"

He heard the moan. They all heard the moan. And it sounded like it was coming from the stage.

"Tall Devil has an excellent idea," McJingles announced. "Let's do 'The Clapping Song'! Mama Claus wants some of this, don't ya?" And then he clapped three times.

"*Ohhhhhhhhhhhhhhhhhhhh!*"

It was a distinctly feminine-sounding voice.

"That's right!" the elf sitting next to him cheered. "You like that, don't ya?" And then he clapped three times. "You're a dirty, saucy, naughty old woman!"

"*OHHHHHHHHHHHHHHHHHHHH!*"

It was a distinctly elderly, feminine-sounding voice.

Wesley turned and looked for Jameson, eyes wide in complete and utter horror at what was unfolding before them.

"Stop!" Jameson shouted and started waving his hands in the air. "No clapping!"

Which only prompted *all* the elves to wave their hands in the air, sing, and start clapping.

"Mrs. Claus!" Wesley rushed toward the stage, yelling her name the entire way. "Mrs. Claus…"

✦ ✦ ✦ ✦

"…is in intensive care." Jameson's voice wavered as he leaned back against the wall of the hallway.

"Intensive care?" Wesley struggled with the words. "How is that even possible? She was fine…ish when they airlifted her out of here. Smiling and short of breath, but fine…ish. The paramedics said it wasn't that bad, or at least not as bad as it could have been."

"And it would have been fine, except one of the little fuckers called ahead and informed the hospital who was on her way in." Jameson sighed. "They really do love her, you know? And he wanted her to have the red carpet treatment."

"What happened?"

"The entire staff gathered at the entrance."

"And?"

"They applauded."

"Oh Christ." Wesley covered his face with his hands.

"Fortunately, the…um…thing, such as it is with the motor in it, acted like a pacemaker and kept her heart beating."

"Then I guess we kind of saved her life."

"After putting it in danger?" Jameson shook his head. "Yeah, that's the spin I'm going to put on it if they ever find out we had anything to do with it, which I hope they never do."

"Of all the people who could have been stealing prototype dildos, why'd it have to be her?"

"She's old, not dead. Just because somebody's up there in age doesn't mean they aren't horny," he explained. "Besides, it's not like they get much excitement these days. Santa can't even watch one of those *Expendables* movies with Sylvester Stallone without taking a nitroglycerin pill, and even then he's having other things go wrong. So's she. Another year or two and we'll be calling them *The Dependsables*."

"This is going to be a long night." Wesley glanced at his watch. "All right, it's eleven thirty. Want to split up for a bit and regroup at Warehouse Six in an hour and a half?"

"Yeah, that's fine. Twinkles sent me a text earlier saying he urgently needs to see me in one of the transit tunnels below Warehouse Fourteen. I thought those were still closed for maintenance, so maybe he found something he wants to report."

"Or maybe he wants to get you alone," Wesley added, smiling weakly.

"Please. I was only kidding yesterday when I asked if you'd ever thought about having sex with an elf." He turned and started walking toward the far end. "Besides, it's Twinkles. He's so goddamn short, he needed a ladder to reach manhood."

✧ ✧ ✧ ✧

Wesley paced up and down the corridor for a full minute, doing his best to look worried, withdrawn, and restless, all within view of a security camera. He silently counted another twenty seconds, then glanced at his watch. It was 11:36 p.m. Perfect! He had work to do.

His body language changed entirely, and he raced down the corridor, through one of the warehouses that wasn't running a third shift, down into the lower level, and through several transit tunnels. He knew it like the back of his hand after having studied the maps SHIT provided him. It's what wasn't showing on the maps that he wanted. To anyone outside the company, or outside the elves and the Kringles, there was a section that looked like it was just another storage area. Nobody ever really spent much time in the warehouses farthest away, so with very little foot traffic, it made the perfect place to keep something hidden. In this case, it was a cemetery.

The elves would sometimes talk about one of their own who'd passed away or even one of the reindeer, but seldom would one ever hear where they were buried. It was pretty rare that one passed away, which made it kind of a big deal when it happened. Also, it was rumored that a place of honor existed where the local deceased were buried, but it was always mentioned in the lightest of hushed whispers, and nobody dared give away its location. It was the one thing even the elves held sacred.

It took several minutes for Wesley to navigate the maze he needed to take from where he'd been to the door where he needed to be. The security cameras throughout Santa's workshop were monitored in one area, but the system itself was divided into two. That way, if one system went down, failed, or went into maintenance mode—which maintenance mode was performed once a day—the other system remained operational. The camera systems were also divided up so that at least the majority of the warehouses and halls could still be monitored when one was down.

Fortunately, there was room for maneuvering if one knew what one was doing.

One did.

The door itself had "Warehouse 57.1" spray-painted on it using the usual toy font stencils. That in itself wasn't a giveaway, since some of the warehouses had been rebuilt or renovated to accommodate new lines of items, which meant those warehouses were given a new level indicator next to their actual number. What gave this particular door away as the one he wanted was that it was freezing to the touch. No warehouse existed on the other side of it. The elements awaited him, as did the end of his very, very long journey.

Wesley tried the doorknob. Locked, just like he knew it would be, so he knelt down and studied the keyhole. All the warehouses took an electronic keycard to unlock, though there was an actual master non-electronic key backup just in case. The door here, though, had a fake electronic keycard lock. If somebody wound up there by mistake, they'd soon discover they couldn't get in, think it was broken, and go on their merry way. If they were there on purpose, they still wouldn't get in and would only wind up frustrated, especially if they had a copy of the master key, since that, too, wouldn't work.

This took a very, very special key, one that only a select few had. Santa and the missus had a copy, of course, and one elf in particular who was referred to in hushed voices over the years as the "key master". And this particular key master always kept it sewn on the inside of the vest he wore each and every day he went to work.

"Thank you, McJingles."

Wesley pulled an antique key out of his pocket. It really hadn't taken much to lift it from the elf while yanking him off the table before the Town Hall meeting began. Someone was going to be in a panic when they discovered it was missing, but that—hopefully—wouldn't be for a while yet.

He inserted the key, turned it to the right, listened for the click, turned it to the left, waited for an additional click, then pushed on it. The door creaked open and he felt a rush of frigid night air blow around him, making him shiver. The light jacket he had on definitely wasn't going to be much help, so the sooner he got done what he came there to do, the better. He checked his watch again: 11:51 p.m.

Wesley made his way through the snowy, eerily silent grounds and read all the tombstones as he went. Deceased reindeer appeared to be on the left—Humper, Humped, Rammer, Rammed, Blue-Balls, Red-Balls, No-Balls, Blitzed—and elves on the right—Woozy, Pickled, Spritzer, Spritzed, Tweezer, Pounder, Pounded, Hammered, Ulf. He stared at that last one for a couple of moments, his left eyebrow raised. None of them were who he was looking for, and there were many more he hadn't read yet.

The moon peeked out from behind the clouds and the light reflected off something in the distance. Wesley slowly turned and looked in its direction, the breath leaving his body when his eyes came to rest on the full-size statue of a young man about his age, but with the saddest expression he'd ever seen. He stumbled, momentarily losing all his strength when he recognized the face. It was the first solid proof that this wasn't just some sick figment of his imagination.

His strength returned, and he quickly made his way to within ten feet of the statue. Where there'd been writing on the surface of it had been slightly worn away over time. What he could make out was:

ETHAN T(illegible) KRIN(illegible)
JULY 19, 1886 - JULY 19, 1914

BE(illegible) SON
SINGING WITH THE AN(illegible)
WITH AN UNFULFILLED HEART

Wesley's own heart ached reading the stone, and while he was tempted to give in to the moment, fall to his knees, and let the emotions wash over him, he only had a couple of minutes before midnight and the hundredth anniversary of the man's death. This was what he'd spent so much time training and readying himself for. This was where the tide of a life turned, including his own.

"Harrumph!" He cleared his throat, pulled an envelope out of his pants pocket, and tore it open. The woman, the one with the brilliant green eyes, multicolored hair, handmade top hat, and twenty earrings, had told him that he had to recite the passages exactly as they were written, otherwise things could go terribly wrong. This was some powerful mojo. As for the passages themselves…

"Oh, fuck me," he muttered, reading them over in his head first. "Are you kidding me with this?" All he had to do was insert the correct name.

"Ethan Kringle, who once was alive, who took the dive because the love in his heart wasn't able to thrive. Hear me now before you say *ciao*. I know you'll never have a frau, so remember your Tao, and come back from beyond… wow." Wesley rolled his eyes and started counting the ways he'd make T.C. Blue pay if this didn't work the way she'd promised. "My feelings for you are no trick, twenty-eight years I've saved this for you…my wick…my dove, for you to prick me with your needle of love. Hear these words of genius and know that I long to covet your hot, throbbing… sereneness. Because I've got it, yeah, baby, I've got it. I'm your Venus. I'm your fire, your tear dryer.

"By the power of Glamberts who are many and fey, I speak these names of power for you to obey. Oh, Army of Lovers, and oh, Bronski Beat. Oh, Culture Club, Dead or Alive, Erasure, and the sounds to which we used to beat our meat. Oh, Frankie Goes to Hollywood, Scissor Sisters, and Soft Cell, music that made our loins swell. Oh, Right Said Fred, oh, Pansy Division, who made us glad our parents believed in circumcision. Bring back my Ethan Kringle, sans his frock, so that I may refill and slide down his large gigantic…clock…of life."

He had the strangest feeling he was seriously being punked, but it only lasted a moment, right up until a light glow began emanating from the large stone in front of him. The light grew brighter and brighter, then moved out and away, toward him, and began to coalesce into a shape. There was no sound, no heat, and nothing natural about it. The figure pulsed and light faded, turning to flesh in the process. What was left was a very nude twenty-eight-year-old man with short ginger hair who stood for a moment, then started to collapse, shivering.

Wesley leaped into action and caught him before he hit the ground. Ethan was lukewarm at best, and wouldn't stay that way for long. He gently set the man down, took his jacket off, and wrapped it around the naked man's shoulders. He then picked the unconscious body up and moved as quickly as he could to the door. Hopefully nobody would see them since it would only start rumors. Heck, there was already a new rumor going around the place in the last hour about a support group for misfit toys.

Because that's just what the place needed.

✧ ✧ ✧ ✧

The elves not on a work shift were busy holding an all-night vigil for Mrs. Claus in the Commons while the salaried workers had gone up to bed, wondering if the events of the evening would affect their quarterly bonus and wondering if wondering that would land them on Santa's naughty list… and not the good naughty list either.

Wesley had no trouble carrying Ethan back to his room in terms of actually running into anyone or being seen by the security cameras after the other ones went down for maintenance and the first system went back online. Hefting six feet, one hundred fifty pounds of newly revived flesh a bit of distance was certainly going to leave him feeling the strain in the morning. Fortunately, the entire operation had gone just as smoothly as his friend in Japan had told him it would.

He laid Ethan gently down on the bed and brought the covers up to just below his neck, then felt his forehead. The man was a normal temperature again and sleeping peacefully. The waking hours would be more difficult. T.C. Blue had explained to him that it would take the body and mind a day or two to reintegrate itself, which would be chaotic at first. Eventually, though, the confusion would dissipate and the man's memory would start to come back. Wesley just needed to keep him hidden long enough for that to happen.

Jameson never showed up at Warehouse Six when he was supposed to, so Wesley continued to run back up to his room to check on Ethan. He left a plastic cup of water near the bed on the nightstand, next to the book he was reading, J.P. Barnaby's *Painting Fire on the Air*, turned on some soft music, and talked soothingly to him, reassuring him that all would be okay and to just sleep. He couldn't help but run his hands through Ethan's hair. It was a timid gesture at first, then grew more confident, considering what had just happened to bring the man back into the world.

This was magic come true. It was the world's most asinine spell he'd ever had to recite, but it turned out to be magic nevertheless, and that somehow seemed appropriate for Santa's Workshop at the North Pole.

Wesley was just closing his door as quietly as he could when he turned around and came face to face with his partner, nearly making him scream in surprise, but more because of how his partner looked than almost getting caught with Santa's son sleeping in his room.

"What happened?"

"You know when you said Twinkles might want to have his wicked way with me?" Jameson was three sheets to the wind. "Well, he did…want to," he clarified, which might explain why his pants and shirt only had scratch and claw marks instead of being ripped in half. "I don't know how you know all this shit, but have you ever seen the inside of an elf den of debauchery? You know the rumors? They aren't exaggerating! It's as fucked up as you can imagine, and there's some things in there I can't even identify…and I watch some pretty weird shit!"

"You're drunk."

"You would be, too, if you saw what I did, then ran like hell to escape from…from Purgatory Pixie's Pleasure Pit of Porn."

"Then you didn't give in?" Wesley could only begin to imagine the things that were almost done to the man, and he actually had to fight the urge to giggle.

"I was tempted," Jameson admitted and stumbled backward before using the wall to steady himself. "The things he whispered in my ear…the things he wanted to do…the toys he wanted to use…the amount of time he was willing to take…his throbbing elfhood… You've no idea how close I came to letting him, but then he made a big mistake. *Huge!*"

"What?"

"He wanted information about you." The man smirked. "And I wouldn't give it to him."

"What did he want to know?" Wesley asked the obvious question.

"He thinks I've seen you naked. They *all* think I've seen you naked. And they're *all* willing to do whatever it takes to get me to share the information." He exhaled loudly and looked around him, momentarily unsure where the hell he was.

"Then since you've never actually seen me naked"—Wesley tried to help the man focus—"why didn't you just let them do some of those things to you and string him along?" It seemed logical.

"Because the little goblins are smarter than that. He was only willing to do that after I gave him the information. I know. I asked." He giggled, hiccupped, looked around to make sure they were alone in the hallway, then leaned in closer. "It's like they're little people…only mini-people…with mini-brains, but genetically enhanced to be as smart as we are!"

"Well, as smart as you are anyway."

"Exactly! Yes. Yes. As smart as me." Jameson pointed to his head to emphasize whatever point he thought he was making. "But I didn't give you up."

"You couldn't give me up."

"You're missing the point, as usual. I didn't give you up, meaning I figure I'm due a little compensation."

"You want me to file your report tonight with mine?" Wesley offered. "It's probably a good idea if I do them anyway since you don't want to go into the office drunk. We'll call that appropriate compensation."

"No!" Jameson stumbled right up to his partner and stood chest to chest with him. "I want to fuck you. If they think I've seen you naked, then I should actually see you naked so I can tell them I haven't seen you naked. It's only fair."

"I agree." Wesley surprised him by giving in so readily. "Tell you what, meet me in your room in an hour."

"You're not going to get out of it that easily," Jameson purred. "I want to fuck you right here, right now, and in your own bed."

"Excuse me?" Wesley crossed his arms. "Let's think about this for a moment, shall we? We just got done working an eight-hour shift. We've used the bathroom multiple times, we've been sweating, we're nasty, we're gross, and you just want to throw down and start fucking without first taking a shower and doing some prep work? What do you think this is? A J.P. Barnaby romance novel? We don't do things like that in the real world."

"Okay." Jameson sulked. "Fine. You're right." He turned and started stumbling down the hallway. "I'll just go up to my room, take a shower, get this wonderful new lube out I confiscated from one of the engineer's lockers and…maybe take a nap first because I am really, really…"

And then he fell down, unconscious.

"Swell."

❖ ❖ ❖ ❖

It took two hours before Wesley was able to return to his room. Not only did he have to carry Jameson back to his room—he left him fully clothed on the bed, but couldn't resist leaving an elf hat he'd found in the elevator sticking out of the man's pants zipper—but he also had to go and file their reports for the night. Fortunately, because everybody was concerned about Mrs. Claus, nobody started any trouble. It was probably the least eventful night they'd had since…well, since sometime before he started. There were some holes in the report he filed for his partner, but nobody was going to be going through them with a fine-tooth comb.

Ethan was still asleep when he walked in and quietly shut the door. Maybe the music was helping, or maybe being gone a hundred years was making him a little jet-lagged. Either way, Wesley knew he himself was going to need some sleep if things turned a bit chaotic later. Some of the water he'd left had been drunk, and the book on the nightstand looked as if it had been moved.

He took a quick shower, dried off, and carefully laid down next to the man he'd been dreaming about since he was old enough to remember his dreams. It took a few minutes to get up the nerve, but he finally moved into a spooning position with Ethan and wrapped his arms around him, pulling him close. Then, a few minutes later, he craned his neck forward and kissed the man's ear. It wasn't sexual, but rather sensual and familiar.

Wesley had no idea how much of his dreams had been real, but if Ethan remembered even a fraction of them, then they'd be sleeping this way for many, many years to come. Wesley had longed to be this intimate with someone flesh and blood all his life, someone who wouldn't be gone when he woke up in the morning. He wanted the intimacy with Ethan. He longed for the familiarity, the scent of his body, the warmth of his flesh pressed up against his own, and the beauty of not mistaking sex for what they actually shared for decades between them.

"Tooooooouch…meeeeeee…heeeeeeere…" Ethan's voice was ragged, uncontrolled, and barely coherent, yet he grabbed Wesley's hand and placed it on the one part of him more awake than the rest.

"Umm…" Wesley mumbled, eyes wide open in surprise. "Awkward."

❖ ❖ ❖ ❖

When Ethan woke up, it was as if he'd just been born… sort of. Nothing looked familiar to him; he was disoriented, couldn't make heads or tails out of anything in the private dormitory room, couldn't put words to what he saw, and he was frustrated by all of it. Wesley tried for an hour to get him dressed on the chance somebody stopped by. It was a rare, rare occasion when someone did, and it was often a mistake, but it happened. Ethan refused to cooperate. So nude he stayed, though he did allow himself to be towel dried after his shower. He also caught on that Wesley was trying to help.

Truth be told, Wesley's presence was the only thing that calmed him down. Well, that and playing anything by The Motels or singer/songwriter Martha Davis's solo work. And when Ethan calmed down and stopped fussing, that's when the "toooooooooch meeeeee heeeeeere" or "tooooooouuuuuuch thiiiiiiiiiis" started. It did follow that a hundred years in limbo was bound to leave someone feeling a bit…hormonal. Or maybe he'd been reading the book on the nightstand.

Wesley spoke very soothingly to him, told him it would be all right soon enough, and that he needed to get rest to let his body and mind sync up. It wasn't so much what he was saying as how he was saying it. He also brought some food up from the Commons and fed Ethan bits and pieces of fruit and vegetables, things that would help his body. Wesley left a couple pieces of fruit on the bedside table in case Ethan got hungry during Wesley's work shift. Ethan would hopefully just sleep. A day of fussing really took it out of him.

It was quarter after seven when Wesley walked into the security office and found Jameson hard at work fixing the holes in his report from the previous night, plus swearing his head off.

"Goddammit." He typed something in, then threw the mouse across the desk in frustration. "Shit!"

"What's the matter?" Wesley watched the spectacle with a small amount of amusement. It served his partner right after drinking on the job and being hungover.

"I think one of the gremlins was in here looking at last night's report, then infected my computer." Jameson leaned back in his chair and glared at the screen.

"With what?"

"The Mo-Mo Thompson virus."

"That's one I've never heard of. What's it do?"

"Every time I click on something and open up a new window or program, a pair of elf breasts pop up and cover the entire screen."

"Those little ass burglars." Wesley figured it had to have been Sparkle, but how the hell did the little tick get into a secure area? "Can't you just run a virus scan and have it removed?"

"I tried that," Jameson informed him matter-of-factly.

"And?"

"It made the breasts lactate."

"That's disgusting." Wesley sat down at the next console, turned the computer on, and entered his password. "Any news on Mrs. Claus?"

"Yeah. Word came in a couple of hours ago that she's going to be just fine. I stopped by your room to tell you and thank you for making sure I got in last night—that's all still a bit blurry, by the way—but you were so busy being lonely and listening to your music, you never heard me knock."

"I'm not lonely."

"Yes, you are," Jameson told him.

"What makes you think I'm lonely?"

"When you're locked in your room listening to 'Only the Lonely,' it tells the rest of the world that you're lonely."

"Or maybe it says I like The Motels. Martha Davis writes a lot of romantic songs."

"'Shame'? 'Take the L'? 'My Love Stops Here'? 'Suddenly Last Summer'?" Jameson stared at him and waited for another bullshit explanation.

"Okay." Wesley realized his partner might have a point. Maybe some or all of the songs he'd been playing weren't exactly romantic, but they had calmed Ethan down. "Exactly how fucking long were you standing outside my door?"

"Not that long, and not the point."

"Yes, it is, and long enough to come up with a playlist?" Wesley deflected. "That's a little creepy."

"Now you're just deflecting." Jameson's computer beeped. "Son of a bitch." He turned and stared at the screen. "Oh, hey! I think I got it removed." Then it beeped again. "This is just wrong."

"What is it?"

"Elf balls." He hung his head down in defeat. "I'm now staring at elf balls."

✧ ✧ ✧ ✧

The first half of the shift went off without a hitch. The elves were relieved about Mrs. Claus, were tired from their vigil, in good spirits, and therefore behaved. Wesley and Jameson made all their second-shift rounds, then did a quick preliminary of third shift before heading back to the office to file the first half of their reports. Fortunately, IT had managed to rid the computer of its curiously adaptive virus. No boobs or balls stared at them, lactated, or ejaculated by the time they arrived.

Wesley went right to work filling out what warehouses they'd observed and a few things to follow up on while Jameson checked e-mail for any alerts they needed to be aware of.

"Hey," Jameson called over to him, "you didn't happen to be anywhere near Warehouse Fifty-Seven last night, did you?"

"Actually..." Wesley thought about lying, but then figured that would be silly since it was entirely possible someone could have seen him, and then they'd be suspicious right off the bat if he denied it. "Yes, I was. Why?"

"What were you doing all the way out there?"

"It was a quiet night, and when's the best time for someone to try and get away with something?" Wesley turned and looked his partner right in the eyes, definitely the sign of someone who wasn't guilty of something. "On a quiet night. I didn't think we should let our guard down, so

I headed toward the outer regions, and that happened to be where I ended up. Now, why?"

"Well, your instincts were right on. Big surprise." Jameson studied the e-mail. "They're not saying anything specific, but upper management is looking into something that happened out that way last night and they must want to find out bad. We're all expected to verify our whereabouts, and then they'll figure out whether or not to question us further."

"You might not want to mention where you were," Wesley suggested. "And we know Twinkles sure as hell isn't going to mention it."

"This may come as a surprise, but I'm not entirely stupid. A little slow? Yes. Stupid? No." He leaned back in his chair.

"Meaning?"

"Is there something you want to tell me?"

"Like what?" Wesley looked him right in the eye again, reinforcing that he was telling the truth. "Because I can't think of anything."

"I've heard the rumors. I have a pretty good idea what's around Warehouse Fifty-Seven. Now what were you really doing out there?"

Bzzzzzzzzzz.

Wesley looked at the name on the caller ID, then turned the phone on speaker.

"Security. What can we do for you, Barbara?"

"Don't dodge the question," Jameson whispered.

"I'm on the intercom with Barbara," Wesley whispered back, pointing out the obvious.

"I'm waiting for my escort with the payroll. Can you please send Adkins and Eric over?"

"Of course. I'll contact them now."

"Thank you."

Wesley hit the button that turned the speaker off, then picked up the phone to call the other two security officers, only Jameson leaned over and put his finger down on the disconnect button, killing the dial tone.

"What did you do? I want you to tell me, or I'm going straight to management."

"And tell them what happened with Twinkles?" Wesley somehow didn't see that happening. "Plus, how you got drunk?"

"Something tells me whatever you did is far worse."

And then there was that.

"Okay." Wesley sighed and set the phone back down. "Yes, I was at Warehouse Fifty-Seven last night. Yes, the rumors are true. Yes, there's a cemetery there where elves, reindeer, and Santa's son, Ethan, are buried."

"So you broke in to the cemetery for what? To take pictures? Take keepsakes to sell on the black market?" Jameson's expression hardened, and his voice rose in anger.

"I'm not a thief," Wesley snapped. "What I did, I did out of love." The look on his face softened at the thought of who was in his room and hopefully sleeping. "The hundredth anniversary of Ethan's death is today, so I only had a small window of opportunity in which to act last night."

"You dug him up?" Jameson's eyes opened wide.

"You're not slow," Wesley confided, "you're a fucking moron. No, I didn't dig him up. I performed a ritual and brought him back from the other side."

"You did *what*?"

"I kind of reincarnated him, because it wasn't his time to die back then, like in that Shelley Long movie *Hello Again*."

"Reincarnated him?" Jameson's jaw dropped. He started to say something else, nothing came out, so he closed his mouth, then opened it again, and still nothing came out. Finally: "You don't do that at the North Pole! Think about where we are. It's one thing to set off a vibrator in your elderly boss's equally elderly wife that she's using illegally, but it's another to bring their kid back to life. You turned *A Christmas Story* into *Night of the Living Dead*!"

"I did not!" *Bzzzzzzzzzz.* "Hold on." Wesley grabbed the receiver. "Yes? They're coming to get you, Barbara." He hung up and cocked his head to one side, more than aware of the movie he'd just inadvertently quoted, which was compounded by the knowing look his partner was giving him. "Oh, fuck off."

"How is it even possible you did what you say you did?" Jameson expected to hear the words "black magic" or something about an ancient curse or having the power over life and death, or vampires, witches, warlocks, werewolves, weresheep, horse shifters...or some such stuff. Instead...

"I met a girl, T.C. Blue, at an Adam Lambert concert, who told me how to do it and what to say."

"Are you fucking kidding me? Some random girl you met at a concert told you how to resurrect someone who's been dead for a hundred years?"

"She's not just some random girl," Wesley clarified. "I told you, her name is T.C. But, yeah. She said she does it all the time."

"And you believed her?"

"She's never lied to me before."

"You never met her before."

"Then there was no reason for her to start."

"How do two people even begin a conversation like that?" Jameson couldn't even begin to fathom it. "'Hi. I'm here to see Adam Lambert sing. By the way, do you know how to raise the dead?' 'Why yes, yes I do! Because my name is T.C. Blue. Let me tell you how it's done since I just happen to do it all the time!'"

"I'm suddenly not liking this other side of you," Wesley informed his partner. "It's coming across as slightly two-faced, and that means any man you marry is one day going to be getting hitched to a bigamist."

"You really have no idea just how much high ground you've lost, do you?" Jameson stood up. "We'll talk about this later, and believe me, we *will* talk about it. But you have to call Adkins and Eric to escort Barbara, and we have rounds to make before the little gremlins think they can start getting away with shit."

"Speaking of the knob jockeys, I have an idea who we can start with regarding who may have accessed your computer and left you the virus."

"Of course you do. I keep forgetting you're psychic."

✧ ✧ ✧ ✧

It had to be Warehouse Thirteen. As if their luck wasn't bad enough, that particular warehouse was the most behind due to an increase in production, meaning pretty much every troublemaker on third shift was there. Not that they weren't all troublemakers, but here they were in large numbers, and that typically spelled disaster.

Wesley had hoped to catch Cosmo Danky Dimples in one of the emptier warehouses by himself, only Murphy and his Law struck again.

"What do you want to do?" Jameson asked while trying to formulate a plan in his own head and coming up empty. He was sure there was a joke in that, so he was glad he hadn't mentioned it out loud.

"I have an idea." Wesley's stoic expression gave no indication of what he was thinking. "Remember that story you told me about the horny Afghan Hound getting loose?"

"Yeah, but there's no guarantee it ever actually happened."

"Then let's find out. You hang out by the door that goes to the designated emergency shelter, and I'll go make the announcement. By the way, be careful with Cosmo. He's not like the other elves. This one can go comment for comment with us, so we may have to double up and cut his shit off real quick."

"I'll follow your lead."

They split up, and while Jameson casually strolled over to the area near the shelter door, Wesley ducked into the foreelf's office, picked up the phone, and dialed the code that would access only Warehouse Thirteen's intercom system. There was no sense disrupting everyone else, and the phone he was using couldn't be traced since the announcement wasn't going facility-wide.

squee

"Attention associates in Warehouse Thirteen, one of the Afghan Hound studs has escaped from the kennel and is heading in your direction. Please head to the nearest emergency shelter until he has been safely apprehended. If you see him, do not attempt to talk, pet, or look in him in the eyes. He was recently injected with dog hormones and is looking to mate. Thank you for your cooperation."

"Not again!" a voice screamed out. "Oh blinking Christmas bulb anal beads, not again!"

Okay, so it was a true story.

Wesley poked his head out the door and watched a flurry of terrified, highly annoyed elves scurrying toward the emergency door that led to the reinforced shelter. Jameson, meanwhile, had already opened it and was ushering people through as quickly as he could. Well, up until one elf anyway.

"Not you, elftard." He pulled Cosmo away from the others and to the side. "We need to have a word."

"At least it'll be a short word since you're not smart enough to know many of the bigger ones," Cosmo quipped. "Can I go now, dull, dumb, and demented? You can look those words up later if you ask nicely for help, you sad excuse for a primate's wet dream."

"Mouthy little motherelfer, isn't he?" Wesley asked from behind Cosmo, surprising the worker.

"Tall Devil?" Cosmo jumped, momentarily surprised, then pointed to Jameson. "Highway here didn't tell me you wanted a word. You didn't know that about him, did you? They've been calling him Highway since he was born because, as you know, that's where most accidents happen."

"We're not in the mood." Jameson shut the door to the emergency area, then crossed his arms and put on his best poker face. "At all."

"Well, if you two wanted a private session with me, you simply had to ask." Cosmo giggled. "I can only please one of you at a time, though, but there's enough of me to go around. Believe me, I'm *that* big."

"Well, believe me, it's hard to take someone seriously who's so short he can't tell the difference between a footache or a headache," Wesley mused. "We'll pass."

"What does this look like?" Jameson held his phone up and showed the elf a picture he'd taken of his computer screen in the office with the elf boobs displayed.

"Oh, what does this look like?" Cosmo dropped his pants and underwear, then gyrated his hips.

The two security guards looked at each other in silent acknowledgement. This nut needed to be cracked, and it would have to be done quickly.

"It looks like a pimple with a pulse," Wesley said, unsmiling.

"Your dick's so small," Jameson continued, "you'll never be half the man your mother was."

"What the fuck?" Cosmo made himself dizzy looking back and forth between them.

"You've got less meat in your pants than you'll find in a vegetarian restaurant."

"I hope for your sake your dick gets bigger in cold water."

"I heard one of the interns subpoenaed it in court and the judge threw it out for lack of evidence."

"All right!" Cosmo shouted. "Jesus Christ, Gandalf, and Mussolini. Do the two of you have to be so brutal?"

"I'm constantly surprised at the amount of bullshit we have to cut through in order to have a meaningful conversation with one of you," Wesley admitted. "We just decided to save some time. Isn't it amazing what happens when a plan comes together?"

"Now"—Jameson held his phone up again—"the picture?"

"Officially?" Cosmo pulled his pants back up. "I don't know what you're talking about. Unofficially? Nobody else possesses the skills to pull that off but me."

"I know."

"He knows. He always knows. So, unofficially"—Jameson followed the elf's train of thought—"what would someone sneak in and look for on my computer?"

"Last night's report, of course." The elf shifted his gaze to Wesley. "You know why, Tall Devil. We may seem like just a bunch of horny perverted gremlins to all of you, but we watch when something matters. You were somewhere you never should have been last night, someplace we consider private and sacred. We don't know how you knew about it or why you were there, but we know something happened. We just don't know what."

"You always were the smart one." Wesley smirked. "And you always made sure the family was taken care of. When Santa overextended himself, you were there. When Mrs. Claus needed extracurricular stimulation, you made sure she got it, though from now on, I'd stay away from the prototypes the engineers have been developing. But the one person you couldn't help is the one thing you always blamed yourself for, and it was never your fault."

"You can't know these things." Cosmo stood there, slack-jawed. "You can't."

"What the hell are you talking about?" Jameson was lost.

"It was never within your power to make his heart whole, no matter how hard you tried. And you did try." Wesley put his hand on the elf's shoulder. "He loved you for that."

"Seriously," his partner demanded, "how do you know this shit?"

"It's hard to kill an elf, and we live a very, very long time, but the grief of losing him almost did me in. Most of your kind are ugly, but Ethan was something special, even for a ginger. Well, especially for a ginger, because, really, who wants to have sex with a ginger?

"He had a smile that lit up a workshop from the time he was old enough to run around the toy rooms, eyes that twinkled like his father's, and a nature gentler than his mother's. The young man he grew into was a sight to behold, tall and muscular, and even more handsome than he was as a child, which we never thought was possible. If he wasn't Santa's son, we'd have been tapping that like a US Senator's page!"

"Then it'll come as such a relief Wesley here brought him back to life," Jameson interjected, feeling like he finally knew something somebody else didn't.

"Ethan"—Cosmo turned white as snow—"is alive?"

"Yup." Wesley really didn't know how else to answer.

"T.C. Blue!" The elf started getting his color back. "You found T.C. and she told you what to do, didn't she?"

"Ha." Wesley turned to his partner. "I told you she wasn't just some random person. And she probably really *has* done this before."

"Still doesn't explain why upper management is inquiring about last night," Jameson changed the subject.

"Actually, it does." Cosmo sobered up. "We put the bug in their ear, which means the three of us need to talk if we're going to figure out how to solve this."

"And by 'we' when you refer to putting the bug in upper management's ear, you mean…" Wesley asked.

"Yeah, me," the elf admitted. "You people would be less annoying if you were smarter. I've watched that moron in HR stare at frozen juice cans just because they have the word 'concentrate' on them."

"We know," Jameson agreed. "She ain't right."

✧ ✧ ✧ ✧

"All right, give us the short version of everything leading up to last night," Cosmo said, sitting down with the two security guards at the table located farthest away from the other elves. The animal alert had been called off, and everyone was back to work, so they had half an hour before the room filled with folks for first break.

"This goes way back," Wesley began. "I've been dreaming of Ethan ever since I knew what dreams were, and I had no idea his presence each and every night wasn't normal. It's like our souls had touched after he passed away and before I was born, and I carried that connection with me. I knew all about this place as it was back then and about all the elves, because he showed me in my dreams. In turn, I learned how to show him my life."

"That's how you always know everything." Jameson put the missing piece together. "You have inside information. He's your significant other."

"We realized in time that the kind of relationship it was turning into was something that could never be real. We would always be separated by the waking world, and because of that, Ethan wanted more for me than he himself had. He showed me how lonely he was here. He was loved and surrounded by love, but there was a part of him that was never whole and couldn't be. Relationships like the one he needed just weren't available in that time and in this place. He died of an unfulfilled and broken heart, and that's something he refused to let happen to me.

"As much as he wanted me to have a life with someone whose arms I could fall asleep and wake up in, I wanted that person to be him. I started reading up on all sorts of ancient rituals and…anything I could find. It wasn't until I met T.C. Blue two years ago that I discovered we had a small window of opportunity to make it real. Last night marked the one hundredth year of Ethan's passing. If I hadn't completed the ritual by midnight, I'd never have been able to bring him back. But I did and it worked."

"Have his mind and body aligned yet?" Cosmo asked.

"No. It's going to take a little more time."

"And what if they find him before he's…aligned?" Jameson asked, not really sure if he was even asking the right question or how much he was truly understanding.

"Ethan needs time alone and with me in order to help create and maintain an environment that helps him balance. If his parents see him before he's whole again, it'll be traumatic for everyone."

"I realize this is going to sound like a dick thing to say," his partner prefaced before continuing, "but you've never struck me as someone even remotely romantic, nurturing or, at times, even human. Now we're supposed to buy that you're all these things and somehow soul mates with Santa Claus's deceased, recently resurrected son?"

"The IQ of lint here has a point." Cosmo pointed at Jameson.

"The only way I was going to be able get a look at this place, study the layout and security systems, and better know the habits of everybody working here was to do it at a distance. The closer people are to you, the more involved they want to be with your life. The farther away they are, the easier it is to get them to avoid you."

"Devious!" Cosmo approved. "You could be an elf."

"Hardly," Jameson countered. "He'd never steal the straw from his mother's kennel."

"God, I hope you and your siblings are sterile." The elf turned from Jameson back to Wesley. "How did you even get into the cemetery anyway?"

"I have this friend who's in Japan right now and he's dating a Butt Nin—" He caught himself. "Never mind. Suffice it to say someone gave me a few lessons in how to lift a key, and I knew exactly which elf would have the one I was looking for."

"McJingles," the elf whispered.

"But what we really need to know right now, though, is what upper management knows about last night. What did you tell them?"

Cosmo grinned, then explained.

❖ ❖ ❖ ❖

Jameson and Wesley had word waiting for them that they were being summoned to the security conference center an hour after their shift ended. That gave them just enough time to go back to their rooms, shower, and prepare themselves.

Wesley lay down next to Ethan after drying off and getting dressed. He put his arm around him and snugged up close. The man wasn't jerking around nearly as much and seemed more at ease with his surroundings. Wesley noticed him staring at things in the room from time to time and trying to put together what they were, more patiently than before. It was coming back to him a little at a time. These were definitely good signs, though the book was no longer on the nightstand. Oddly enough, Wesley found it under the pillow. Had Ethan been reading J.P. Barnaby?

"Wannnnnnnnnt...miiiiiiiiiiiiine...innnnnnnn...yoooooooooourssss..."

Ethan reached behind him, grabbed Wesley's crotch, and moved it closer to his rear end.

Why yes, yes, he had.

"When you're better," Wesley whispered, "and after I've gone to the bathroom and prepped. Remember? We've had many conversations about this. Cleanliness is a gay man's motto."

"Jayyyyyyyyyy... Peeeeeeeee... Barrrrrnaaaaaaabyyyyyyy..."

"...is going to receive an e-mail from me about adding douching to her novels," Wesley promised.

"Mooooommmmmm...Daaaaaaaaaaaad..."

"They're here," he soothed Ethan. "We'll go to see them as soon as you're better."

"Hooooooooooome..."

"You are home, and you're safe." Wesley glanced at his watch. "I have to go for just a little while, but then I'll be back and we'll spend the day together, just you and me. I'll bring you something to eat, too, and we can talk."

"Moooooommmm...Daaaaaaad...Wessssssssley... hoooooome..."

Wesley got out of the bed and padded over to the phone. He'd promised Jameson he'd page him before he headed down to where they were supposed to report. Unfortunately, while he could remember what to dial to make an announcement in a specific warehouse, he'd never managed to remember the special number for the entire facility, living quarters and warehouses in all. Instead, he picked the phone up and dialed the security office.

"Hey, Java? What's the number to page the entire facility?" He wrote it down on a Post-it note next to the phone. "Got it, thanks." Wesley put the phone down, waited a couple of seconds and then picked it up again.

"Phooooooooooooone?"

"Yes"—he turned and smiled at Ethan, who was watching him intently—"phone. That's good, Ethan! It's coming back to you." Wesley then dialed the number Java had given him.

squee

"*Jameson Wallace, please report to the Security Conference Center. Jameson Wallace, Security Conference Center.*" And that's where he should have left it, but he didn't. "*McJingles, please report to the proctologist's office. They found your head. McJingles, proctologist's office, found head.*"

✧ ✧ ✧ ✧

"Are you ready for this?" Jameson asked when they met up outside the conference center.

"Piece of cake," Wesley assured him. "If there's one thing I know about, it's how the world's worst management company works. There's always one figurehead in charge who everybody else is trying to impress and suck up to. Nobody cares what your answers are as long as they get to ask the questions, though they will frequently try to make it seem like you're not giving the right answer. Again, it's to try and impress the boss. They've gotten where they are, enjoy the power and salary, and will do anything to keep it. And because of this, you'd be amazed at what you can get away with saying to them because they're really not listening."

"That's not true."

"Sure it is." He opened the door and ushered his partner in.

"By the way—" Jameson leaned in closer. "—I about shit when you mentioned McJingles in your announcement."

"And the people waiting for us inside won't even mention it." Wesley smiled. "Watch and learn."

They entered a small office with an administrative assistant who ushered them right into the large conference room. There was a table with two chairs for them; then those were surrounded by other tables with eight men in suits sitting behind them. Wesley recognized the one in the middle from his picture above the Letter from the Chief of Security Operations in newsletters they received. He was the head honcho. The others? Window dressing.

"Security Intern Wesley Lee and Security Officer Jameson Wallace reporting as requested," Wesley broke the silence.

"And you're two minutes early," the first one on the left remarked. "We appreciate punctuality and that you were looking out for your partner when you paged him."

The two guards exchanged a quick, knowing look and sly smile when the man failed to mention the second part of the page.

"Please have a seat and we'll—"

squee

"We'll wait for a moment." No announcement followed. "Okay, then. I turn these proceedings over to Chief of Security Operations Reid."

"Let's come right to the point, gentlemen." The man in the middle, obviously Reid, folded his hands in front of him. "Do you know how—"

squee

They all waited, but nothing followed.

"Do you know how a Deluxe Ally Blue Blunt Instrument of Orificial Pleasure Palace Pleasing G-Spot Stimulator Simulator prototype found its way into Mrs. Claus?"

"I'm going to have to say 'carefully', I hope." Wesley turned to Jameson. "That was the buzz anyway, wouldn't you agree?"

"Definitely"—he did—"and we've been very careful to keep a firm grip on the throbbing pulse of gossip around here."

"That's not very funny," the man on the far right chastised them. "And you're purposely missing the point of the question."

"No, sir." Wesley turned and stared at him, eye to eye. "I'm not. You are. Do you really think one of us put a dildo up Mrs. Ho Ho Ho's hooha? Does that sound like something anyone working here would have the opportunity or desire to do? And don't you think she might have noticed? So, no, we're not missing the point."

squee

"Is somebody playing around on the intercom system?" Reid asked nobody in particular. "Or are they testing it?"

And nobody answered.

"Were either of you down by Warehouse Fifty-Seven last night?" the man on the left asked.

"I was. He wasn't," Wesley answered.

"And what were you doing there?"

"My job."

"Since you seem to be the one with all the answers," the man just to the right of Reid piped up, "let me ask if you're familiar with the name Ethan Titus Kringle?"

"No." And it wasn't a lie. Ethan had never told Wesley what his middle name was, and after hearing it, he understood why.

squee

They paused. Still nothing.

"Then you're not familiar with this person?" the man to the left of Reid chimed in.

"That's what I said." Wesley felt horrible for Jameson right about now, but his partner was doing exactly what he should: staying silent. "Should I be?"

"Perhaps you know him by a nickname?" the man pressed. "After all, don't you yourself go by a nickname?"

"The elves gave me the nickname Tall Devil, which is Swedish for 'incredibly well hung' in Cantonese. I didn't give it to myself, but it's entirely possible I've met an elf named Ethan if he was using a nickname. Would you care to tell me what it is so I can more accurately answer your question?"

"We never said he was an elf."

"And you never told me what his nickname is either." Wesley actually wanted to know. Calling Ethan something familiar like that might help him remember, which would in turn help speed up the healing process. Plus, in all honesty, he was legitimately curious what it was.

"It's—"

squee

"Eeeeeeee Teeeeeee… phooooone hooooooooome…"

"Oh, fuck my life."

✧ ✧ ✧ ✧

The meeting only lasted another couple of minutes, at which time the Chief of Security Operations was seething and demanded nobody in particular track down the "fucking elf" who was playing with the intercom system. And if they couldn't, he demanded they turn the system off until they did.

Nobody, once again, listened.

As Wesley had told Jameson they would, the suits in the meeting didn't pay any attention to what had been said, and instead focused on making sure they got to ask questions and follow-ups and that Reid acknowledged they were asking questions and following up. Whatever the group hoped to get out of the meeting ended with them thinking the two guards weren't who they were looking for.

The two men waited in the small office with the administrative assistant for the executives to file out first. Wesley said good-bye to each of them as they passed by, starting with Reid.

"Merry Christmas...merry Christmas...merry Christmas...thank you very much...fuck you very much...fuck you with his...see if you can find your own...happy Kwanzaa."

And then they were all gone.

"Okay." Jameson looked impressed. "You may have a point. They really don't hear a damn thing, do they?"

"I told you. *Worst...management...company...ever.*"

"What do we do now?"

"First"—Wesley smiled warmly—"thank you for sticking by me. I know you had less than honorable intentions regarding my virtue, so I appreciate you backing off on the whole 'I want to fuck you' thing. I couldn't have acted on it even if I'd wanted to, and I didn't because, well, you're no Ethan or—"

"Remember that thing I told you about regarding not acting like you're human?"

"Right. I have to get upstairs and stop Ethan from picking the phone up again."

squee

"Seriously?"

❖ ❖ ❖ ❖

Jameson agreed to get a hold of Cosmo and watch the hall until Wesley figured out if he needed to move Ethan to another room. It all depended on whether or not someone in security had traced the calls to the facility's main paging system. If not, no problem. If they did, Jameson and Cosmo would stall them.

Wesley opened the door and found Ethan standing in the center of the room wearing only a pair of white 2(X)IST Stretch No-Show briefs. He momentarily forgot to breathe at the sight before him, mostly because Ethan had been having issues standing on his own since being brought to the room, and also because Cosmo was right: the man was truly beautiful. Breathtaking even. Every part of his body was perfectly accentuated, and that perfection most likely included the bits that couldn't be seen. Dreams had been one thing, but to have him standing upright on his own before Wesley, an inch taller than himself and now flesh and blood, was a whole other matter.

"Wesley."

It wasn't a question, wasn't uncertain, or through clouded eyes.

"Ethan?" Wesley fought back a lump in his throat, but couldn't do anything about the tears welling in his eyes.

They took a tentative step toward each other, then slowly extended their arms, connected, and pulled each other in. Wesley felt the warmth of Ethan's shoulder on his face and Ethan the warmth of Wesley's body. They stood there for several minutes just holding each other, feeling the strength in each other, and listening to each other breathe, neither believing it was finally real.

"Jesus Christ," Cosmo's voice interrupted them from the door, "now I want to fuck both of them."

"You know, Cosmo," Jameson, standing next to the elf, said, "with you being so low to the ground, it's no wonder your mind is always in the gutter."

"Your inferiority complex is completely justified."

"I worship the ground you'll be buried under."

"Son?"

"You're not my father," Jameson snapped.

"I'm not the one who said it, asshat," Cosmo countered, then turned around to see who was standing behind them. "Aw, shit."

"What?" Jameson continued staring at Wesley and Ethan hugging.

"Big man in red," Cosmo whispered. "Big man in red."

"Oh, that kind of 'aw, shit'." Jameson leaned forward. "Guys…you might want to save that for later. Ethan's dad is here."

"Father?" Ethan broke their embrace, smiled at the man standing in the doorway, then reached out and held Wesley's hand.

Santa, who was dressed in a regular pair of red work overalls, was too spellbound by the sight of his son standing there alive and well to even take notice of the fact he was only wearing a pair of designer underwear, had been hugging one of the workers, and was now holding the man's hand.

"Is it really you?"

"It is," Ethan whispered.

"I can't believe…" Santa's voice wavered. "Your mother and I never forgave ourselves when we lost you, but we never knew how to save you." He nodded several times. "Maybe you just needed that one person we couldn't find at the time who's here now. Only a supreme act of true love could bring you back. Tell me, my son, what woman here at the North Pole finally reached your heart and rescued you from the abyss?"

"That would be me," Wesley informed him.

"Who could possess such feminine wiles and magic that could cross into the afterlife, bewitch you, and bring you back to us? Who do your mother and I have to thank?"

Wesley raised his hand. "Still me."

"What beacon of healing, tender, effeminate light and nature could soothe your soul and make your heart yearn for life again after all these years?"

"We could do this allllll day." Wesley rested his free hand on his hip. "And the answer is still going to be the same."

"*You?*"

"If it helps, Father," Ethan offered, "he's a bottom. Your son hasn't taken it up the—"

"He means I prefer the bottom bunk in a bunk bed if we had bunk beds here," Wesley interrupted and explained, "which we don't, but I'll be putting a work order in for one as soon as possible." He quickly turned to Ethan. "For the record, I'm pretty sure your dad wasn't fishing for information about our nonexistent sex life."

"Don't be silly. He needs to know these things." Ethan looked back toward his father. "Wesley and I love each other."

"Platonically." Wesley giggled nervously. "It started out that way, and it's still very much that way because of the whole 'he hasn't been alive for a hundred years' thing. Not to say that it won't turn into something romantic—probably today and with your blessing, of course—since I think there's definitely chemistry between us. But for the record, we haven't laid a hand on each other in an inappropriate way."

Santa stared at one, then the other, then back again, completely befuddled.

"What Wesley means to say is that I plan to mount him as soon as we're alone and he's had another shower."

"And when Ethan says mount"—the two of them *really* needed to have a discussion about discretion, especially with Wesley explaining the unwritten rule to Ethan about not sleeping with the boss's son—"that's slang for he's going to help me hang some pictures up in my room, because, as you can see for yourself, I'm very minimalist and he's…well, he's been looking at white walls for a hundred years and wouldn't mind a little color."

"No," Ethan corrected him. "I mean I'm going to use some of the lube Jameson slipped me when neither of you were paying attention and thrust my cock deep inside you until you beg me to coat your insides with my semen."

"That's it!" Wesley put his foot down. "You are off the J.P. Barnaby novels until further notice." Ethan must have gotten to the bathroom scene in *Painting Fire on the Air*.

"Is this true?" Santa asked.

"Yes, I fully plan on mounting him."

"He means the being in love part…I hope," Wesley clarified through clenched teeth, "otherwise your father is a little pervy."

"Oh, then in that case, yes, Father. We're in love." Ethan gazed at Wesley, tears forming in his eyes. "He found me, healed my heart, gave me hope, and brought me back. I am his."

Santa stared at the two of them for a short time, his face finally softening.

"All right," he conceded. "As long as you're happy and he's the one taking it up the ass"—he gestured toward Wesley—"the elves won't get any ideas with you, I can live with it, and I'm sure your mother can too. Do you want me to tell her, or do you want to once she's discharged from the hospital?"

"Why's Mom in the hospital?"

"Well, son—" Santa took a breath. "—someone took a Deluxe Ally Blue Blunt Instrument of Orificial Pleasure Palace Pleasing G-Spot Stimulator Simulator and installed a vibrating motor inside it that responds to clapping. It took her to her special place, and she almost didn't return from it."

"Who would do such a vile thing?" Ethan demanded, glaring at the two security men in the room.

"I'm sure whoever the bastards are," Wesley offered, "they're very remorseful. Wouldn't you say, Jameson?"

"I think they're too scared shitless not to be," his partner agreed.

✧ ✧ ✧ ✧

"I think we can safely leave these two alone for a while." Santa closed the door behind him and joined the remaining security guard and elf out in the hall. "Besides, it's time to watch my latest download and take my little blue Benadryl pill."

"Viagra," Cosmo corrected him.

"Viagra, yes." Santa giggled and ambled down the hall toward the elevator.

"It's been a hell of a couple of days." Jameson sighed. "I just want to go back to my room and sleep until it's the weekend."

"You should do that"—Cosmo liked the idea—"because I'd rather pass a kidney stone than stand here with you for another minute." A noise reached their ears. "What the..." He tilted his head to one side. "I swear I just heard the tinkling of a bell."

"You did."

"Is it me, or is it getting louder?" The elf stood there, puzzled. "It's gone from tiny bells to those ones the street peddlers use."

"It's the lube I gave Ethan." Jameson chuckled. "It's a prototype. The more it heats up due to use, the louder the sound it makes. I only managed to get it up to a cow bell myself."

"Shocking. Oh, for the love of soft pretzel sticks and hot fudge, it's like the fucking bells of St. Mary's in there now!" Cosmo put his hands over his ears, and the two quickly headed toward the elevator in hot pursuit of Santa.

"I guess one of them didn't need to take that second shower after all."

The doors had already closed by the time they got there—the big man in red must have really wanted that Viagra—and when they opened again, the head of HR stepped out.

"Have either of you seen Santa?" Barbara asked. "I heard he was up here and..." She turned toward the racket coming from down the hall. "What the hell is that noise?"

"Those are the sounds of sex," Cosmo informed her. "Search your furthest, most distant memories. It'll come back to you."

"Barbara, I've always wanted to ask you this. Is it true what they say about your middle name?" Jameson distracted her before she had a chance to respond to the elf's insult.

"Yes. It's Bettina."

"Bettina?" Cosmo rolled his eyes. "Your name is Barbara Bettina Barletta? Your initials are BBB?"

"I am the living embodiment of the Better Business Bureau, which is why I knew I was destined for greatness in Human Resources."

"And you consider being the head of HR in one of the most desolate places on Earth surrounded by sexually molested interns, horny elves trying to fuck almost anything that moves, a dildo-thieving Christmas matriarch, and a Viagra-popping, granny-porn-watching Christmas patriarch to be the epitome of employment?" The words rolled out Jameson's mouth before he had any idea what he was saying.

"You're turning into your partner." She didn't sound impressed.

"Thank you!" He grinned from ear to ear.

"That wasn't a compliment." And with that, Barbara set off down the hall toward the noise. "Santa? Are you still up here? Santa?"

"Yes, it was." It didn't matter she couldn't hear him. It was still a compliment whether she knew it or not.

Jameson and Cosmo stepped into the elevator and started the descent toward the main floor.

"You're either constipated or you're thinking." The elf looked up and studied the guard's face. "It's really difficult to tell with you."

"I was thinking that it's going to be a little sad for them when Wesley dies before Ethan."

"What do you mean?"

"Well, Santa's a couple hundred years old, as is Mrs. Claus, so I'm assuming Ethan will live an equally long life." Jameson bit his upper lip for a moment, then continued, "Wesley's just a regular ol' human being, minus when he opens his mouth."

"I'm pretty sure Wesley has a very long life ahead of him," Cosmo said.

"How do you know?"

"Elves live a very, very long time, and there's a unique side effect when we mate with one of your kind without protection."

The elevator doors opened, and they stepped out into the main hallway.

"Are you saying one of you is really Ethan's father?"

"Don't be disgusting." Cosmo made retching noises. "Can you imagine one of us up there in Mrs. Claus's moistness… well, when it actually was still moist?" He gagged again. "Let's just say that Santa was kinda cute in his younger days, and not always entirely straight. One of us may have been a little turned on, there may have been a night of drinking involved, and some questionable judgment. Then he met the missus, but the three of them are friends now. Santa passed our little gift on to her, and she in turn passed it on to her son during pregnancy. And based on what was going on back in the room we just left, I'm pretty sure Ethan's passed it on to Wesley by now. Possibly even twice."

"Well, it's a wonderful lube."

"I'm sure it helped. You know, play your cards right, and you might live to be a couple hundred years old yourself," Cosmo teased. "Sure, you may be one of those idiot savants minus the savant, but I've known lesser men in your species."

"Cosmo"—Jameson reached down and took the elf's hand—"I think this is the beginning of a beautiful friendship."

So with the twist of a lube cap,

And no worries about getting the clap,

Off they went about their mounting without fear they might injure,

Thus ends our tale of a security intern from Missouri and his reincarnated ginger.

But for all those who heard the delicious noise,

Knew it was just a little hardcore mating between the boys.

And when Santa sat down on his fanny a short time later, somewhat forlorn,

He exclaimed, "Now where the hell did I put my Viagra and granny porn?"

OVERNIGHT DELIVERY

JEVOCAS GREEN

The week before Christmas. One of the busiest retail weeks of the year. People scrambling around everywhere to find that special gift, that toy that would make their child or loved one smile on Christmas Day as they sat beneath the tree and unwrapped the gaudy, over-the-top wrapping paper hiding their prize.

"That'll be $24.99," Justin Scott said to a very disgruntled woman in his checkout line. It was a busy day in Barney's Toy Box, and this woman was determined to make it worse. Justin, no more than maybe twenty-two or twenty-three, with straight brown hair that seemed to sweep in front of his face constantly, stood there prepared to hear this woman give him the business. He tossed his head to clear his thick locks from his eyes as he listened to the woman bellowing at him.

"$24.99 for a freaking *doll?!*" the woman barked back to Justin, who adjusted his glasses and tried to ignore the woman's rudeness.

Justin had just been promoted to Assistant Manager and was simply covering another employee's register while they were on break. He'd seen many people like this woman during the day, and he was quite done with it to be honest. But he figured he'd try and kill her with kindness and smile through it.

"Well, ma'am, unfortunately that *is* the price. It's actually marked down for our Christmas blowout sale, but if you like, I could—"

"I don't care what the sale is, this is overpriced! You can *keep* your goddamn doll!" the woman snapped back, cutting Justin off before he could offer another solution.

Justin sighed with frustration as the coworker he was covering for returned.

"What'd I miss?" Henry asked as he smiled cluelessly at Justin.

All Justin could do was stare at his fellow employee blankly and walk away.

✧ ✧ ✧ ✧

The day moved on, and tons of people came and went from the store. Finally it was time to close up shop. Justin was definitely worn out by the screaming children and their uncaring parents, some of whom had left their little *darlings* in the store to run amuck while they did their last-minute shopping in other stores nearby. Justin began turning out the lights in the store. As he cleared one aisle, he scooped up a brown teddy bear some small child or careless adult had tossed aside during the rampage. Looking it over, Justin recognized a certain calmness in the sewn-on button eyes of this plush little bear. Justin released a sigh of relief to himself, reflecting on the busier than normal day that had finally come to an end. He was ready to get closed up and leave as he reshelved the teddy bear.

Just as Justin turned the sign on the front door from Open to Closed, his boss approached. He was a short, middle-aged, balding man, slightly overweight and probably

Italian, who smelled of cigars and salami. Justin and his coworkers joked how he closely resembled Danny DiVito. His boss pulled on a long coat as he made his way toward Justin and managed to wedge his plump, putrid presence between him and the door.

"Good work there today, Justin," his boss exclaimed with a low, gravelly voice, that sounded like he'd smoked his whole life and had a patch of phlegm just at the back of his throat but never bothered to cough. Justin always fought to not grimace when they spoke.

"Thanks, Mr. Godleski, I really appreciate it." Justin was fighting *really* hard not to think about his voice.

"Good, good. Hey listen, I've got a shipment of toys coming in. Special items that were on back order. It's that new life-size Kent doll. I need you to receive 'em tonight."

"But Mr. Godleski, I had plans with—"

"It'll have to wait, these things need to be checked in tonight. You'll just have to do it! Or if you'd rather your Christmas be spent out of a job…"

Justin realized that his boss had him by the balls on this one. Reluctantly, and rolling his eyes out of exasperation, he nodded in agreement.

"Good boy. That's why I promoted you." Mr. Godleski chuckled in a low bubbly chortle that sounded nothing short of a slowly draining pipe. "Make sure it's done by morning. Have a good night!" Mr. Godleski added as he put his half-smoked cigar to his mouth and lit it.

Justin could barely believe his boss was pawning this off on him at the last minute. He watched from the doorway as Mr. Godleski hopped in his car and sped away.

Justin closed the door, defeated and depressed. He turned off the front store lights to let people know the store was officially closed. His evening plans were now completely ruined. Justin pulled out his cell phone and called up his best friend to let her know.

"Hello?" she answered.

"Tara? Hey, it's Justin." Justin rested the phone between his cheek and shoulder as he began pulling register trays out and counting money.

"Hey, Justin! We still hitting the pub tonight?"

"Sadly no."

"Please tell me you're joking. We planned for this all week!"

"I know…" Justin said, removing the final tray and counting the money.

"You know you are missing out on Xander. I finally convinced him to come tonight."

"Are you *serious*?! The *one time* he finally shows up… Ugh!"

Frustrated, Justin stacked the register trays on top of each other and headed upstairs to the office to put them in the safe.

"This was totally your prime opportunity! At this rate, you are *never* gonna get your dick for Christmas. You must wanna keep your dry spell going for another seven months."

Justin made his way to the safe and opened it, his expression drooping from the disappointment.

"I know! Trust me, it's definitely driving me insane. I feel really bad about this, but my boss is making me stay late at the toy store for a shipment. He threatened my job, Tara! So I really have no choice."

"Ugh, that ugly old fart is *such* an *asshole*! Well, I guess we'll have to take a rain check, then. I'll see if I can convince Xander to make a repeat appearance."

Justin, so disgusted by having to bail on his friend, opened the safe and thrust the trays of money in haphazardly, then slammed the safe shut.

"Yeah, I guess so. Drink one for me, okay? Love you."

"You bet, babe. Love you too. Sorry your boss is a dick. I'll catch you later and tell you all about how sexy Xander is," Tara joked, making Justin chuckle through his frustration.

"Thanks, you're a real peach," Justin uttered with dry sarcasm. "Talk to you later," Justin added before hanging up the phone.

No sooner had Justin pocketed his phone, than he heard a loud thud from downstairs. Startled, he turned around, his hair sweeping quickly before his glasses. Justin could feel his heart racing in his throat. He was the only person in the store. What the fuck was that noise?

Taking a moment to collect himself, Justin made his way out of the messy office and into the stairwell.

Normally, the stairwell wouldn't creep him out, but there was something about the dimly lit passageway that unnerved him after hearing that noise. Justin crept down slowly, waiting intermittently to see if he would hear the noise again. Silence. Justin reached the hallway that led to the front of the store, and an eerie chill came over him, and he was sure it wasn't due to the cold weather outside.

Justin made his way through the checkout aisles near the front of the store. Still no one. But now he could see out the front window. The streets were quiet in the quaint, sleepy town. Snow covered the streets and cars like a child tucked in at night. The sky seemed really clear and still, and the moon brightened the otherwise dimly lit pavement. People made their final trips home for the night, past the decorations on street lamps and storefronts that lined the block.

The light from the sign overhead for Barney's Toy Box shone through the snow-kissed window onto Justin's face. He pressed his hand against the glass, and it fogged slightly from the warmth against the cold surface.

But even with the beautiful sight of the calm winter evening before him, the noise still worried him. Justin walked farther into the room. There was really nowhere anyone could hide in. From where he stood between two of the three register lanes, he could see down all the aisles on either side of the store.

"Okay, this is fucking weird," Justin said to himself under his breath. He crept forward a little more, and out of the corner of his eye, he saw it. A long box wrapped in shimmering blue paper sat on the counter as if it had been there the entire time.

"Where the fuck did this come from?" Justin blurted. The randomness of this box appearing out of nowhere really alarmed him.

Justin bravely approached the box, which seemed to be illuminated, as if it had a spotlight aimed its way and *wanted* Justin to open it. The store was eerily quiet. Justin checked his surroundings—still no one around, and still no clue how the box had been left without him realizing it.

Justin's palms were sweaty as he approached, close enough to reach for the blue box. Then all at once, there was a knock at the door. Justin's gaze darted to the front entrance to see the shadowy figure of a delivery guy standing there rubbing his hand against his hip to try and keep warm. The man was wrapped up tight, his dreadlocks tucked into the collar of his thick coat and his toboggan pulled snugly onto his head. He stood there patiently, clipboard in hand.

Justin gave another quizzical look at the blue box, then turned and headed toward the door to let in the freezing courier. Justin quickly unlocked the door and let the poor man in.

"Thank you, thank you!" the delivery guy exclaimed as he passed through the threshold of the toy store. "It's getting really cold out there." He laughed, and Justin smiled, then closed the door behind him.

"No problem. So, are you here to deliver the expected shipment?" Justin questioned, looking out the window and seeing there were several very tall boxes leaned against the far outside wall.

"Yep. The new line of life-size Kent dolls. All ready to go." The delivery guy explained and presented his clipboard to Justin, drawing his attention from the merchandise outside.

"They should be a hit! Fully poseable, they stand on their own, and even move their arms and head! They'll probably sell themselves!"

"I don't doubt it." Justin chuckled as he signed off for the product.

"Well, where do you want me to set up?"

"Over near the Brittany Dreamhouses. There's a section cleared out for them."

With that, the courier was off. One by one the tall blue boxes rolled in containing the life-size Kent dolls. Justin had never really been a doll person, but something about *this* doll was different. It looked so real. They'd given Kent a strong, chiseled jaw with a slight five o'clock shadow. Blue eyes and medium brown, lightly tousled hair. He wore a flannel button-up shirt and blue jeans. Man, these designers knew what they were doing. They even left the top couple buttons of Kent's shirt undone so the perfect pec man-cleavage he had going on could be seen.

Shit, Justin thought to himself. *If this were a real guy, I'd be trying to fuck his brains out right now.*

Justin stood out of the way of the delivery guy while he brought in the last of the Kents, staring at how legitimately lifelike they appeared.

"All set," the delivery guy exclaimed.

"Huh? Oh, okay, good. Thank you," Justin responded, snapping out of his daze.

"Cool. Well, I'm gonna take off."

"Awesome, thanks! Take care," Justin said while walking the delivery guy to the door and seeing him off. As the delivery guy hopped into his truck and drove away, Justin locked the door and returned his attention to the Kent doll.

The delivery guy had taken one out of the box to set up for display. It seemed to stare straight into Justin's eyes as he approached. His smile was perfect, all dimples and white teeth.

"Man, they did a good job with you." Justin moved closer and could now see that the doll's hands and arms were quite muscular and manly. Even his forearms had the little raised veins on them. Justin reached out and touched the doll's hand. It was surprisingly soft. They must have used a foam latex outer shell to make it appear more realistic. He ran his fingers up the Kent doll's forearm, feeling the various veins molded into the material. He traced the doll's arm up to the opened buttons that displayed Kent's chest.

Justin couldn't resist; he opened another couple of the buttons, revealing more and more of the doll's chiseled physique, including abs cut so hard they could probably break boards. Justin released a gasp of astonishment as he ran his fingers across the doll's perfect body. As much as Justin understood this was an inanimate object, he couldn't help but get turned on by how sexy it was.

"God, you're perfect." Justin stared as he continued dragging his fingers across the doll's ripples and creases.

"Why can't I ever have a guy like you?"

"Good *Lord*, you're a pathetic waste, ya know that?"

Startled by an unfamiliar voice, Justin's gaze darted in the direction of the sound, wide-eyed to see a rather short impish creature standing atop the register where he'd found the blue present earlier.

"What…who…who the fuck are you?" Justin said, slightly frightened. "How did you get in here?"

"Oh great, another scared queen. Look, the name's McJingles, and I'm an elf if you couldn't tell that just by looking at me." McJingles motioned to his attire, a loose white and red Christmas-y shirt and a mini Santa hat. "They make me wear this shit, ya know."

"What do you want?"

"What do I want? Well, that list is much longer and would take more time than we have here tonight. And trust me, I'd much rather be *anywhere* besides here with Coward the Fag."

"Excuse me?" Justin said angrily, storming over to the imp. "Who the fuck do you think you're talking to?"

"Whoa, easy there, twinkletoes. I'm not here to start nothin', I'm here to help you out."

"So far it seems like you're just getting your rocks off by pissing me the fuck off!"

"Interesting choice of words there," McJingles said as he hopped across the counter to stand next to Justin. He put his arm around Justin's shoulder and walked him closer to the box. "You see, I'm here to fix a dilemma you seem to be facing."

"Dilemma? What dilemma?" Justin asked, pulling away from the imp.

"I see subtlety is wasted on you," jested the imp sarcastically. "Your seven-month itch, sir."

"What?"

"Your barren wasteland?"

"Not following."

"The thirst of the Sahara? *Come on*, man."

"What are you talking about?"

"*Jeez*. Do I have to spell it out for you?" McJingles said, obviously agitated at Justin's cluelessness. "I'm here to fix your 'dry spell,' genius."

"Dry spell? Oh…"

I think Justin's getting it.

"OH!"

He just got it.

"Ohhhhh…"

Yep, just clicked.

"Wow, you are a piece of work, ya know that?" McJingles stabbed.

"Look, thanks for wanting to fix my 'little problem' and all, but I don't think you're my type…or even my species, for that matter…"

"Ya cut me deep, son, ya cut me deep," McJingles proclaimed statistically. "No, you cock-deprived fool, I'm here to help you get laid. But not with me. Hell, once you go elf, you'll stop playing with yourself."

"What does that even mean?"

"I don't know, still a work in progress on that one. But here. This is for you."

McJingles picked up the blue box and handed it over to Justin.

"Wait, you put this here?"

"Give the man a prize. Jesus, you are not a bright one, are you?"

Justin took the box and cautiously unwrapped it. After opening the cardboard flaps and peering inside, he found glowing back at him a huge glowing nine-inch blue dildo. Looking it over, it appeared to have all the natural curves and veining and the head was nice and firm.

"I mean, this is an amazing dildo, but how does this fix my problem?" Justin asked, lowering the box with disappointment. "My issue is finding a guy who wants to fuck me. I could go *home* and use a dildo."

"Well gee, that explains a lot," McJingles fired again. Justin glared at him.

"No, *genius*," McJingles started. "You obviously don't know the power of Christmas magic, do you?"

With that, McJingles led Justin over to the display model of the Kent doll that he had earlier been fondling.

"Okay, I don't have all night, so here's the deal," McJingles said, impatiently taking the dildo out of the box and slapping it in Justin's hand.

"That dildo in your hands is no ordinary dildo. It's an enchanted dildo. It will grant life to any object you connect it to, and then it will fuck you into submission."

Justin looked down at the dildo in wonder and then considered the Kent doll again.

"And since you've been basically eye-fucking and molesting this Kent doll since it got here, I figure I know what you'll be using it on."

"What are you saying?"

"What I'm *saying*, princess, is that you need to quench your fucking thirst!" With that, McJingles opened the Kent doll's jeans, revealing the blank space where a penis *should* be. "These things don't exactly come anatomically correct."

Justin was shocked at the situation presented before him, but his wonder intensified by what was in his hand. The hornier he got, the more the dildo glowed.

"This can't be real…" Justin stated, pondering what he should do.

"Well, technically it isn't, seeing as though Kent is made out of plastic and latex, but you can change that. The minute you give him your cock, he will become real and he will reward you with fucking your brains out! Your choice."

Justin was overwhelmed with excitement. He stepped closer to the Kent doll, then knelt down before it. Looking up over the ripples of Kent's stomach and the cliff of his pecs, Justin could see the pronounced chin of Kent smiling even from that angle. How badly he wanted to be fucked, and it looked like he was about to get his wish.

Justin took a firm grip on the illuminated neon blue dildo and brought the end with the balls up to the blank crotch of the Kent doll. The dildo seemed to glow brighter the closer it got. Finally, with a great suction, the dildo popped into place, and suddenly the entire Kent doll started to glow just as brightly as the dildo. Justin stood and backed away, unsure of what was happening.

"It…it's working!" Justin said in amazement at the spectacle before him.

"*Oh*, I forgot that there is one catch…"

"You say this *now*?"

"Details, nothing major."

"What? What *catch*?"

"You only have him till sunrise. Once the sun hits the Kent doll in the morning, the dildo will become a normal dildo and fall off, and the Kent doll will return to being just a toy."

Justin glanced at McJingles, concerned, then turned his gaze to the clock on the wall, which read midnight.

"Well, I have six hours till sunrise... I had better make them count, I suppose," Justin exclaimed, taking off his apron and glasses, then tossing them aside.

"Well, someone's an eager beaver."

Justin turned back to the glowing figure and looked him over. He smiled, thinking about the beautiful man that would soon emerge from the blue light. In anticipation, Justin knelt once again before the glowing dildo, ready to greet the phallus with wet, warm lips. As he assumed the position, the light began to subside as if it were peeling away from the tip of his cock and over the rest of his body.

The light cleared the head of the cock, leaving behind a gorged, plump, pink mushroom top, followed by a hard thick shaft that continued down to a full, low-hanging set of balls. Justin looked up as the light moved up the doll's abs and chest. Finally, the glow moved over its head, the doll's chest rising and flexing, even the abs tensing. The Kent doll took his first breath. Justin's eyes widened in amazement as Kent gazed down at him, his piercing blue eyes finally real and melting Justin. The expression of wanting in Justin's eyes was overpowering.

Kent appeared to recognize the desire Justin felt burning inside, and could only smile, his beautiful pearly whites sparkling as his plump lips parted to expose them.

Justin was certain he had never seen a more beautiful or perfect man in all his life. They certainly didn't make them like that around there. He could *only* have gotten this one that was shipped from Taiwan.

Kent could see the shock on Justin's face and wanted to assure him that all was well. He knelt down to Justin's level, then stared into Justin's greenish-hazel eyes. Not averting his gaze, he finished removing his already opened flannel shirt.

After his shirt was gone, Kent cradled the back of Justin's head, gently running his fingers through his brown locks, then pulled him in slowly. Justin didn't resist as Kent swept his other hand to the small of his back and drew him in to kiss him.

Justin's eyes widened suddenly, then slowly closed as he gave in to the seduction. Justin ran his hands up Kent's arms, his triceps and biceps tensing at his touch. Kent's arms were so strong, his skin even softer than before the change. This was really happening. Justin was amazed at how wonderful Kent's lips felt against his. They were the perfect balance of soft and firm. Kent's tongue gently massaged his own, and Justin eased into giving himself to Kent's embrace.

✧ ✧ ✧ ✧

McJingles stood nearby, pleased at what he'd done. Then in a blink, he vanished, leaving the two to have at it.

✧ ✧ ✧ ✧

Kent pulled away from the kiss and smiled at Justin again, then began unbuttoning Justin's shirt and pulling it off of him. Kent began kissing Justin's abs up to his nipples, which he stopped to suck. Justin moaned in pleasure, feeling Kent's lips on his skin. In one motion, Kent scooped Justin up and sat him on a nearby gift-wrapping counter, then went to work taking Justin's pants off.

"Oh my God," Justin said, amazed at what had just happened. Kent's hard, throbbing, thick cock pulsated from how ready it was to be inside Justin. Justin wanted the same thing. To help Kent out, he pulled off his shoes and socks, then his pants.

Kent appeared to like what he had been given to play with so Justin planted his feet on the edge of the counter and parted his legs, giving Kent full access to his now rock-hard cock, which lay against Justin's stomach up to his navel.

Kent put his hands on both of Justin's thighs, rubbing his smooth skin down to where his cock and balls were located. With a glance to Justin for approval, which Justin *obviously* obliged, Kent took Justin's cock into his warm, wet mouth. Justin arched in ecstasy as Kent took huge strokes of his cock in and out of his mouth. Up and down. At one point, Kent took Justin's cock all the way into his mouth and down his throat. Justin couldn't contain himself. He grabbed the back of Kent's head and began thrusting into Kent's mouth.

To Justin's surprise, Kent didn't appear to mind this, since he gripped Justin's ass cheeks and assisted him in pounding his own face. Justin was so close. Justin knew that at any moment he would cum, but he stopped himself. Panting hard, pulling his cock from Kent's mouth, he paused the action.

"I don't want to cum yet… I want you inside me when I cum."

"As you wish," Kent said, his voice low and smooth.

Justin's eyes widened at the fact that he could talk too.

"Full of surprises tonight, aren't you?" Justin smiled.

"The best is yet to come," Kent replied. And with that, he dropped his pants all the way, revealing his muscular thighs and calves. His legs were hairless and looked as if he'd been swimming and running his entire life.

"Bless you, Taiwan, bless you!" Justin exclaimed as Kent pulled him to the edge of the counter.

Kent continued exploring Justin's body with his tongue, his warm, wet mouth tracing every line of Justin's abs, down to the crest of his crotch, then back up his Adonis belt. Then one after the other, he pleasured Justin's balls, after which he proceeded farther down toward his puckering entrance. Justin so desperately wanted something in him, and happily Kent obliged by sticking his tongue inside him.

A jolt went through Justin as Kent's tongue pushed deeper into his hole. His body shuddered and convulsed with each movement. After a time pleasuring Justin's candy box, Kent returned to Justin's cock. Justin bit his lip, remembering how close he came to coming last time Kent sucked him. But to Justin's surprise, that wasn't the only thing his new plaything had in store. Kent started preparing Justin for what was soon to invade his precious snow cave. One…two…then three fingers slid into Justin. He let out a moan of pleasure as Kent massaged him inside and devoured his cock outside.

Justin's moans were getting more and more frantic as the sensations Kent provided overtook him. All Justin could do was wrap his legs around Kent's shoulders and grab the back of Kent's thick hair as the doll made Justin's cock his own peppermint stick.

But Justin was anxious to have Kent's Yule log buried deep within his chimney stack. Kent glanced up to meet Justin's gaze just as he had Justin's member buried deep in his throat. Justin's expression apparently told him all he needed to know.

Kent pulled off Justin's rod and prepared to mount the table. His cock dripped with his precum, falling perfectly on Justin's hole… Drip…drip…drip. *Damn*, Justin thought, *he's even self-lubricating too!*

Without breaking eye contact, Kent inched his large cock down to Justin's wanting orifice. He then slowly eased into him. Justin flung his head back, wanting to scream, but nothing came out. First the head, then slowly the shaft, inch by inch he could feel it sliding in, until every thick and veiny bit of Kent's cock was inside him.

Justin let out a gasp as Kent began thrusting into him deeper and deeper, opening Justin up more than he'd ever been opened in his life. Justin could feel every curve and bend of Kent's cock invading him as Kent pounded away at him.

His abs tensed each time, and still, he didn't break eye contact with Justin.

Justin's face softened and strained in turns as he accepted Kent's Christmas gift. Suddenly, Kent flipped him on his side, holding Justin's left knee to Kent's chest and bracing his knees on either side of Justin. Kent plowed in, and it felt as if he had found a way to get even deeper into him. Justin let out a moan of pleasure like he never had before. No one had fucked him this hard or this deep.

As the time went on, he realized how much he wanted to keep Kent, but knew he couldn't. So he just let Kent fuck him on through the night, position after position.

✧ ✧ ✧ ✧

By 5:00 am, Justin's body had been folded more than an origami snowflake. But he couldn't get enough of Kent's beautiful cock. Now, nearing the first light of the morning, Kent still had not cum yet! Or if he had cum, he hadn't told Justin and just had one hell of a refractory period. Justin wanted him to, though. He wanted to cum with Kent, and he wanted it badly.

After one position that Kent had twisted Justin into that could only be described as the atomic pretzel, Justin unfolded himself and locked gazes with Kent, pulling him down and kissing him once more. It was a deep passionate kiss that was nothing short of spectacular. Upon pulling away, Justin again stared into Kent's eyes.

"Make me cum."

"As you wish."

The response alone was almost enough to make Justin explode right there. Kent lifted himself off Justin and parted Justin's legs even more. Kent then slowly pulled his cock out till just the head remained inside Justin. All at once, Kent slammed the whole length in, making Justin let out a loud moan.

"Oh... My... *God*!" Justin exclaimed. Three long thrusts and suddenly an eruption of creamy nog blasted from his cock. But just as soon as Justin erupted, Kent pulled out his cock, laying it next to Justin's resting member and released his bountiful load as well.

By the end of it, Justin was so covered in cum, he looked like a giant marshmallow had exploded all over him. The two of them collapsed on the gift-wrapping counter and enjoyed the sticky mess together, giggling.

"Did I please you?" Kent asked very honestly and without pretense.

"Are you kidding me? I haven't been fucked like that in…well…ever," Justin exclaimed, gazing at Kent's now blushing face.

"I am pleased that I could give you so much joy."

"Yeah…me too." Justin glanced up at the clock and realized it was almost 6:00 am. A tear fell down Justin's cheek, and Kent caught it with his finger, appearing puzzled.

"You are leaking. A tear? What is wrong?"

"It's nothing."

"I do not believe that at all," Kent said directly.

For a toy doll that had only been a real boy for a little over five hours, Kent was surprisingly perceptive.

"It's just…I…I don't think I will ever have someone like you ever again.

Once daybreak comes, I'll lose you…forever. And that is really tearing me up right now. I know we pretty much just met. And well…you're a plastic doll brought to life by magic, but you've made me feel things tonight that I don't think I'll ever feel again…ever. And it sucks because I can't keep you."

"I am sorry that I cannot stay. I, too, feel a connection with you even with the only fleeting life given to me. But there is one thing that can be done."

Sudden hope filled Justin.

"Keep the piece that gave me life, and once every Christmas, I'll return to you. And for that night, I am yours."

"You mean I can see you again?"

"Yes, but only once during Christmas. No other time will have the magic to bring me back. But until then, I want you to find someone that can make you happy when I am not around. Don't let me be your only happiness."

Another tear fell from Justin's eye as he accepted what Kent was telling him.

Kent gazed out the window and up at the sky where the light of the sun made its way over the horizon. Worry crossed his face. Turning to look out the window too, Justin panicked slightly. Kent stood quickly and began to put his shoes and pants back on, then pulled his shirt over his shoulders. His cock still hung from his open pants, surprisingly still erect. Justin covered himself with a nearby piece of cloth meant for wrapping, then stood to face Kent.

"Please, please, don't leave."

"You are very beautiful, Justin. You deserve to be as happy as you just were all the time. Find that happiness. And until I see you next time, good-bye."

Tears filled Justin's eyes as he reached up and kissed Kent. The sun broke over the buildings and light spilled into the toy store. As it passed over Kent, he returned to plastic, leaving just the Kent doll standing there with his smiling expression. Lastly, Kent's cock finally returned to its previous appearance, a normal blue dildo. The phallus fell off, hitting the floor with a thud.

Justin turned back to stare the sun as if it had betrayed him. But he understood the lesson that he'd needed here. He took the piece of cloth from around him and proceeded to clean the jizz off himself and Kent's chest. He then buttoned up his shirt and pants. And thought about what he'd just experienced.

A little later, Justin wedged the Kent doll, sitting upright, into his backseat and put the now rewrapped dildo on the seat next to him. Justin regarded Kent's face and smiled back at the plastic smile and bright eyes on the doll.

It was almost time to open the shop. And Justin managed to get everything back to pristine order. Upon entering the main area, he noticed that a couple of the employees had arrived.

Justin went to the front door and let them in. They greeted each other, then headed toward the break area to clock in and prepare for the day. Last to arrive was Mr. Godleski. He pulled up to the door in his car, and Justin leaned on the doorframe, rolling his eyes and awaiting his phlegm-filled greeting.

"Ah! Justin, m'boy!"

"Morning, Mr. Godleski."

Ugh…that gurgling voice again, Justin thought to himself.

"Everything go well last night?"

"Peachy. All the Kent dolls have been inventoried… all but one."

The two of them walked to the area of the display where there were ten Kent dolls standing together.

"One," Mr. Godleski scoffed. "What happened to the one?"

"Well, there was a defect, sir, so I marked it as damaged and took it."

"You took it?"

"I figure all it'd do is get tossed anyway. I plan on giving it to my nephew. He'll love it." Justin smiled at Mr. Godleski, fighting back nausea from his voice.

"Well…I suppose. You *did* stay and get them all checked in. It's the least I can do. But don't make this a habit."

"Yes, sir." Justin beamed.

A line of customers were beginning to amass outside the doors. That put Mr. Godleski on alert.

"All right, get to your stations, fire up those registers. We've got toys to sell. Let's *go*."

With that, all the employees scrambled out to their registers and stations. Becky headed to gift wrap and just as she was about to plant herself on the stool behind the counter, Justin grinned at her as he used a rag to wipe a spot he'd missed the night before. He then pocketed the rag and walked away without explaining.

Justin began making his rounds through the store, counting inventory and checking on shelf placement of items. The usual. But he couldn't shake what Kent had said to him about finding happiness. As Justin rounded the corner to the main part of the store again, he was met by a tall, slender blond with striking green eyes and wearing a pea coat and scarf, holding two coffees.

"Xander?" Justin asked, shocked that the man was standing before him.

"Morning. Figured you could use a little liquid courage for the day."

"Oh my God, you have no idea," Justin said, taking a big sip of coffee.

"I was, uh, sad not to see you out last night. It wasn't the same without you."

"Yeah, I really did wanna go. But duty calls, I suppose."

"Yeah, I suppose," Xander agreed, smiling shyly at Justin. Justin blushed at the thought.

"What?" Justin asked coyly.

"Nothing, it's just…" There was a long pause as Xander seemed to search for his next word. Then with a nervous sigh, Xander leaned in and kissed Justin passionately. Justin fell into the kiss willingly. He'd wanted this a long time, but shock befell him as he pulled away.

"Xander… I…I don't understand."

"This is what I was hoping would happen last night. I wanted to tell you how I feel. I've avoided coming out this whole time because I didn't think you would want me, and I didn't want to chance it."

"Wow." Justin took a moment to collect himself after hearing this information.

"Well, I do. And have for a long time," Justin replied, then pulled Xander in for another kiss. Xander beamed.

"Ha! Great!" Xander blushed. "Feel up to a take-two tonight?" Xander asked.

"Sure, dinner? That Italian place downtown sound good?"

"It's a date!" Xander exclaimed. "Okay, well, I'll leave you to your managerial duties."

"Thank you for the coffee." Justin chuckled. "I'll see you tonight."

As Xander walked away, Justin noticed Mr. McJingles standing there smiling. Justin's eyes widened as he glanced around and then back to the little man, but…he was gone. For a brief moment, Justin stood perplexed, but then he realized this was what Mr. McJingles had planned all along. He simply wanted him to believe in himself first. Believe that he'd find happiness. And once he believed, love would surely follow.

"Well done, McJingles. Well done." Justin smiled as he watched Xander's car pull away, then headed back to work.

THE ISLE OF MISFIT SEX TOYS

J.P. BARNABY

"It's enough already, by Claus. Why do they keep playing Christmas carols?" Bob sat back against the discarded sofa he'd salvaged from one of Santa's old storage units behind the workshop. "Let It Snow" drifted from the open vent above them, and he initiated the protocol used to close his eyes. It took less than a second, but the plastic drifted down over the optical circuits in his sockets. He might have looked like an elf, but beauty, as they say, is only skin-deep. Or, at least, polyethylene deep, anyway.

"I don't know. I k-k-k-k-kind of like this s-s-s-s-song," Buzz stuttered from his place in the circle.

"We might as well get started." Bob sighed. "Is everyone here?" He directed the question to the room, and Dil turned on yet another lantern in their tomb-like home. It would have been depressing in the utility closet of Santa's workshop if it weren't for the alternative. They were all cast-off misfit toys destined for the junk pile. Then Bob rescued them and found a safe place for every toy to live. They considered him their king, but he just wanted someone to abate the crushing loneliness.

"I think so, Bob."

Toys began to push odds and ends into a circle, nothing the humans or even the elves would see as organization, but someplace for them to sit, nonetheless. Boxes for the less fortunate, but some more industrious toys found bean bags and even doll furniture to sit on. Each of the toys settled into their place, some with more difficulty than others, but eventually, the room quieted. They'd worked their little circle up to six toys. Sometimes they had more, sometimes less, but for the time being, six seemed like a comfortable number.

Bob stood at the head of the circle, next to the severed doll's head that had rolled into their hideaway a few months back.

"We're all here for the same reason," Bob started, and a hush fell over their little group, broken only by the uncontrolled, intermittent buzzing noise they'd all learned to ignore. "My name is Bob, Battery Operated Boyfriend, designed for a single purpose, one that I can no longer fulfill. Once considered an advanced robotics pleasure toy, now I'm no longer…fully functional, but I'm okay with that. The trilithium battery that powers my neural substructure will keep me running for another hundred years, so I have to find my new purpose. That is my goal, to find my new purpose. Who wants to go next?"

"I w-w-w-w-w-will."

"Okay, Buzz, go ahead."

"Yay, Buzz," two tiny silver spheres chimed in, and Buzz smiled.

"My name is B-B-B-B-Buzz, and I've been here for about a m-m-m-m-month. Like Bob, I was d-d-d-d-designed for a p-pretty specific p-purpose. I m-m-m-massage things." The small spheres on the right giggled, but Buzz continued as if he hadn't heard. "I w-w-w-wanna learn to c-c-c-control my stut-t-stutter."

"Thank you, Buzz," Bob said quietly. "Now, since you found his introduction so funny, Wally, maybe you guys should go next."

"I'm Wally and he's Ben," Wally announced.

"Wally, do we have to go through this every time?" Bob asked with a quiet sigh.

"What? We have to say our names every time, even though we all know each other. Why put him through his fears?" He had a hard time making his tinny little voice sound angry, especially with the smooth expression across the metallic surface of his ball face.

"It's okay," Ben interrupted. "We know what our joint purpose is. Our biggest fear is that we'll be separated and lost."

Wally rolled to the left, and if Wally and Ben had hands, they'd have joined them.

"Yes, yes, and we all know that Dil the dildo is terrified of the dark. Can we move on to more pressing business like finding a place to live that doesn't smell like cabbage?" the severed head asked. "I'd also really like to do something about being more mobile. Maybe a skateboard and some arms?"

"Candy, I understand how you're feeling, but your body deflated. We don't even know where it is. As for the arms, what exactly are we going to attach them to?" Bob asked patiently, like they hadn't had that same argument every week.

"Oh, that's easy for you to say, Mr. Not Fully Functional. At least you can get up and walk around. At least you can get away from the insanity and stand at the door watching where we *should* be."

As a whole, the group turned toward the door that led into Santa's workshop. Though he hated himself for it, Bob felt a longing in his actuators that just wouldn't die. During the brief time he'd been with Christelpher, the elf who'd created him, they'd been happy. Then his elf slipped at the top of the present-wrapping machine, probably because of the lube that had seemed permanently on his hands. He fell, pointed ears over belled shoes, across the conveyer belt and into the machine. He came out with bows in places they had no reason to be and ribbon wrapped so tightly around his neck he'd been blue as a Smurf. In fact, they'd thought he *was* a Smurf toy for a few minutes, until the horrible truth had dawned.

Bob still thought of Christelpher often, especially in the dark of night as he wished for the comfort of his slick hands and the whispers of love.

"Hey, Bob, you want to get your head back in the game here? We were talking about how to get ourselves tossed into one of those present sacks and out of here."

"This isn't a good idea. What happens when some eight-year-old girl ends up with us?" Wally asked with a smooth expression.

"Oh look, Mommy, I got marbles," Candy cried in an unnaturally high girly voice. "I'm a broken doll, and you, Bob, can climb down off the shelf and find yourself a Ken doll. We can all find a place outside this room."

Bob turned toward the cracked sliver of mirror lying against the wall and considered his elven reflection. No one outside the Pole would want a sex toy that looked like an elf. He wasn't even sure anyone here would, especially one that didn't work. It didn't matter where he went, but he could at least help the others.

"Okay, the key is getting to the present-wrapping machine…"

✧ ✧ ✧ ✧

Dale dropped to his knees and wrapped his fingers around Biff's throbbing elfhood.

"I want to suck you like a thick, sweet candy cane," Dale told him from between Biff's spread legs, the tips of Biff's shoes pointing the way up to paradise. When the tiny warm mouth sank onto Biff's dick, it was like the day after Christmas.

"Relph Elf, what in Santa's name are you doing?"

The voice shattered the dizzying arousal that was buzzing through his body at the words on the page. He rolled up the elf-printed magazine and tried to hide it in his back pocket. A back pocket he couldn't find because his pants were around his tiny little ankles.

"Are you kidding me here? Santa is going to run you over with the sleigh if he catches you stroking your pole while you're still on the clock. Dude, save it for quitting time. And a stroke mag? Really?" Adelf stood with his hands on wide hips, his stare penetrating Relph's self-righteous defensiveness. Silver hair poked out of his bell-tipped hat, set above his stern expression. As usual, Adelf's perfect uniform wouldn't dare show a crease or stain. Relph scowled as he pulled down his shirt to hide its unkempt appearance and went on the offensive.

"Shut up, you have a wife at home. I don't have anyone. Do you know how lonely it is year after year? Damn it, Adelf, I'm one hundred fifty-two years old, and I've never had someone to love. Sure, quick hand jobs, maybe a few blow jobs in the back of the sleigh, but nothing that's been real." Relph reached down and snagged the top of his velvet pants, pulling them up short, toned legs.

"Plus," Relph continued, "who in their right mind gives us velvet clothes? I spend my whole day wanting to hump my own pants."

"I've never seen such a horny elf. You're going to end up in your parents' basement addicted to porn or swinging on the hardware over at The Pole. I can't believe you subscribe to *On the Shelf*."

"What else am I going to do? It's not like there's a huge selection of jolly elves donning gay apparel."

"I think you'd be surprised. You're just not looking in the right places. One isn't just going to fall out of the sky and land on your dick."

A whistle sounded in the background, indicating the end of their shift. Adelf sighed long and loud, while Relph just gazed over the production floor. Why did it matter if the workday ended? He didn't have anything to go home to. For a long time, he wished he could work all the time. Not for the money, but so he'd have something to do instead of reclining on his bed while reading some skin magazine and wishing for something he couldn't have.

"Come on, the wife isn't home tonight. She's off doing a book club thing with some of the other wives. They're reading *Fifty Shades of Elf* this month. Trust me, I need a drink."

"Fine, but first, let me take an elfie."

"For what?"

"I heard about this new site Elf 4 Elf. Maybe I can end up with a hookup later."

"You missed the whole point of our conversation."

"I didn't miss it. I ignored it. There's a difference."

"Whatever, I want some eggnog. Let's go."

Relph followed the older elf down a flight of carpeted stairs toward the main part of the workshop. Since he'd met his quota about an hour before, Relph had gone to find some peace and quiet. His mind had traveled back to his last lonely hookup, one thing led to another, and he'd found a magazine in one hand and his dick in the other. It wasn't even about the sex, though he couldn't articulate that effectively to Adelf. He wanted a connection—a deep, throbbing connection.

The Pole, the only gay bar in Santa's Village, sat on the edge of the world, backlit by the northern lights. Smaller than most of the bars on the landing strip, it gave off a Claus-trophobic feel, but remained the only place to find hot nubile elf bodies writhing together in peppermint-scented lube. The bouncer on the door, a less than jolly elf named Gelfrey, glared at Relph as he took their cover charge.

"You, no touching the dancers. It took us two weeks to replace that table." His scowl gave Relph a shiver, and he nodded, afraid of what the elf would say if he tried to argue that the dancer might have been a little plump for that particular piece of furniture. Instead, he simply shuffled past and headed for the bar. He didn't have any interest in touching the dancers. They only cared about the money. He wanted someone to care about him.

A slight barmaid with a reindeer tattoo on her bicep came over to take their orders. Relph didn't recognize her from his infrequent trips to the bar, so he hadn't gotten into any trouble with her yet. She smiled at him, pushing spikes of blonde hair back from her eyes. Red and green lights reflected off the mirrored shelves gave her face an unearthly glow.

"What'll it be, guys?" She had a deep voice, much deeper than he'd have expected in a woman. Relph blinked once—twice—and then realized that the barmaid wasn't a woman at all, but a carefully made-up guy. Cross-dressing elves were pretty rare, even at The Pole. Relph didn't really see the attraction, but to each his, or her, own.

Relph smiled back.

"I'll take a whiskey eggnog," Relph said and then turned to Adelf, who stared openmouthed at the barmaid.

"Dude," Relph said, poking his friend in the side. "What do you want to drink?"

"I… Oh, I'm sorry. I'll take the same."

The barmaid rolled her heavily shadowed eyes and went off to fix their drinks.

"What the hell, man?"

"He's a dude. In a dress."

"You should try it sometime, a bit of air might do your balls some good."

Adelf sputtered, choking on his own spit, and Relph smiled.

Maybe tonight would turn out okay after all.

✧ ✧ ✧ ✧

"So, the trick is getting up those stairs without anyone seeing. We only have about two weeks, so we need to figure that out first. We also need to make sure that all the pieces and parts stay together. We can't let Ben and Wally go into different packages." Bob took notes on the reverse side of some torn wrapping paper. Dil looked over his shoulder, his head nudging Bob's cheek.

"Dude, if I wanted a dick in my face, I'd get on my knees." Bob snorted.

"Sorry. Sorry. I'm just…nervous. I'm having reservations about being in a present like that…in the dark…by myself. Maybe it would just be better if I stayed behind and—" Dil stopped, his fear overpowering speech.

"Stayed behind and what?" Candy asked with a huff of impatience. "Prop yourself up in a corner and watch the world go by? Don't you want to get *out* of here and live?"

"I don't…I don't know…"

"Candy, not everyone wants the same things you do," Bob chastised. "I mean look at me, I'm a sex doll who looks like an elf. Except for someone with an elf fetish, who in the greater world would want me? They'd just stick me on a shelf somewhere. I don't know that I'm going either."

"Bob, you're going to help us, but stay behind?"

"I haven't decided yet."

"Oh, honey." Candy's voice turned from annoying to pitying in an instant, forcing Bob to turn away. The last thing he wanted was someone's pity. He looked over the plans again for something to do.

"We need to find some kind of bag to put Ben and Wally in so they don't get separated. We should also throw some barrettes, combs, and stuff in with you, Candy. We want whoever gets you to keep you."

"You're really putting a lot of thought into this," Dil said, dropping down onto one of the beanbag chairs near the door.

"Well, yeah, you guys are my friends. I want you to be happy."

"We want you to be happy too."

"I don't know what would make me happy." Bob glanced out over the workshop floor at the elves busy and bustling around, carrying toys and pieces of toys to the assembly line. They were focused, driven toward that goal of Christmas just around the corner. The middle-of-the-day shift seemed the best time to get through the chaos unseen. If they went at night when things were slower, someone would certainly stop them.

He took a step toward the door and then another. When he reached the shadow of the frame, he stopped at the collective intake of breath behind him. The group gasp made the constant carols seem quiet in comparison. Without turning, he stopped and waited. It took a minute, but someone came to stand at his elbow.

"Y-y-y-y-y-y-you can't g-g-g-g-g-go out there, B-b-b-b-b-bob," Buzz said, and Bob had a feeling if Buzz'd had hands, his friend would have grabbed his arm. Instead, he simply implored Bob with his voice.

"I have to. If we're going to plan any more, I need to derive a safe path to the machine and see how to get into it." If he were perfectly honest with himself, Bob didn't want to go anywhere near that machine, not after his Christelpher lost his life there. He could still see the bit of ribbon in Christelpher's blond hair and bits of wrapping paper stuffed in places paper had no reason to be. How he fell in naked, no one would ever know. No one, but Bob, who had been bent over the railing when Christelpher slipped. If he'd just been faster… But, he'd left those thoughts behind long ago. Now it was time to help his friends.

He could do this.

He *had* to do this.

Bob swerved around Buzz and crept out into the workshop. The light, the colors, and the noise hit him like a blow across his digital senses. Lenses behind his eyes adjusted to the bright, chaotic atmosphere, and he saw everything at once, input flooding into his processors. Hardwood floors bounced sound back against the sensors vibrating in his elf-shaped ears. His shoes whispered against the floor, the sound lost in the cacophony of noise as he snuck past a workbench and behind the backs of elves toiling with hammers against wooden trucks and cars.

The drawer above his head opened, and he scampered away, nearly losing his footing on the slick wood. The elves, of course, had rubberized shoes, but as a pleasure bot, he had no need for such luxuries. His path cleared as another elf carried a stack of doll arms too high for her to see around. Bob got a glimpse of her long flaxen hair as she whipped by on her way to yet another workbench.

He dodged runaway toy frogs and meandering toy dogs. It took nearly half an hour, but eventually, he climbed a flight of stairs he hadn't been near in too many years to count. Each step upward took him back another year in time until he reached the top where he came face to…well, face to dick with someone. An elf stood near the machine with his pants down, his hand wrapped around his dick, and a transcendent expression on his beautiful, flushed face. Bob stared; he couldn't help himself.

The elf's hand flew over his dick, thick for an elf, but still a good length. Bob couldn't help but wonder how it would feel inside him. It had been years since he'd been filled. Dil had offered a few times, halfheartedly, but Bob couldn't even think about it. So he'd gone without. An empty loneliness ate away at him as he watched the elf's body flush, his cock red and leaking. He reached out a hand. Just a touch, that's all he wanted.

"Fuck," the elf whispered, and his grip stuttered on his shaft as cum shot out and landed on Bob's face. He sputtered as the hot fluid splattered across his synthetic skin. The elf's eyes flew open, wide in surprise and fear. Bob turned, wiping the worst of the release from his eyes, and stumbled down the stairs. The elf whispered something behind him, but Bob didn't slow. In fact, he scampered all the way back to their closet hideaway.

"Bob, did you find out what you—" Dil asked but stopped as he caught sight of Bob's face, still covered in a sticky film.

"Oh my God, is that…" Candy trailed off as Bob pushed past her and into his small room. The door slammed behind him, louder than he'd intended, as he grabbed a blanket off the empty spool that once held ribbon.

What the fuck just happened?

✧ ✧ ✧ ✧

What the fuck just happened?

Relph jerked his pants back up around his waist and stared at the spot the…elf—something—had just vacated. The thing looked like an elf, but he had skin like some kind of doll. He'd heard of elves making themselves sex toys, but it had been decades before, and management seemed to frown on using spare parts to fashion themselves something to fuck. Or maybe it was just the steel pipe and soft latex he'd taken from the robotics department for something to stick his dick in.

He used the sleeve of his uniform to swipe at the semen on his hand and the bit that had landed on the floor before jogging down the stairs after the elf robot. It seemed strange, but he wanted to apologize. He'd never unintentionally ejaculated on anyone before. Though, he didn't know if the thing had feelings. If it did, he wanted to say he was sorry. At the bottom of the stairs, he searched wildly around, his heart throbbing against his Adam's apple.

Nothing.

The whistle sounded, indicating the end of his workday, and he went in the opposite direction of the door, searching. Getting on his hands and knees, he looking under the workbenches, but saw nothing, not even a lock of synthetic hair.

"Any particular reason you're crawling around on the floor?"

Relph glanced up to see Adelf standing above him, a curious expression stretching across his broad face. The chaos around them started again, the sound pressing in on his little pointed ears as he searched again for the stranger.

"Have you ever heard of an elf making a replica of himself as a doll? Something close to a living, breathing doll?" Relph asked as he climbed to his feet and accepted the fact he wouldn't find what he was looking for right then. Instead, he glanced over at Adelf and stopped at his friend's fearful expression.

"What?" he asked and put a hand out to touch Adelf's arm, but the older elf grabbed him and pulled him toward a cleaning cubby. Relph didn't protest, didn't struggle, but merely followed as he tried to figure out the intensity he'd seen in Adelf's gaze.

"There was one," Adelf started as he pulled the door closed behind them. "Years ago, an elf stole parts from different departments in our workshop. He was a strange one, always so quiet, but smart. He built most of the communications equipment in the control room. Anyway, he built this robot. Santa didn't like it, but since the elf kept up all of their electronics, he didn't want to upset the sleigh, so to speak."

"What happened to the elf?" Relph had a feeling he wasn't going to like the end of the story.

"I don't know for sure. Stories say that he got depressed because he'd never found an elf mate, only his toy. Others say that they were having sex up on the walkway. But somehow, the elf fell into the present-wrapper, and well, he didn't survive." Adelf put a hand over his heart in solidarity with the fallen elf.

"What happened to the toy?"

"No one knows. It disappeared after the accident. Why are you asking these things, Relph? This was long before your time here."

"I think I saw it—the toy."

"What? Why would you say that?"

"I was up near the top of the present-wrapper. When I looked up, something stood at the top of the stairs. It looked like an elf, but wasn't. It had the skin of a doll, but walked and breathed like an elf. I didn't know what to do. It ran and I ran after it, but I lost it in all the chaos."

"Are you sure?"

"Yeah, I'm sure. Who forgets a living doll?"

"We need to tell Santa."

"No." Relph hadn't meant for it to come out as a shout, but Adelf winced at the sound.

"What do you mean?"

"I want to find it first. It seemed… I don't know, kinda sad."

"It's a sex toy. How can it feel sad?"

"I don't know, but if it does have feelings, I don't want them to destroy it."

"Okay."

"Okay, that's it?" Relph asked, suspicion churning in his gut.

"I remember him, and I think he's at least partly sentient. I don't want anyone to kill him either. We'll figure it out."

A tingle along the back of Relph's spine told him Adelf wasn't telling him the truth. Something felt off about their conversation. He needed to find the elf toy and quickly before Adelf rounded up other elves and maybe even Santa himself to hunt down the toy and hurt it. He remembered the wonder and kindness in the toy's expression. If he could have someone look at him like that all the time, he'd be a very happy elf indeed.

✧ ✧ ✧ ✧

"Bob, are you okay?" Dil asked, leaning against his friend as they sat in the common area of their little closet. They were alone while the others were off collecting things they would need for the big escape. They worked in pairs, supplementing each other's weaknesses. Bob had already found most of the items on his list: a bag for Ben and Wally and foam cushioning for Buzz. He still needed to find a tiny flashlight for Dil, and everything would be ready for Santa's run the following night.

"Yeah, Dil, I'm fine." He sighed, the sound coming long and harsh from his mechanical lips.

"You want to tell me what happened on the present-wrapper? I know something spooked you." Dil settled in a little closer, intent on hearing the story. They'd been close friends since Bob had rescued him from a trash receptacle outside one of the elf bunkhouses. The poor guy shook for nearly an hour after Bob brought him to the safety of the supply closet. He'd had nightmares for much longer, but with the help of their therapy sessions, he'd started to find a place with them.

"I saw someone up there. At first, I thought it was *him*, but that's impossible. He's been dead for years. Then I noticed that this elf's hair was darker, his eyes blue instead of brown."

"Why did you think it was him?"

"He was standing at the top of the stairs jacking off. Christelpher used to do that too, or ask me to do it. He got very bored on his shifts because they didn't give him much to do. He was an electronics guy, not really a present-wrapping guy. That's why we were having sex up there the day he died."

"Okay, so it wasn't him. What did you do?"

"I didn't do anything. When he came, I freaked out and ran."

"What did you want to do, Bob?"

"What do you mean?"

"You're a sex toy. You're built to pleasure an elf…"

"I…I don't know," Bob admitted. Deep down in the core of his circuitry, he had wanted to stay and pleasure the elf. He wanted to feel that cock inside him. He wanted to touch and suck. For so long, he had been *needing*; the desperate craving made him ache. The fact that he couldn't, that there was something *wrong* with him, made it that much worse.

"I think you do know."

"Fine, what do you want to hear? That I miss it?" Bob's voice cracked, an out-of-control sound not normal for his perfectly calibrated speakers. St. Nick, he really was falling apart.

"Do you?"

"Of course I do! I miss being touched and held. I miss being needed."

"We need you," Dil whispered, but Bob couldn't hear that right then. Nothing made sense.

"I have to get out of here for a while. I'm going to go find the last thing on my list. We need to be ready tomorrow."

"You mean you need to have us ready tomorrow. You're really not going, are you?"

Bob didn't answer; he merely pushed past Dil and headed for the door out onto the main workshop floor. In twenty-four hours, he'd be alone again, and he had no idea how to deal with that. Leaving Dil in the shadows of their closet, Bob peeked out and saw no one.

His slippers whispered across the hardwood floor once more as he set off for the utility area of the workshop. He'd seen it with Christelpher all those years ago, but they could have moved things around since then. Instead, he wandered with his head down, peeking around the edges of his old hat. They'd changed the style of elf clothes since Christelpher dressed him. He felt out of place, like a neon sign advertising two-headed puppies in a strip club.

The first room, the main workshop, contained all the handmade toys and the present-wrapper, but when he moved on to one of the side rooms, he found stacks of severed limbs and a bucket of heads, the tiny eyes rolled back until only the whites remained. The doll room always creeped him out; it felt like the scene from a horror movie. A line of elves, mostly female, stood assembling and dressing the dolls. They dropped them into a huge rolling bin at the end of the line where they lay like a mass grave.

Bob hurried into the next room, keeping his head down to avoid suspicion. This room held tons of computer servers and hundreds of disc drives. He didn't understand until he saw the discs being popped out and packed into video game cases. A couple of elves stood before an enormous screen, waiting for something Bob couldn't even imagine. They moved their arms in the air, following the human on the screen and then, after an immeasurable period, started to dance. They mimicked the human's steps, looking more like epileptic marionettes than elves. Bob tried not to laugh, but a snicker escaped, and he ran for the door. Thankfully, they were more into the game than the source of the noise.

It was in the third room he found something he was looking for and something he wasn't. As he entered, the elf nearest the door, the same elf who had left him a mess, turned toward him and nearly fell off his stool. The tiny flashlight he'd been using to check the inside of a large turtle-shaped toy box clattered against the wood. The elf grabbed it, glanced around at the other elves, still absorbed in their tasks, and turned to a rather large elf sitting on the floor disassembling a shelving unit that tilted to one side.

"Adelf, I need to get the hot glue gun out of my locker. I'll be right back," he called, holding up one finger to Bob, asking him to wait. Adelf merely grunted, not even looking up as the elf tucked the flashlight into his pocket.

❖ ❖ ❖ ❖

Relph couldn't believe it. He dropped his flashlight into the outer pocket of his uniform and made his way to the door. The elf toy looked the same as he had the day before, minus Relph's jizz on the thing's face. On *his* face. Relph believed Adelf's story about the inventor, so the toy must have at least some feelings, some sentience. He couldn't continue to call the toy an "it"; the word felt all wrong on his lips. Though, looking at the slender elf in front of him, he could imagine something that would feel perfect on them.

"Let's duck in here so we can talk," Relph said, not quite touching the toy's arm but leading him to one of the cleaning cubbies down the hall. His palms sweat as he closed the door behind them and pulled out the flashlight to find the room's overhead switch.

"What's your name?" Relph flipped up the switch to see the toy pressed against the cubby's back wall. He looked like a frightened puppy, and Relph clenched his hands at his sides to keep from comforting the elf.

"Bob," the toy whispered.

"It's okay, I'm not going to hurt you or turn you in. I just want to talk."

"We don't even know each other."

"I blew jizz on your face. I'd say that makes us acquainted." Relph's nervous laughter filled the small, dank space. He moved one of the mop buckets over so he could take a step toward Bob, who in turn took a step farther into the corner.

"Okay, I won't come closer. Just…what are you doing out here? Adelf said no one has seen you for years and years. Did you leave? Why did you come back?"

"I didn't leave," Bob said, shivering against the cold wall. "I've been hiding."

"So why come out of hiding now?"

"I was looking for a flashlight." He glanced down at Relph's hand where he still held the tiny device.

"Let me get this straight. You came out of a century-long exile to find a flashlight?"

"Yes."

Bob's eyes weren't like the eyes of a normal elf, and Relph couldn't tell if the toy was lying to him or not, but there had to be more to the story.

"Can I ask you a question now?" Bob asked, and Relph just nodded, startled, the sweating back in his palms.

"Why were you up there masturbating?" Bob rested an arm on one of the shelves, obviously a bit more comfortable now that the humiliation tables had turned. It took a long time for Relph to come up with an answer to that question, but Bob waited patiently. It seemed like he had nowhere else to be.

"I was…bored, no…" Relph switched tracks because something in his gut told him to tell the whole truth, that after being alone for so many years, maybe Bob would understand. "I was lonely. I've been lonely for a very long time."

"I know how that feels. I've been alone since…since *he* died."

"Your creator?"

"Yes."

"It's a pretty heavy thing to make another elf, do you know why he…?"

"For sex. I was created as a pleasure toy."

"Oh."

"Well, I *was* a pleasure toy. Now I'm just a broken toy," Bob muttered and looked away. The closet shrank around them with the admission, making everything seem so very close.

"I'm a pretty good machinist. You want me to take a look?" Relph asked, stretching a hand out toward Bob's pants.

"Whoa, dude. You and I aren't *that* friendly." Bob slapped his hand away, and Relph's face flamed.

"I'm so sorry, I didn't think—"

"You thought that since I'm a sex toy, it's just fine for you to put your hands on me?"

"*No!* Of course not. I...I don't know what I thought, actually. I just...you look so sad. I wanted to make you happier." This time, it was Relph's turn to look away. "I've been alone for so long. I think I'm beyond the ability to be happy. I wanted someone else to be."

When Relph raised his head again, Bob was watching him furtively but didn't move away again.

"Well, I... Okay, you've been honest with me. I should probably be honest with you. There are a few other toys, different kinds of toys, who have been cast out. Like me, they really don't have a purpose anymore. We thought maybe if we could get them into the present-wrapper and out into the world, they could be useful again," Bob said, the words tumbling out like candy from Santa's hidden stash. If toys could blush, his face would have been red as the big man's suit.

"Wait, so you have a group of sex toys looking to get wrapped and given to children as gifts? Isn't that a little... sick?"

"The children wouldn't know they were sex toys. Only their context gives them away."

"That's a very good point. But what about you? You don't want to go out into the world?"

"Who would want an elf sex doll?"

"I would." The words were out before Relph could stop them. Just for good measure, he slapped a hand over his mouth before anything else could escape.

"What?"

Relph shook his head furiously, keeping his hand clamped tight over his lips. A rush of heat swirled in his face and chest. He couldn't believe he'd actually said that aloud.

To his utter disbelief, Bob took one step toward him and then another. Eventually, he stood within arm's length of Relph and held out a hand. Unsure what Bob wanted, Relph didn't move. Bob took another step until their bodies were touching. Relph couldn't help the erection that started deep in his groin and filled his dick with slow, aching pleasure.

"You really weren't kidding, were you?" Bob asked as he slid a finger down from Relph's face, over his chest, and to his rapidly swelling cock. The elf could do nothing but nod in mute fascination.

"I'm sorry I can't do the same for you," Bob whispered. "It's not that I don't find you attractive, because I do. But…"

"But?" The word escaped as a croak from Relph's freed lips.

"I haven't been able to get hard in years."

"Let's, um, let's get you back to your friends before one of us does something we'll regret. Are you looking to get into the present-wrapper close to time for Santa's flight tomorrow night?"

"Yes, I don't want them to have to be in those things any longer than they need to. They wrap presents up until the evening if previous years are any indication."

"I'll help you get up there and in to the machine. Don't worry about that. I have clearance to be up there. If no one sees your face, they'll never know you're not an elf. Then, maybe after everything is over, you and I can get to know each other a little?"

"I'd like that."

Bob brushed past him, and Relph's cock jumped at the contact. He handed the toy his flashlight and then crept to the door and peeked out.

"Where are you and your friends hiding so I can help you get to the machine?"

Relph watched something play across Bob's face, but couldn't quite place it. It wasn't distrust exactly, but maybe something more like indecision.

"We're in the supply cabinet off the main workshop room."

"Okay, I'll be there about six thirty tomorrow night."

"Thank you, Relph."

He opened the door and stepped aside to let Bob through. In a fit of impulse, he kissed Bob on the side of the neck.

"What was your creator's name?"

"Christelpher."

"See you tomorrow night."

"Goodnight, Relph."

✧ ✧ ✧ ✧

Bob scrambled back to the closet, resting his back against the frame to catch the breath he didn't really need, his world shifting as he stared wildly around the room. His friends, the other misfit toys, stared back, their expressions frightened. The flashlight, all but forgotten in his tiny hand, remained the only tangible reminder of his talk with Relph. If he hadn't had it, Bob might have considered it a dream. The spark of hope burned bright in his tiny little mechanical belly.

"Are you okay, Bob?" Candy asked without her usual snark and heat. Instead, Bob looked into her face where it sat propped in one of the beanbag chairs and saw compassion.

"Yeah, I'm okay. I ran into an elf, but it's fine. He wants to help us."

"Wh-wh-wh-wh-wh-why would an elf w-w-w-want to he-he-help us?" Buzz asked.

"Yeah, they're the ones who threw us away," Dil growled in an unusual expression of anger.

"This one is different, I think. And he gave me this for your box," Bob said, holding up the tiny flashlight. "We'll tape it to your side and turn it on right before you go into the wrapping machine. It should stay on until you're opened the next morning."

Dil's eyes went wide, and he gasped. "I like the elf. Let's keep him."

Bob laughed, longer and louder than he had in a long time.

✧ ✧ ✧ ✧

That night, they stayed in a close circle, reminiscing about their time together. If they wanted to go out into the world and make something of themselves, they needed to split up, but the pain of it was hard to bear.

"Oh, and that time Ben rolled out into the workshop by accident. Remember? You guys were playing, and he just went right out the door? I don't think I'd ever seen Bob crawl that fast," Candy cried, rolling right off the beanbag chair and onto the filthy tile. It didn't faze her since she landed face up, but Bob chuckled as he grabbed her up and dropped her back in her seat.

"We don't want your hair to get dirty before your big trip," Bob teased.

"You remember Candy and that bowl of Jell-O?" Dil could barely breathe with the force of his laughter.

"Guys, I can hear you all the way out to the first workbench. Thank Nicholas they're too busy to notice."

The room froze with the sound of an outsider within their midst—not just an outsider, but an elf. Bob didn't think he'd ever heard them so quiet before. They stared at each other, one to the next, before turning all eyes on him.

"You t-t-t-t-told him wh-wh-wh-where…" Buzz started, but Dil became impatient and finished Buzz's question.

"You told him where we were?"

"He wants to help."

"Help us into the incinerator, maybe," Cindy piped in. "I'm a broken toy. Do you know what happens to broken toys in Santa's workshop? It's not some romantic notion of putting me back together again. Broken toys get disposed of, and they get tossed by *elves*."

"Guys—"

Relph cut off Bob with a hand to his arm.

"How about if I fix Bob? Would that show you that I want to help?" he asked, and the room fell silent again. The clenching and unclenching of Bob's hands was the only movement, the only life, as he worked to process Relph's claim. Fix him? Was it even possible?

"How…how can you fix me?" Bob asked, not waiting for the rest of the room to come back from the shock of Relph's bold question.

"I spent the afternoon in the archives researching Christelpher's work. If I'm right, you're not broken, you're empty," he explained.

"Empty?"

Relph pulled a surprisingly large bottle of lube out of the drawstring bag on his shoulder, and a tingle of nerves shot through Bob's stomach.

"Turn around, drop your pants, and bend over," Relph said, popping the top on the bottle of lube.

"I'm sorry?" Bob asked, his ocular lenses wide as he backed away.

"According to the design specs left behind by your creator, you get hard because of lube being forced into your penis. When you ejaculate, you lose some of that lube. Christelpher must have filled it from time to time. Do you not remember?"

Bob closed his eyes and accessed the memory files he'd stored in the lowest level of his memory banks, the ones that wouldn't resurface unless he brought them back to his primary banks. He didn't want to think about Christelpher or what they'd shared. It upset him. It made him feel so lonely. After a few minutes, the playback showed his creator filling those tanks Relph mentioned. It had been erotic play with him bent over the bed, spread for his creator as he used some kind of device to fill him.

"I remember."

"Do you want to try it?" Relph asked, his voice careful and unsure.

"Yes, but not here." Bob glanced around the room at his friends who all stared at him, obviously waiting for him to drop his pants and give them a show. "We can go in my room."

"Don't hurry back," Candy told him with a wink, and if he'd had blood, it would have rushed to his face. Candy appeared to be the only one unconcerned about him going off with an elf. Dil rolled a bit closer, and Buzz vibrated darkly.

"Guys," he said to Dil and Buzz, "I'll be right in here. If he wanted to hurt us, he'd just have told them where we are. If something happens to me, you know the plan. Get to the present-wrapping machine and get out."

"Nothing is going to happen to you. Why do you have to go all James Elf on me? I don't want my shiz shaken *or* stirred. I just want to help. Seriously. This isn't *Mission: Impossible*," Relph said and headed toward the room Bob pointed out. Bob followed, noticing the elf's tight ass encased in velvet as he did so. He wondered if that velvet felt as soft as it looked.

"Okay," Bob said as he closed the sliding door behind them and lit a few of the small candles on his bedside table. "Is that enough light?"

Relph froze. In the soft candlelight of the tiny room, Bob's skin took on a soft sheen, a healthy glow of life.

"I… Maybe we should…"

"Yeah, where should I…?"

"Let's just…"

Relph bumped Bob's arm as he reached for one of the candles, and Bob's arm tingled with an electric charge, one he didn't think came from his internal power source. His sensors must be misaligned, because the room heated for no apparent reason, and he became painfully aware of his own body. His entire body became erect even though his cock couldn't get hard.

"Why don't you get undressed from the waist down and bend over the side of the bed there. I'll try to make this quick and easy." Relph held out an arm toward the bed, and Bob moved over to stand beside the rumpled blanket. He'd dropped an old couch cushion on top of a low coffee table, everything discarded from the remodel of Santa's private quarters. Somehow, knowing that the big man himself had sat on the cushion helped him to sleep at night.

Bob untied the cinch at his waist, and the ragged cotton pants he'd worn his entire life fell to the ground, leaving nothing beneath but his cobbled-together body. With trepidation, he kicked the pants to the side and stood half-naked in front of the elf. It took a long, painful moment for him to be able to bend over the bed and bare himself, even though something deep inside his programming made him want it.

"Spread your legs wider," Relph whispered, and Bob opened himself further for the elf's inspection. Careful fingers explored the tender spot between his legs just in front of the opening Christelpher built for his own purposes.

He closed his eyes against the blinding pleasure, wishing his dick would get hard.

✧ ✧ ✧ ✧

Relph searched for the button, trying to ignore the low moans issuing from Bob's mechanical throat. It took a few tries in the low light, but eventually, a compartment on the toy's body opened, revealing the reservoir. He reached to the low table next to him and picked up the large bottle of lube he'd picked up from the village store. The clerk had given him a long funny look because of the size of the bottle, but if it helped Bob, a little discomfort would be worth it.

The opening on the lube lined up perfectly with the opening of the small compartment. He pressed the pieces together and squeezed the bottle, transferring the lube from the bottle to Bob's stores. Bob moaned, a desperate sound, as Relph filled him. It took a few minutes, long and nearly painfully hard moments, for Relph to empty the bottle of lube into Bob.

"I'm done. Stand up and let's see if it worked."

Bob stood slowly, almost too slowly, and shook his head as if to adjust his sensors. When his body cleared the bed, Relph saw the massive erection protruding from Bob's body. Pre-cum, or in Bob's case, excess lube, drizzled from the tip, and Relph couldn't stop himself from rubbing the liquid into the shaft with long, careful strokes. Bob thrust his hips forward with a groan.

"Please," he whispered, his synthetic body closer to Relph than it had ever been. "It's been so long."

"Do you want to top or bottom?" Relph whispered back, the heat of Bob's body searing his skin.

"I don't know what that means," Bob said and took a step back. The fog of arousal didn't clear from Relph's mind.

"Do you want me to take you, or do you want to take me?"

"I want you inside me. Christelpher added a sensor there that makes it feel so good for me."

"Elves have that too." Relph chuckled and turned Bob back toward the bed. "Are you sure you want me to—?"

"I've never wanted anything so much," Bob confirmed and bent back over the bed, his legs spread and his upper body braced on his forearms.

Relph reached beneath Bob, gathered some of the lube leaking from his dick, and used it to slick his entrance. He slid his small fingers as deep as he could into Bob, trying to find that little button he'd mentioned. When Bob bucked against the bed, humping his cock into the covers, Relph figured he'd found it. It was in a similar location to an elf's prostate.

Bob's cock fit perfectly in his hand as he reached down once more to stroke it. The perfect arch of his partner's back, the quiet invitation, made Relph's dick throb and his balls ache. He needed to be buried hard and deep into the sweet ass he'd been playing with. He needed to fill it, to stretch it for real.

Relph stretched Bob's tender opening with his fingers, not knowing if it was necessary, but not taking a chance to hurt him. Bob whimpered as he spread himself wider. By Claus, Relph loved that sight.

The skin of Bob's neck felt soft under his lips as he kissed it. He smelled like candy canes, pine needles, and pure joy. The head of Relph's dick pressed against the small hole made specifically for this purpose. For a moment, he could ignore the fact that someone else had constructed Bob and pretend someone made Bob just for him. It drove him crazy with a frenzied need.

The slide of his cock into Bob's ass brought a warmth like the sun breaking through clouds on Christmas morning. Tight, wet heat engulfed him, setting his soul ablaze. If a lifetime of porn taught him anything, it was to start with short strokes. The friction brought him close to his pinnacle far too quickly. He rubbed Bob's hip and pushed deeper.

"Yeah...deeper. God, that's good," Bob murmured, fisting his worn blanket. He pushed back ever so slightly, and Relph bottomed out with a groan. His hands fit in the perfect grooves of Bob's hips, pulling him back hard and fast, riding his pleasure.

"You like that?" he confirmed.

"It's been so long."

"It's too good. I'm not going to last," Relph admitted as he pressed Bob harder into the mattress with the force of his thrusts.

"There's a button," Bob started before a deep thrust caught his breath. "Oh... There's a button on the underside of my shaft near the base. Press it when you're ready for me to come."

"Really?"

"Yeah, so when you feel it start, just press that button."

Relph closed his eyes and lost himself to the pleasure. He gave himself over to the thrusts and to the clench of Bob around him. Something inside warmed as they made love in the bowels of Santa's workshop. Something might have even thawed. He'd felt frozen inside all his life. But now, he felt...whole.

A spasm in his groin warned Relph that the time to push that button had come. He slid his hand down from Bob's hip, between his lover's spread legs. He stroked Bob's cock a few times using the lube still leaking from the tip. Finally, when his own orgasm burned through him, he found the button with his index finger and pressed it hard. Bob gasped his name before clenching around him with a cry.

"You're mine," he whispered against Bob's ear as he filled his lover with seed and lube leaked over his hand onto the bed. It was but a fraction of the amount with which he'd filled Bob's tank, so Bob should function for a long while before needing a refill.

"Yours," Bob agreed. "I don't want to be alone again."

Bob collapsed onto the bed, and Relph helped him shift up to put his head on the pillow.

"Lay with me," Bob whispered. Relph's little elf heart clenched at the rest, and he crawled onto the tiny cushion, pulling Bob hard against his chest.

"I'm not going anywhere," he whispered.

❖ ❖ ❖ ❖

I'm not going anywhere. The sentiment resonated somewhere between his fake Adam's apple and the sensors in his nipples, near where he would have had a heart. He hadn't heard those kinds of words, felt those kinds of emotions in over a century. So many years, in fact, that even those memories were archived, accessed only when he had great need.

Relph snored softly beside him, having fallen asleep shortly after they were both spent. He knew he'd have to go out into the main room and face the others, but right then, he didn't have the strength. Right then, he had the fortitude only to wrap his arms tighter around the elf and hold on for dear life. His entire world would shift with his friends' escape. He would be alone again.

A quiet knock on the door changed his decision in an instant. He couldn't ignore the knock and abandon his friends on the eve of them leaving his life forever. It took a little maneuvering to get out from under Relph's arm without waking him, but he managed. When he lifted himself off the cushion, however, the elf's eyes opened.

"Hey," Relph said with a slow, sleepy smile.

"Hang on, there's someone at the door," Bob whispered as he returned the smile and added a small kiss. He kicked his discarded pants out of the way and crept over to the door in the low light of the room. Only the bed and a small table lay within its walls, nothing in the way of comfort.

He cracked open the door and hid his naked lower half behind it. Dil stood there with a look of apprehension.

"Everything okay in there? He isn't hurting you? We heard some...strange sounds."

"No, Dil, everything is fine. I promise. We'll be out in a bit."

He closed the door in Dil's wary face and shuffled back to the bed where a completely bemused elf watched him. Relph's blond hair spilled over his face without the hat that lay abandoned on the floor somewhere.

"Strange sounds, huh? I think we may have frightened your friends."

"They'll get over it."

"Well, my dear Bob. I think we may have another problem to face now."

"What do you mean?" Apprehension slid into his belly like the lube had into his tank earlier. It lay heavy and thick inside his chest.

"We're totally on the naughty list," Relph deadpanned. The stress and enormity of the past few days caught up with Bob in that moment, and laughter bubbled out of the speaker in his throat. It swelled until he thought tears might follow.

"I think you may be right." He didn't have the emotional capacity of a real elf, but Christelpher programmed him with intuitive AI because he wanted a companion, not just a toy. That programming had lain dormant for years, just waiting for someone to bring it to the forefront again.

"You're worried about tomorrow," Relph said. The tingle in Bob's chest intensified as Relph pushed the synthetic hair back from Bob's eyes. He reached up and stroked the elf's cheek.

"It's not just tomorrow, but all the tomorrows."

"Look, I know we're not well acquainted. Making love doesn't really help you get to know someone, but I want to. If you're willing."

"Yeah, I'm willing," Bob whispered against the elf's skin.

"We should get some rest. Tomorrow is a big day," Relph said and wrapped his arms tighter around Bob.

"Would you…I mean, would you like to…you know, stay?" Bob stuttered, as if his neural processors were not quite attached correctly to the speaker in his throat.

"I'd like that."

They huddled closer on the cushion, their bodies melding together as if they came from a single mold.

One heart.

One mind.

One soul.

✧ ✧ ✧ ✧

"Are you guys ready?" Bob asked, his hand tightly grasped in Relph's as they stood in the common room. Ben and Wally had been packed closely into a red velvet stocking, the top cinched to keep them together. A tight red ribbon held the flashlight at Dil's side; they'd turn on the beam just before he went into the machine. A tight cocoon of bubble wrap muffled Buzz's occasional uncontrolled vibrations, and Relph had tightly coiled Cindy's hair, her new fancy barrettes in a see-through pouch at her side. They were ready.

"R-r-r-ready."

They gave a nervous chuckle of laughter at the muffled answer.

"Okay, the bin is just outside the door. I'll set each of you in there, and Bob and I will carry you up to the present-wrapper. Simple and quiet. Then each of you will make your way out into the world." Relph sounded confident, but Bob heard the quaver in his voice. He wasn't convinced the plan would work.

"You okay? This is going to work, right?" Bob whispered.

"Oh, it's not that. Tonight is going to be chaos. They'll go out the door, I'm just worried about what will happen when they get there."

"Yeah, me too, but we have to try."

"And you're sure you don't want to go with them?"

"I am now."

Relph leaned in and gave Bob a quiet kiss before jogging to the entrance of the closet. He grabbed the bin, tossed the lid aside, and brought it back to the safety of the group. They laid each toy carefully in the bottom, making sure not to muss Candy's perfect hair.

"You guys okay?" Relph asked.

"Good to go," Dil said as the others wriggled a little in their new packaging. Bob hummed the theme to *Mission: Impossible* as they crept out of the closet, each of them holding one of the bin handles. Relph giggled, a sound born more of nerves than actual humor.

They made it to the first workshop table where a harried-looking elf in purple velvet swiped extra pieces off the workbench and into an open drawer. He muttered quietly to himself about how he always had extra pieces left over after assembly. They caught something about it not being his fault, and how the stuff wouldn't fall apart when the kids got it, really it wouldn't.

Relph ducked a little lower as they passed the table, a laugh caught in his eyes. Bob followed, trying to keep his face angled away from the group of elves mercilessly whipping the last of their toys into shape for the night's toy run.

They passed another table where an elf in blue sat cursing a car with only three wheels, and yet another sat in tears over a bicycle with no seat. They heard her sobbing to her supervisor, confused about the location of the seat. He told her, not unkindly, that toys didn't just get up and move and maybe she'd been working a little too hard. Bob laughed outright at that, and they turned into the last aisle and headed toward the machine.

Relph slid into a line of elves waiting to take their stacks of toys up to the machine. They stood behind a girl in green who could barely corral all of the dolls in her arms. Each little face seemed to be turned in a different direction, and Bob could see a few Mary Jane shoes peeking out above her arm. Bob was about to ask if they could help when he saw Relph go very pale.

"What is it?" he whispered.

"Adelf is on the line tonight. I didn't think it was his year, but maybe I counted wrong." Relph jerked his head to indicate a plump elf in a bright silver velvet uniform. "He'll know I'm not supposed to be up there tonight."

"Okay, don't panic. We can get through this." If Bob could sweat, he'd have been wet all over. "We don't want to get you in trouble."

"I don't care about getting in trouble. I'm scared he might turn you in to Santa or get rid of your friends."

"Turn me in to Santa?"

"You went into hiding after Christelpher's accident. I just assumed you were hiding from Santa."

"I don't know what I was hiding from. But let's focus on the problem."

They moved up another few stairs and were now halfway up. Adelf stood just ten or so steps above them talking with one of the other elves on the line.

"I have an idea," Bob whispered. "See if you can get the elf in front of us to toss a couple of her dolls in the bin on top of them." Relph looked at him for a moment, and then his face broke into a grim smile.

"I won't give you up. Even if they throw me into exile. I'd rather live with the abominable snowman in the woods with you than stay here without you."

"With luck, we won't have to worry about that. Just ask her."

"Hey, Stelphanie, looks like you've been busy tonight," Relph commented calmly, as if he were just trying to make small talk while they waited in line.

"Oh, hey, Relph. Yeah, lots of little girls looking for dolls this year. I've been working since October."

"Wow. Hey, you know, our bin isn't that full. You want to throw some of those in here? We can help you carry them," he said with a shrug. Bob filed a note in his memory banks never to play poker with Relph.

"That would be awesome, my arms are killing me. Thank you," she squeaked and tossed half her haul into the bin. Buzz vibrated at the sudden startling weight on him, and Stelphanie's eyes widened.

"We have those balls that vibrate. You know the ones with the ferret thing inside?" Relph covered quickly.

"Oh, those are cool," she said and launched into a diatribe of toy design and child market research the likes of which no one had ever seen. It carried them all the way to the top of the stairs, or that could have been the hot air she let off. Wow, the woman liked to talk.

"Well, Relph, what do we have here?" Adelf asked as they stepped onto the platform. His tired eyes skimmed over the dolls in the bin and then over Bob. They lingered on Bob's old-style clothes, fixing on his face when Bob refused to look at him directly.

"We…we were just…"

"I thought you were on the day shift. In fact, I know I saw you over on the mechanics floor." Adelf took a step forward, his hand reaching for the dolls.

"Oh, that's my fault," Stelphanie said, shifting her remaining dolls to the other arm so she could gesticulate unhindered. "Relphie here was just walking by and asked me if I needed help with my dolls. They were in such demand this year. I don't know how I would have gotten them up here by myself. It was really very sweet of him." It took a full minute of her eye batting for Bob to realize she didn't have something there. She was flirting with Relph. If he hadn't been trying to fulfill the dreams of his closest friends, he might have initiated his growling program. Apparently, Christelpher had wanted to do some puppy play at one point. That program didn't get used much.

"Well, that was very kind of you, Relph. You guys go ahead up."

They followed Stelphanie up to the opening of the machine, and Bob swayed. He hated being on that platform. An image of Relph tripping, just as Christelpher had, and going head-first into the machine made him whimper behind the bin.

"It's okay, Bob. We'll be out of here in a jiffy. Why don't you stand back by the railing?" Relph asked, pulling the bin from his stiff fingers. Bob took a step back and grabbed on to the railing behind his back with both hands.

"Okay," Relph whispered just loud enough for Bob to hear. "What the hell was that, Stelphanie? I thought you were a lesbian?"

"I am, but that old codger has been trying to set you up with a woman and me up with a man for so damn long, I thought that might distract him so you and your friend could get up here long enough to do what you needed to do."

"Thank you."

"No biggie. You and I have been friends for a long time, man. We gotta stick together."

Bob laughed, the hysterical laughter that preceded tears. Relph grabbed each of Bob's carefully packaged friends in turn, wished them luck, and dropped them into the present machine. Each time, he wrote something down on the inside of his hand with a marker. The lump stuck in Bob's throat around good-byes he'd already said in the common room.

And then, they were gone.

"We just made it. It's loading up the sleigh now," Relph whispered and grabbed Bob's hand to lead him to the second set of stairs. He pulled the velvet rope away for a moment to admit them both, and then they were leaving.

"I hope they're going to be okay. Please, let them find good homes," Bob whispered back, and Relph squeezed his hand.

"I took down the RFID tag numbers for each package. We can go up to the control room and listen to them being opened."

"You're kidding?"

"Nope, I put in the RFID tracking system myself."

"When should we go up?"

"Let's go now. It's just old Wendelf up there. He won't care. In fact, get him talking about cookies and milk and he'll explain to you how the whole concept of Thanksgiving is just a ruse to shift focus from Christmas and diminish the power of childhood beliefs. It's actually rather fascinating."

Bob laughed, lighter and freer than he'd felt in years.

✧ ✧ ✧ ✧

"Okay, Relph, your RFID tags are coming up for the scan. Are you ready?" Wendelf asked and hit a series of buttons on the most complex electronic system board Relph had ever seen. It had taken him forever to get through all the design specs in order to install it. Every time he looked at it, his heart raced and jolted with pride.

"Tag 37A038h9 is up first."

"That's Ben and Wally," Relph said, consulting the list still written on the inside of his hand. Damn, it would take forever to get the permanent marker off his skin. Good thing they hadn't been caught; the guilt would have been written all over him…literally.

"Let's turn up the speakers," Wendelf said, and they heard a shredding sound. Relph recognized it as the ripping of wrapping paper by excited children.

"Oh, Mummy, I got marbles. They're all metal and shiny. I love them, thank you," a little boy cried with such excitement and joy Relph had to smile.

"That's going to make Ben and Wally really happy," Bob said, wiping his face. Relph didn't know if his new lover could actually cry, but he didn't say anything. Wendelf hit another series of buttons and another section of the board lit up.

"We've got RFID 92G635r6," he read off the code and looked up at Relph.

"Okay, that's Candy."

Static came in through the speakers, louder than the unwrapping of the presents, and Wendelf made a few adjustments to the equipment to clear it up.

"This one dropped in…Detroit," he said, pulling up the coordinates of the tag.

"Mama, oh Mama, I got a dolly head. It's got hair thingies too. Oh, we'll have so much fun. Look at her hair, Mama. Isn't she pretty?"

Relph could almost imagine the joyful look on Candy's face as she finally found a home. He'd only known the other toys for a very short time, but they meant the world to Bob, and judging by his friend's expression, nothing on Earth would have made him happier.

"RFID 66J161q4."

"That's Buzz," Relph said with a hesitant look at Bob. It would be very difficult to pass off a giant powder blue vibrator as a child's toy. They both held their breath as voices broke through the static.

"Mommy, Mommy, I got a unicorn horn, Mommy. Isn't it cool? I've always wanted to be a unicorn," a tiny voice cried into the still morning. Relph couldn't tell if the voice was male or female, but it definitely sounded young.

"Let me see, honey," an older female voice, the sound laced with confusion.

"Oh my God, David! David! Did you screw up the tags? Do you see what she has? Did you? Oh Jesus, it's vibrating. It's… Oh my God!"

Relph couldn't suppress a laugh as he took in the expression on Bob's face. It was a tempest somewhere between amusement and horror.

"David," the woman's voice whispered. "I love it. We'll play with it later…upstairs after she goes to bed. Put it in my bedside table before she sees it again. I'll distract her with the My Little Ponies."

Bob cracked up, the laugh shooting from him, sounding more like a sneeze.

"That just leaves Dil," he said, trying to hold in the laughter.

"Here it comes." Wendelf pulled up the last tag on his screen.

"Oh, Dad, look! I got a gun with a scope! How cool is that?"

"Uhm, son… This thing may shoot something, but I don't think it's gonna be bullets."

FOR FOX SAKE

T.C. BLUE

CHAPTER ONE

Run-run-run, hide-hide-hide, quiet-Yoshi-quiet! Almost there, almost free!

Every quick, desperate, dashing step burned like fire, the soles of his feet leaving red smears behind, but Yoshi embraced the pain. Hells, he embraced being able to actually feel it after so long lost in the hazy gray. A grayness full of hands and voices, somehow disembodied while still seeming all too real.

The marble was cold under his aching feet, but it felt good. Soothing, in a way, but also bracing. The last kept him from stopping to rest, though the drugs still in his system made him want to do just that. Every chair and bench he passed in his stumbling run seemed to beckon to him, promising sweet minutes or hours of calm, easing respite, offering a break from the activity no one in his position should be engaged in. Ignoring the urge to let go and sit down, then curl up and sleep was difficult, but he managed. Mostly by digging his nails roughly into his own palms whenever the desire got too strong, but whatever. It worked. He was still moving, wasn't he?

"Where do you think you're going, Yoshi-chan? There's nothing for you that way. Come back to your rooms now."

The bitch-vixen sounded amused, but Yoshi didn't stop or even slow down to look back. Of course she was amused, laughing at him. Maybe she even had the right. It wasn't the first time he'd thought to escape, but he'd never made it out of his bower before.

He'd also never managed to hide the fact that he wasn't drinking the special wine until this time, so if he had any luck at all, maybe he could pull it off. All he needed to do was get outside. If he could just do that—just leave the Den under his own power—he would try to shift, and if he shifted, he'd be able to run faster, hide better. He'd be able to disappear, even if it was into whatever human city this particular Den existed in. After that…maybe he could find his way home. He was already banking on a fistful of maybes. What was one more?

"I'm losing patience with this game, Yoshi-chan. Be a good little male and stop. Come on! I'll talk to the Vixen Prime about getting you a new necklace. Something sparkly. Stop! Now!"

He almost did just that out of force of habit. Almost gave up at the less than pleased tone she'd used. His staggering, wobbly progress slowed for a moment, but then he reminded himself what would happen if he gave in to the conditioning, to the generations of tradition pressing down on his head, incorporeal but weighty nonetheless.

"No," he tried to shout, but it came out more as a breathless mumble. "No. I'd rather die trying to get away than live as your Lady's…anything."

Inari help him, but he was almost out of steam. Pretending to eat and drink for the last four days had let him become aware enough to run, and the shower he'd snuck had helped too, but he'd planned on being gone before she noticed. Before anyone noticed. Clearly, he'd been too optimistic.

That he'd been wrong wasn't the surprising part. He'd been wrong before, many a time. What he hadn't been, in longer than he could remember, was an optimist, probably because it didn't seem to work out for him when he tried.

No. Hells with that. Don't let her inside my head. Don't listen. Keep moving. Run-run-run. Hide-hide-hide. Be loud now. No need to sneak. She's already found me, but she won't run. I will. I can. Faster, Yoshi. Faster!

He did his best, his sore, bloody feet slapping faster, harder against the marble. He didn't hiss with the pain, still treasuring it, still somewhat excited to be feeling something—even that—with immediacy rather than at a drug-induced remove. If he could feel pain, though, could he feel other things? Could he tell where…?

It hurt more than his feet at first, trying to access the part of his mind that let him shift, that let him *See*. It felt like trying to force open a door with rusty hinges, though he'd shifted a few times since he'd been dragged to this Den—the last of many. The drugs kept him compliant, for the most part. He'd been able to shift, but only with help and permission. He would still be able to shift on his own, he hoped, but that wasn't his goal at the moment.

No, right then he was focused on keeping his feet moving and not running into anything that might stop him or let the bitch-vixen catch up…and getting at his damnable *Sight*, which he wasn't supposed to even have and definitely hadn't been allowed to use in far too long. It lived—not the right word, but Yoshi hadn't had the same lessons he would have if he'd been born female, so he didn't have the terms. The point was the *Sight*-trigger lived next to the *shift*-trigger. He knew he could still shift, and that had to mean he could still *See*. It had to!

"What are you doing, Yoshi-chan!" The bitch-vixen finally seemed to realize he wasn't going to obey. Or else she somehow sensed him reaching for his *Sight*. Either way, she sounded even more unhappy than she had a few moments earlier when trying to bribe him with jewelry. "Stop that this instant! Whatever you're up to, it's unacceptable! Don't make me call the Guard!"

His head was spinning from some combination of running while starving and forcing that rusty door open again, but he still managed to stay on his feet. The threat of the Guard was good one, but he couldn't let that stop him. By the time the bitch-vixen pulled any of the Guard from the Vixen Prime's audience room, Yoshi would be either gone or fully defeated. He could worry about the Guard later. Or not, depending. He wouldn't be worrying about anything at all if they stopped him. The drugs would see to that.

Something glimmered at the far edge of the ether. Something shiny and bright that called to him just as soon as he accessed his *Sight*. It grew brighter and brighter as the pain in his head lessened, and Yoshi ran toward it.

He wasn't sure how he could be running toward its physical location when the shimmering flicker of brightness in his mind wasn't physical at all, but he knew he was. He could feel it, somehow, the closer he got, feel its energy and something wonderfully capricious but not quite conscious wrapped up in all that sparkle. The closer he got to it, the better he felt…or rather, the more like himself he felt. The Yoshi he thought he'd been before being traded away.

"You will stop and return to your bower!" The bitch-vixen actually sounded frantic, but Yoshi didn't care. Hells, he barely even noticed. He was too caught up in the sparkling *thing* he *Saw*. He still didn't know what it was, but he wanted it. Oh yes, did he ever want it!

He vaguely registered pushing through doors he shouldn't have been able to open, judging by the unbecoming squawking sounds from the bitch-vixen, but it didn't seem important. Nor did it matter when, a good minute later, Yoshi heard several members of the Den's Guard shouting at him to stop, to lie down on the blessedly cool marble and put his hands behind his head. He thought they were too complacent with their authority, but he didn't lie down. He didn't even *slow* down.

One more doorway appeared before him, and this one he saw clearly. It seemed out of place in the mostly modern Den, and Yoshi suspected it went somewhere important. He couldn't imagine that the Vixen Prime of this Den would have left it as it was when she'd remodeled the rest unless it was somehow essential. He was about to find out, because that was where he needed to be.

The shining, shimmering, beautifully mischievous energy he *Saw-felt-needed* was behind that door. It was calling him, wanting to show him…something. Something amazing, right there behind the arched carved ebony wood doors. All he had to do was reach out and turn the ornate silver handle that sparkled with tiny hematite gems.

"No! Yoshi-chan! Don't touch that! You don't know what—"

"Try to stop me," Yoshi said, still softer than he would have liked, still desperate. "Even if opening this door kills me, it'll be better than staying here. I don't want to die right now, but being *here* hasn't been anything like living. I'll take my chances."

Freedom would be good enough, though Yoshi couldn't pretend that he didn't want to be happy. Even if that never happened, freedom would be enough. And if he died…well, at least he'd be away from this Den and the latest in the line of Vixen Primes who'd owned him. He didn't remember, exactly, but he thought there'd been more than one.

"You're defaulting on your contract! Your Den will suffer!" The bitch-vixen said it like it mattered. As though his own Den hadn't rented him out like a car or a pet. Perhaps repeatedly.

Yoshi turned slightly, tearing his eyes away from the door, and was surprised to see five of the Guard nearby, though none of them seemed willing to approach. Then he saw one of them blow a sedative dart his way, but the dart veered to the side before it got within six feet of him. Cool.

He didn't know why that had happened, but he didn't care, either. Anything that kept them from drugging him again was welcome in Yoshi's book.

"If my Den suffers even *half* as much as I've suffered with you, it won't be anywhere close to enough. I would have defaulted the day after I got here if you hadn't been keeping me sedated, but since I couldn't… Yeah. Make them suffer. Go to war with them. That might punish you *both* enough to make me happy. But probably not."

He ignored the bitch-vixen and the uniformed Guards in favor of turning back to the door behind which his future lay. Whether that future could be counted in seconds or centuries was irrelevant. He would be free.

The door opened easily, and lights danced in his vision, both sight and *Sight* dazzled as he stepped blindly across the threshold and the world…disappeared.

✧ ✧ ✧ ✧

Inari, he was cold. That was all Yoshi could think when he woke. He was cold, and he must have kicked off his fur blankets again. That was the only thing that made sense. Except the voices were confusing and maybe he wasn't really awake. There was no way there would be two other males in his bower. The Den didn't have that many males and the bitch-vixen would never put them all together, so he was dreaming. That was why there were male voices saying things that didn't make any sense. It had to be.

"Well, what did you want me to do? Leave him out in the snow so he could die on our doorstep? Honestly, Will." Snarky and sarcastic, that one.

The other voice was less pointed, but no less mocking. "Uh-huh. And your sudden urge to help has nothing to do with him being a cute little thing."

"You think he's cute?"

"I know *you* do, Kris. And from the way you're looking at him, you're considering the merits of bestiality too."

A loud *Pfffft* from the first voice was followed immediately by "As if. It's just ears and a few tails. The rest of him is human-like. I don't think that counts as bestiality."

"So you *are* thinking about it. I knew it!" The one Yoshi's brain had decided to call Will sounded much more entertained than annoyed.

"What?" Kris sounded confused for a moment. "Not at all. I'm just saying that when someone is a good ninety-eight percent human-looking, you can't really say that sleeping with them would be bestiality. I might be wondering whether he barks or meows in the heat of passion, but I'm not really anxious to find out through personal experience. It's an academic kind of curiosity."

Will snorted. "Right. Because you're working on your thesis. So you took him in. What are you planning to do with him now? He belongs to Inari. The last thing we need is to get into a shouting match with him-her over one of his-her people. And your grandfather wouldn't like it, either."

"True." Kris sighed. "Of course, Grandfather also wouldn't try to kill him—and me—for fun, unlike someone else's grandparent. Sorry, but remind me who Inari is again? I can't keep track of all the gods and things."

"You mean you *won't*," Will said, adding, "You could, but you don't want to. Like that time you 'couldn't' clean out the garage, then wanted to know why you couldn't get the snowmobile out."

"I was busy! Grandfather likes it when I take my work seriously, and—"

"And there was a *90210* marathon on that week," Will interrupted, but he was clearly amused. In fact, there was a smile in his voice that Yoshi wished he could see. He almost opened his eyes, but stopped at the last second, sure that doing so would wake him from the strange but funny dream he was sunk in. "You still haven't answered me, though. What are you going to do with him now? He still stinks of the nexus, in case you didn't know. Someone's going to sniff him out sooner or later—probably sooner—and even if they don't, there's still that little Inari problem."

Yoshi wanted to speak up then, to tell the men that Inari didn't give a single shit about him. Not even his location, much less his happiness and wellbeing. If Inari cared at all, Yoshi wouldn't have needed to escape in the first place, would he? But it was just a dream, and he was so tired. So very, very tired, and so incredibly…not cold anymore, or not really. Cooler than was entirely comfortable, but not cold.

"I'll ask McJingles to see about his feet and get him some appropriate clothing; then I guess we'll have to send him on his way. As much as I hate saying you're not wrong, we really can't afford to have any issues with Inari, whoever he or she is."

"Japanese God of Kitsune, among other things," Will answered. "And you still haven't said I'm right. You know that, don't you?"

A soft chuckle left the one called Kris. "Fine. *I'm right.* Happy now?" Then Yoshi felt a touch on his forehead and heard Kris murmur, "Sleep. Sleep deep and wake well."

After that, he knew nothing. Until he woke screaming, surrounded by streaks of light in every color imaginable and some that were entirely new, all set against a backdrop of the deepest black Yoshi had ever seen.

There was no wind, though he had the sensation of falling fast and hard, from where and to where, he didn't know.

The screaming seemed to go on forever, though he hadn't taken a single breath, and just when he'd decided that he was going to be stuck in whatever hellish place he'd been consigned to—and that it really wasn't any worse than his time at the possibly numerous Dens he'd been contracted with—it stopped. Suddenly and without warning. It just... *stopped.*

"What the...?" He blinked, and in that tiny split second, the blackness and lights were gone, leaving him standing in front of the boarded-up doorway of a seemingly abandoned building as the sun perched just to the left of the steeple of the church-turned-medical-clinic across the street. "What the Hells!"

It couldn't be, and yet it looked like... No. There was no way that he'd spent almost five years trying to escape his personal Hell and dove into whatever had been behind that ebony door, only to end up in Madison. No way he'd somehow woken up across from Saint Grublath's, in the same damned town he'd grown up in. The town where his own Den was located.

He shuddered, wondering how long it had been since he'd escaped, and whether his own Vixen Prime knew yet that he'd broken contract. Inari help him, but he needed to get the Hells out of Madison. Out of California entirely, and even that might not be enough.

He groaned, crossing his arms to hug himself, and discovered he wasn't wearing the loose silk shorts he'd worn while getting away from the other Den. He hadn't had a choice about that. It was all he'd been allowed to wear there. The Vixen Prime had liked him to be...accessible at all times. He shuddered again, then forced himself to stop.

He was free. Free and nowhere near Arizona, or wherever, anymore. Free and fully covered in black leather that probably looked really good on him. It fit nicely, from what he could tell, and matched his hair. It likely made his eyes pop too. He was even wearing a pair of square-toed boots like the ones he'd owned before the seemingly endless rounds of contracts had started.

And that was when he realized that his feet didn't hurt. They'd been bleeding during his escape, torn and cut by the sharp rocks that made up the floor of the only corridor exiting his rooms. The boots he currently wore would have kept his skin whole, but he hadn't been allowed footwear. He'd cut himself badly crossing that fifty-foot walkway, but he couldn't feel even a twinge of pain. It was weird. Then again, his whole day had been strange, starting with his escape, then having that odd dream...unless it hadn't been a dream. Yoshi thought he remembered something about clothes and looking at his feet, or...something. If it hadn't been a dream, then...

Then nothing. It didn't matter. He was free. He was clothed. His feet felt fine.

Sure, he was apparently in Madison, but he could work with that. He'd had a few bolt-holes in town, back in the good old days. If he was lucky, at least one of them had gone undiscovered by his own people, as well as the homeless, both human and non. And if Inari loved him even a little, one of those bolt-holes just might be able to give Yoshi a way out of town before his home Den even knew he was there.

CHAPTER TWO

"Something's wrong."

The words left Nick even as the old-fashioned silver bells hanging above the door of the one non-Starbucks coffee shop in town jingled. The other customers sitting in Madison Marketplace probably couldn't tell the difference, but Nick knew from bells, and there was a frantic sound to the otherwise cheery ringing that set his teeth on edge. Pol's too, because his friend's usually open, happy expression was suddenly closed and sharp, though that was more likely to be due to Nick's statement, as Pol couldn't read the bells at all, be they physical or not. Not the way Nick could.

"It better not be Jeff again," Pol grumbled, standing up quickly. The large paper cup of fresh black coffee steamed on the table, and Pol grabbed it like it was an afterthought. "Waste not, want not," he added.

Nick snorted as he left the table himself. "I'm so glad you're thinking about your caffeine addiction instead of Jeff. Let's go. He can't be far."

To be fair, Jeff did tend to get into trouble on a fairly regular basis, though he rarely caused it. There were just certain sorts of people who saw Jeff and made assumptions. Like Jeff was weak. Like the guy was as young as he looked.

Like he was an easy target for whatever issues said people might have. None of that was Jeff's fault. He couldn't help looking like he did. Even in jeans and flannel shirts, there were those who wanted to satisfy one of the two basic needs by either fighting or fucking him. That Jeff wasn't really interested in either of those things was apparently immaterial. People, almost always men, still tried.

Jeff was very good at taking care of himself, but it was possible that a group had cornered him. His odds were less good if there were more than two people coming at him at once.

Nick grabbed his own coffee and stalked from the small shop on Pol's heels. "Just remember it's not his fault," Nick ordered, as he did every time Jeff needed help.

"Of course it is." Pol sounded convinced as he stopped on the sidewalk. "If he didn't keep going off on his own when we're away from home, he wouldn't have these kinds of problems. Where is he?"

It was in Nick's nature to argue, but they might not have time for that right then. Instead, he bit his tongue and listened hard, focusing for one distinct peal now that the real bells had broken through his thoughts and made him aware of the internal chiming he'd almost missed.

Just the faintest jingle reached him, though it had an odd echo in his mind, and he nodded, frowning. "This way," he said, turning to the left. "It's farther than I thought from the sound of things. We should hurry."

✧ ✧ ✧ ✧

The small, internal sound-sensation grew louder as Nick blazed a path through pedestrians out for a stroll or hustling about on business. Pol was clearly just as impatient, considering the way he kept trying to surge ahead, only to stop with obvious frustration to let Nick catch up.

"I can't help it," Nick groused at Pol's latest semiglare. "If I go too fast, I can't hear him."

Pol grumbled. "I know, I know. I just don't want anything bad to happen to him. Or not too bad. Maybe just enough that he'll stop running around on his own. You know."

Yeah, Nick knew all right. Pol and Jeff had been dancing around each other for years. Some days, Nick wished they'd just stop screwing around and start screwing, but that wasn't up to him, damn it. The blatant sexual tension between the two didn't generally cause problems, so he couldn't just order them to get their shit together. He wasn't that kind of boss. Even if he had been, they were his friends, and that lent them a certain latitude.

"This way." Nick turned at the next side street and walked quickly, tracing the sound-sense another block before slowing at the mouth of an alley. "God. What is it with Jeff and alleys? I swear he thinks there's some sort of treasure hiding in them. It's always damned alleys!"

Pol snorted. "Except that time with the abandoned factory. That wasn't fun, either. But that wasn't here in Madison. I like the California weather way better than the constant snow back home too."

Nick would have replied, but the sounds of a scuffle and a muffled shout reached him just as the mental pealing became discordant and jangly. "Now!"

He didn't wait for Pol to go first, though he should have. He was sure to hear about that later, and deservedly so. Making sure Nick didn't do anything monumentally stupid—like running into a dark alley where something bad was happening without even checking to see what the situation might be—was part of Pol's job. Even so, Nick would be damned if he was going to stand out on the street and let Pol, and possibly Jeff, take all the risk. Or all the damage, if it came to that. Thus, he stormed into the alley, ready for anything. Anything but what he found there.

He wasn't the only one, judging by the sudden unrestrained laughter that left Pol. Not that Nick could blame him. He was hard pressed not to indulge in a fair bit of excessive merriment himself. It wasn't every day that he expected the worst, only to be surprised by…

"Cats. Really? You're chiming like an entire symphony because of a few cats?" Okay, Nick was laughing. So what?

Jeff glared but didn't stop the muttering Nick was only just noticing. It was Pol's suddenly anxious observation, "It looks more like a few hundred, Nick. And is that a boot?" that forced Nick to look more closely.

Nick followed the direction of Pol's pointing and frowned, his own laughter vanishing almost as quickly as Pol's had. "Oh hell." It was a boot, all right. More specifically, it was a black boot with a toe that would have been pointy if it hadn't been squared off at the tip. Nick owned a pair like that, though he rarely wore them anymore. They'd been out of style for years, and while he wasn't a slave to fashion, he did stay on top of what was in and out. It would never do to attend a meeting wearing anything that might imply he was struggling to make ends meet, and those boots would definitely announce just that. Which had nothing to do with the boot sticking out from under the pile of cats.

"I don't think it's just a boot," Nick said when the boot moved, seemingly on its own. "I'm pretty sure it's attached to a person."

"Don't be ridiculous. Why would a person be rolling around in an alley under a giant pile of cats?" Pol sounded just as baffled as he looked when Nick glanced his way. "That would be insane. And really unsanitary." His face screwed up into what Nick privately called Pol's ick-face.

"Well, it makes more sense than Jeff standing in an alley trying to chant a bunch of cats into submission for fun, right?" Pol wasn't an idiot. Nick had to remind himself of that at least once a week, but it was true. Pol just wasn't very good at making leaps of logic on the fly. He had too many things going on in his head that were connected with his job: watching every angle, keeping track of who was where, coordinating transportation and lodgings when they traveled…keeping an eye on Jeff without seeming to be keeping an eye on Jeff, which wasn't really part of Pol's job, but still. Poor Pol had to be exhausted. Throw something like a writhing pile of cats and a boot at him, and Pol saw just that. Cats and a boot. He tended to be a fair bit literal when focused on something other than what was right in front of him.

Pol frowned but nodded after a moment. "I guess so. Let's get whoever it is out from under all that pussy."

Yeah, there was a reason Pol was on permanent guard duty instead of dealing with customers, as Nick had discovered the one and only time Pol had filled in with the customer service department. That last sentence pretty much summed it up.

"Feel free." Nick couldn't help grinning as Pol stepped forward to try just that. He caught Jeff glaring at him, even while the chanting continued, but Nick couldn't quite bring himself to feel guilty. Not even while his eyes finished adjusting to the dimness provided by the one bare bulb above what was clearly a back door onto the alleyway and he saw the bloody, half-healed scratches on Jeff's arms and face. Instead, he found his earlier mirth returning as Pol waded in.

"Come on, pussies, leave the nice person alone, okay?" Pol sounded like the kindest, gentlest voice of reason ever. Coaxing and soothing were plain in his voice, right up until he tried to lift the closest cat from the writhing pile. Then the sweetly calm tone changed dramatically.

"Hey! Stop that! Ow! Don't bite, I'm only—Ow! I'm trying to hel— Ow, damn it! I'm gonna kill you and make—Ow! Gods! Stop that, damn it! Slippers! I'm gonna make you into fuzzy slipp—Ow!"

Yeah, there was zero chance of Nick being able to catch his breath soon.

Pol finally admitted defeat and moved away from the big mound of squirming cats, saying "Ow, damn it! Those pussies have teeth! And claws too! Sharp ones!"

Nick really couldn't breathe, he was laughing so hard. That Pol clearly didn't understand *why* he was laughing only made him laugh harder even as he watched the scratches and bites on Pol's arms, neck and face start to heal. And all the while, Jeff glared like he was going to kick them both in the basket just as soon as he finished his chant.

Even being Jeff's boss, Nick wasn't sure Jeff wouldn't do it, and that actually helped him to…not *stop* laughing, but at least tone it down a bit.

✧ ✧ ✧ ✧

By the time Jeff's chant started to work, Nick was thoroughly bored with the alley. He was even more tired of Pol's whining, regardless of how amusing it still was.

"I don't get it," Pol muttered, leaning against one brick wall as a few of the cats shook themselves and strolled off as though their work there was done. "I always thought pussies were soft and sweet, but it was like they wanted to eat me up. I just wanted to get them off that guy, girl, whatever."

"Guy," Nick said, sure of it from the boots alone. Not just the style, but the size. He'd met very few women—biological, born-that-way women, he meant—who wore a men's size ten. "Don't feel bad," he added. "I'm pretty sure the cats are Spelled. It's not really normal for what seems like every cat in town to swarm a human. Poor guy must have really pissed someone off."

Nick frowned as Jeff's chant grew louder and the alley seemed to squeeze in around them. "Someone strong," he added, grimacing as pressure built in his ears. He popped his jaw repeatedly, but it didn't help.

Jeff became louder still and shouted out a hiss-spit-snarl that seemed to suspend time for just a split second.

That was what it felt like, anyway, because the world went quiet and still, then rushed back into motion with an almost audible snap. The furry exodus struck immediately, and Nick could only imagine what anyone on the sidewalk must think at seeing so many cats streaming from the mouth of one alley. It probably looked like someone had opened a fire hose and sprayed it out into the street.

"Are you both stupid?" Jeff sounded just as prickly as his sharp gaze implied. "I needed help, not two bumbling morons who would just run in and try to peel the damned cats off the guy! And even when you saw that I was trying to break the cycle, you just stood there! What, you're both too good to mix your energy with mine so maybe—just maybe—breaking that damned curse would have taken less time? Not to mention I'm exhausted now! Feline *gravitas* is damnably hard to wrangle even without needing to free some random victim from a well-wrought curse! Gods. I'd kick your asses, but I just don't have the strength right now."

It was only when Jeff's voice died out that Nick saw how gray Jeff's skin had become. Granted, the alley wasn't exactly well lit, but still. He should have paid closer attention and not let himself be so distracted by Pol's unintentionally hilarious comments. The mere fact that Jeff was taking him to task should have told him just how worn out the guy was. They were good friends, but Jeff generally mentioned Nick's shortcomings in a more diplomatic fashion.

"Sorry, Jeff." Pol sounded more than sorry. He sounded like he was getting ready to open a vein, damn it. "I just. Every time I've tried to help you before, you yelled at me because you could do stuff yourself. Sorry. Um, there's still cats, but you probably know that, right?"

Jeff snorted and stumbled over to the wall opposite Pol. It was kind of sweet how the two of them gravitated toward each other but never got too close. Sweet but stupid.

"Prince Headbasher and his court live here. This is their alley. They aren't about to leave just because I broke the curse on… Wait. The Cursed. Is it still alive?" Jeff looked mildly curious but also like he didn't care enough to find out himself.

"I'll check." Nick smiled a little. "Pol, get over there and help Jeff. Feed him some energy or something. I don't like how gray he is." Pol started to say something, but Nick spoke over him, saying, "There's no way this guy is any sort of threat, okay? Even if he might be at some other time, right now he's suffering from being smothered in cats. Assuming he's even still breathing."

There was a chance that the guy was dead after spending at least ten minutes under an undulating blanket of felines who'd seemed to either have it in for him or like him to an unnatural degree. As Nick moved closer, he saw that Pol had been right. Being stuck under a pile of cats was definitely unsanitary, because while the guy—Nick had been right; the person was male—didn't seem to be scratched or bitten, he was covered in hair of every color and length, and he smelled like…well, like a litter box, as well as something more bitter. Apparently cats liked to mark their territory too.

"Ugh." Nick grimaced but knelt down beside the still form. "Let me guess. Pied Piper curse, but tweaked for felines?"

"Yeah." Jeff's voice was slightly muffled, but Nick didn't bother to look. He suspected that Pol was helping Jeff in ways Jeff hadn't expected, but whatever. None of his business. "The Caster must like him, or at least not hate him much. It could have been rats. Or roaches. Or any number of things."

Oh gross. But Jeff was right. The poor guy had gotten off easy.

"Or else whoever did it resonates better with felines." Pol sounded smug enough that Nick looked over his shoulder. Once he did, he couldn't decide whether the smugness was because Pol had made a valid point about Casters or because Jeff was letting Pol hold him up and cushion him from the bricks. Maybe both.

He looked back at the man covered in cat hair and urine and wrinkled his nose again at the smell. "He's breathing," Nick observed out loud for the benefit of his friends. With the question of life settled, he turned the man over, and somehow everything changed.

"Hells. It's him." Nick took a long, deep breath to slow his suddenly racing heart. "He's back."

"Oh good," Jeff replied, and while he still sounded irritable and exhausted, he also seemed…something. Unhappy, maybe. Or worried. "That's sure to go well. No, really. It'll be super!" Yeah, that degree of chipper could only be sarcastic.

The sad part was that Jeff was right. Nick knew it just as much as Jeff obviously did, though that did nothing to stop Nick from stooping to gather the man up into his arms.

"We'll take him home," he said carefully, well aware that he might be making the third biggest mistake of his life. "I can't just leave him here, you know? No matter how much you probably think I should." And as Nick was the boss, Jeff and Pol went along with it. Silently, in Pol's case, and with much grumbling and sniping in Jeff's, but that was normal. Normal enough that Nick paid it no mind as they left the alley, Pol supporting Jeff while Nick held on to the unconscious man as though he might break. As though they *both* might break, because Nick wasn't feeling anything but fragile right then, damn it all.

CHAPTER THREE

He hated passing out. Inari, did he hate it. Of course, he also hated cats, but Inari hadn't done a single thing to keep his occasionally faithful worshiper from being attacked and borderline molested by what had seemed a metric ton of the things.

Yoshi could only be glad he'd been fully clothed when the attack began. Otherwise, who knew what he might be covered in, aside from the pungent urine he smelled much more strongly than he really wanted to.

"She's going to regret this," he grumbled, his entire body sore from being chased and pounced on. He ached more right then than he had during his escape, damn it.

Inari help him, but Kameko was going down. "Maybe not today, maybe not tomorrow, but soon."

"And for the rest of her life?" The laughing voice surprised him from his thoughts. It also alerted him that he must have really been out of it if he hadn't realized that not only were the cats gone, but he wasn't lying in that alley anymore, either.

Yoshi forced down the panic as he opened his eyes and found himself inside…somewhere. In a bed. A very nice bed and fully clothed, but still. The surge of fear was harder to suppress this time, but he managed it. He needed to be strong; especially when he didn't know what was going on. If he couldn't actually *be* strong, he could at least sound it, the way he used to back in the day.

"The rest of her life measures to about five minutes after I track her down. I'm going to kill her," he added sharply, in case his first sentence had been too oblique. "I'm going to kill her hard. Siccing a million cats on me is way more than I deserve."

"I'm not sure planning a murder out loud is the best way to *not* seem like a psycho," said the man sitting on the edge of the bed, watching him closely. "But I'm glad you're not dead, so I'm willing to cut you some slack. I wasn't even sure you were still breathing once we got the cats off you."

Another voice, this one from across the room, had Yoshi's eyes darting to the doorway. "I've never seen anyone be such a pussy magnet before. It was crazy. And those pussies were mean, but I guess they didn't hurt you. Maybe because of all that leather, huh?"

Okay, the guy by the door was obviously brain damaged. He also had scratches on his face and a couple other marks that looked like they might be bites, though more healed than seemed reasonable, but that was irrelevant.

Yoshi hoped the mentally challenged man wasn't going to get tetanus or rabies, but it wasn't really his problem. He'd never asked for help, had he? Of course not. No one had ever been willing to help him before. It was a hope he'd grown out of early.

He wasn't at all clear on how the two men had managed to snatch him away from the cats. Kameko wasn't the sort to pull any punches, and what she'd done… Well, it should have lasted until morning. Dusk to dawn, or dawn to dusk.

That was just the way her particular sucktastic screw-Yoshi-over spells worked. It had been a while since the last time he'd been a target—of hers, anyway—but he remembered that much clearly.

It didn't seem likely that this group of men would have been able to do anything about Kameko's curse. Not if they were just what they seemed, and that meant...what, exactly?

Yoshi didn't know, but one thing he was sure of—until he knew how he'd ended up in an unknown bed with two strangers in the room and *without* a million cats, he couldn't trust them. Not even a little bit. That didn't mean he couldn't pretend to, though.

"It'll take more than a few cats to kill me," Yoshi said, a good five seconds after the man's words. "And ew. I smell like a cathouse." He wrinkled his nose, well aware he looked adorable when he did that. He wished he didn't, but try as he might, he'd never been able to make himself look rougher, less fine and refined. Maybe in another twenty or sixty years, his outsides would catch up with his insides, but he wasn't holding his breath. Except he wished he could. The cat stench might kill him where the actual cats hadn't even come close.

"Who are you, and where are we?" He probably should have asked that first, but he hadn't wanted to show how freaked out he was. Even so, he'd escaped from drugged-stupid servitude once. He thought—hoped—he could do it again if he had to. And the men weren't giving off any kind of predatory vibes. Yoshi was very good at recognizing those types, though perhaps not when he'd been the star attraction at an all-cats love-in. Still, he didn't think they were dangerous to him, once he'd calmed a bit more.

The man sitting beside him laughed yet again. Inari, the man was just too flipping jolly for words, wasn't he? Or not, because he spoke, saying, "You really don't know, do you? No, of course you don't. Never mind. I'm Nick. My friend is Pol." He looked a little bit confused, too, though Yoshi didn't know why.

"And I'm Jeff. The *other* friend. The one who *saved your ass*." The new voice came from behind the one Nick called Pol. It wasn't until Pol moved aside that Yoshi saw the new arrival.

"Jeff!" Nick sounded like he was scolding the guy. "He's—"

"I heard," Jeff snapped. "I'm not sure I believe it, but I'll play along."

About the same height as Pol, Jeff was much more slender. Not that Pol was overly bulky or anything, just muscular and solidly built. They were both attractive enough, as far as Yoshi was concerned. Not his type, granted, but not at all bad, though the bags under Jeff's eyes would count as carry-on luggage if the guy ever flew. Nick, on the other hand… Oh, he was exactly Yoshi's type. Too much so for it to be an accident. It was a good thing he already knew better than to trust the guys, though. If he hadn't, Nick probably could have talked him into anything.

"Do you have a name, or are you one of those guys who wants to be called 'dude' all the time?" Wow, Jeff had snarky, pissy, bitchy, and suspicious—while seeming perfectly reasonable—down to an art form. Yoshi wondered whether the guy would be willing to give him lessons. His people wouldn't know what to think if Yoshi went home having mastered the ability to imply a great big *screw you* while actually saying good morning. Then again, his people wouldn't know what to do if Yoshi went home at all. Other than punish him some more before renting him out to the highest bidder. Again.

"Well?" Jeff's tone was sharper than before, and that took some skill too. Yoshi almost checked himself for wounds, but the guy next to him—Nick—laughed yet again.

"You know how… I mean, you can probably tell by now that Jeff gets irritable when he's tired, and right now, he's really, really tired. It's been a long day." Nick smiled a strange little smile that somehow seemed more hopeless than happy. "So are we going with 'dude'?"

Yoshi rolled his eyes, doing his best to remember how to interact with people who weren't actively taking advantage of him. That he knew of, anyway.

"Please. I know we're in California and there's a beach less than ten miles away, but the first person to call me 'dude' is going to be in for a rude awakening if they expect me to respond with anything other than heartfelt derision." He furrowed his brow. "Not that there's such a thing as an *un*-rude awakening when someone else causes it, but that's immaterial. My name is Yoshi." He let his frown vanish and put on the sunniest smile he could dredge up. The men hadn't offered last names so Yoshi didn't feel bad for lying just a little when he continued, saying, "Yoshiro Genko, if we're being formal. I suppose I should thank you for helping me back there. It was a… Let's call it an unusual situation. Even so, I'd still like to know where we are." Good. He sounded like a relatively normal person rather than a drugged-out contract slave. He sounded stronger than he felt, but that was a bonus.

Nick's smile grew in size, but not pleasure. It still only made him better looking, damn it, in so many ways.

So while Nick was saying, "You were unconscious, so we decided to bring you to our place. I figured you'd either wake up soon and would rather do that somewhere that wasn't an alley…or you wouldn't and we'd need to call in a doctor or get you to a hospital. Either way, we couldn't just leave you there," Yoshi was cataloging the man's appeal.

Even with him sitting on the edge of the bed, Yoshi could tell that Nick was tall. Not insanely so, but probably around six feet, give or take an inch. A little bit taller than Yoshi himself, anyway, judging by their similar positions and the small disparity while seated.

Nick's hair and brows, the first of which was wavy and almost hit his shoulders and the latter of which were bold, slashing statements that suited the man, were a medium-dark brown, like fine mink, and Yoshi knew from mink. Nick's eyes were a few shades lighter and showed small specks of near-gold around the pupils and at the edges of his irises. Yoshi wondered whether that gold would intensify when the man's pupils expanded, say in darkness or possibly arousal, but he would never know.

Strong cheekbones, a straight nose that was saved from seeming severe by the small upturn at the end. A light red—not to be mistaken for pink—mouth that was full and wide above a somewhat square jaw finished out the picture, which was only enhanced by the lightly tanned tone of Nick's skin.

Yoshi felt almost too refined with his own deep, shiny black curls that covered his ears, his pale, porcelain skin, and odd violet eyes, with the classic features of his heritage. He would have paid to be more like Nick. More...real. More erection-inducing, because his cock was definitely trying to firm up, just from looking at Nick. Stench of cat...stuff... aside, Yoshi couldn't help being distracted by his reaction to cataloging Nick.

"Um..." What was the question? Had there even been a question?

Jeff snorted. "Oh, we totally could have left him there. I even said so, if you'll recall. But no. You just had to be all 'it's him, let's take him home with us,' didn't you? I swear, when this ends up biting you on the butt, don't come crying to me, Nick! I mean it!"

Yoshi didn't really understand what Jeff had against him, but it didn't matter. It was enough to know that the guy—one of Nick's friends, apparently—didn't want him there. The other one, Pol, hadn't said anything, so he either agreed with Jeff or didn't care, and Inari knew Yoshi wasn't going to stay anywhere he wasn't wanted.

"Fine," he said bluntly. "I'll just be going, then." He tried to get up but didn't make it far. Between his aching body and the way Nick seemed so distressed, he only made it about a foot closer to the side of the bed.

"Works for me. I can give you a ride to anywhere that's not here." Jeff sounded just as snarky, pissy, and bitchy as before, but that wasn't the problem. The problem was... Yoshi didn't actually have anywhere to go. Not really.

He shifted on the bed, and the motion released a strong scent of cat. So strong, it made Yoshi want to puke. He didn't, of course, but he wanted to.

"I'll need to make some calls," Yoshi finally said, and he sounded shaky, even to himself. He was still unsettled, though, and that was reason enough to be off balance and out of sorts. That and the sudden realization that if this was real—if he wasn't actually dreaming or hallucinating—he'd cut ties to his own Den with his actions and didn't have anyone he *could* call. "Maybe I can just go back downtown. Find a room." With a shower. Inari, please let there be a shower in his future.

"Oh man!" Pol looked disappointed. Sounded it, too. "So you want us to just take you back? But what if the pussies attack again? Jeff barely managed to break that pussy-magnet curse the first time. I don't know if he can do it again without hurting himself, and I don't want him to get hurt, Yoshi."

Oh, Inari. Brain damaged or not, there was something about the way Pol said all that. Something that told Yoshi the man had feelings for Jeff. It was more than a little bit strange to him, because how in the universe could anyone ever get fixated on someone so prickly, but that was the least of Yoshi's concerns right then.

What was bothering him was the way Pol made it sound like Jeff had broken Kameko's spell all by himself, because that just wasn't possible. There was no way anyone could have done that and still have enough personal *gravitas* to not only still be standing, but be a huge, vocal pain in the ass, too.

"No one's going anywhere," Nick announced. "Especially not you, Jeff. If Yoshi really wants to go back into town, I'll have someone *else* drive him. Right now, though? I want you to go relax, Jeff. Soak in the hot tub for a while, and for the gods' sakes, eat something! You'll be hurting tomorrow if you don't, and *I* don't feel like putting up with your 'poor me' attitude yet again. You know better than to overextend yourself like that. Pol, make sure he doesn't fall asleep in there and drown. I'll handle Yoshi."

Damn his body for taking those words at face value, because Yoshi's cock was definitely doing exactly that. Yoshi had to bury his nose beneath the cat-pungent collar of his leather jacket and inhale four times, deeply, just so his big head could resume operating the meat-machine. Thank Inari the feline urine hadn't managed to soak through, though. Yoshi wasn't sure he would have been able to stand it if his skin were damp and stinking, too. He took a few more long, deep breaths, willing his cock to relax, though it seemed reluctant, which was odd. All the drugs and such during his contracted times had been meant to make him—or more specifically, his cock—interested in playing but had rarely been even slightly effective. To have his dick expressing an interest all on its own was somewhat disturbing, though Yoshi didn't know why. Still, the deliberate, deep whiffs had his dick quiescently limp. Thank Inari.

By the time he'd managed that, Jeff had started grumbling something about the hot tub switching off at random. Yoshi imagined that the tub was only one of the things Jeff turned off on a daily basis, and he didn't mean by pressing a button.

So, okay. Jeff probably turned off everything, and every*one*, aside from Pol, who was obviously challenged. It was a shame, because Jeff was…pretty, Yoshi decided as he rolled from the bed and stretched, trying to unkink his back after the constant assault of many, many little cat feet.

Jeff was pretty, and Pol… Well, looking at Pol, Yoshi couldn't imagine that he had any trouble finding partners of either sex, no matter how slow the man might be. Even amongst Yoshi's people, Pol would be in a certain degree of demand. Not for breeding, granted, but for fun? Hells, yeah. In fact, Yoshi couldn't imagine turning the guy down himself. Pol might be stupid, but he was well made and shaped right in both body and face by his maker, whichever god had been involved.

That gentle and approving hand hadn't extended to the man's hair, apparently, because he had none on his head, aside from eyebrows, but Pol was still nice to look at. It looked like he'd be even nicer to touch.

"Hey! Vagabond!" Jeff's snapping voice pulled him from his contemplation of Pol's form. "Don't get any ideas about anything! You're here as a guest, until you and your filthy *skins* can be decontaminated. After that, you can be on your way, and with any luck you'll never darken our doorstep again."

"Jeff!" Nick seemed annoyed as he pushed up from the edge of the mattress. "Is it really necessary to be such an asshat? Yoshi's—"

"Wearing more leather than any one person actually needs, and stinking up the place at the same time?" Jeff's tired eyes narrowed enough that Yoshi wondered whether they might start emitting death-rays. If they did, those beams would probably be diverted by the giant bags under the guy's eyes, though, so he wasn't *too* worried. As long as Nick, who seemed to be in charge, wasn't going to kick him out of wherever the Hells they were on Jeff's say-so, Yoshi could manage, and for whatever reason, he didn't think Nick would do that.

"I'll call Farad to come up for the clothes," Nick replied easily, seeming far calmer than Jeff was. "That'll take care of the smell, especially once Yoshi washes up. And this is *my* room, anyway, so you don't really need to concern yourself with any lingering, um…stench."

Jeff snarled, though Yoshi wasn't sure how. It wasn't a sound that human throats could generally produce. It was still a snarl, though.

"See, I'm not sure the stink is from the cats. I think it might just be the vagabond's natural, rotten scent. But it's none of my business, right?"

Inari. What was the man's problem? Yoshi hadn't done anything but be Spelled by Kameko. He'd never asked Jeff and the others to save him. They had, but still. Even worse—the thing that was bothering him the most right then—was being called a vagabond.

He might be covered in cat hair that had adhered to the feline fluids, but he was fully clothed, and in items that actually went together. He was miles away from tatterdemalion status, even if he still didn't know why he'd ended up in leather after the dream that clearly hadn't been a dream. He'd think about that later, though, because at the moment he was too busy trying to figure out what the Hells was going on. Aside from the way he and Jeff were sparring, because that part of things was clear as vodka.

"It'll be a pleasure to see the last of you as soon as possible!" Yoshi didn't really mean that, of course, because while he'd just met the men, he sort of liked them. Even jerky Jeff. He just wasn't about to say so. They were also the only people he knew—in the loosest possible sense—who hadn't drugged and imprisoned him so he could *service* someone, but he wasn't thinking about that. He couldn't. Not without losing control, and he might like the men, but he for damned sure didn't trust them enough to drop his guard around them.

"I mean that sincerely," he added. "It'll be a *pleasure*."

Jeff turned and muttered something, Yoshi couldn't tell what, then the man smiled an annoyingly bright smile. "Not the word I'd use if I were you, but okay. Nick? We'll be around when you come to your senses and send that… *Yoshi*…off to wherever he came back from."

Yoshi grinned as Jeff stalked off, with the slow one right behind. Whatever might be going on with Pol's mind, the man could move fast as all get-out when it suited him.

"So. I guess it's just you and me," Yoshi murmured, looking up the scant couple of inches into Nick's eyes. He didn't usually go for humans, but there was something about Nick and his people that was appealing. Mostly Nick. "Was Jeff just being a bitch or is there really a chance of showering and possibly having these clothes cleaned? I'd probably kill for a shower, and even a set of sweats right now. I will be in your debt."

He hated saying that last, but he had to. A debt owed needed to be acknowledged, no matter how much Yoshi didn't want to. Inari knew how he'd repay any debt at all, much less a major one. He had nothing, aside from what he was wearing.

Nick grinned and gestured toward the door the other two hadn't left through. "No debt," Nick said, releasing him from obligation as though it was nothing. Gods. "I'll have to talk with Farad about the clothes thing, but even if we can't take care of your stuff tonight, I know for a fact that we can do better than borrowed sweats. I'll show you where you can get cleaned up."

Nick seemed to take his duties as host seriously, because five seconds and ten feet or so later, Yoshi found himself in the truly luxurious bathroom that connected to the suite Yoshi had been stinking up. Jeff was right about that much, regardless of how it hurt Yoshi to admit it, even silently.

"Feel free to use whatever towels and toiletries you like," Nick said, his voice pulling Yoshi from his thoughts. Then Nick nodded at a tall, narrow door beside the sink in the large bathroom. "There's a good assortment in there. If you'll just leave your dirty things outside the door before you bathe, they'll be dealt with. That includes your boots, if you want. The service here is pretty amazing. Farad's folk are meticulous and perfectionists. They'll do you right. Like I said before, you should have your things back within a few hours. By morning at the latest, and if not, I'll make sure you have something else to wear. I think you'll be fine."

Yoshi smiled slightly before forcing himself to meet Nick's gold-flecked eyes. "Sounds like. Do you have someone to come wash my back for me, too? I have this one spot between my shoulder blades that's a little hard to reach." He broadened his smile to show he was teasing, but the grin faded when he noticed the sudden heat in Nick's stare. The man's eyes really did become more gold when his pupils were wide. It was hotter than it should have been and had Yoshi's body reacting yet again. Inari, his cock was popping up and down like a jack-in-the-box.

"I'd offer, but you've already had a rough night. Just put your things outside the door, and I'll make sure to leave you something to wear, okay?"

"But I..." Yoshi stopped talking then. There wasn't any point, considering Nick's rapid retreat. The bathroom door was closing by the time he got those two words out.

It had to be the stink of cat piss, Yoshi decided as he struggled his way out of the damp leather that only smelled worse as time went by. Why else would a guy who was apparently attracted to him make a run for it when Yoshi implied, jokingly or not, that he wouldn't mind someone, by which he'd meant Nick, joining him in the shower?

Nick didn't know—*couldn't* know—how undeserving Yoshi was of any sort of interest...could he? He couldn't know that Yoshi had deliberately, and with flagrant disregard, violated the terms of his contract to the point that the contract itself had probably burst into flames.

It wasn't possible that Nick would know, because no one knew Yoshi was free. Aside from the Arizona Den, because he'd escaped from there...and obviously his *own* Den, right there in Madison, California. And whoever might have heard and passed it on, because people did love to gossip, and...

"Gods. People are so weird."

Not as weird as Yoshi's own Clan, who'd been the ones to contract him out in the first place. More than once, if his hazy perceptions had been correct, but that might have been the drugs.

Of everything that had happened in the last several hours, it was that—not being able to remember his own relatively recent history—that truly scared him. He should know what he'd done and been through, and what had led up to his time as a…contracted breeder, because that was what it all amounted to. Shouldn't he?

Yoshi was reasonably sure that he should, and yet he didn't. He tried to focus as he stripped out of the leather and left it outside the bathroom door, but the lure of Nick's shower proved to be too strong, considering Yoshi's usual fastidious nature.

He was more than a little bit disgusted by how filthy he'd been, as well as for how long, but he was actually excited about the idea of soaking in the deep, oval tub after he finished washing the gross-nasty-stinky off. Even thinking about being clean made him happy.

So did the notion of replaying every moment with the unexpectedly appealing Nick. And if he ended up treating himself to a little bit of pleasure while thinking about the so-intriguing man, Yoshi wasn't going to feel even a little bit guilty.

Hells, he literally couldn't remember the last time he'd had an orgasm. He also couldn't recall the last time he'd *wanted* to.

Something about that seemed wrong, but he would think about it later. Right then he was more interested in getting wet and soapy. Soapy enough that he'd be able to slip and slide down even the most poorly paved street without getting more than a scratch or two.

Inari help him, but he couldn't think about anything else at the moment. He was barely even holding *that* thought, his head was spinning so much.

CHAPTER FOUR

Jeff and Pol were waiting for him down the hall, but that wasn't unexpected. Nick was just happy that they'd been willing to leave the bedroom. Yoshi had seemed more than a little bit nervous, though Nick was sure he hadn't been meant to recognize that. Then again, Yoshi seemed to think they were strangers, and maybe they were, after thirty years of no contact. They'd been the opposite of strangers once, though. Before…

"He disappeared," Jeff said, hissing with obvious fury. "He just *vanished*, and when he turns up again out of nowhere, after *three decades*, your first impulse is to bring him home with you? What the Hells is wrong with you, Nick? You should have left him in that damned alley. I should have *made you!*"

Nick wanted to be angry. Wanted to respond with shouts and curses and possibly even flying fists. He really *wanted* to, but he couldn't. Even if he'd had the energy… which he didn't, because sometime between finding Yoshi and leaving him to bathe, Nick had become so exhausted himself, he couldn't manage more than a quiet tone… Well, even if Nick had been something other than beat right then,

Jeff had a point. It wasn't necessarily a good point, but it was definitely a point. Hells, Pol even looked like he agreed.

"You could have *tried*." Nick kept moving, walking past Jeff and Pol and heading down the hall toward the communal kitchen for the floor. "I understand that you're offended on my behalf," he added, even as he pushed through the swinging door into the kitchen proper. "I'd probably be the same if you were in my position, but..."

"*But* nothing! That tacky little hobo just wanders back into your life and you...what? You're fine with it? No. I'm not having it." Jeff frowned deeply, though Nick noticed the expression did nothing to stop him from opening the freezer and removing the bottle of emergency vodka from its depths. "This isn't happening, Nick. You were a complete wreck after he took off. If you do this, I won't be sticking around to clean up the nasty mess he leaves behind."

"I think Jeff's right." Pol seemed just as distracted as earlier, which was a little bit surprising. It was one thing when they were out and about, but Pol was generally more on the ball when his attention wasn't split by watching for security threats. "And he's been gone for a long time. He doesn't even act the same. How do you know he's not dangerous now?"

Well, that explained it.

"I don't." Nick wasn't fond of that answer, but he wasn't willing to lie. Not to Pol, and not to Jeff. "But he doesn't remember me. Any of us. Pol, you were across the room, but when his eyes first opened, there was no... I don't know. I could tell he didn't recognize me, and..."

Pol frowned, though not as deeply as Jeff was still doing. "He looked scared. Probably would have smelled it, too, but who could tell when he was covered with all that pussy?"

One nose-wrinkle later, Pol went on. "But what happened to make him not remember?"

Jeff snarled, but softly, and pulled glasses from the cupboard beside the stove. "I can't believe either one of you is buying into his act. Because it has to be an act! He dates you for almost a year, Nick, then poof! Gone! And—"

"And all of a sudden he's back. I know. You've said it at least ten times, now." Nick sighed. "Maybe you're right. Maybe he's playing me for some unknown reason. Except he didn't just disappear from *my* life, Jeff. He vanished *completely*. None of our old friends ever saw him again, and none of our old enemies, either. You know Marchand, at least, had his people watching Yoshi's home Den for years, until I paid him back. He probably had informants inside, too, and if *he* couldn't find Yoshi, then Yoshi was gone in a way people just don't do for something as trivial as breaking up with someone. And…he said his name was Genko. Not Katsumi, but *Genko*. I know he was lying about that. I could see it in his face. He never could lie to me worth a damn, you know? But *he* knew it, too, or he did before. So why would he lie about his name if he knew it would just make me suspicious? So, no. He doesn't know me. Doesn't… Gods. He doesn't remember. You know what he was to me. What we were to each other. Recognized or not, you know what we were. Something happened. Something…bad."

Nick sipped the clear, sharp liquid in the glass Jeff gave him and waited until Jeff had swallowed his own drink and poured another.

"Fine," Jeff said, grudgingly. "I still say he could have left town, but… Name aside, he wouldn't have stayed away from his own Den for that long without even visiting. I guess. Not if he could help it."

"You want me to drop *Sight* on him?" Pol finally seemed less distracted, though still not entirely himself. "I couldn't before, because Jeff was breaking the pussy curse—"

"*Pied Piper* curse," Jeff snarked, but Pol just grinned and continued.

"Jeff was breaking *the curse*. There was way too much energy flying around. Not that I would use *Sight* outside anyway, but you know. I couldn't have even if I wanted to, but I didn't want to." Pol's grin turned sheepish. "Your Grandpa's awesome, Nick, but he'd punish me bad if I let anything happen to you. Worse than bad, since I'm more naughty than nice."

That surprised a laugh out of Nick. Not because Pol was wrong, but because the man rarely admitted it out loud.

"You're in good company," Nick responded, patting Pol's arm. "We're all more likely to be on one list than the other. Even—or especially—Jeff." He winked at Pol, hoping to encourage him to join in teasing Jeff, but it didn't happen. Instead, Jeff snorted.

"Let's make fun of my shady past and dubious genes later, shall we? Right now, I think it's more important to decide what we're going to do about your…*Yoshi*. I vote for letting Pol do his *Sight* thing. I'm too worn out to *See* reliably, and…" Jeff tossed back some more vodka and made a face. "I'm not feeling at all neutral about him. It's possible that I might manipulate the *gravitas* without meaning to and *See* something that isn't there. Or *not See* something that is. I don't trust myself to be impartial after what you went through when he left. Or vanished. Whatever we're calling it. Pol's more likely to *See* clearly."

"Uh… I really don't know what to say to that." Nick had never heard Jeff step away from anything. For him to do so right then was beyond odd.

Jeff poured—and drank—more liquor. "I don't like this," he said bluntly, "and I don't trust him. I don't want him within ten miles of you, much less right down the hall. That's bound to affect my perceptions in *Sight*." Jeff's lip curled, then he added, "It's not just that I'm tired, or even that I think I might hate him for what he did to you. It's also... Shit, Nick. Pol's just plain better at *Sight* than I am. I may only be admitting that part because I'm tired, though. Or a little bit drunk. It could be either. I'll deny it if you ever repeat it."

Nick chuckled. "Deny what? I didn't hear anything."

"Um, Jeff said my *Sight* is better than his, Nick. You were standing right there!" But there was a certain sparkle in Pol's eyes that said he was joking. Playing along with the not-terribly-bright persona he wore so often when his attention was split.

"Sorry, must have missed it," Nick replied, still grinning. "So, how do we want to do this? Yoshi's either showering or taking a bath. Can one of you call down to Farad's department and let him know there's an outfit requiring his unequaled attentions outside my bathroom door? And that he should leave a change of clothes there, as well? After that, we'll sit down and see what we can figure out. Does that work for you?"

"I'll call Farad," Pol said quickly, smiling again. "I need to thank him for my birthday present anyway."

Jeff growled, so softly Nick suspected he wasn't meant to notice. "Of course you do," he grumbled, and Nick was entirely sure Jeff didn't know he was speaking out loud. Then, "I have a feeling tonight is going to be long on liquor and short on sleep," said in Jeff's more usual tone, convinced him of it.

Yeah, Jeff still had a poorly hidden thing for Pol…and Pol likely knew it, considering Nick hadn't heard anything about Farad giving Pol a birthday gift, and he *would* have heard. Pol's birthday was well over a month past.

Good for Pol, he decided. Maybe it would even be good for Jeff, assuming Jeff didn't realize how accustomed he'd become to underestimating Pol in the last few decades. It might be interesting to watch Pol make Jeff chase *him* for a change.

That was something to consider later, though. Right then, Nick had some plotting and planning to do, which meant he needed Jeff at his best, rather than mostly wilted from breaking the Pied Piper curse.

That being so, he waited while Jeff dug in the freezer for another bottle, then followed him to the long table set against the far wall. He sat down beside Jeff and accepted another few fingers of clear booze in his glass before setting it down on the wood and extending his arm.

"You need to recharge," Nick said to Jeff's suddenly wide-eyed stare, "and Pol already fed you enough *gravitas* through the ether. I know it'd be more ideal to absorb it from the Workshop, but that'd probably take all night and at least half of tomorrow and I'm not sure we have that kind of time. Especially if whatever you're suspecting—because I know you suspect something—happens. So recharge, Jeff. I need you at the top of your game."

Jeff's teeth didn't hurt going in. It was only when they were fully seated in the crook of his arm that Nick felt the pain. Even that was short-lived, though, because Jeff only fed for ten seconds or so and was just as careful as he'd been every other time he'd recharged from Nick.

In the wild—meaning the world outside Nick's family—Jeff's kind were more feral. Not that Jeff had an actual *kind*. As far as Nick—and his grandfather, and every archive they had—knew, Jeff's parents had been the only instance of a love match between dark elf and what the humans called vampyre. They'd been unlucky enough to be caught out during the Inquisition, leaving Jeff an orphan, but they'd been *smart* enough to leave him behind on the one night when they'd been pressed into service like nearly all Grandfather's employees. There was something about the Workshop, be it Nick's or his family's, that eased the wildness within…or possibly something that was missing outside. No one was quite sure about that part. Whatever it was, it didn't matter.

Jeff was the only one of his kind, and by his very nature, slightly wicked. He'd been one of Nick's closest friends from before Nick could even remember, and if being that close meant the occasional nip-and-suck—and a few adventures that had ended with a need for bail money—then so be it.

Helping Jeff recharge did nothing to alleviate Nick's own exhaustion, but then he heard Pol clattering about at the other end of the kitchen, followed by the loud, grating sound of coffee being ground. "Thank gods. Pol, remind me to give you a raise for thinking of coffee."

Pol smiled and shrugged, setting about making the ground beans into liquid alertness. "Give it to Farad. He figured you had to be almost unconscious because you didn't say what size clothes to bring up while he takes care of the leather. I told him 'Yoshi-sized,' so everything's fine."

Oh gods. Everything was so far from fine, Nick didn't even have a referent. He'd forgotten how much Farad had loved to dress Yoshi. To design for him, though Farad wasn't actually a designer. Nick *wished* the *cofgoda* would design! Their clothing department would sell out with every catalog if he did; Nick was sure of it. Farad wasn't interested, or so he said, but…

"Nick?" He startled, shaking his head a bit. "Coffee. Black. You can have cream and sugar later, okay?"

Gods bless Pol, because Nick wasn't sure he hadn't been about to doze off, eyes open and midcrisis. "Fine. So what do you think is going on, Jeff? And how soon can we get Pol in to *See* Yoshi? And does Pol need to absorb some *gravitas*, or is he all right? Pol?"

"I'm good." Pol seemed sure. "All I did was share a little energy with Jeff, and he wouldn't take enough to count. I'm fine."

Nick wasn't so sure. Not until Pol sat down and offered up another grin, this one toothier than those previous.

"No offense," Pol added, "because I love you like a third cousin, twice-removed, but I don't much want to suck anything out of your body, Nick. I mean, we're friends and all, but you're my boss, too, and that would just be weird. The sucking, I mean. Since we're not actually related and stuff. Or, you know, dating or whatever. And I can just tap into the web if I need to, so…yeah, I'm definitely good. I'm good."

If he hadn't been so used to the way Pol phrased things, Nick would have been laughing hard enough that speaking would have been a dream. As it was, he almost couldn't because of the look on Jeff's face. Nick thought that was due to Pol having said anything at all about sucking things in relation to dating, but it was still none of his business. If they all got through this mess with Yoshi intact, he might just have to kick Jeff in the ass…and make sure Pol was nearby to catch him. Still, for the moment…

"Okay. So what do we think, guys? If Yoshi really doesn't remember me or *us*—and yes, that 'if' was for your benefit,

Jeff—and he's been away from his own Den for the last three decades, what could have happened? Did someone kidnap him? Hold him for ransom? What do you think?"

Gods knew whether they'd figure anything out, but even aimless theorizing had to be better than doing nothing at all.

CHAPTER FIVE

Inari, he finally felt clean. Blessedly, beautifully, wonderfully clean!

Yoshi hadn't felt so fresh in…he didn't know how long. Yet it seemed odd, somehow, that just thirty minutes or so under the strong, rain-like flow from the strangely large showerhead contained within the unusually big stall could have made such a difference. Not even the following soak in the hot, bubbling water of the Jacuzzi tub should have improved his outlook quite so much, and yet he couldn't deny that he felt changed, in a way.

Stronger. Less timid, though he'd been doing his best to appear at least self-possessed with the three men. No. They had names, and he needed to use them. After however long he'd spent being treated as a *thing*, Yoshi couldn't handle not using names when he knew them. Not without feeling guilty, so… He'd been making an effort to seem confident with Nick, Pol, and Jeff. Mostly Nick.

He didn't know why, but while he'd been cleaning up, Nick had been more and more on his mind, and not simply because he found the man so physically appealing. There was something, in retrospect, about the way Nick had looked at him; the way Nick had spoken to him. Something that had portions of more than just Yoshi's body taking notice. Something Yoshi liked. A lot.

He couldn't quite define it. He thought it might be that Nick looked at him as though he was worthwhile…or maybe that Nick didn't seem to want to control him. Maybe it was just that when Yoshi had more or less suggested that Nick stay and wash his back—by which Yoshi had meant much more than mere washing—Nick had said no. Even while Nick's eyes and face had said yes, Nick's mouth, Nick's voice, had said no. And Nick had walked away.

Yoshi shouldn't have found that appealing, even before his oddly cleansing shower and following bath in the Jacuzzi tub. *Oddly cleansing* in that they seemed to have washed away some of the second-guessing and desperation that had become so familiar to him since… Since when?

It was a puzzle, and Yoshi hated puzzles. Or not really, because when they involved words or cardboard pieces that needed to be fit together, Yoshi *liked* puzzles. At least he thought he did. He couldn't remember the last time he'd done one, but that was probably because he'd been so dru…

No, no, no, don't think about it, or you'll wake up and see this is just another fantasy! Stay asleep, Yoshi! Don't think about reality, because this is so much better! There's a beautiful man with gold-flecked eyes, and when he looks at you, he seems to care! Don't think about any of the away-De—the before! It doesn't matter! Stay with the right now!

"I love puzzles." He still wasn't sure, but it was better than thinking too much or too hard about anything else. "I love puzzles and showers and especially bath tubs with jets. I love thick, soft towels I can use by myself. I love being able to *wrap* myself in towels without hands trying to stop me or dragging them away. I love feeling alive and aware!" Yoshi shivered, then forced himself to whisper on, "I love that this dream is so much better than my life, and that Kameko can't get to me here…and I'll do whatever I have to, to stay."

Inari help him, but he meant it. When he finally woke up, he would find a way to first return to and then stay in the dream for long enough that when it ended he'd be lost completely. Dead inside, with no chance of resuscitation. Because this dream was too good. Too perfect to let go.

Part of him was trying to insist that it *wasn't* a dream, but Yoshi knew better. Even with the remembered, recent sensation of water, and the towel that was still wrapped around him, he knew better. He could feel reality pressing in around him, trying to convince him to wake up, but he wasn't going to. Didn't want to. He didn't even want to open the bathroom door to see what sort of clothing his dreaming mind might have conjured up.

Everything around him was imaginary, but he wanted it to be real. Wanted to feel like it was true, the way he had just a short while earlier. He *needed* that. Needed it like air.

The towel fell to the warm tile floor as Yoshi made himself move toward the tub.

His knees tried to give out after just a few steps, and he redirected his stumbling path to the shower stall that was at least four feet closer. If he hadn't felt a sharp lance of pain as he reached it, he would have sighed with relief.

As it was, he doubled over, crying out as much as he could while robbed of breath, and the next thing he knew, there were arms around him, holding him up. A strong body, fully clothed, pressed against his back. A voice, gentle even while sounding frantic, soothing him as much as Yoshi figured he *could* be soothed while feeling like something was simultaneously trying to gnaw its way into and out of his stomach.

"Calm, dearheart. Calm. Just try to breathe, okay? Slow and steady. With me. In… Out… In… Out…"

I know how to breathe, you moron! He wanted to say it but couldn't, which possibly meant he really *didn't* know how. Then, "Come on. Come, on, Yosh. Three steps, okay? That's all. Just three. Work with me, love. One…"

Hardest thing Yoshi had ever done. Aside from trying to escape the Den he was currently trapped and dreaming in.

"Two… Come on, sweetheart, take another step for me!"

Only because the person—man—was calling him kind, gentle names. He would try harder for *love* and *sweetheart*, sounding so sincerely meant, than he ever would for *pretty* or *stud*. *They'd* only and ever been used to trick him.

One more step left him shaking, shuddering as his body tried to shut down, but that voice was still there, those arms held him…and while he was still fully naked, the body supporting him was no less clothed than it had been three or four years earlier, when it had asked him to take that first step.

"One more, Yoshi. Just one more, and I promise—I swear to you, on my grandfather's name!—that you can rest, okay? Just give me one more step. Lift your foot this time, honey. You need to be entirely willing, and that means I can't do anything more than support you the way I'm doing. You need to lift your own feet."

Inari, he couldn't. It was too much work. Even thinking about raising *one* foot high enough to enter the shower had him ready to topple over and sleep the sleep of the near-dead. Having to do it twice…? That wasn't even possible, and Yoshi knew it, even if nobody else did.

"Can't," he somehow managed to whisper. "Sorry, Nickolai. Can't." Who the Hells was Nickolai? Fuck if he knew. Fuck if he cared, either. He just wanted to sleep, damn it, even if that seemed strange, considering he'd just woken up from being unconscious, what? Two, maybe three hours earlier?

It didn't make sense, except…he was dreaming. Everything made sense in dreams. Even the guy holding him up being able to hear his thoughts, because the next thing Yoshi heard was "You're not dreaming! You're not even asleep! You're Yoshi and I'm Nick and I know you don't remember me all the way, but you just called me Nickolai, and that has to mean it's all still inside your head, somewhere! So lift your fucking feet, you annoying sack of Kitsune! Step into the damned shower! Running water doesn't break many spells, but it for damned sure *weakens* plenty of them! *Lift your fucking feet, or I'll never blow you again, Yoshi*! I mean it! *Never*!"

It was a ridiculous thing to say. Yoshi didn't know how he knew that, but he felt it as deep and solidly as he knew his own name. "Will so," he whispered, somehow managing to smile at the irritated groan that answered him.

"Only if you're not dead, dearheart. Now, please. Lift your feet for me. Even if you feel like it'll kill you, okay? Because you have to, Yosh. For me."

Inari knew how, but Yoshi felt himself moving. Felt one trembling leg rise, toes scraping against the raised lip of the huge shower stall. He almost fell when his foot twisted against the tiled shower floor, but those arms—Nick's arms—supported him just enough to keep him upright.

"One more, Yoshi. Gods, you're doing so well! Just one more foot, and I'm already so proud. You were always amazing; I never forgot that, even when I wanted to. Come on, Yoshi. You can do it! I know you can!"

Yoshi wasn't anything like as sure as the man sounded. He wasn't even sure he hadn't passed from dream to nightmare. What he did know was that he would never get any rest until he did what Nick said. The man seemed determined to nag him into submission.

The second foot seemed to take forever. It also took whatever strength he'd had left because he'd barely managed to drag the sensitive arch of his foot over that hard edge when he felt like his heart stopped. Then there was water pouring down over him, warm and accompanied by words that seemed very, very wrong, simply because they felt so right. So unexpected, but good.

"Gods, I knew you could do it! You were always so damned determined when you wanted to be. Amazing, Yoshi! I don't know if anyone else could have done what you just did, which just proves you were right, way back when you said being stubborn was part of your charm. Gods!"

He couldn't remember the last time being stubborn had gotten him anything other than drugged harder and punished more. Even if he was just dreaming, it felt so nice to think he'd done something right. Less than a minute later, the steady rain soaking him became a pulsing torrent, slightly cooler than mere moments earlier, and Yoshi… woke up.

He fought the sensation, tried to stay dazed and foggy, but it was no use. The water was obviously real and was being used to rob him of the small bit of comfort he'd somehow managed to find. "No…" His groaning moan echoed from the gray and black subway tiles and he cringed, but the arms were still around him, still holding him up, and he felt… wet fabric against his skin. Too coarse to be silk and not spongy the way leather would be when wet, and those arms felt the same and the voice hadn't stopped, though it had gone from encouraging him loudly to murmuring against his hair, and…

"You. You're real? This. I'm not. This is real? Not more drugs? Not a trick? I really escaped?" Inari help him, but the hope was the hardest thing to handle. It had been so long since he'd truly felt anything like it, it took him a few seconds to recognize it, and even then he wasn't sure if it would help or harm him, in the end. "This is real," he said again, when the one holding him—not a female, because he felt solid male beneath the sodden fabric against his back—didn't laugh, or push him to his knees, or slam him against the tiles. "I. How much? All of it? Or is this… No. This can't be a different part of that terrible other-Den. It just *can't*."

A snort came from outside the glass wall of the shower stall. "We should be so lucky. No, I'm afraid this is all real. So is Nick. Sadly, you are, too."

Yoshi's bleary eyes tracked more slowly than he would have liked, even as he slowly became even more aware. He felt himself frowning, though he didn't know if it was because of what the blond man had said or the fact that he hadn't been part of Yoshi's dream, nightmare, whatever.

"Right back at you," Yoshi managed, though he could barely hear himself over the water, so who knew whether John? No, Jeff. He didn't know whether *Jeff* had heard him. "Can I…I'm naked. I need to get out of the shower and—"

"No!" Okay, Nick had heard him just fine, because even though he was clearly and strongly disagreeing with the last, he'd also started to chuckle at what Yoshi'd said to Jeff. "Sorry. I didn't mean to yell. But you can't get out yet, okay? Pol needs to look at you first."

Yoshi's hands immediately covered his most personal bits, even though he knew it was a bit late. "He's seen enough!" Inari, his voice was much stronger already. Good. "I'm not going to be the star of some naked peep show!" Never again, damn it.

Pol, who Yoshi hadn't even noticed until he moved—and that was saying something because Pol wasn't in any way a small or nondescript man—made a sound that could only be called a giggle.

"Not like that! I need to *See* you. You can wear a towel if you want, but it's gonna get really, really wet."

"Here." Jeff shoved a towel through the open shower door. "And don't flatter yourself, vagabond. The only one of us who'd want to see you naked is in the exact wrong position to manage it. Cover yourself and let Nick get out of there. His *gravitas* will mess with Pol's *Seeing*."

Everything went far too quickly then, with Yoshi wrapping the towel around himself and grimacing as it became heavier than cotton should be, even when soaked. Nick stepped away, and Yoshi felt cold, despite the steaming water. He felt colder still when Pol leveled an intent stare at him for close to ten seconds before shuddering and stumbling backwards, only Jeff's quick movement and the bathroom vanity keeping Pol upright.

"Just stay there, Yoshi, okay?" Pol sounded shaky but determined. "Try not to move too much. All that water's making it hard enough to *See,* and there's something way weird on you. I'm gonna try to get a feel for it so I can follow it, okay? It'll be easier if you can hold still, no matter how much I know you want to fidget. You're not even good at being peaceful when you're sleeping, but try, okay? It'll make it easier for me."

Inari! Did that mean Pol's *Sight* was strong enough to *See* through running water? He'd been waiting to be told to shut the flow off. Then again, he'd also assumed that Pol was staring just to familiarize himself with Yoshi's physical shape, which would help with *Seeing*. But Pol had been using *Sight*, water and all, and Yoshi didn't even know how to feel about that, aside from equal parts scared and impressed. Scared because that amount of raw power in the hands of someone as…*not* smart as Pol was an accident waiting to happen, and impressed because Pol might actually be that strong.

"I can be as still as a statue," Yoshi promised, right before proving it. And all the while, his mind was racing, wondering what, exactly, had happened to him, and why Pol seemed to know his sleeping habits. Unless the guy meant the time Yoshi'd spent unconscious after the not-dreamed cat-attack. That must be it, he decided, barely even breathing as Pol stared at him, eyes flicking back and forth and up and down in a way Yoshi had never seen before… except it seemed just the tiniest bit familiar, which made no sense at all, considering he'd only just met the guy.

✧ ✧ ✧ ✧

The water was still warm. That was possibly the only good thing about being stuck in the shower wearing nothing but the unpleasantly heavy towel. It really was heavy, too, and seemed to be growing more so with each passing second.

Yoshi's arms had started to ache from holding the damned thing up after less than five minutes. After ten, he'd barely been able to manage, which was when Jeff—because Nick and Pol had left him alone with the guy who hated him, and Yoshi planned to remember that for later—had dragged some sort of folding single-person bench from the closet that held the towels and such. Yoshi wasn't sure why he hadn't noticed it when he'd first opened that door to choose shampoo and conditioner, except he hadn't really been paying much attention to things that wouldn't get him clean.

Another five minutes, during which the ache in his arms faded, and Yoshi was less achy but more than slightly impatient.

"How long am I supposed to stay in here? I'm getting all...pruney. And bored." He fiddled with the water knobs, just to have something to do.

He'd tried to sound curious, rather than demanding, but either he'd failed or Jeff hated him, because the guy snorted.

"It's not exactly a laugh-a-minute for me either, sunshine." Okay, the guy hated him. Yoshi didn't know why, but it probably didn't matter. Maybe it was because of Nick, though.

Once that thought had entered his head, Yoshi became sure of it. The guy, pretty as he was, was probably either with Nick or trying to be. Seeing Nick pay so much attention to someone else, not to mention sharing a semi-naked shower with them...? Yeah. Yoshi would be pissed off and hating, too. In fact, he was kind of pissed off and hating Jeff for even thinking of Nick that way. As a prospective...whatever.

"You know—" he started before cutting himself off. "Wait. Never mind. Sorry. I'm being crazy." It wasn't any of his business whether Jeff was interested in Nick, no matter how much he felt like it was. "Let me try this again. I'm pretty sure I can't spend the rest of my life in this shower, and the water is starting to make my eyes hurt. And my skin. And pretty much everything. I can probably last another..."

He paused, forcing himself to think back to the last Den while trying not to let the emotions associated with remembering take him over. "I'd say a few hours, at most. After that, I might start trying to drown myself." Yoshi did his best not to shudder. He failed, even though the water he was under was warm, this time. "I need... Please, okay? Can you *please* tell me how much longer? I just—"

Jeff's brow was furrowed when he leaned closer to the open shower stall door. He sounded just as pissy as ever, though.

"It'll take as long as it takes. If there's any justice in this world, and I know for a fact that there is, you'll suffer as much as Nick's done all this time. He may not show it, but you came close to breaking him. Too close. And *he* may be dumb as a post where you're concerned, but I'm not. You can feel free to shut up now, by the way. I have zero sympathy for your plight."

It shouldn't have mattered. He shouldn't have cared what Jeff said. Yoshi knew that. Yet somehow, it hurt. Almost as much as the way Nick had looked at him before leaving the bathroom with Pol.

That look—equal parts disappointment, hope, and sorrow—had started a low, deep pain in Yoshi's chest, and he still didn't know "Why?"

"Why what." Jeff's tone made it clear that he didn't want an answer. That he didn't even want to be there in the first place, and that only led Yoshi to more questions, like...

"Why everything! Why am I still here! Why are you guys helping me, if that's even what you're doing! And why do I keep feeling like I should know what's going on when I don't have a single clue?" His own voice was making him dizzy with the way it bounced around the shower stall, even though it was slightly hushed by the flowing water, and he tweaked the water pressure in an effort to reduce the echoing tones. "Also, what are you? All of you! Because I thought you were human before, but humans can't break curses and *See*, and especially not through running water! I just. What the Hells is going on, and why do you hate me so much? You don't even *know* me!"

Inari help him, he was teary-eyed. Tired and sore inside and frustrated, yes, but worse than that was the confusion, the overwhelming sense that nothing was right or ever would be again.

"I should have just stayed at that Den," he whispered, for his own benefit. "At least I knew my place there. It was a *crappy* place, but it was mine." He couldn't even remember why he'd been so determined to escape, anymore. Or why he hadn't just used his less-drugged time to end himself. He could have done that. It wouldn't even have been difficult. He'd just been so sure that there was something more, out in the world. Someplace he could be free and maybe happy, or at least not *un*happy. "Maybe the drugs would have killed me. That wouldn't have been so bad."

Jeff snorted. "Oh good. We're going for drama. That'd work better on Nick, so you might want to try again when he's here."

Yoshi sighed and slouched on the bench, releasing the water knobs. "Why bother? Why don't you just get me my clothes, okay? I'll go away, and you can stop hating me."

"You'll die."

"Ha! Kameko doesn't want me dead. She wants me out there in that other-Den earning whatever stud fee she negotiated for my 'services.' I'm no use to her dead. No matter how much I… Never mind. Just…never mind."

There was no point in fighting anymore. No point in anything. Jeff didn't give a shit, and Inari had obviously abandoned him. Hells, Inari hadn't paid Yoshi any mind in ages, considering. What sort of God would let someone be sold off, or even just rented, for that matter? Not one who cared.

"Just let me go. I'll go back, and everyone will be happy. I'll be out of your life, and Nick's, and my Den won't be stuck with whatever penalties were built into the contract I broke by escaping, and… Maybe if I get lucky they'll mess up the dosage and that'll be that." It was starting to sound good, really. And so much easier than fighting.

He started to lose himself in the idea of slowly vanishing, of fading away inside while the rest of him went on, and while it wasn't ideal, it had to be better than…

"Hey!" he shrieked, yipping at the end of the word. "What the Hells?"

Jeff, wet and angry, kept hold of the cold water knob he'd obviously just twisted to full. "They're right. Gods damn it, they're right! Shit!" Yoshi watched, eyes stinging, as Jeff twisted the other knob—the one for hot—all the way, as well. The increase in water pressure made it feel like tiny, cold but quickly warming hail stones were pelting Yoshi without end. "Tell me again how you want to go fulfill whatever ridiculous contract you were talking about."

"It makes sense," Yoshi answered, slightly breathless from the shock of cold followed by the changed, more intense pressure. "Everyone's lives would be easier if I just… went… Wait. What the Hells was I saying? But it makes sense, doesn't it? *Does* it…?" Inari, he was lost. "I don't know what's happening to me. I think… I think I'm losing my mind. I don't know…" Anything. He didn't know *anything*. Not anymore.

CHAPTER SIX

"We have a problem."

Nick groaned and leaned forward, elbows resting on the kitchen table. "Great. Another one. Just what we need. And wait. Why aren't you in the bathroom with Yoshi?" Gods knew what the weird cloud Pol had *Seen* around Yoshi meant, but it wasn't good. That much was a given. The spectral cord leading away from Yoshi and to…something too far away to *See* made that much clear. "He knows to stay under the water, right? No, of course he does. He's not a stupid man."

"Fox," Jeff said sharply. "He's not a stupid *fox*. Or he never was before. Now? Not so much with the smart. It's sad, Nick. We were just hanging out. You know, in the shower for him, outside it for me. And I wasn't really sure he wasn't playing you. I mean, you have zero common sense where he's concerned. He could probably convince you that a penguin was really a waiter in a tux, if he wanted to."

"Sometimes a penguin *is* a waiter in a tux. Is there a reason you're wet?" Jeff hadn't been wet when Nick had left him in the bathroom; Nick was sure of it. "Unless you drowned him, but that's not easy to do in a shower." He shook his head. "Gods, I need more coffee. Okay, what's our new problem, and why did you leave him alone?"

Jeff frowned and looked down at himself, presumably to see just how damp he was.

Nick was sure of it when Jeff's lips twisted into a clearly disgusted grimace. "He's been Spelled. Not the curse!" Yeah, Jeff knew him too well. "This is something else. Probably whatever Pol *Saw*. I never did get to hear about that, by the way. You two just ditched me in there to watch your little fox."

Nick closed his eyes for a moment, then speared Jeff with a sharp stare. "Yeah, we did. Be a dick about it later. We already know it's some sort of spell. Pol didn't recognize it. All he could tell me is that it's 'muddy' and 'tangled' and 'dark,' whatever that means with Spelling. Oh, and it's got some sort of feeder arm going off to…somewhere. Pol's out with some of the factory security guys, trying to track it. If we can find the source, maybe we can do something about it."

"Doubtful." Jeff looked angry, all of a sudden. "Whoever Spelled him did it a long time ago, Nick, and they're good. Really, really *good*. And unless I miss my guess, they've renewed it regularly. That's the only way I can think of for him to be Spelled so hard that he tried to turn off the water, even when he knew why he shouldn't."

"What the fuck?"

Nick felt his heart sinking lower and lower as Jeff grabbed a beer from the fridge and proceeded to tell him a story that should have been fiction but wasn't.

"He said he wanted to go back?" Gods, what if he really did? What if Nick was wrong about what they'd been to each other, and without those memories, Yoshi couldn't see anything worthwhile in him? But no. That was the uncertainty of three decades apart, sneaking into his brain and making him question.

"He said it would 'make everyone's lives easier.' *Not* that he wanted to." Jeff was as snarky and bitchy as usual, and that actually helped. Things couldn't be entirely fucked up if Jeff was being his normal self. "Then I jumped into the shower and turned the water on full-blast, and he got confused. Like he wasn't sure what he was saying or why. It took a few minutes, but he seemed to get his shit together again. So, yes. I'd say we have another problem. He can't stay in the shower forever. Even if he could, there's no guarantee that it'd do much good, long-term, but for right now, he's not going anywhere."

"Hells."

Jeff nodded. "There's more, too. I'm not sure if it helps, but this Kameko he mentioned…"

The rest of what Jeff said had Nick quietly fuming, even if he didn't understand it all. How in the worlds could anyone rent Yoshi out? How could that even be an option? And for what? He hoped to gods that he'd misheard, or that Jeff had when he claimed Yoshi'd said *stud services*.

Nick was well acquainted with most of the cultural differences between his kind and Yoshi's, but he'd never heard that Kitsune practiced contracted prostitution; not even for breeding purposes.

Not to mention, "But Yoshi's gay! And we're… I mean, he would never sign that sort of contract when he wouldn't be able to, um…perform. He can be shifty and crafty and more clever about twisting things than should be possible, but even he wouldn't promise something he could never, ever deliver!"

At least, Nick didn't think so. Unless there was something in it for Yoshi, but Nick couldn't see what.

"He mentioned drugs," Jeff said, looking just as disgusted as he sounded. "And escaping some Den somewhere, gods know how, so I'm going to go out on a limb and say none of it was voluntary, aside from breaking out."

Nick couldn't help the full-body shudder that rolled through him then. If he hadn't known better, he would have sworn that his skin was trying to crawl right off his flesh so it could huddle in a twitching pile in a corner somewhere. And okay, that mental image was slightly creepy, even to him.

"I don't even know what to say to that." He really didn't. Not when it was Jeff he'd be talking to. If Jeff was right, though, and whoever had taken advantage of Yoshi were standing there? Oh, Nick would have lots of things to tell them. Even more things to do to them.

"I guess I'm surprised he told you anything at all, considering how you've been treating him." Yeah. That wasn't exactly important, but it seemed odd.

Jeff blushed for the first time in years, as far as Nick could recall. "I might have been pushing him. I know I said I agreed with you about something happening when he disappeared, but it just seemed too pat. The more time went by, the less likely it seemed that he didn't have some sort of agenda. So I was extra assholey to him and he cracked, but not the way I thought he would. Then I felt bad, and it was like all that suspicion just drained away." A discomfited expression crossed Jeff's face. "I think I was just worn out from breaking the curse and not thinking right. I'll apologize to him later. After he's allowed out of the shower."

"Oh Hells! I forgot! We've been standing here talking while he's alone! He could have—"

"No." Jeff's hand on his arm and determined head shake stopped Nick. "I may be your administrative supervisor, but

I know how to use a screwdriver, and I know you keep some tools in the bottom of the towel closet. Your shower knobs are in your nightstand drawer, and Farad's keeping Yoshi company. He showed up about five seconds after Yoshi stopped talking to me, and I'm fairly sure he custom made the clothes he brought for your fox. Last time I checked, Klaas Act didn't have any silver pants or shirts in production with the clothing division."

Nick chuckled, though it felt forced. "He always did love dressing Yoshi. Then again, Yoshi was always willing to be flawless in whatever Farad came up with, so they're probably fine for now. I'm just… Gods, Jeff. I hate just sitting around."

Jeff shrugged. "So don't. Go talk to him. Hells, shower with him if you think that'll help. Staying away from him isn't going to make Pol find anything any sooner."

"Speaking of Pol," Nick started, and Jeff turned away.

"We're *not* speaking of Pol. Not the way you want to." Jeff set his empty beer bottle on the counter and pulled another from the fridge. "If you want to mind some business that's actually yours, maybe you should take some food to your vagabond. Gods know when he ate last, and to be honest, Nick? He looks like he's lost at least twenty pounds, now that I'm thinking about it." Jeff shrugged and opened the new beer. "He has some questions, too. Have fun feeding him in the shower!"

Nick glared, but it did nothing to stop Jeff from strolling out of the kitchen as though Nick wasn't even there. "Someone needs to be reminded which of us is the boss, here," he muttered, but he was smiling slightly, too. Some days Jeff was a huge pain, but Nick wouldn't trade him for an entire tribe of yes-men. And sometimes, Jeff actually gave great advice. Like feeding Yoshi, and possibly having a conversation.

If Yoshi had questions, it could only be in Nick's best interests to answer them. He hoped so, anyway.

❖ ❖ ❖ ❖

Farad wasn't happy. Nick could tell that much just from looking at the man. If anything, Farad was as close to going *cofdiabhal* as Nick had ever seen. The small but powerful male was livid.

"Skin! Bones! Small flesh! Master Yoshi is sick, Master Nick! Skin! Bones! *Small flesh*! And asking only for boots and pants! Boots and pants and boots and pants! Who has done this thing?"

It was almost funny, hearing that degree of outrage in the lilting, old-world cadence that was Farad's by birth, but the near-red gleam in the *cofgoda's* eyes was anything but amusing. It was dangerous, as Nick and his family—and a small town in Germany that no longer existed—had reason to know. When a truly old House God was edging toward tipping into House Devil mode, laughter was the least appropriate response.

"I don't know," Nick answered quickly, balancing the loaded tray precariously with one hand while the other dropped to rest on Farad's shoulder. "We only found him again today, and he's not well. We're going to make him better, though. I promise." Even if it killed him, by which Nick meant if it killed *him*, not Yoshi. "As for the 'boots and pants,' I'm guessing he's tired of being naked by now. And wet. He probably wants to get out of here, you know?"

The red tinge grew stronger in Farad's eyes. "Out? *Away*? No! Master Yoshi will stay! He belongs here."

"I can hear you, you know, and I'm right here! It's up to me if I stay or go." Yoshi sounded grumpy, but that was far better than what Jeff had told him earlier, so grumpy-Yoshi was Nick's favorite thing right then. Which did nothing to derail Farad's looming combustion.

"You will stay. *Because you belong here!*" Yeah, Farad seemed surer than sure. So sure, Nick thought he might chase after Yoshi and tackle him by hugging him around the knees if Yoshi tried to leave again while Farad was anywhere nearby.

Nick did laugh then. Just a small chuckle at the mental image, but it seemed to derail Farad's growing ire, and as that was what Nick had been going for, he considered it a success.

"He does, Farad." Nick nodded. "But somebody's done something to him. He's been Spelled. Pol's working on following it back to its Maker so we can work out how to break it. Until then, Yoshi doesn't remember us, okay? So if he's been acting like he didn't know you, it's because he doesn't right now. But he will." Gods, Nick hoped so. "Jeff said you made Yoshi a new outfit. Silver?" He arched both brows. "Are you sure about that?"

Farad gasped, as though his taste had never been questioned before, and maybe it hadn't. Either way, the small remaining bit of red faded from the *cofgoda's* eyes.

"You will see," he said strongly. "When Master Yoshi is no longer wet, you will see. The silver will be perfect. I merely need to do some tailoring, to accommodate for the weight Master Yoshi has been robbed of. Yes. I can do that. It won't even take more than an hour. I will not rush, considering the current situation, yes? So I will return later with Master Yoshi's new clothes."

Nick smiled. "I'm sure he'll love that. In the meantime, do you think one of your staff could bring up some sweats or something? By the time we can let him out of the shower, he'll probably need to sleep, and while I'm sure the silver is lovely, I don't know that it would suit as pajamas."

The small, wizened, one-time god cocked his head. Nick tensed slightly when his eyes narrowed, but then Farad grinned a huge, diamond-toothed grin.

"I may have something that will let him from the water sooner. Allow me to check with Jeniffer. I will return, Master Yoshi and Master Nick!"

This time, when Nick laughed, it was a true, loud laugh—probably the first he'd really meant since he and the guys had found Yoshi. There was just something about the way Farad was so certain that had Nick feeling as optimistic as he'd been trying to seem.

Farad might not be a major god. Might never have been, even in his heyday. There was still something beyond comforting in knowing a god of whatever stature was determined to help.

"I brought you some food," Nick said, hoping the offering would act as his apology for talking with Farad as though Yoshi hadn't been there. "I'm so sorry. I should have offered before. It's just that everything seemed to happen so fast, and then there's the thing with finding out you've been Spelled, and we've all sort of been running around like headless chickens, so…" He stopped himself and shook his head. "Sorry. What I meant to say was 'After everything you've been through, you must be hungry. I brought you some food. I should have done it before, but I didn't. My bad.' Of course, it would have been better if I'd just led with that, but I didn't. So, are you?"

"Huh?" Yoshi sounded choked, but not in distress, which seemed a little odd, out of bed. Then a small, yipping noise made its way through the sounds of water and weight of steam in the air, and Nick blinked.

"Are you laughing at me?" It came out more baffled than demanding. "Really? I just faced off against a pissed off *cofgoda*, and I brought you food—which said *cofgoda* obviously knows you need as much as *I* do—and you're laughing at me?"

Another yip sounded, then Yoshi asked, "Who says I'm laughing?"

Nick snorted, even though that was more Jeff's thing. "I do. I know exactly what that kind of yip in that tone of voice means, dearheart. Fortunately, I've never really minded having you laugh at me. It's kind of cute." He smirked, well aware of just how much Yoshi didn't like being called the C-word. Not that Yoshi's antipathy for it changed anything. He *was* cute, damn it. And beautiful in a way that most men never could be.

It was the sudden silence from the shower stall that told Nick he'd said too much. Damn it! Why couldn't he just keep his mouth shut?

"Yosh?" And there he went again, talking when he should just be quiet. "You okay?"

No words answered him. Just a small, whining sound that he barely heard. He did hear it, though, and it was enough to have him moving to the vanity and setting the tray down before approaching the stall door.

"Yoshi?"

Gods, it was sad, seeing Yoshi curled up as much as possible on the tiny little bench seat Nick had bought the last time his brother, Kris, had visited. He hadn't wanted to know why Kris—and Will, of course, because Will was a permanent fixture in Kris's life—needed a shower bench. He still didn't want to know. The memory of Will's smirk when Kris had asked for said item was enough answer. Nick had made a point of eradicating the memory of the bench's existence from his mind and shoved it into the back of the towel closet, just to make it that much easier to forget. Clearly someone, probably Jeff, had decided Yoshi needed it. Looking at Yoshi right then, Nick thought Jeff had been right.

He'd been in dry clothes for less than three hours, but Nick didn't even hesitate. He walked right into the shower, ignoring the pounding water, which at full-force was more pummeling than soothing, and went to his knees on the tiles.

His hands rose, and while he wanted to put them on Yoshi's naked knees, he forced himself to shift them higher, resting on the soaked towel covering Yoshi's thighs. "Yosh? Tell me what you need, okay? Please, sweetheart. I'll do everything I can to make sure you get it. I swear."

"You… You keep calling me that." Yoshi sounded breathless, but Nick wasn't sure whether that was because he was, or because he was whispering. "D-dearheart and s-sweetheart. And you're acting like you kn-know me, and it's freaking me out."

Nick squeezed his eyes shut against the urge to cry. "I'm sorry. I'll stop, okay? It's just…" What? Habit, though it had been years? Well, yeah, but he couldn't say so. That would only freak Yoshi out more. "I do know you, though," he went on, crossing mental fingers that the truth was the way to go. "We used to be... Gods, Yoshi, we belonged to each other. It was only for a year, but it was so damned good. Then you disappeared and I almost lost my mind trying to find you."

He rubbed Yoshi's legs lightly through the sodden cotton. "It was like you'd never even existed. I mean, all our friends remembered you, of course, but you were just *gone*. After a few years, they all told me to move on. Mostly because you were so *very* gone that no one had even seen you, much less heard from you. I guess I started to believe it myself, except not really. There just wasn't anything I could think of doing to find you, after a while. Scrying didn't work. *Finding spells* didn't work, even though I had a ton of your things. I even hired a few private investigators, but they didn't find even a hint of you, and that doesn't matter anymore."

Reddened violet eyes peered up at him from beneath Yoshi's wet hair. "I. It doesn't?"

Nick did his best to smile, even as he shook his head. "It doesn't. Because you're here now, by whatever method, and I know you didn't want to go. I wondered for a while, but seeing you again..." He swallowed roughly. "I know you don't remember me. I'm guessing that's part of why you were Spelled. To make you forget. But Pol's hunting down whoever Spelled you, and he'll find them. If not tonight, then tomorrow, or the day after that, or whenever. But he'll find them and we'll make them break the Spelling, and then..."

"And th-then?" Yoshi was still barely looking at him from behind that dripping hair, but that was fine; that was good. It beat the merry Hells out of Yoshi *not* looking at him.

"And then you'll remember. Or you won't," Nick added, just for the sake of honesty. "Either way, you'll be out from under it, and that can't be anything but good. And if you still don't remember, I guess I'll just have to court you again." He smiled, doing his best to hide how much he truly wanted Yoshi to be the Yoshi he knew. "It could be fun, right? There's nothing like a good courting to get a guy's blood racing."

Yoshi's eyes widened behind the hair. Then they narrowed. "I'm not going to do anything until you answer my questions. Um, okay?"

The begging tone at the end had Nick about to lose it, because this wasn't his Yoshi. *His* Yoshi would have demanded answers, not pleaded for them. Even so, the little Nick knew about what Yoshi had been through since they'd parted told him that he needed to answer whatever questions Yoshi wanted to ask…and even if the Yoshi before him ended up being the only Yoshi he could have, well… *Any* Yoshi was better than none at all.

"Okay," Nick agreed, thumbs sliding carefully over the wet towel covering Yoshi's thighs. "I'd like you to eat something first, though. I brought lamb."

The speed with which Yoshi's sharp little canines emerged should have been funny. Would have been, any other time. Right then, though, Nick wasn't amused. Encouraged, yes. Amused? No.

"If you can stand up, I'll move your bench closer to the door. That way, you can eat but still be somewhat protected by the running water."

"I. Okay," Yoshi mumbled, and Nick stood, trying to ignore the water that ran from his own clothing. Gods, he had it bad, but that was only to be expected. What wasn't expected was that Yoshi hadn't given any indication of being as attracted as Nick was.

If things had changed that much, then Nick wouldn't push it. Not yet, anyway. Soon, though. Very, very soon.

CHAPTER SEVEN

Oh, Inari! Lamb! Raw, bloody *lamb*!

It tasted so much better than Yoshi remembered. Meaty, yes, but also sweet. Tender, as thinly as it was sliced, and he couldn't quite figure why Nick would have thin-sliced lamb on hand, but he also couldn't bring himself to care too much since he was ravenous.

He knew he was writhing on the repositioned seat. Knew he was making odd rumbling sounds as Nick hand-fed him thin slices of cold flesh. He couldn't seem to help it, and Nick didn't seem to mind. If anything, Nick fed him faster when he rumbled.

The food—mostly meat, but every few bites Nick switched it up by giving him a baby carrot or broccoli floret—went a long way toward clearing his mind. The water still pouring down over him went a long way toward annoying him.

"I might go crazy, or crazier, if I have to stay under running water for more than another hour," he said carefully, during a break in the feeding. He actually liked the way Nick was offering individual bits to him, but that didn't change anything. He wanted out of the shower, for fuck's sake. He felt sodden and soggy and more than slightly pathetic, even without the question of whether it was Nick or Yoshi himself who was crazy. Nick had at least been able to change into dry sweatpants, which only had Yoshi feeling more resentful than he liked.

Regardless of that, the more time he spent under the shower spray, the better he felt; especially with food—real food—in his belly. His mind didn't seem so fuzzy anymore, and he didn't feel even slightly guilty for planning and executing his own bumbling escape from the other-Den. He even remembered what the bitch-vixen had said about his home Den being in breach of contract, but he didn't care. He remembered not caring at the time, and he still didn't.

"Farad said he might have a solution to the running water dilemma." Nick set the tray down on the floor beside the shower door. Then he smiled, and everything Yoshi had been trying to ignore—every bit of desire and need, every wish to grab the man and wrap around him—became less idea and more necessity.

"I don't care," Yoshi said, everything within him aching desperately for Nick. "Sorry, but I don't! I need out of this shower, okay? Now!" Not only was he tired of being wet, but now that he was feeling more himself, he couldn't help but realize just how wretched he must look. Hells, he was surprised Nick was able to stand looking at him at all. Drowned rat wasn't a good look on anyone. Drowned *fox* could only be worse.

Nick frowned, his head already shaking, and Yoshi knew he wasn't going to like what the man said, before Nick spoke a single word.

Not safe. Running water. Forgetting spell. Blah-blah-blah. He would have cut Nick off, but there was something about his voice, some tone or timbre, that soothed Yoshi's desperation, because he was definitely desperate. Desperate to be dry, yes, but also to make a better impression on Nick, whom he…what?

He couldn't say he knew Nick, or even liked him, although Nick had been incredibly nice so far. Nicer than Yoshi thought he would be himself, if some random stranger he'd rescued started being as high maintenance as Yoshi'd been from the first. But if Nick was right, then they weren't strangers. If Nick wasn't lying—and that was a big *if*—they'd been friends once. More than friends. Much, much more.

"You said 'years.' Before." Yoshi didn't have a single problem with interrupting Nick's list of reasons to stay wet. Not once he'd started repeating himself. "You said you looked for me for *years*. How long… I mean, time was kind of messed up at the other-Den. I'm not sure…"

Whatever he'd been expecting, Nick's growled "just over thirty years" wasn't it. The anger shining from Nick's eyes was just as shocking as Nick's claim. "I almost gave up. Or maybe I did. I don't know."

"No. No, it can't have been. Thirty years? No. It felt like… I don't know, but not thirty years!" Inari help him, had he really been gone that long? How was that even possible? The bitch-vixen had said he was under contract, but reproductive contracts didn't run that long; not ever! Six human years or until gestation began. Not three fucking decades! Three decades he didn't even remember!

"What the fuck?" Had they drugged him that much? Enough that he'd missed the passage of time? It didn't seem possible.

Nick nodded. "Exactly. 'What the fuck' is *exactly* what I'm going to find out, just as soon as Pol finds whoever Spelled you, Yosh. But that's for later. For right now, how do you feel? Aside from soggy and cranky." Nick offered up a smile, but Yoshi could see how forced it was. Even so, he kind of appreciated the effort.

"I'm okay." He wasn't, really, but he was far better than he'd been earlier. Still wet and not getting any drier as the shower ran, but still. "I guess…this past we have. The one you mentioned. That's why you're trying to help me, isn't it? Because you think I'm… Thirty years? *Years*. Really?" He couldn't manage to wrap his mind around that. "And we were together. Before."

"We were." Nick's smile went from forced to wistful in about one point three seconds. "We weren't the perfect couple or anything. Gods, we fought like cats and dogs, sometimes. But we never went to bed angry and we always had each other's back." He chuckled. "You know how they say there's a honeymoon phase at the beginning of any new relationship?"

Yoshi nodded, even though he wasn't sure he'd ever really heard that. Then again, he'd never spent a whole lot of time amongst humans. One of which he was fairly sure Nick wasn't. If the curse-breaking and *Seeing* weren't enough—and to be fair, it had been Nick's friends who'd done that, rather than Nick himself—the way Nick was talking about three decades gone by while looking much younger than any human who'd been bouncing around Madison thirty years earlier could possibly be? That was more than enough to support the suspicion that seemed more fact than theory.

"Well, we never had that. The honeymoon phase." Nick laughed again, though no more loudly. "We had the *honeymoon-from-Hells* phase, because we drove each other the bad kind of crazy for a while, but there was just so much heat between us. Fire. So we fought and fuc… Um. Let's just say it took us some time to learn how to compromise. But we did and we were good together. Then we were amazing.

We made promises, Yosh. Serious promises. Forever was mentioned, more than once. Then you were gone, and it was so hard to keep believing, you know? Especially with so many people telling me that forever must have meant something different to you, or even worse, that I'd brought it on myself for getting involved with one of your kind."

Oh, he wanted to wipe the sadness from Nick's eyes. And the anger buried beneath it. For some reason, Yoshi didn't think the anger was for him, though. Not when Nick still seemed to feel the separation he was talking about as though it had happened thirty days earlier, rather than years. Even so, Nick had given him the perfect opening.

"My kind." It wasn't a question. Nick obviously knew, just as Jeff did. The raw meat had been a dead giveaway. "How did you… Never mind. You knew from before. I must have told you." He was starting to confuse himself, damn it. First with his emotional schizophrenia, and next with trying to phrase things the right way for a past he didn't remember.

Nick shook his head. "Not exactly, but the night we met, when I took you home with me? You flashed canines and popped furry ears and three tails every time you came. The tails were especially…flexible. It took me about five minutes to figure out what you were, after that night, and I made a point of learning everything I could. I had to. You wore me out so much, I slept for two days, afterward. And I wanted to do it again, which we totally did."

Inari help him, but Nick wasn't lying. Yoshi really hadn't been able to control himself back then. He might still be unable, but he wasn't sure. He hadn't had an orgasm—that he remembered—since…he had no idea when. Not including earlier in the same shower he was starting to hate.

"I wish I could remember that," Yoshi murmured, before he'd been aware that he was going to say anything at all. Still, in for a rabbit, in for a fat hen. "I'll bet you're great in bed. Strong and kind. Gentle but forceful." That was the type that had always turned his crank, so to speak.

"Not so kind and gentle that first night." Nick's smile, while small, was anything but sheepish. "You'd been teasing me all night long. By the time we got back to my place, I was so desperate for you, I would have robbed a bank or slapped someone's granny if it would have gotten you naked any faster. And that's saying a lot. My family isn't big on naughtiness. You, on the other hand? The naughty made you yowl."

It was the exaggerated waggling of Nick's brows that made Yoshi laugh. He was glad, though. As long as he was laughing, he couldn't embarrass himself by asking if Nick would consider giving him a demonstration. Or ten. Ten would be nice. *And naughty.*

He still wasn't entirely sure about what Nick was, but Yoshi thought it might be enough to know Nick wasn't human. That Nick had mentioned being naughty, not once but twice, meant something; Yoshi was sure of it. But sitting there on a folding bench under pouring water, with Nick just a foot or so away and half naked, Yoshi didn't much care. Angel or devil or something in between, Nick was Nick, and Yoshi…liked that. Liked that even the tiny bit Nick had just told him had helped him forget about the water running over him. Inari, he was afraid he was getting used to it.

"I yowled?" Yoshi did his best to sound skeptical. "I don't think so. I've never yowled a day in my life."

"Oh, you yowled. A lot." Nick's lips curved into a smug, prideful little smirk that fully convinced Yoshi that the man was telling the truth. No one could fake that self-satisfied expression. "There was this spot on your back, right above your tails. Every time I touched you there, you wriggled like a fish on a line."

"I don't wriggle!" Yoshi tried his hardest not to crack a smile, or Inari forbid, laugh again, but it was a close thing. "I don't!"

Nick's small grin faded slightly, but not entirely. "Maybe not anymore, but you used to. For me."

"But what about—"

A loud throat-clearing from the bathroom doorway, followed immediately by, "Jeniffer is brilliant. She knew just what Master Yoshi needs and was able to cobble it together more quickly than expected," interrupted him, but Yoshi didn't care. If Farad had really come through with something to let him get out of the damned shower, the *cofgoda*, as Nick had called the small man earlier, was welcome to cut off every single thing Yoshi tried to say for the next year.

"Um, Jeniffer is…?" It seemed polite to ask, though Yoshi wasn't sure why he was trying, except…Farad seemed to know him just as much as Nick, Jeff, and Pol did. Not in the same way as Nick, Yoshi hoped, because Farad seemed like a nice man, but *so* not Yoshi's type…and his mind was spinning. Probably because of the chance to be dry again.

"Jeniffer is Farad's niece." Nick's faded smile grew, and Yoshi wondered why he wasn't surprised by the way Nick's happier expression made *him* happy, too. "She oversees production of our clothing line, and you've never seen anyone so quick and capable with a needle and thread. Aside from Farad, of course."

"All she knows is from me," Farad boasted, clearly proud of Jeniffer's abilities. "Other than the hat she's sent for Master Yoshi. We will need to try it, but her mother taught her well before Jeniffer chose to pursue her current path."

Yoshi blinked and cocked his head. "What does that mea—"

"It is a very good hat," Farad announced, interrupting again. "I would have made it silver, to match the outfit you will wear soon, Master Yoshi, but this will suffice until morning. We must test it to ensure that it works, Master Nick."

Yoshi looked at the folded bit of fabric in Farad's hands and groaned silently. There was no way he would look like anything but a fool while wearing that, but he remembered what Nick had said about not wanting to piss Farad off, so he merely clutched the wet towel more tightly around his own waist and levered himself up from the folding bench he'd been perched on for so long he thought he might have adhered to it.

"If it'll get me out of this shower, I'll wear one of those bobbly glitter-ball antenna headbands." He meant it, too. "So let's get started with whatever testing we need to do." Inari, he hoped Farad was right, because now he had his hopes up. Just the idea of being dry and fully clothed had his heart racing. Not as much as the idea of being dry and fully clothed while Nick undressed him, but one step at a time.

❖ ❖ ❖ ❖

The hat, if one could call it that, seemed to be doing the trick, or at least the lining Farad's niece had sewn into it was. Yoshi didn't know how rubber layered over fine mesh chainmail and stitched into a red and black plaid hunters cap—with, Inari help him, fake fur trim—was making a difference, but he didn't *have* to know. Nick said it was working, and so did Jeff, who'd come back from wherever he'd gone earlier. The subtly silver pants and shirt Farad had brought were beautiful, though. They fit like a dream. Unfortunately, they had the effect of making the hat seem even worse, from what Yoshi could tell by his reflection in the big, strange mirror on the bedroom wall.

Why anyone would hang a rectangular mirror horizontally, he didn't know. Of course, he also didn't get why it was black instead of reflective silver like the mirror in the bathroom, but whatever. He was just glad to be out of both shower and bathroom, finally.

"He's still not having any weird, poor-me mood swings," Jeff said loudly, as though Nick wasn't just a few feet away, and that should have bothered Yoshi, but it didn't. He was starting to suspect that Jeff was being annoying on purpose. It would make sense, considering how impossible it seemed for someone to be so aggravating by accident.

"I might start if you don't shut up," Yoshi muttered. He turned a bright smile on Jeff. "So it works. Yay. What do we do now? Being out of the shower is great, but I've never really been a hat guy. Not even for this super-attractive plaid thing. Um, not that I'm complaining. I just can't help wondering if I'm going to be stuck with hats, all day every day, for the rest of my life."

Jeff snorted. "However long that might be. Anyone who's strong enough to keep you Spelled for thirty years, even while you were drugged, probably won't be happy when we find them and make them release you. So look on the bright side, vagabond. Maybe they'll kill you and you won't have to worry about hat-hair ever again!"

It was Jeff's overly cheerful smile that had Yoshi laughing, even while Nick bit out a disgruntled sounding "Hey!" Then Nick seemed to notice that Yoshi was laughing and chuckled a bit, too. "Okay. Apparently all it took for you two to get along was a pile of cats, a nasty spell, an incredibly long shower, and the equivalent of a tin foil hat. Good to know."

Yoshi's laugh turned into more of a raspy yipping, and he stuck his tongue out at Nick. "It's not tin foil!"

"No... It's flannel. *Plaid* flannel. Usually bought by customers planning on dressing as *Cletus the Slack Jawed Yokel* for Halloween." Jeff smirked. "It somehow suits you. Speaking of Pol, which we actually weren't, shouldn't he have lost the trail by now and come crawling back with his tail between his legs?"

"Pol has a tail?" Yoshi knew his eyes were wide under the flipped up fur flap at the front of his hideous new hat. "What is he? Not a shifter or I would have known, but what else has a tail, other than my kind? And I *know* he's not one of *me*. All our males are documented from birth. There's no way he's *Kitsune*."

"Relax, fox-o-rama, it's a figure of speech." Jeff's eye roll was a thing of beauty. If beauty was irritating as all Hells. "What do you mean, you would have known? You were passed out, then freaking out. You barely even knew your own name."

Yoshi shrugged. "Shifters all have this thing. Like a look." He shrugged again. "I don't know. It doesn't matter, I guess, because Pol's not a shifter and there aren't that many of them in Madison anyway. Or weren't."

Jeff huffed out a grunt. "Whatever. Where's Pol?" He looked at Nick, though Yoshi wasn't sure why. Nick seemed to understand, though, because he closed his eyes and appeared to be concentrating on...something. "Well? Nick?"

"Give me a minute, Jeff!" Nick's eyes snapped open, and he shot Jeff the closest thing to a glare that Yoshi'd seen from him. "It's not like I have him on GPS. I need to find the currents, since he's not chiming like you were before. It's harder for me to find you guys when you're not stressing or scared, and you know it."

"See, you could have just said 'he's fine, Jeff, there's nothing bad happening to him,' but no. That would be too easy, right?" Jeff frowned then, stopping his snarky, bitchy commentary in what Yoshi thought was midstream. "Wait. I shouldn't have said that. I think I'm just tired. It's been a really long day and a half. That was all me, Nick. Sorry."

It was kind of fascinating, watching Nick and Jeff interact. Yoshi thought they might be almost like brothers. They looked nothing alike, of course, but that didn't matter. They were close in a way Yoshi envied. Inari knew he would have loved to have had a brother, but with males being so rare amongst his kind, the idea of more than one male being born to the same vixen was absurd. Not even every Den had a male, which was exactly why males were contracted out. Sure, females of Yoshi's kind could reproduce with males of any species because the Kitsune strain won out, but kits born of two Kitsune were very highly prized, and considered especially blessed. Sometimes they were also especially dangerous, but that was a whole other issue.

"You could just call him, you know." Nick looked almost as teasing as he sounded. "I'm sure he'd stop whatever he's doing to answer you."

The interesting thing was the way Jeff's face turned slightly pink before he turned away. "We're not talking about that. In fact, we haven't talked about it for the entire time your hillbilly impersonator was gone. So…what, Nick? You think that now's the right time to get into why that's not going to happen? Because I can think of about a million other things we should be more worried about than whether Pol will answer my calls."

Yoshi felt his brow furrowing just a bit. "But I thought you said you didn't know where he was."

"I don't."

"Um, so how would you know what number to call? You can't just call every pay phone in Madison and hope he answers, right? Or I guess you could, but that would take forever. Especially if he's not standing still…"

Jeff blinked. "Are you insane?"

"Thirty years!" Nick said sharply, and Jeff's eyes widened so far and fast, Yoshi thought someone might have punched the man in the stomach. "Not everyone had a cell phone back then. Cut him some slack."

"Cell phone. You mean those mobile ones? They're huge! And expensive!" Yoshi was horrified. "Why would anyone carry one of those around all the time? They don't even fit into pockets!" He'd been a little bit envious of those who had them, but then he'd used one for the first time and hated it. He couldn't even imagine having to lug something the size of a brick with him all day. Poor Pol. No wonder he was brain damaged. Those enormous gadgets had to be radioactive or something. He shuddered. Regular telephones were just fine, as far as he was concerned.

Something beeped, and Yoshi hid a smug grin. Even with all his talk of cell phones, Nick had a beeper instead. Good. At least the guy wasn't going to start drooling like Pol probably did from the radioactive waves or whatever.

The thing Nick pulled from his pocket wasn't like any beeper Yoshi'd seen before. Judging by the way it lit up when Nick touched the front of it, the design had clearly changed since Yoshi had last seen one. He was kind of curious to get his hands on it, though. It was so shiny and glowy and bright!

"Pol's back," Nick said after looking at the beeper. "He needs me to meet him downstairs. Apparently something came up while he was out, and we may have an issue. Jeff, I need you to keep Yoshi company. Show him the kitchen, okay? He can't possibly be full. I'll be back as soon as I can."

"Nick…" Jeff sounded like he was warning the man, but that couldn't be right. Nick was the boss, wasn't he?

"I mean it, Jeff. Play nice. Yoshi, I'll be back as soon as I can, okay?" Nick somehow crossed the few feet between them in what seemed like a split second, which had Yoshi stunned. Then he leaned close and just barely brushed his lips across Yoshi's cheekbone before turning and heading for the door.

"I'm not fragile!" Yoshi announced, but he wasn't sure Nick heard him. Probably not, considering that small graze against his skin had taken a good few seconds to recover from, and by then, Nick was already gone. "I'm not," he muttered, well aware that he was lying even to himself. He *was* feeling brittle inside, but he figured he probably would until he knew what had happened to him while he'd been gone…and what he'd been made to forget.

"Oh, Nickolai," he muttered, before forcing himself to look away from the door. When he did, he found Jeff looking at him as though he'd just grown another head. "What?"

Jeff's brows rose and the man smiled, but it wasn't the sly, smug smile Yoshi had grown used to. Instead, it was a simple smile; friendly, even.

"I just realized you don't know anything." Jeff shrugged when Yoshi hissed, which was far from the reaction he'd hoped for. "Except that Nick is short for Nickolai, apparently, but I digress. Do you really not know about technology now? Cable TV, wireless internet, none of it? Gods, have you been living under a rock all this time?"

Yoshi swallowed roughly, trying to dislodge the knot of emotion so suddenly in his throat. "I wouldn't call it *living*," he finally answered, feeling sick. "I can't. I mean, I really *can't* believe I was gone for so long. It felt like less. I guess because of the drugs. But I never saw…I mean, there was no television, nothing like that, so yes. I really don't know about technology anymore. Why?"

Jeff laughed, but nicely. At least he wasn't calling Yoshi stupid for his ignorance. That was a change from what he thought he was used to.

"I have so much to teach you, young *padawan*. Let's start with cell phones!"

Oh, Inari. He had a feeling he was going to regret admitting to his lack of familiarity with everything after the mid-eighties. Then again, things couldn't have changed *that* much, could they?

CHAPTER EIGHT

Nick couldn't tell, right at first, whether the figure Pol loomed over was male or female. Largely due to the sheer quantity of straps and tape wrapped around it, in addition to the rope tying it to the chair. He could see that whoever it was had red hair, and that said hair was very long—long enough to cover the person's face—but that didn't really mean anything. Most Fae were partial to long hair, as well as a number of other types in Madison, regardless of gender. It didn't much matter right then whether the person was male or female, anyway. What mattered was the sneer on Pol's face whenever he looked down at his captive.

"Pol? Do I need to get our legal staff ready to bail you out when you get arrested for kidnapping?" Nick tried to smile but it felt more like a grimace. "I thought you were chasing whatever you *Saw*, not planning a hostile extraction." Yeah, that sounded better than *what the fuck have you done, you moron*, didn't it?

"This is what Spelled Yoshi." *This*. Not him or her, but *this*. Gods, that wasn't good. Not even a little bit. "It was following its own tether. I'm guessing it was trying to get to Yoshi before he could escape. *Again*. That's how we found it, so we took it down."

The dangerous gleam in Pol's eyes was startling. Mainly because it had been so long since Nick had seen it, even in Pol's capacity as his personal guard and chief of security for Klaas Act Enterprises.

"And now, here you are. With our unwilling guest."

Pol shrugged, as though he and his men hadn't snatched someone off the street, tied them up, and dragged them back to the building like a sack of…something.

"It's either responsible for what's wrong with Yoshi or it's working for whoever is. I thought you'd want to find out before I kill it. Where's Jeff?"

"With Yoshi. Your text said you had information and wanted me to meet you down here. I didn't think you wanted Jeff, too." Hells, this whole situation had clusterfuck written all over it.

"Both of them." Pol nodded sharply, or as sharply as Nick recalled him ever doing. "Seeing this *thing* might jog Yoshi's memory, and Jeff's better at questioning than I am. I'd rather just kill it and see whether that fixes things, but if it doesn't…"

"Then we're back to square one. Or worse," Nick said, nodding as though Pol wasn't talking about killing someone, right there in the basement of their building. "If this is just an agent for whoever Spelled him, then the Caster would still be out there and probably on his guard once his agent was dead. They're probably connected somehow, so it's a good thing you didn't kill whoever this is."

Pol frowned, but at least he lost the sneer. "I didn't think of that. Can Jeff come down now? And Yoshi. I need to get this done, okay?"

Thank gods. Pol was starting to come down from whatever hunter's-high he'd been on. He didn't sound as cold and clinical as he'd seemed at first. It was slow going, but it was a good thing, and if having Jeff there could move it along faster, Nick was all for it.

He was less comfortable with putting Yoshi in a room with the person who'd possibly Spelled him, but he didn't see any way around it, because Pol was right. Seeing the bound figure might jar something loose for Yoshi, or maybe he'd at least be able to recognize whoever it was.

"Yeah. Go ahead and text Jeff. Tell him to bring Yoshi and get down here. Meanwhile, I want to get a good look at this…" He moved closer and leaned down, then started to drag the hair back from the bowed head, hoping to see the person's face. What he *hadn't* been hoping for, or even imagining in anything but his worst nightmares, was the sudden emergence of pointed ears that matched the red hair. "Oh Hells. Damn it, Pol! You just kidnapped a *Kitsune*!"

He'd heard Yoshi mention someone from the Den, a vixen named Kameko, more than once in the last couple days, but Nick had thought she'd only been responsible for the curse. Yoshi had even implied as much. If the same person had also Spelled Yoshi and was part of Yoshi's home Den, then…

For fuck's sake, the trouble never ended. It just got deeper and deeper.

✧ ✧ ✧ ✧

He'd had to change clothes, of course. One simply didn't welcome the Vixen Prime of the local Den into one's home, or rather into the salon just off the lobby of one's building—especially after one's staff kidnapped a member of said Den—without observing protocol. It was just a bad idea, unless one actually wanted to go to war with another species of Other, as Jeff had just finished reminding him for about the fifth time in twenty minutes.

"Which *one* doesn't," Nick grumbled, trying to loosen his tie without destroying the careful knot. "Grandfather would burst a vein."

"And your brother would lord it over you for the next millennium, at least," Jeff added, obviously understanding what he meant. "Every time you talked to him, all you'd hear is 'Hey, remember that time when you single-handedly destroyed eight hundred years of peaceful coexistence? Because *I* do. Hey, Grandfather, remember when Nick pulled chaos from order? Wasn't that amazing? He's sooooo talented!' It would be the exact opposite of fun. Plus, your Grandfather would get that disappointed look, and we *all* hate that."

Ugh. Jeff was right. Nick still almost wanted to curse Pol out. He'd actually done so at first, though silently. But in the time it had taken to attire himself appropriately and talk with Jeff about what was happening while Yoshi listened and looked lost, Nick had changed his mind. Pol's actions had created problems, yes. Probably more problems than they even knew about yet. That didn't change the facts, though.

"Siobhan's standing by with the wine, right?" State visits on a half-hour's notice were no one's forte. State visits from the head of the local Den in response to someone being snatched off the street were even worse, as far as Nick could tell, and the Vixen Prime wasn't even there yet.

"Yes, Siobhan's got the wine. She'll enter from the back hallway once you've greeted the VP. She'll pour for you both, you'll give the VP first choice of glasses, and it's red wine, so try not to spill it, okay, Nick? Unless you're bleeding. At that point, the rug will already be ruined, so a glass or two of wine won't matter."

Nick groaned. "So not the time for snarky fun, Jeff. Seriously."

"Um, is this really dangerous?" Yoshi was biting his own bottom lip when Nick looked over. "It sounds dangerous, but Jeff's being a dick, so that makes it seem like it's maybe not?"

Ah, Hells. Poor Yoshi must want to just run away and hide. Nick did, and he hadn't been through half of what Yoshi had in the last little while.

"It'll be fine, dearheart," Nick murmured, moving closer. He raised one hand and rested it on Yoshi's shoulder, offering the best smile he could manage. "I just need to make it clear to the Vixen Prime that *my* people didn't know they were stealing away one of *her* people. That we weren't targeting *Kitsune*, but rather hunting for the person who Spelled you."

He expected that part to go well enough, though the Vixen Prime would likely demand certain compensations. He wasn't entirely sure about how the VP would take hearing that the same *Kitsune* who'd been taken was the one who'd done the Spelling. That it wasn't so much mistaken identity as *correct* identity, in which the villain also happened to be one of the VP's subjects. Then again, she might already know all that. Hells, she probably did. The Vixen Prime made a point of knowing about every project her people got involved in, and this—what had been done to Yoshi—was definitely a project.

The best Nick could hope for was to pay a penalty and convince her that Yoshi belonged with him, rather than back at the Den or *contracted out* again. He would pay whatever fines she felt necessary, but if she tried to take Yoshi… That was something Nick really *would* go to war over. Or to New Mexico. He could do that, too.

"She's here." Pol sounded sheepish as he spoke from the doorway. "Stalwart is bringing her and her guards through the wards. Castelan will take the guards for refreshments since we do still have a treaty in place, while Stalwart brings the Vixen Prime to us."

Nick took a deep breath and stepped away from Yoshi. "Okay," he said, exhaling roughly. "Places, everyone. Let's do this thing."

✧ ✧ ✧ ✧

In the end, it would all seem anticlimactic. In the moment, it seemed very much the opposite.

The Vixen Prime of the Madison Den—call me Akane, if you like, she'd said—was relatively reasonable. Things almost went easily, though not quite. Especially when Nick and Jeff showed her to the room in the basement of the building and she saw the *Kitsune* Pol had subdued.

"Kameko," Akane said, a wealth of shocked disappointment in her tone. "I don't know what kind of craziness you've gotten yourself into, daughter, but it doesn't reflect well on you that you were caught."

"That bitch-vixen sold me, or at least rented me out!" Yoshi sounded…well, less pissed off than Nick would have expected. Of course he also didn't expect the Vixen Prime's response.

"You are a male, Yoshiro," she replied, as though it was the most reasonable thing in the world. "Your primary purpose is to be attractive and breed. Also, you're Kameko's first cousin. If your nature didn't cause you to do as you are meant to, your familial bonds should have."

"I…" Yoshi was obviously stunned. Not as much as Nick would have been if his…what? Aunt? Something like that if Kameko was Yoshi's cousin and Akane's daughter… But whatever. Nick would have been shocked to hear any sort of relative talk about him as though he was simply an asset.

"Really?" He hadn't planned to interrupt, but he'd for damned sure done just that. "You're fine with your daughter selling your…what, nephew?" The Vixen Prime nodded so slightly Nick would have missed it if he hadn't been watching for some kind of reaction.

"Okay. He's your nephew." He growled. Just a little, and mostly to let his anger out, but Akane heard him. It was obvious from the way she glared. "So you don't have any problem with your daughter *Spelling* your nephew. You're fine with him being a *prisoner* for the last thirty human years. And you don't give a single shit that he's so very, very gay that he can't even begin to function with a female, no matter her race. *Kitsune* or otherwise. Thirty years, entrapped to the point of despair. Until he starved and dehydrated himself for almost a week," Yoshi had told him that much, "because he needed to either get away or die." Gods, Nick could imagine it. Easily.

"Then he forced his weak, thirsty body to run," he went on, still glaring at the Vixen Prime while Jeff and Pol stood behind him. "He forced himself to ignore whatever implorations were thrown at him by the bitch-vixen, as he called her, of the 'other-Den.' He escaped. Then he was nearly smothered in cats because your *daughter* sent a Pied Piper curse after him. And that's fine with you. You don't see any reason for any of that to be an issue."

The Vixen Prime's sculpted red brows rose slightly, and she cocked her head. In that moment, Nick saw the resemblance to Yoshi, not that he would ever say so.

"It's clear that you have no understanding of how things work within Dens," she said, her voice more condescending than Nick ever would have thought possible. "Yoshi may have chosen to enter into a contract, which he obviously did, but if he were, as you say, unable to function with females, he and the contracted Den would have been able to agree to terminate. As he didn't do that, he's in violation of his own sworn word. He signed the contract, which obviously means he thought he could perform."

"Not if he was under the influence at the time!"

Jeff wasn't technically allowed to speak right then. A State visit from the VP of the Madison Den pretty much implied that the Vixen Prime and Nick would be doing all the talking. Even so, Nick couldn't bring himself to do more than sigh.

"I don't know what that means." Akane's sea-blue eyes narrowed slightly.

"It means that your so-perfect *spawn* sold him off to people who kept him drugged the entire time!" Jeff didn't sound even close to as snarky as Nick knew he could be. Yet. "Did you know *that*? Is that common for your people? Because I'm a mix of two of the most feared species there are, and even *my* family wouldn't do what that heinous bitch did to Yoshi. Not even close."

There was a period of time during which the Vixen Prime, Akane, clearly didn't believe what she was hearing. Nick assumed it was more that she didn't *want* to believe. Eventually, she asked Kameko—her daughter and Under-Vixen, who was still taped, tied and chained to the chair in the large but mostly bare basement room—and Kameko surprised not just Nick himself, but Akane, too, if Nick was any judge.

"You didn't ensure that those suggesting the contract were willing to abide by the laws of our kind, daughter?"

Gods, Akane sounded so disappointed, but there was a small tone of steel in her voice.

"No." The bitch-vixen spoke for the first time.

"No," Yoshi echoed, his voice like broken glass, but soft. So very, very soft.

It was the closest thing to a whisper, without actually being one, that Nick could imagine. He almost said something, but he didn't have the chance, because that was when Yoshi apparently sacked up, clearly pushing past his own horribly unnatural reticence and recent, inexplicably retiring nature.

"Why? Why, Kameko? I mean, I know we had our moments, but why would you…"

Gods, Nick wanted to do nothing more than go to Yoshi. To wrap him in his arms. To hold him close until that absurdity faded and Yoshi noticed just how right they felt together…again. He *couldn't* do it, but he wanted to. He also wanted this Yoshi—the one who didn't know him—to be able to stand up for himself, so while Nick didn't let himself step in, he did rest one hand on Yoshi's back. Then the bitch-Vixen—Under-Vixen, really, and Nick figured he might worry about that later, but right then he was more concerned with Yoshi—laughed a dry, barking laugh from her position in the chair, restrained by tape and straps and rope.

"Why *wouldn't* I?" She glared, even bound as she was. "Ask instead why I would! Why you're allowed to do nothing, to be nothing! Why a puling *male* can float through life without a single responsibility or even a thought in his head, while *I* have to always do as I'm told and take care of everything no one else wants to handle!" Her glare shifted to him, and Nick grimaced at the vicious gleam he saw there.

"Ask why he had to be born male!" Kameko wasn't even slowing down. "He should have been female! *He* should have been born of the right gender to be my mother's heir! But instead, it's all up to me! And what did *he* do? He ran out and found himself an Inari-blessed *mate*, when I have no hope of anything like that! So, yes! I didn't insist on the other Dens following our laws! I Spelled him, and I told them he was violent and needed to be subdued. And I'd do it again!"

It was the sheer hatred in her voice that stunned Nick. Judging by Akane's expression, she was equally shocked. Yoshi, however… Oh gods. Yoshi looked like someone had just run him through with a rather large sword.

"But you… You were like a sister to me." He sounded just as wrecked as he looked.

"And you were and still are an offensive creature. I'm glad I stole your memories. Do you hear me, Yoshi? I'm *glad*!" Kameko seemed completely sincere. Right up until Nick noticed wet trails of tears sliding down from her eyes.

After that, the Vixen Prime put her foot down. From the look in her eyes, Nick thought Kameko might be lucky that foot wasn't put down on the young *Kitsune* woman's throat.

"You will remove all Spelling from your cousin. Immediately." Akane's stark stare wasn't one Nick would ever want aimed his way. "There are two ways to accomplish that. I believe we would both prefer the voluntary method, but either way, you *will* unSpell Yoshi."

More trouble came when Jeff spoke up again, arguing that the Den owed Yoshi for what Kameko had done. Then still more when the Vixen Prime realized that Yoshi wouldn't be returning to the Den.

"He may not remember it, and maybe he never will, but he made me promises, Akane. I expect him to fulfill them." Nick refused to be moved on that point, even when she mentioned that Yoshi's company would generate a lot of income for the Den, as escort if he truly couldn't function as a breeder. Not that her plans mattered to Nick. In fact, "Only if he's free to enter those sort of arrangements, not to mention willing," Nick insisted. "Which I doubt he is, considering what he's been through."

"Nick's right!" Yoshi didn't look anything like as sure as he sounded, but that was fine. At least Nick could be sure he didn't want to go back.

"Quiet!" Akane snapped it out. "You're not to interrupt while Mr. Klaas and I are deciding your future. Someone give him something shiny so we can have a peaceful discussion."

✧ ✧ ✧ ✧

"I can't believe she actually said that." Pol seemed baffled. "It's Yoshi's life, right? How can she be all…" He shrugged.

"He's male," Jeff said, snarky as ever. "And it's not like she's any less of a dictator with her own daughter, is it? I mean, just listen to them!"

Nick couldn't argue with that, because even though the door to the basement room was only open a crack, they could all very clearly hear Akane chastising Kameko. Hells, Yoshi was so clearly disturbed by it all that he was sitting on the floor and leaning against the wall as though it was the only thing keeping him from being a twitching pile of fear. Whether that fear was because of his aunt or due to the fact that things weren't quite settled yet, Nick didn't know, but settled or not… He wasn't going to let the Vixen Prime leave the building with Yoshi in tow. No matter what.

It was then that he felt it. Felt the deep-down, shuddering sensation of chiming, in a tone so low, it could only belong to one person. "Oh gods," he groaned, wishing he could dig a hole and hide inside it. "Grandfather's opening our portal from his end. Shit!"

Pol startled and suddenly looked guilty, but that was normal enough, considering.

It was Jeff who really surprised Nick, and he did so by laughing for a good five seconds before saying, "Oh good. I almost feel sorry for the Vixen Prime and that bitch of a daughter of hers. Only almost."

Less than a minute later, large, boot-clad feet stomped from the elevator, and Nick had to force himself to meet his grandfather's eyes. "Um, hey, Gramps! What's going on?"

A booming laugh answered him immediately, but as soon as Nick tried to join in, it vanished as though it had never been. "What's going on is that I haven't been keeping a close enough eye on what you've been up to, Nickolai! Your actions have put us precariously close to unsettling the carefully negotiated balance between species, and you know it! What do you have to say for yourself?"

He didn't even think about it. Maybe he should have, but he didn't.

Instead, Nick stopped thinking at all and spilled everything he was feeling, starting with "I'm not the one who Spelled Yoshi! I'm not the one who kept him hidden in some strange Den, or series of Dens, for the last thirty years! It wasn't me who stole his memory, either! But he got away and I found my way to him, and that has to mean something! It has to mean he's meant to be here and that he's still… We're still…" Nick frowned. "He's still mine. We promised each other, Grandfather! Me to him and him to me, forever, and that doesn't change, damn it! It just… doesn't," he finished.

Grandfather's bright eyes narrowed slightly, and Nick watched as he stroked his white beard, the way Gramps always did while deep in thought. Not lengthy thought, but definitely deep, because it was only ten seconds or so later that he spoke again.

"You mean that. Interesting. It would explain why your brother hasn't commented on your fickle nature for the last little while. I'll even admit that I expected you to let it go and move on, regardless of your promises. You wouldn't have been the first of my line to do so, when abandoned."

Nick frowned. "I wasn't abandoned. He didn't leave me. He was *stolen*. And okay, I might have looked at a few other men over the decades. I may even have wanted a couple of them. But not enough, Grandfather. Not when the one I love was missing." He sighed. "If he'd just taken off and left me behind, he would have a least sent a postcard to break up with me. I don't think I *ever* really thought he'd left me. And he didn't. But that's our drama, not yours, so please don't think I'm not happy to see you, because I am, but… Why are you here?"

Grandfather chuckled, sounding far merrier than he had even a few moments earlier. "Because my grandson's husband is returned, and *someone*—someone whose name rhymes with Mamego—has been very, very naughty. She really shouldn't have interfered with my family."

"But—" Jeff started to say something, gods knew what, but Grandfather cut him off.

"You boys go on upstairs. I'll deal with this. Yoshi looks like he needs a hug, at the very least. And don't worry. Everything will be fine. I guarantee it." Grandfather smiled.

"Trust me. It'll be best if you're not here for my talk with the *Kitsune*."

Nick didn't have any idea about what that was supposed to mean, but Gramps never lied, or not to him, anyway. Also, Grandfather could be scary when thwarted. Sure, he was generally pretty damned jolly, but Nick didn't want to be on his bad side. Ever.

Then Grandfather moved closer to Yoshi. He bent down and lifted the smaller form easily. "Here," he said, and Nick accepted Yoshi from him, confused by Yoshi's lack of reaction. "I think your mate is a little shell-shocked. It's been a difficult day or two. It'd be best if he went to sleep. It'll make it easier on him when that damnable spell is removed. Allow me."

Nick didn't have a chance to stop him. Mostly because it was in Grandfather's nature to move incredibly quickly when he chose to. He barely even saw his grandfather's hand rise. He didn't know it had until he saw it resting on Yoshi's forehead and heard Gramps murmur, "Sleep, Yoshi. Sleep deep and wake well."

CHAPTER NINE

Yoshi woke slowly and hummed out a soft, contented murmur as he stretched slightly beneath the soft cotton sheets. He felt a small, short-lived flash of fear when he realized he was naked, but pushed it away because it didn't make sense. There was nothing to be afraid of in being naked; especially when he could feel Nick close by. They weren't quite touching, but he could sense the heat of the man, radiating from just a few inches away. He *felt* him, felt that indefinable sense of *Nick*.

"Mmm, Nickolai," he rumbled softly, in his kind's equivalent of a purr, "What time is it?"

"You're awake!" Nick sounded relieved, though Inari knew why. "How are you feeling?"

Yoshi rolled onto his back and gazed at Nick, smiling right up until he noticed how tired he looked. "Nickolai, what's wrong? You look… Hells, were you up all night again working on that stupid marketing plan? How many times have I told you not to do that? I didn't even get laid last night, damn it, and that was in our vows! Sex every night! I put that in there for a reason!"

Nick didn't say something snarky or sarcastic the way Yoshi expected. Instead, Nick just stared at him, wide-eyed, before bursting into laughter.

"What? What's so funny?"

"Not funny," Nick finally answered. "I'm just happy, Yosh. You're back, and gods, I'm so fucking happy right now!"

That grin always disarmed him. Always made him smile, too. Even in the middle of one of their epic arguments, Nick could derail the entire thing with just one of those grins. He didn't do it often, because Inari knew Nick loved arguing just as much as Yoshi did. Sometimes their arguments became full-on fights, but somehow Yoshi never worried that their clashes would hurt their relationship. Good thing, too, since he'd gone and married the still-grinning buffoon.

"O…kay?" He pitched his tone to the *you're-crazy* side of things, but that was fine, too. Nick was used to it, considering—or should be, after close to a year. "Where am I supposed to be back from? Because you said 'you're back' like I went on vacation without you."

The grin faded from Nick's face, and Yoshi frowned. "Nick?"

"What's the last thing you remember before waking up just now, love? Please, Yosh. It's important." If Nick hadn't said it so seriously, Yoshi would have laughed. As it was, he furrowed his brow and thought about it.

"We were arguing. Again." That was a given, really. "I took off to get some air, and possibly dinner, and then I…" Then he what? He should know that, shouldn't he? "Oh right. I ran into Bettina, one of the Den guards, and…" And nothing. "After that, I came home." He must have, considering he was in bed with Nick, except…

"Why don't I know this? Inari, Nickolai, what the merry Hells happened last night?"

Nick smiled again, but it looked sickly and weak. "Think harder, Yosh," he said, and when he reached out, Yoshi went to him, curling against him the way he always had, but it felt different, somehow. "Gods, I wish I could let you… Just think harder. We were fighting about meeting each other's families. You thought it was a bad idea."

Yoshi nodded, his cheek rubbing lightly against Nick's chest, and it felt like heaven to be that close to Nick again, after so long. Except a night wasn't long. Not really.

"It's a *terrible* idea," he muttered sincerely. "Families are never a good thing. Number one cause of splitting up."

Besides which, Nick didn't have anything his aunt wanted. She would insist that Yoshi abandon Nick and take up with someone who had more to offer. Hells, she was starting to make noises about Yoshi doing his duty to the Den. Hearing that he'd gone and married Nick would likely have her so livid she'd steam. Then she'd somehow leverage her way into owning whatever Nick managed to acquire, especially if the toy store he and Nick had started ever really took off.

"You were only half right." Nick's heart was racing beneath Yoshi's cheek, and that would have been fine if they'd been aroused. As it was, it was more worrisome than exciting. "*Your* family is a nightmare. Fortunately, Gramps stepped in last night, and Akane won't be coming near you again. Neither will your cousin." Nick made a sound that might have been a barked laugh, except it was softer than a bark and not amused the way a laugh would be. "Actually, I'm not sure Kameko will be getting close to anyone at all for the foreseeable future. What she did to you was…"

Nick shivered, and Yoshi was about to ask why when a sharp, vicious pain shot through his brain, as though he'd been stabbed in the head with a hot needle. He shouted something and knew he flailed, but Nick held him close, held him safe. Even through the sudden agony and nauseating rush of memory, he felt safe with Nick. He always had.

✧ ✧ ✧ ✧

It could have been minutes or hours that his brain was pummeled with hazy, warped images of the other-Den, or possibly Dens, that he was only then remembering. Yoshi didn't know which. It felt like it lasted forever.

Kept in bowers, treated like a dimwitted child, dosed with something he felt sick just thinking about, and that wasn't the worst of it. No, the worst part was that he'd forgotten—*been made to forget!*—Nick.

He remembered wanting to escape and failing to try, thanks to the drugs. He also remembered wanting to die and even trying to plan how he could manage it, more than once. He remembered deciding, for whatever reason, to have one more go at making a run for it. That there had to be something better out in the world.

Maybe—just maybe, because Yoshi truly hadn't remembered Nick at all, even when Nick, Jeff, and Pol had rescued him—some part of him, below conscious memory, knew. Knew that Nick was out there and that if he could just get to Nick, things would be better.

He couldn't swear to it, but he wanted to think so.

"I'm going to kill her so dead, dead will only be a fond memory," he whispered when the throbbing pain subsided to a manageable level. "She stole… Inari! How could she do that to me?"

Then another wave of memory struck, this time of the night before and the things Kameko had said. Unlike then, her words only made him angry, now that he truly knew what she'd done.

"Forget that. Killing's too good for her. I…I'm so sorry, Nickolai. I never should have walked out while we were fighting. I just…" He shrugged helplessly, or as much as he could with Nick still holding him close.

"It's not your fault, dearheart." Nick seemed so sincere. "It wasn't the first time. You had no way of knowing that… bitch-vixen was even thinking about punishing you. For being you, I guess." Yoshi sighed softly but almost happily at the light kiss Nick gave him on the temple. "And I know she's your cousin, but I seriously think she might be a little insane. And bitter."

Yoshi couldn't help snorting at that. "You *think*? A *little*? That's like saying Jeff's a little snarky, or Pol's a little focused on whatever he's doing at any given time." Nick chuckled softly, and Yoshi did, too. Not really because he'd been joking—he hadn't—but because it was just so amazing to hear Nick laugh again, while knowing exactly who and what Nick was to him.

"So you stayed here. I mean, after I was gone." *Well, duh. Way to sound stupid.*

"Of course I did. It's our place. *Ours.*" Nick's hold loosened and Yoshi almost complained, but then Nick rolled them and stared down into Yoshi's eyes. He was grinning again, which had its usual effect. "I always hoped you'd come back, some day. Even when I thought I doubted it, I didn't really. So I went ahead with everything we talked about, Yosh. I finished building our toy store, and since I didn't have anything else to occupy my time, it became a lot more than we ever imagined."

Yoshi squirmed a little. "It's been thirty years, Nickolai. How could you think—"

"I know. I know, okay? The plan didn't call for a clothing line, or books and DVDs, or even the more fetish-oriented stuff, but there was a market for it and still is, so—" This time Yoshi interrupted.

"How could you think I want to talk about *business* when I've missed out on three decades worth of sex! Inari, Nickolai! My balls used to go blue after a day! How do you think they feel now that I'm home and there's a chance of you reminding me how good sex can be?"

He didn't mention the extremely fuzzy sort-of memories in which he suspected vixens of the other-Den-or-Dens had tried to make him able to do his so-called job. He wasn't sure whether those vague impressions were real or had been one of the repeating drug-induced nightmares he'd had. He didn't want to know either. What he wanted was for things to go back to normal. He wanted Nick. Needed him.

"Please, Nickolai," he murmured. "Remind me. Pl—"

Nick's mouth was hot against his. Rough, too. Like the first time they'd been together, and countless other times. Their kiss was wet and deep, Nick's tongue spearing into his mouth as though it was aiming for his soul, and Yoshi was fairly sure he reached it.

It took him a moment to get up to speed, but once he did, he was all in.

Hands grasping tightly, bruising skin and drawing sharp, short, swallowed cries from them both. Cries that were eaten, taken in and savored. Bodies pressed so close and tight that not even a whisper of air came between them.

"I don't want to hurt you," Nick said on a long moan.

Yoshi just bucked up harder, legs opening as far as they were able, even as he gasped out, "You won't!" But even if Nick did, he welcomed that. What did he care for a little pain when there would be so much pleasure? And there *would* be pleasure. There always had been with Nick. Always.

He managed to hold on when Nick moved away for a scant moment and returned with a tube of the necessary. Held on even more while Nick opened him up, and Inari help him, but he felt like a virgin again, his body was so tight. So tight but so ready, too, as Nick's fingers danced inside him, pushing small sounds from him that he would have been embarrassed by with anyone else, but there *was* no one else. Hadn't been since the first night with Nick, and never would be again.

Finally, Yoshi couldn't stand it anymore. One more second, one more twist of those elegant digits inside him and he would come apart. Not empty, but not full in the way he needed to be.

"Damn it, Nickolai, now! Please, Nick, please!" Yeah, nothing got to Nick like being begged in bed. Yoshi remembered that part even more clearly than the rest, and while he was sure certain things about Nick had changed while they'd been apart, that wasn't one of them.

His heart thundered wildly in his chest as Nick positioned himself, and when that long-missed, fully-desired hard heat pressed at him, Yoshi forced his body to relax, to take it in, to welcome it home.

The relaxation didn't last, of course, and that was a good thing because once Nick started to move, the last thing Yoshi wanted to be was relaxed. Nick obviously didn't want to be either, and he showed it with thrusts and bites and harsh, shuddering breaths against Yoshi's skin, which was entirely fair since Yoshi was right there with him. They shook and writhed, bodies bowing and heaving, and it was the best damned thing Yoshi had ever felt. It felt even better when his ears and tails burst out, proving that Nick still affected him just like he'd always done. Yeah, that was the best feeling ever.

It would be, he figured, until the next time, which would undoubtedly raise the bar on *best*. Again.

✧ ✧ ✧ ✧

"My understanding," Nick said, as they took their time in the shower, hands tracing soapy trails over skin, "is that you refused your cousin's demands that you accept the contracts, based mostly upon our bonding."

"So she made me forget you and I signed." He wished he could still be horrified, but after three days of recovering—most of which had been spent in bed with Nick, and that was the best kind of recovery ever—he'd decided to not worry too much about it. That didn't mean he wouldn't periodically obsess over Kameko's actions and whether he'd done something to cause them, but he wasn't going to spend every minute of the rest of his life doing so. It hurt, yes. He'd seen her grow up. He remembered when she'd been a tiny, feral thing who'd alternately referred to him as Cousin and Idiot-Male. He'd loved her then and still did, but Kameko had done him a favor, of sorts, when she'd Spelled him. Or rather when the spell broke. She'd opened his eyes to the truth.

He did still love her. Some part of him always would. They'd been the youngest members of their Den for more than two centuries. But either Kameko was flawed or she was sick. Either way, she clearly didn't love *him*, and while it might take a while, eventually Yoshi would be able to accept that emotionally, rather than just intellectually. Nick would help. He knew that much for sure. Nick always helped him; sometimes without even knowing it.

"Yeah," Nick agreed, though he didn't seem happy about it. "She cheated and tried to find a way around our bonding. If she'd just… You know what? Never mind. It's irrelevant."

"Okay." He leaned against Nick, his head on Nick's shoulder as he stroked soap over that strong back. It wasn't irrelevant. Nor was it something that could be erased with a simple *never mind*. Yoshi was thinking it too, after all. Thinking that if he'd just let Nick meet his aunt and cousin—officially—that maybe everything could have been avoided. Sure, the Den would currently own at least half of Nick's business, but Kameko never would have had the nerve to take the steps she'd taken. Not with the Vixen Prime knowing about Yoshi and Nick, and especially not with Akane aware of just who and what Nick was.

"It is," Nick insisted, though Yoshi wasn't sure how he knew there were questions about that in Yoshi's mind. "You're here now, and we're going to be fine, right?"

Yoshi nodded against Nick's shoulder and inhaled the scent of his mate.

"Then that's what matters. I refuse to be angry anymore. It was one thing to be bitter and sour on the inside while you were gone, but you're here, Yosh, and that has to be the most important thing. Besides, your people didn't get away without consequences, according to what Kris told me."

Right. Kris. Nick's brother. Inari help him, but he really might have to meet the rest of Nick's family, since his own was most likely just as done with him as he was with them.

"Oh?"

"Yep." Nick spun Yoshi around, rinsing him under the water, and Yoshi laughed, not fighting it. He still didn't want to spend any longer than necessary in the shower, and Inari help him, he was never wearing another hat again. Ever. Especially not a plaid one. "Gramps apparently made peace between your people and mine by granting your aunt a Christmas Wish."

Yoshi groaned. "Because offering a wish to an impulsive Vixen Prime doesn't have *disaster* written all over it. I mean, she's good at running things, I guess. As good as any Kitsune, anyway, but we're not really the most structured group." That was why they had contracts. Because unless there was something in writing, his kind frequently just changed their minds about things. Yoshi wasn't any sort of exception, either. Except about Nick. He hadn't changed his mind about *him* for even a second. He was keeping Nick, or possibly being kept. Whichever.

Nick chuckled, and Yoshi followed him from the shower once they'd fully rinsed and the water was shut off. "No, but you *are* clever. *Kitsune* are. Just not as clever as Gramps. With him, it's not so much what you wish for, but the way you word it. He always knows what you mean, but interpretation is up to him. I think he bases it on which list you're on, and your position on said list."

Oh, Inari. "What did Akane wish for?" He already had a bad feeling about it. Even the thick, soft towels didn't offer any comfort, though he did still enjoy that they were blessedly dry. Wet towels—fully wet ones—held no appeal anymore, and likely never would. Bad associations, there.

"She wished for more males to be born to your home Den." Nick was already nodding and smiling a less than pleasant smirk even before Yoshi groaned. "You know, it's in her nature to be a bit naughty, so Gramps probably won't fulfill her wish too harshly. If it were Kameko's wish, on the other hand… Heh. But anyway. If you're dry now," Nick went on, that smirk changing to something sweeter and hotter, "why don't you go see whether there's anything good on TV? I'll join you in a few minutes. I need to shave. I don't want to give you any more beard burn, dearheart."

Yoshi rolled his eyes but accepted the change of subject. "Fine, but you know I don't mind the stubble. See you in a minute." He really didn't mind the small abrasions. Or the bruises from fingers and hard, sucking kisses against his skin. He wasn't ready to fight with Nick over something so minor, though. Not yet. Maybe in a few weeks or years, when the sheer relief of being back where he belonged became familiar.

He kissed Nick lightly, then left the bathroom, only to find himself staring at the rumpled, twisted sheets on the big bed. Inari, they'd barely left it since Yoshi's memories reintegrated into his conscious mind. The entire room smelled of sex and Nick, and Yoshi hoped it always would.

He dropped the damp towel on the floor and kicked it toward the corner, where a growing pile of same lurked, and he made a mental note to remind Nick that they needed to let the building's cleaning staff in at some point, but not yet. Not even that day, or at least not for a good number of hours, as the scent and recollection of the last few days had Yoshi's body reacting hungrily.

"You don't mind if we need a bath later, right, Nickolai?" He was grinning as he called out the question. "I have a sudden desire to get all sweaty and smelly again."

He heard Nick's answering growl, as well as Nick's words.

There wasn't much chance of Yoshi ever missing "I'm shaving! You'll have to get yourself ready, love."

The lube in the nightstand on Yoshi's side of the bed had been finished off before their shower, but that was fine. Yoshi was utterly certain that there was more in Nick's nightstand. As it turned out, he was right, which he discovered when he yanked the drawer open with a bit too much force.

The drawer flew from the frame of the nightstand, spilling all manner of items across the floor to join the drawer itself. Yoshi yelped and blinked once before trying to sit down on the edge of the bed…and missing.

"What the…?" he muttered from his unplanned seat on the rug, picking up one of the items to examine it; then he started to laugh the hard, yipping laugh that only slipped out when he was truly beyond amused. He probably sounded hysterical, or maybe just insane, but he couldn't help it. Then Nick ran in through the bathroom doorway, large blobs of shaving cream still on his face, and Yoshi only laughed harder.

CHAPTER TEN

One second, he was shaving and smirking slightly, which was difficult to manage at the same time, and the next, he'd dropped his razor—thankfully without cutting himself—and ran into the bedroom.

Nick didn't know what he'd expected to see there, but Yoshi had sounded startled. A second or so later, Nick had heard something that he would have mistaken for choking if he hadn't heard it before. Hells, the first time he'd heard Yoshi laugh in that particularly unusual manner, he'd thought the poor guy was coughing up a hairball.

He'd been wrong about that, of course, as Yoshi had gone to great pains to make clear. That had actually been their third, or maybe fourth fight, and making up with each other had been just as incredible as it ever and always was.

This time, the sound had disarmed him. Scared him a little, for some reason. Maybe because Yoshi wasn't so quick to laugh anymore…or fight, it seemed, but he didn't really mind that. They'd get back to their own normal eventually, or possibly shape a *new* normal from the way their experiences while apart had changed them. Nick wasn't sure which, but he didn't much care, either. They would be fine.

What he cared about at the moment was that he'd raced into the bedroom to fix or slay whatever was wrong, only to find Yoshi rasping out even more of those hiss-barks when he caught sight of Nick.

"What the Hells...?" Then he saw what Yoshi was holding and had to laugh, himself.

"Ugh. *Fifty Shades of Elf.* That's not mine!" Nick wondered if he sounded as disgruntled as he felt when Yoshi looked unsure. "Seriously, Yosh. Look inside. Not the story, but the first page."

Yoshi hesitated.

"Oh please!" Gods, Nick was almost begging. He hated begging. Except not really. Not with Yoshi. *Even so...* "I know it's been a while, but you can't honestly believe I've changed so much that I'd read something like that. Just open the cover if you need proof."

Yoshi took him at his word, thankfully, because Nick watched him flip the cover back. He saw Yoshi's brow furrow slightly, too. He nearly laughed yet again when those pretty eyes darted to him, then back to the book, because he knew exactly what Yoshi was seeing.

"Um, okay. Who uses bookplates with the Little Mermaid on them? Other than six-year-old human girls?" Yeah, Yoshi sounded confused. "And...and what's with all the names?"

Nick did chuckle then, some of his usual good humor restored by Yoshi's obvious, horrified bafflement. "Well, I'm guessing the first one—McJingles—was the original owner, but then someone named...what was it? Melvin? Whatever." He shrugged slightly. "I suppose McJingles gave it to Melvin, because McJingles's name has a big X through it. Somehow Pol got his hands on it and crossed out Melvin, and..." Nick chuckled again. "Well, you see what Pol did."

"Added his own name with a whole bunch of little hearts around it? Yeah, I see that. I don't get why it's in your drawer, though. Your sex drawer! Do you use it as some kind of instruction manual, or—"

"No! Gods, no!" Nick was honestly disgusted by the notion that Yoshi might really think that. "I found Pol reading it and taking notes, of all things, and you remember how Pol always was about Jeff, right? Well, that hasn't changed, and I had this sudden flash of Pol deciding the things in that gods-awful book might convince Jeff to give him a chance. That would be the exact wrong thing to do, considering some of Jeff's issues, and would probably start some sort of monumental drama that would end up involving the whole staff, so I confiscated it. That drawer is the one place Pol would never look, so I figured it'd be safe there until Pol forgot about it."

Yoshi didn't seem convinced, so Nick went on, adding, "Um, that was two months ago. I've been a little busy since then."

"I haven't read it. Obviously." Yoshi's nose wrinkled and he put the book down on the floor. Nick thought he detected a bit of distaste in the way Yoshi wiped his fingers against the rug. "There was something about it on that channel. Um…"

"MPA?" Nick arched one brow, even as he leaned down to offer Yoshi a hand up. "Madison Private Access? I bet it was Sunshine's talk show, but if I was awake, I probably wasn't paying attention to the television." No, if he'd been awake, he would have been completely absorbed with watching Yoshi, who moved almost as much as anyone on screen. The guy was still prone to twitching and fidgeting, just as he'd been before their separation.

Yoshi shrugged, once he was on his feet, and Nick grinned at the way he pressed close. "Some vampyre chick. I remember thinking she had a weird name for a vamp, so you're probably right. Whatever she and her guests were saying, I sort of got the impression that it's not a book I want to read."

Nick chuckled, staring into Yoshi's insanely beautiful violet eyes. "I'm not sure you could sit still long enough to read more than a page or two, but if you could, you'd be right. It's…" He made a face. "You know what? Let's not talk about it anymore, okay?"

"That's completely fine with me. The less I have to think about Pol, and how he has designs of Jeff's throbbing elfhood, the better. Can we talk about you finishing shaving now? Unless that's whipped cream on your face, I don't want to lick it off." Yoshi's eyes were shining almost as much as Nick remembered from the old days, and it had Nick feeling even better about their future. If Yoshi could get past what had happened to him, Nick for damned sure could, too.

"We'll do that whipped cream thing later," Nick murmured. "Let me go finish up, and I'll be back in a couple minutes." He paused, purely for effect. "And didn't you have something to be doing, too? I seem to recall that it involved you and lube, and possibly some fingers." Gods, yes. Please, yes.

Yoshi was smirking in a way that almost worried Nick when he pulled away, but that devilish gleam was still there.

"Fingers? Okay," he answered, sounding smug as all Hells. "It seems a shame, considering all the pretty toys you have, though."

Gods. Nick shivered with sudden heat at the thought of Yoshi using the mentioned items. "Next time," he suggested, even as he fought the urge to grab Yoshi and kiss him mindless, regardless of the damned shaving cream.

"They're on the floor. They'll need a good cleaning before we do that. Gods. I'll just go and…"

He rushed, almost nicking himself more than a few times, and when he strode back into the bedroom, cock hard and just as ready to feel Yoshi as the rest of him, he did that. He felt Yoshi with every part of himself, and it was beautiful. Blissful. Fulfilling for every part of him, but mostly his heart, because that was the part of him that had missed Yoshi the most.

✦ ✦ ✦ ✦

The video call to introduce Yoshi to Grandfather, Kris, and Will went well enough. Yoshi hadn't run from the room screaming, in any case. Nick was a little surprised to hear that Kris and Will had already met Yoshi, if it could be called meeting when Yoshi hadn't said a word. He was a lot *more* surprised to learn that Yoshi had somehow managed to travel by the nexus, but that was something to think about later. Right then all that mattered was that Yoshi seemed to like the family. Cautiously, but that made sense, considering Yoshi's own familial dynamics.

"I think we should do it again." Nick laughed when Yoshi turned wide eyes on him. "Not that, dearheart, or not yet." They were still damp with sweat, and Nick, at least, needed a bit of recovery time. "I meant I think we should get married again. Legally, this time, since we can do that now."

"Why?" Gods, Yoshi looked good, all worn out. Hair a mess, black furry ears poking up through it and tails swishing lightly behind him. "It's not like the human laws apply to us."

Nick grinned. "True, but we've been through a lot. I think it'd be nice if you married me again. Besides, after everything that's happened, I think our people would love a party, and what better reason is there to have one?" And he wanted to be sure that everyone knew he and Yoshi were joined. Bonded. Just in case Kameko ever decided to try something again. Assuming she ever had the chance, Nick wouldn't put it past her.

"Besides, Farad would explode with excitement if he could plan a wedding for us. You know he would."

Yoshi chuckled a little. "Inari. He so would. Are you sure you want to, though? I'm not… I mean, even without clear memories of being away, I'm not the same, Nickolai. I wouldn't blame you if…" He shrugged.

That, right there, was the other reason Nick wanted to do it. Because he hated that little edge of uncertainty in his love's eyes and voice. It didn't show often, but he wanted it gone, or at least soothed away.

"You're perfect." Nick pulled Yoshi closer, skin to skin, and stroked one hand over Yoshi's mobile tails. "Perfect for me, just like you've always been. If you marry me again, I won't have to worry that you've outgrown me. So, you see, it's a purely selfish request."

One of those choked-sounding yipping laughs emerged then, and Yoshi rolled his eyes. "Well, as long as it's solely for your benefit, I suppose I'll have to say yes."

Maybe he didn't need that much recovery time after all, Nick decided. In fact, he didn't need any at all.

"Always be mine, Yosh," he murmured as he pushed deep. "Always, okay?"

Yoshi's response was clear in the way he moved, but Nick still felt a surge of happiness flood through him when Yoshi answered with "Always. Now fuck me, for fuck's sake!"

Forever and ever. For fox sake, indeed.

THE END

TRADEMARK ACKNOWLEDGEMENT

THE HALF LIFE OF PUMPKIN PIE

The author acknowledges the trademark status and trademark owners of the following wordmarks mentioned in this work of fiction:

Muppet: Henson Associates, Inc.

Oscar the Grouch: Sesame Workshop

Toys for Tots: Marine Toys for Tots Foundation

Barbie: Mattel, Inc.

Tonka: Hasbro, Inc.

TRADEMARK ACKNOWLEDGEMENT

ELF CONFIDENCE

The author acknowledges the trademark status and trademark owners of the following wordmarks mentioned in this work of fiction:

Amazon: Amazon Technologies, Inc.

Snap, Crackle, Pop: Kellogg North America Company

M&M: Mars, Incorporated

Keebler: Kellogg North America Company

Kreacher: Warner Bros. Entertainment Inc.

Catwoman: DC Comics

Public Broadcast System: Public Broadcasting Service

Plexiglas: Arkema France

McDonald's: McDonald's Corporation

Hallelujah Chorus: DreamWorks Animation L.L.C.

Facebook: Facebook, Inc.

Betty Crocker: General Mills, Inc.

Twitter: Twitter, Inc.

Instagram: Instagram, LLC

TRADEMARK ACKNOWLEDGEMENT
IT'S A WONDERFUL LUBE

The author acknowledges the trademark status and trademark owners of the following wordmarks mentioned in this work of fiction:

Black & Decker: The Black & Decker Corporation

SyFy: Universal City Studios LLC

Percocet: Endo Pharmaceuticals Inc.

Post-it: 3M Company

Benadryl: Johnson & Johnson

Viagra: Pfizer Inc.

Better Business Bureau: Council of Better Business Bureaus, Inc.

TRADEMARK ACKNOWLEDGEMENT
THE ISLE OF MISFIT SEX TOYS

The author acknowledges the trademark status and trademark owners of the following wordmarks mentioned in this work of fiction:

Smurf: Studio Peyo S.A.

Ken: Mattel, Inc.

Jell-O: Kraft Food Global Brands LLC

My Little Ponies: Hasbro, Inc.

Mission Impossible: Paramount Pictures Corporation

TRADEMARK ACKNOWLEDGEMENT

FOR FOX SAKE

The author acknowledges the trademark status and trademark owners of the following wordmarks mentioned in this work of fiction:

Starbucks: Starbucks Corporation

ABOUT THE AUTHORS

SHAE CONNOR

Shae Connor lives in Atlanta, where she's a lackadaisical government worker for a living and writes erotic romance under the cover of night. She's been making up stories for as long as she can remember, but it took her a long time to figure out that maybe she should start writing them down. First published by Dreamspinner Press in 2010, Shae adds a new notch on her bedpost each time another story is unleashed onto an unsuspecting universe. When she does manage to tear herself away from her laptop, Shae enjoys running, hiking, cooking, and traveling, not necessarily in that order.

You can find her hanging out on Twitter most any time @shaeconnor, or occasionally on her website at www.shaeconnorwrites.com, but for the direct route, you can email her at shaeconnorwrites@gmail.com.

Facebook: https://www.facebook.com/shaeconnorwrites

Twitter: @shaeconnor

Goodreads: http://www.goodreads.com/author/show/4409037.Shae_Connor

Website: www.shaeconnorwrites.com

ALSO BY SHAE CONNOR

Sand & Water
En Fuego
Model Student
Accidental Love
Butt Pirates in Space (anthology)
Butt Ninjas From Hell (anthology)

ABOUT THE AUTHORS

KIERNAN KELLY

Kiernan Kelly lives in the wilds of the alligator-infested U.S. Southeast, slathered in SPF 45, drinking tropical, hi-octane concoctions served by thong-clad cabana boys.

Actually, the truth is that she spends her time locked in the dark recesses of her office, writing gay erotic romance while chained to a temperamental laptop, drinking coffee, and *dreaming* about thong-clad cabana boys.Sigh.

Links to the full body of Kiernan's works in both print and e-format may be found at her website, www.KiernanKelly.com.

Facebook: http://www.facebook.com/kiernan.kelly

Twitter: @kiernankelly

Goodreads: https://www.goodreads.com/KiernanKelly

Website: www.KiernanKelly.com

Amazon author page: https://www.amazon.com/author/kiernan_kelly

ALSO BY KIERNAN KELLY

Riding Heartbreak Road
In Bear Country
In Bear Country II: The Barbary Coast
Seti's Heart
Outland
In Their Own Skins: Shifting Sands
In Their Own Skins: The Mark of Cain
In Their Own Skins: Uncaged
Cornfed
Vyper
A Weapon of Opportunity
Fifty Gays of Shade (editor and contributor)

In addition, a plethora of short stories and novellas through a variety of houses.

ABOUT THE AUTHORS

KAGE ALAN

Kage Alan lives in a suburb of Detroit, MI with his husband, named Honorable Husband, and their fish and shrimp, who are affectionately named and answer to "fish" or "shrimp". He enjoys leaving Fangoria Magazine out in the open in the bathroom knowing full well that Honorable Husband can't resist looking at the awful pictures and asking if they own the movies…that he'll NEVER watch. Kage lives in fear of his husband's Hong Kong Grandmonster and is the author of A Funny Thing Happened on the Way to My Sexual Orientation, Andy Stevenson Vs. the Lord of the Loins, Gaylias: Operation Thunderspell and the short story Spacehunters: Master Elite and the Maternal Order of Loganites Beyond Uranus featured in the Butt Pirates In Space anthology.

Facebook: www.facebook.com/kagealan

Twitter: www.twitter.com/kagealan

Goodreads: https://www.goodreads.com/author/show/2007812.Kage_Alan

Website: www.kagealan.com

ALSO BY KAGE

A Funny Thing Happened on the Way to My Sexual Orientation

Andy Stevenson Vs. the Lord of the Loins

Gaylias: Operation Thunderspell

Spacehunters: Master Elite and the Maternal Order of Loganites Beyond Uranus
Featured in the *Butt Pirates In Space* anthology

Twink Ninja Tiger, Flaxen Buns of Fury
Featured in the *Butt Ninjas From Hell* anthology

ABOUT THE AUTHORS

JEVOCAS GREEN

Born and raised in Atlanta, GA, Jevocas Green, 'Java' to his peers, new to the writing world, debuts this, his first published work "The Vagabond and the Soldier." This temptuous tale came from his love of old wu-shu films and his fascination with the Asian culture. Early on, when Java was invited to guest write on the 'Butt Ninjas from Hell' anthology at 2013's Outlanta Con, he realized that he wanted to do a tale with a bit more heart but still keeping that edgy sex appeal and melding them into an unusual and unconventional love story. Incorporating elements of bondage, BDSM and sensory stimulation, and forming a bond between these two characters that would bring you into their decadent world. Known better for his work as a local Atlanta actor and filmmaker, and work with beauty and visual effects makeup, Java is no stranger to the debaucherous. For over a decade, he has been wowing audiences as 'Dr. Frank N. Furter' with the Atlanta Rocky Horror Picture Show Shadow Cast, "LIPS DOWN ON DIXIE." Java has also lent his writing talents to several short films, independent features and webseries.' He is also co-founder and co-owner of his own film production company, Jymeni Productions, LLC. This is only the beginning for the novice writer. It will be very exciting to see what fresh stories brew to mind for this up-and-coming new author.

Facebook: https://www.facebook.com/pages/Jevocas-Green/186789994666228

Twitter: https://twitter.com/TheJavaKitty

ABOUT THE AUTHORS

J.P. BARNABY

J. P. Barnaby, an award-winning gay romance novelist, is the author of over a dozen books including the Little Boy Lost series, the Forbidden Room series, and Aaron. As a bisexual woman, J.P. is a proud member of the GLBT community both online and in her small town on the outskirts of Chicago. A member of Mensa, she is described as brilliant but troubled, sweet but introverted, and talented but deviant. She spends her days writing software and her nights writing erotica, which is, of course, far more interesting. The spare time that she carves out between her career and her novels is spent reading about the concept of love, which, like some of her characters, she has never quite figured out for herself.

Facebook: https://www.facebook.com/JPBarnaby

Twitter: https://twitter.com/JPBarnaby

Goodreads: http://www.goodreads.com/JPBarnaby

Website: http://www.JPBarnaby.com

ALSO BY J.P. BARNABY

The Survivor Books
Aaron
Painting Fire on the Air

The Little Boy Lost Series
Enlightened
Abandoned
Vanished
Discovered
Escaped
Sacrificed

The Forbidden Room Series
The Forbidden Room
A House of Cards
The Perfect Tree

The Working Boy Series
Charlie: Rent Boy
Andy: Go-Go Boy
Vinny: Porn Star

Novellas
Mastering the Ride
Bane of Boston

Short Stories
Papi
His Heart's Desire, 'Twas a Dark and Delicious
Christmas: Manlove Edition

ABOUT THE AUTHORS

T.C. BLUE

Contrary to popular opinion, T.C. Blue was not raised by wolves. Nor did she spring, fully formed, from the forehead of a god, instead entering the world in the usual manner.

A true jack of all trades and master of none (otherwise known as flighty and unable to make a decision and stick with it), she currently resides near the east coast where she does her best to avoid politics and religions as a general rule.

T.C. can usually be found sitting in front of her computer, trying to wrangle rabid and numerous plot bunnies, though her muses insist that she not be too hard on the poor little fluffy things. (Poor little fluffy things with sharp teeth and claws, but whatever. Muses don't seem to care much about the possible bloodshed if the bunnies think T.C.'s not writing quickly enough.)

Facebook: https://www.facebook.com/profile.php?id=100000896020443

Twitter: @tc_blue

Website: http://tcblue.wordpress.com/

ALSO BY T.C. BLUE

The Farmingdale Gentleman's Club series
A Game of Chances
A Game of Skills
A Game of Hearts
A Game of Schemes.

Torquere Press
The Conventions series
One & One series
Fruit Basket series

The Second Door (stand alone)

Butt Pirates in Space
Butt Ninjas From Hell